UNDER SIEGE

Books by Stephen Coonts

Flight of the Intruder
Final Flight
The Minotaur
Under Siege

STEPHEN COONTS

* * * * * * * * * * * * * * * * * * *

UNDER SIEGE

POCKET BOOKS

New York   London   Toronto   Sydney   Tokyo   Singapore

This novel is a work of fiction. The characters, names, incidents, dialogue, and plot are the products of the author's imagination or are used fictitiously. Some of the characters are named after real public figures holding elective office in the United States Government at the time of this writing, but the descriptions of these characters and the dialogue, opinions, characteristics, and actions attributed to them are purely fictitious. Any other resemblance to actual persons or events is purely coincidental.

 POCKET BOOKS, a division of Simon & Schuster Inc.
1230 Avenue of the Americas, New York, NY 10020

Copyright © 1990 by Stephen P. Coonts

Library of Congress Cataloging-in-Publication Number: 90-62714

All rights reserved, including the right to reproduce
this book or portions thereof in any form whatsoever.
For information address Pocket Books, 1230 Avenue
of the Americas, New York, NY 10020

ISBN: 0-671-72229-8

First Pocket Books hardcover printing October 1990

POCKET and colophon are registered trademarks of
Simon & Schuster Inc.

Printed in the U.S.A.

TO MY PARENTS,
GILBERT AND VIOLET COONTS

UNDER
SIEGE

Government is not eloquence. It is not reason. It is a force. Like fire, a dangerous servant and a fearful master.

—George Washington

Of all the tasks of government, the most basic is to protect its citizens from violence.

—John Foster Dulles

CHAPTER ONE

* * * * * * * * *

WALTER P. Harrington was eastbound on the inner loop of the beltway around Washington, D.C., this December evening, in the leftmost lane. He kept the speedometer needle rock-steady at fifty-five miles per hour. Traffic swirled past him on his right.

Harrington ignored the glares and occasional honks and upthrust fingers from drivers darting into the middle lanes to get around and kept his eyes firmly on the road ahead, though he did occasionally glance at the speedometer to ensure the needle was on the double nickel. It usually was. Maintaining exactly fifty-five was a point of pride with him. He often thought that if the speedometer ever broke he could nail fifty-five anyway. He had had plenty of practice.

He also ignored the car that hung three feet behind his rear bumper flashing its lights repeatedly from low to high beam and back again. His rearview mirror had been carefully adjusted to make such shenanigans futile.

Walter P. Harrington had absolutely no intention of moving into the middle or right-hand lane. He *always* drove in the left-hand lane. Walter P. Harrington was obeying the law. *They* weren't.

The car behind him darted past him on the right, the driver shaking a fist out his window. Harrington didn't even glance at him. Nor did he pay any attention to the next car that eased up behind him, a white four-door Chevrolet Caprice.

In the Chevy were two men wearing surgical gloves. The driver, Vincent Pioche, muttered to his passenger, "It's him, all right. That's his car. A maroon Chrysler. License number's right and everything."

The passenger, Tony Anselmo, swiveled his head carefully, scanning the traffic. "No cops in sight."

"What'cha think?"

"Well, we could just pass him and be waiting for him when he gets home."

"Neighbors, kids," Vinnie Pioche said disgustedly.

Both men sat silently staring at the back of Walter P. Harrington's balding head. "Little jerk driving fifty-five in the left lane," Tony said.

"Yeah, he's an asshole, all right. The problem is, he may swerve right and nail us before we can get by."

"He won't," Tony Anselmo said thoughtfully. "He'll go out like a light. Won't even twitch."

"In his neighborhood, there may be a cop two blocks away and we won't know. Or some broad looking out the window ready to call nine-one-one. A kid screwing his girl under a tree. I hate the fucking suburbs."

They followed Walter P. Harrington for a mile, weighing the risks.

"I dunno, Vinnie."

"In a right-hand curve, with him turning right, when he goes out the car will tend to straighten and go into the concrete median. I'll floor this heap and we'll be by before he smacks it and rebounds."

"If he comes right he'll clip us," Tony objected.

"Not if you do it right. Stick it in his ear." When Tony didn't move, Vinnie glanced at him. That moved him.

Tony Anselmo crawled across the passenger seat back and flopped onto the rear seat. He paused to catch his breath. He was getting too old for this shit and he knew it.

Under a blanket on the floor were two weapons, a twelve-gauge sawed-off pump shotgun and a Remington Model Four Auto Rifle in .30-06 caliber. Both weapons were loaded. After he rolled down the left rear window, Tony Anselmo picked up the rifle and cradled it in his arms. He flicked the crossbolt safety off. The shotgun would be easier, but the buckshot pellets might be deflected by the window glass. It would take two or three shots to be sure, and they didn't have that kind of time.

"Okay," he told Vinnie. "Get in the next lane, pull up beside his rear bumper, and sit there until you see a right curve coming. Try to let some space open up in front of you."

"Got it." Vinnie used his blinker to ease into a space in the traffic on his right. That stream was flowing along at sixty-five to seventy miles per hour but he was still doing fifty-five, so a space quickly opened as the car in front pulled away.

Tony scanned the traffic for police cars. He saw none, nor did he see any cars that might be unmarked cruisers. Harrington was plainly visible, his head about twenty to twenty-five feet away, his hands in the ten-and-two position on his steering wheel. He was concentrating on the road ahead, looking neither left nor right.

"Looks good. Any time."

"Curve coming up. Fifteen seconds. Get ready."

Anselmo scooted to the right side of the car, then leaned left, resting the barrel of the rifle on the ledge of the open window. "I'm ready."

"Five seconds."

Anselmo concentrated on the open sights of the rifle. This was going to be a shot at a bouncing, moving target smaller than a basketball at a range of about a dozen feet, from a bouncing, moving platform. Not a difficult shot, but tricky. An easy shot to miss and wonder why.

"Here we go." Anselmo felt the engine rev. Out of the corner of his eye he saw they were gaining on Harrington's Chrysler.

Then they were there, right alongside, passing with a three or four mile per hour edge, Harrington's head plainly visible. Tony could feel the centrifugal force pushing him toward Harrington's car, feel the Chevy heel slightly.

Tony swung the rifle gently, adjusting for the jolts of the car. His finger tightened on the trigger.

Harrington's head exploded as the rifle bellowed.

Vinnie floored the accelerator and the Chevy began to pull away. As expected, with a dead hand at the wheel, Harrington's car eased left, toward the concrete median barricade.

"Get by, get by," Tony shouted.

In the car immediately behind Pioche, the horrified passenger screamed at her horrified husband behind the wheel. He swerved right as far as he could and still stay in his lane. It wasn't enough. The rear end of Harrington's decelerating Chrysler swung ponderously into the traffic lane as the front ground spectacularly on the concrete barrier. The left rear fender of the maroon Chrysler kissed the left front corner of the swerving vehicle, a gentle impact that merely helped the Chrysler complete its 180-degree spin.

The wife screamed and the husband fought the wheel as their car swept past the Chrysler, which, with its entire right side in contact with the barrier, rapidly ground to a smoking halt as pieces of metal showered the interstate.

In the backseat the two teenagers cursed and looked back at the receding Chrysler. The wife's screams died to sobs. "Did you see that man shooting, Jerry? *Jerry? My God!*"

Behind the wheel of his car Jerry McManus of Owosso, Michigan, strove manfully to keep the vehicle going down the highway in a straight line as he began to feel the full effects of a massive adrenal shock. In front of him the white sedan that contained the gunman accelerated and pulled away. A moment later another vehicle, a van, swung left into the widening gap and McManus lost sight of the gunman.

Jerry McManus had just been driving down the road on the way back to the motel, comfortably following these two cars at fifty-five miles per hour while all the locals played NASCAR in the right lanes and the kids in the backseat hassled each other and his wife gabbled on about her rich great-aunt who lived in Arlington or someplace.

Owosso, Michigan, didn't have any freeways, and even if it had McManus wouldn't have driven them, living as he did immediately behind the gas station that he owned. But now, on the *big* annual vacation, the pilgrimage to the tourist traps of Washington, D.C., that his wife had insisted upon—"it will *broaden* the children, make them understand what America's all about, make them *appreciate* their heritage"—out here on these goddamn racing strips they call beltways, these maniacs are murdering each other with guns. Why in hell can't they do it downtown, around those marble monuments to dead politicians? And to think we took the kids out of school for two weeks for this!

"We're going home," Jerry McManus told his wife grimly.

She looked at him. He had his jaw set.

Behind them the teenagers resumed their interrupted argument. The youngsters had been bickering at each other for the entire week. When in Washington . . .

"We're going home," Jerry said again. "Today."

"Okay," Tony Anselmo said as he rolled up the rear window to staunch the flow of fifty-degree air into the vehicle. "Nobody's following us." He turned his attention to the rifle. "Let's get off at the next exit."

He flipped the box magazine from the weapon and jacked the bolt to clear it. Then he broke it into two pieces and placed it in a shopping bag that also lay on the floor. The magazine, the loose cartridge, and the spent brass all went into the bag.

Vinnie steered the Chevy down the off-ramp and turned right, toward the District. After two blocks he turned into a narrow side street and pulled to the curb in the middle of the block. No vehicles followed.

Tony got out of the car carrying the shopping bag and went around to the trunk. In fifteen seconds he had the license plate slid from its holder and another in place. The original plate, stolen, went into the shopping bag. From the trunk Tony took two cartons of eggs wrapped in plastic. After taking the plastic off, he dumped the eggs into the shopping bag, then threw the plastic wrap on top. Holding the bag shut, he broke the eggs. These were old, old eggs that had never been refrigerated. They would make the bag and its contents stink to high heaven.

Holding the bag firmly shut, he climbed back into the passenger seat, beside the driver.

A half mile from the beltway they saw the tops of a large apartment complex. Vinnie Pioche steered slowly through the parking lot. The dumpster was in back. No pedestrians were about.

Tony Anselmo hopped out, tossed the shopping bag into the dumpster, then got nimbly back into the car. The vehicle was stopped for only fourteen seconds.

Out on the beltway traffic had ground to a halt. A Maryland state trooper arrived within three minutes and blocked the eastbound fast lane with his cruiser. After a quick glance into the remains of the maroon Chrysler, he used his radio to call for an ambulance and the crime lab wagon. Soon another trooper stopped his car behind the first one and began directing traffic.

A curiosity slowdown developed in the westbound lanes, but traffic was still getting through until a third cruiser with lights flashing parked immediately beside the concrete barrier westbound. Traffic on the beltway around the northern edge of Washington, D.C., stopped dead.

Pioche and Anselmo took the Baltimore Parkway into the heart of Washington and found a spot in a parking garage. They had dinner at a small Italian restaurant where they were known. The headwaiter insisted they try a fine red wine from northern Italy, compliments of the house. After the uncorking ceremony, they sipped the cool, robust liquid and languidly studied the menu. They had plenty of time.

Outside on the streets the evening dusk became full darkness and the temperature began to drop. It would get down into the thirties tonight.

The reporter and photographer for *The Washington Post* entered the beltway jam-up from the east, westbound. The police scanner had warned them. After thirty minutes of stop-and-go creeping, the reporter, who was driving, eased the car to a stop in front of the police cruiser halted against the median barrier. The two men exited through the driver's door and stood for a moment staring at the wreckage of the maroon Chrysler on the other side of the barrier. A television chopper was hovering overhead, just high enough so that its downwash created a gentle breeze and cut the fumes from the idling vehicles creeping by.

The reporter approached the plainclothes detective who was in charge, Detective Eddie Milk, who was standing to one side watching. Milk had a meaty face, a tired face, noted the reporter, who wasn't feeling so chipper himself after a long day.

"Hi, Eddie. Some fucking mess, eh?"

Even though Milk knew and tolerated reporters like this young one from the *Post,* he had other things to do at the moment. Milk concentrated his attention on the ambulance attendants, who were placing the remains of Walter P. Harrington on a stretcher. They were in no hurry.

The reporter got a good look. The head was gone from the torso: all that remained was a bloody fragment of tissue on top of the neck. There was no face at all. The photographer had his equipment out and began snapping pictures. He even got a close-up of the corpse, though he knew the editors would never use it.

Milk finally opened up. "At least one shot, maybe more, from the right side of the vehicle. One of them hit the driver smack in the right side of the head. Killed instantly. Can't give you his ID yet. Get it downtown."

"Any witnesses?"

"You kidding?"

"Dope or guns in the car?"

"Not so far."

Jack Yocke, the reporter, was twenty-eight years old, two inches over six feet tall, and he still had a flat stomach. He silently watched the ambulance crew carry the corpse to their ambulance, then pile in and roar away with lights and sirens going.

The *Post* photographer, a dark man clad in jeans and tee-shirt and wearing a ponytail, stood atop the median barrier and aimed his camera down into the front seat of the Chrysler. From where Yocke stood he could see that the left side of the vehicle's interior was covered with blood and tissue. Sights like this used to repulse him, but not now. He thought of them as surefire front-page play in an era when those boring policy stories out of State and the White House and overseas usually had top priority on "the Front."

In the cars creeping past, faces stared blankly at the smashed car, the police, the photographer. Slowly but perceptibly, the speed of the passing vehicles began to increase. The body was gone.

Yocke looked around carefully, at the traffic, at the huge noise fences on the edge of the right of way, and at the tops of the trees beyond. To the west he could just see the spire of the Mormon cathedral.

"An assassination?"

"How would I know?" the cop grunted.

"Rifle or pistol?"

"Rifle. You saw what's left of the driver's head."

"Color of the car that impacted the victim's car?"

"You know I can't tell you that. Check downtown."

"What do we know about the victim?"

"He's dead."

"Gimme a break, Eddie. It's all got to come out anyway and I'm close to a deadline."

The cop regarded Yocke sourly. "All right," he grunted. "Victim's driver's license says he was a male Caucasian, fifty-nine years old, Maryland resident."

"How about his name and address, for Christ's sake! I won't print it until you guys release it. I won't bother the family."

"Don't know you." That was true.

And Yocke didn't know the cop, but the reporter had seen him twice and learned his name and had made the effort to associate the name and face.

"Jack Yocke." He stuck out his hand to shake, but the cop ignored it and curled a lip.

"You kids are ignorant liars. You'd screw me in less than a heartbeat. No."

Jack Yocke shrugged and walked past Harrington's car, looking around the technicians into the bloody interior. The photographer had finished shooting pictures and radioed in to the *Post*'s photo desk. Now he was standing beside the *Post*'s car.

Yocke walked eastward, back along the way the victim had come. He could see where the car had impacted the concrete barrier, scarring it and leaving streaks of paint and chrome. Fragments of headlight and the colored glass of blinkers lay on the pavement amid the dirt and gravel and occasional squashed pop can. He kept his head down and his eyes moving.

He walked on up the road another hundred yards, still looking, past the cars and trucks, breathing the fumes.

The motorists regarded him curiously. Several of them surreptitiously eased their door locks down. One guy in the cab of a truck wanted to question him but he moved on without speaking.

Facing eastward, Yocke could just see the crash site. He looked to the right, the south. Nothing was visible but treetops. Where was the rifleman when he pulled the trigger? He walked back toward the curve, carefully inspecting the naked, gray upthrust branches of the trees.

This was crazy. The guy wasn't up in a tree! Only military snipers did that kind of thing.

Yocke slipped through the standing vehicles to the south side of the road and walked along scanning the terrain which sloped steeply downward to the noise fence. The rifleman could have stood here on the edge of the road, of course, and fired through a gap in traffic. Or—Yocke stopped and looked at the cars—or he could have fired from another vehicle.

Somewhere in this area, then, the Chrysler impacted the median barrier in that curve.

Yocke took a last look around, then trudged back toward the officials around the wreck.

Milk glanced at him. Yocke thanked him, was ignored, motioned to the photographer, then vaulted the barrier.

The photographer got behind the wheel. Looking back over his shoulder, he put the car in motion as Yocke pulled his door closed.

Yocke extracted a small address book from a hip pocket, looked up a number, then dialed the cellular phone.

"Department of Motor Vehicles."

"Bob Lassiter, please."

"Just a moment."

In a few moments the reporter had his man. "Hey Bob. Jack Yocke. Howzit going?"

"Just gimme the number, Jack."

"Bob, I really appreciate your help. It's Maryland, GY3-7097."

Silence. Yocke knew Lassiter was working the computer terminal on his desk. Yocke got his pen ready. In about fifteen seconds Lassiter said, "Okay, plate's on a 1987 Chrysler New Yorker registered to a Walter P. Harrington of 686 Bo Peep Drive, Laurel."

"Bo Peep?"

"Yeah. Cutesy shit like that, probably some cheap subdivision full of fat women addicted to soap operas."

"Spell Harrington."

Lassiter did so.

"Thanks, Bob."

"This is the third time this month, Jack. You promised me the Giants game."

"I know, Bob. I'm working on it."

"Yeah. And try to get better seats than last time. We were down so low all we could see was the asses of the Redskins standing in front of the bench."

"Sure." Yocke broke the connection. Lassiter wouldn't get tickets to the Redskins-Giants game: Yocke had already promised those to a source in the mayor's office.

The reporter made another call. He knew the number. It was *The Washington Post* library where researchers had access to back issues of the paper on microfilm. The indexes were computerized.

"Susan Holley."

"Susan, Jack Yocke. Helluva accident on the beltway. Guy shot in the head. Can you see if we have anything on a Walter P. Harrington of 686 Bo Peep Drive, Laurel, Maryland."

"Bo Peep?"

"Yep. Harrington with two r's. Also, remember that epidemic of freeway shootings out in California a couple years ago? Can you find out if we ever had any of that around Washington?"

"Freeway snipers, you mean?"

"Well, yes, anything we have on motorists blazing away at each other on the freeway."

"I'll call you."

"Thanks."

Yocke hung up. He had a gut feeling Harrington had not been a sniper victim since the terrain offered no obvious vantage point for sniping. Sitting a long distance away and potting some driver was the whole kick for the sniping freaks, Yocke suspected.

Yet the freeway shootouts, didn't those people usually use pistols? He tried to imagine someone using a high-powered rifle on another driver while he kept his own vehicle going straight down the road. That didn't seem too likely, either.

So what was left? The rifleman in another vehicle with a second person driving. An assassination? Just who the hell was the dead man, anyway?

The story for tomorrow morning's paper would be long on drama but short on facts. Getting your head shot off on the beltway was big news. But the following stories would be the tough ones. The who and the why.

He was going to have to try to get hold of Mrs. Harrington, if there was a Mrs., find out where the dead guy had worked, try to sniff out a possible reason someone might have wanted him dead.

"Drugs, you think?" the photographer asked.

"I don't know," Jack Yocke replied. "Never heard of a killing like this one. It had to be a rifle, but there's no vantage point for a rifleman. If it was close range, why didn't he use a pistol or submachine gun?"

"Those heavy drug hitters like the Uzis and Mac-10s," the photographer commented.

"If it had been one of those the car would look like Swiss cheese." Yocke sighed. "It's weird. I've seen quite a few corpses over the last three years. Who did it and why has never been a mystery. Now this."

The photographer had the car southbound on Connecticut Avenue. Yocke was idly watching the storefronts. "In there," he demanded, pointing. "Turn in there."

The photographer, whose name was Harold Dorgan, complied.

"Over there, by that bookstore. I'll be in and out like a rabbit."

"Not again," Dorgan groaned.

"Hey, this won't take a minute." When the car stopped, Yocke stepped out and strode for the door.

It was a small, neighborhood bookstore, maybe twelve hundred square feet, and just now empty of customers. The clerk behind the register was in her mid-to-late twenties, tallish, with a nice figure. She watched Yocke's approach through a pair of large glasses that hung a half inch too far down her nose.

The reporter gave her his nicest smile. "Hi. You the manager?"

"Manager, owner, and stock clerk. May I help you?" She had a rich, clear voice.

"Jack Yocke, *Washington Post.*" He held out his hand and she shook it. "I was wondering if you had any copies of my book, *Politics of Poverty?* If you do, I'd be delighted to autograph them."

"Oh yes. I've seen your byline, Mr. Yocke." She came out from behind the counter. She was wearing flats, so she was even taller than Jack had first thought, only two or three inches shorter than he was. "Over here. I think I have three copies."

"Only two," she said picking them up and handing them to him. "One must have sold."

"Hallelujah." Jack grinned. He used his pen to write, "Best Wishes, Jack Yocke," on the flyleaf of each book.

"Thanks, Ms. . . . ?"

"Tish Samuels."

He handed her the books and watched her put them back on the shelf. No wedding ring.

"How long have you lived in Washington, Mr. Yocke?"

"Little under three years. Came here from a paper in Louisville, Kentucky."

"Like the city?"

"It's interesting," he told her. Actually he loved the city. His usual explanation, which he didn't want to get into just now, was that the city resembles a research hospital containing one or more—usually a lot more—specimens of every disease that affects the body politic: avarice, ambition, selfishness and self-interest, incompetence, stupidity, duplicity, mendacity, lust, poverty, wealth—you name it, Washington has it, and has it in spades. It's all here in its purest form, on public display for anyone with the slightest spark of interest in the human condition to muse upon or study. Washington is El Dorado for the sly and the bold, for every identifiable species of pencil thief and con artist, some in office, some out, all preying on their fellow man.

"Say, Tish," Jack Yocke said, "I've got a party invitation for tomorrow night. How about going with me? I could pick you up after work, or . . ."

She walked back behind the register and gave him an amused half smile. "Thanks anyway, Mr. Yocke. I think not."

Jack lounged against a display case and looked straight into her eyes. "I've been taking a class at Georgetown University and the instructor is throwing an end-of-semester class party. The people in the class hardly know each other, so it's sort of a get-acquainted thing for everyone. Low key. I really would enjoy the pleasure of your company. Please."

"What's the class?"

"Spanish."

Tish Samuels' grin widened. "I close the store at five on Saturday."

"See you then. We'll get a bite somewhere and go party."

Yocke actually was taking Spanish. He had hopes of breaking out of the cop beat and getting sent to Latin America by the foreign desk. This, he hoped, would be a way to leapfrog over endless, boring years on the metro staff where there were too many reporters covering too few stories—few of them worth the front page.

Out in the car Dorgan asked him, "How many books did you sign, anyway? A couple dozen?"

"Naw. She only had two."

"If it takes that long to sign just two, you better never write a best-seller."

By eight p.m. Jack Yocke had learned several things. The *Post* had never before mentioned the late Walter P. Harrington in any of its articles, and the police had brought in the victim's wife to make an identification. She had recognized his wallet and wedding ring, so the victim's name and address were officially released to the press.

Ruing the impulse that had made him tap his Maryland DMV source and renew the man's claim on a pair of Redskins' tickets, Yocke wrote as much as he knew, which wasn't much, and padded the story with all the color he could remember. After he had pushed the right keys to send it on its electronic way to the metro editor, he spent a moment calculating just how many ducats he was in debt. Two pairs for every home game should just about cover it, he concluded. He had a source for tickets, a widow whose husband had bought season tickets years ago when the Redskins weren't so popular. She kept renewing them to maintain the connection with her husband but almost never went to the games herself.

He was getting his assignments at the metro editor's desk when one of the national reporters rushed in with a printout of wire service copy he had read on his computer terminal. "Listen to this, you guys. The Colombians just captured Chano Aldana, the big banana of the Medellín cartel. They're going to extradite him tonight."

Yocke whistled softly.

"Where are they going to hold him?" the editor asked.

"An 'undisclosed' place. The Air Force has a plane on the way down to Bogotá now. Going to bring them back to Miami and turn them over to U.S. marshals. After that, they're all mum."

"I guess the lid's off, now," Yocke said to no one in particular as the national reporter hurried away. "It'll blow off," he added, scanning the big room for Ottmar Mergenthaler, the political columnist with whom he had been having a running argument about the drug issue. Mergenthaler was nowhere in sight.

Just as well, Yocke concluded. The columnist believed, and had written ad nauseam, that traditional law enforcement methods adequately funded and vigorously applied would be sufficient to handle the illegal drug epidemic. Yocke had argued that police and courts didn't have even a sporting chance against the drug syndicates, which he compared to a bloated, gargantuan leech sucking the blood from a dying victim.

The verbal sparring between the talented newcomer, Yocke, and the pro with thirty years of journalism experience had not prevented a friendship. They genuinely liked each other.

As Yocke marshaled his arguments yet again to fire at the man who wasn't there, he took stock of the *Post* newsroom. It was populated by literate, informed, opinionated people, every one of whom subconsciously assumed that Washington was the center of the universe and the *Post* was the axis on which it turned.

This newspaper and *The New York Times* were the career zeniths that every journalist aimed for, Yocke thought, at least those with any ambition. Yocke knew. He had ambition enough for twenty men.

Jack Yocke and the photographer were headed for Laurel to interview the Harringtons' neighbors—and, if possible, the widow herself—when

Vinnie Pioche and Tony Anselmo finished their meal and strode out into the gloom of the Washington evening.

They took their time walking toward the parking garage. A lady of the evening standing on the corner watched them come toward her, took a step their way, then abruptly changed her mind after a good look at Vinnie's face. Tony knew Vinnie pretty well, and he knew that look. It would freeze water.

Once in the car they drove to a garage in Arlington and beeped the horn once in front of the door, which began to open within seconds.

The fat gent inside was smoking a foul cigar. He handed them a pair of keys to a ten-year-old Ford sedan. Tony used one of the keys to open the trunk. Inside was a sawed-off twelve-gauge pump shotgun, a box of twenty-five buckshot cartridges, latex surgical gloves, and two nine-millimeter pistols. They pulled on the gloves before they touched the weapons or the car.

Vinnie stared at the pistols, then ignored them. Tony helped himself to one and made sure the clip was full and there was a round in the chamber while his companion carefully loaded the shotgun, then placed five more cartridges in his right jacket pocket.

Tony slid behind the wheel and started the car. The engine started on the first crank and the gas gauge read full. He let it idle while Vinnie arranged himself in the passenger seat and laid the sawed-off on his lap, the barrel pointed toward the door.

Anselmo nodded at the cigar smoker, who pushed the button for the garage door opener.

"Nice car," Tony said to Vinnie, who didn't reply. He had used up most of his conversational repertoire at dinner, when he had grunted and nodded to acknowledge Tony's occasional comments on the food or the weather.

Vinnie Pioche had the personality of a warthog, Tony reflected yet again as he piloted the car across the Francis Scott Key Bridge back into Washington. Still, a more workmanlike hitter would be hard to find. Through the years, when somebody had a contract and wanted it done just right, with no repercussions, they sent for Vinnie. He was *reliable.* Or he used to be. These days he was getting . . . not goofy . . . but a little out of control, out there on the edge of something that sane men rarely see. Which was precisely why Tony was here. *"Make sure it goes okay, Tony."*

They found a parking place a hundred feet from the row house they wanted, just a block east of Vermont, a mile or so northeast of downtown. Tony killed the lights and the engine. The two men sat silently, watching the street and the occasional car that rattled over the potholes.

Streetlights cast a pale, garish light on the parked cars and the row houses with their little stoops and their flowerpots on second-floor windowsills. This neighborhood was much like home. Here they felt comfortable in a way they never would in the sprawling suburbs with huge lawns and tree-shaded dark places and the winding little lanes that went nowhere in particular.

Tony checked his watch. Thirty minutes or so to wait. Vinnie fondled the shotgun. Tony adjusted the rearview mirror and his testicles and settled lower in his seat.

Twenty-six minutes later a yellow cab slowly passed. Tony watched in the driver's door mirror as the brake lights came on and the cab drifted to a stop in the middle of the block.

"It's them," he said as he started the engine. "Remember, not the woman."

"Yeah. I'll remember."

Vinnie got out of the car and eased the door closed until the latch caught. He held the shotgun low against his right leg, almost behind it, and waited.

Tony watched a man and a woman get out of the cab and the cab get under way. Vinnie started across the street.

No one else on the street. The wind was beginning to pick up and the temperature was dropping. Tony turned in the seat and watched Vinnie cross the street and stride toward the couple, now standing on the stoop, the woman digging in her purse.

Vinnie stopped on the sidewalk fifteen feet away from the couple, raised the shotgun, and as the man turned slightly toward him, fired.

The man sagged backward. Vinnie shot him again as he was falling. The victim fell to the sidewalk, beside the stoop. Vinnie stepped around the stoop and shot him three more times on the ground.

The shotgun blasts were high-pitched cracks, loud even here. The woman stood on the stoop, watching.

A pause, then one more shot, a deeper note.

Now Vinnie was walking this way, replacing the .45 in his shoulder holster, the shotgun held vertically against his left leg.

Anselmo eased the car out of its parking place and waited.

Vinnie Pioche just walked. Lights were coming on, windows opening, a few heads popping out. He didn't look up. He opened the car door and took his seat, and Tony drove away, in no hurry at all.

Just before he turned the corner, Tony Anselmo glanced in the driver's door mirror. The woman was unlocking the door to her town house and looking down off the stoop, down toward the dead man. Well, she had been paid enough and she knew it was coming.

CHAPTER TWO

★ ★ ★ ★ ★ ★ ★ ★ ★

On the flight from Dallas–Fort Worth, Henry Charon sat in a window seat and spent most of his time watching the landscape below and the shadows cast by cumulus clouds. Sitting in the aisle seat, a young lawyer with blow-dried hair and gold cufflinks occupied himself by studying legal documents. He had glanced at Charon when he seated himself, then forgotten about him.

Most people paid little attention to Henry Charon. He liked it that way. People had been looking around and over and through him all his life. Of medium height, with slender, ropey muscles unprotected by the fat layers that encased most other forty-year-old men, Henry Charon lacked even one distinguishing physical feature to attract the eye. As a boy he had been the quiet child teachers forgot about and girls never saw, the youngster who sat and watched others play the recess games. One teacher who did notice him those many years ago had labeled him mildly retarded, an unintentional tribute to the protective shell that, even then, Henry Charon had drawn around himself.

He was not retarded. Far from it. Henry Charon was of above-average intelligence and he was a gifted observer. Most of his fellow humans, he had noted long ago, were curiously fascinated by the trivial and banal. Most people, Henry Charon had concluded years ago, were just plain boring.

Although the lawyer in the aisle seat had ignored his companion, Charon surveyed him carefully. Had he been asked, he could have described the young attorney's attire right down to the design on his cufflinks and the fact that the end of one shoelace was missing its plastic protector.

He had also catalogued the lawyer's face and would recognize him again if he saw him anywhere. This was a skill Charon worked diligently to perfect. He was a hunter of men, and faces were his stock in trade.

He hadn't always been in this line of work, of course, and as he automatically scanned the faces around him and committed them to memory, in one corner of his mind he mused on that fact.

He had grown up on a hard-scrabble ranch in the foothills of the Sangre de Cristo Mountains of New Mexico. His mother had died when he was three and his father had died when he was twenty-four. The only child, Charon inherited the family place. Weeks would pass without his seeing another person. He did the minimum of work on the ranch, tended the cattle when he had to, and hunted all the rest of the time, in season and out.

Since he was twelve years old Henry Charon had hunted all year long. He had never been caught by conservation officers although he had been suspected and they had tried.

Sagging cattle prices in the late '70s and a thrown rod in the engine of his old pickup changed his life. A banker in Santa Fe laid reality on the table. Unless he devised a way to earn additional income Charon was eventually going to lose the ranch. That fall Henry Charon became a hunting guide. He advertised in the Los Angeles and Dallas newspapers and had so many responses he turned people away.

In spite of his taciturn manner and introspective personality, Henry Charon enjoyed immediate success at his new venture. His gentlemen nimrods always saw trophy animals, sometimes several of them. When one of the corporate captains with his shiny, expensive new rifle needed a little help bringing down his deer or elk, the crack of Charon's .30-30 was usually unnoticed amid the magnum blasts. Stories of successful hunts spread quickly through the boardrooms and country clubs of Texas and Southern California. Charon jacked his rates from merely high to outrageous and was still booked for years in advance.

The event that changed his life came in 1984, on the evening before the last day of elk season, as he drank coffee around the campfire with his client, who this year had come alone and paid without quibble the entire fee for a party of four. That was the client's third season.

The client was looking for someone to kill a man. He didn't state it baldly but that was the drift of the conversation. He didn't ask Charon to undertake the chore, yet somehow in the oblique conversation it became unmistakable that the demise of a certain board member at the client's savings and loan would be worth fifty thousand dollars cash, no questions asked.

The client got his elk the next morning and Charon had him on the plane in Santa Fe by six p.m.

Intrigued, Henry Charon thought about it for a week. Really, when one thought about it objectively, it was hunting and hunting was the one thing that he was extraordinarily good at. Finally he packed a canvas bag and headed for Texas.

The whole thing was ridiculously easy. Three days of observation established that the quarry always took the same route to work in his black BMW sedan. Charon went home. From a closet he selected a rifle that one of his clients from the year before had brought along for a backup gun and had left behind.

Three mornings later in Arlington, Texas, the quarry died instantly from a bullet in the head as he drove to work. The police investigation established that the shot must have been fired from a salvage yard almost a hundred and fifty yards away as the victim's car waited at a traffic light. There were no witnesses. A careful search of the salvage yard turned up no clues. Asked to assist, the FBI identified several dozen ex-military snipers as possible suspects. These men were all discreetly questioned and their alibis checked, to no avail. The crime remained unsolved.

Two weeks later the money arrived at the ranch in the Sangre de Cristo in a cardboard box, mailed first class without a return address.

The savings and loan man came to the ranch on two more occasions. He was stout, in his late fifties, and wore custom-made alligator-hide cowboy boots. He sat on the porch in the old rocker and looked at the mountains against the blue sky and talked about how tough times were in Texas since the oil business cratered. On each visit he mentioned the names of men connected with the savings and loan industry in the Dallas–Fort Worth area. The first man subsequently drowned on a fishing trip in Honduras and the other apparently shot himself with a Luger pistol, a family heirloom his father had brought back from World War II, one evening when he was home alone.

The last time Henry Charon saw the original client he brought another man with him, introduced him, then got back into his Mercedes and drove off down the dirt road, dust swirling. The new man's name was Tassone. From Vegas, the savings-and-loan man said.

Tassone was as lean as his chauffeur was fat. He looked over the house and grounds with a deadpan expression and made himself comfortable on the porch. "Awful quiet out here," he observed.

Charon nodded to be sociable. He scanned the hillsides slowly, carefully.

"I hear you got a talent."

Charon again examined the draw where the ranch road went down to the paved road. He shrugged. Tassone had his feet on the rail.

"A man with talent can make a good living," Tassone said. When Charon made no reply, he added, "If he stays alive."

Charon seated himself on the porch rail, one leg up, his hands on his leg. He turned his gaze to Tassone.

"If he's smart enough," the man in the chair said.

Charon stared at the visitor for a moment, as if he were sizing him up. Then he said, "Why don't you take the pistol out of that holster under your jacket and put it on the floor."

"And if I don't?"

Charon uncoiled explosively. He drew the hunting knife from his boot with his right hand and launched himself at the man in the chair, all in the same motion. Before Tassone could move, the knife was at his throat and Charon's face was inches from his.

"If you don't, I'll bury you out here."

"What about Sweet?" Sweet was the Texas savings-and-loan man. "He knows I'm here."

"Sweet will go in the same hole. He'll be easy to find. He just drove about a mile down the road and stopped. He's sitting down there now, waiting for you."

"Reach under my coat and help yourself to the gun."

Charon did so, then moved back to the rail. The pistol was a small automatic, a Walther, in .380 caliber. He thumbed the cartridges from the clip, jacked the shell from the chamber, then tossed the weapon back to Tassone.

With his eyes on Charon, Tassone holstered the gun. "How'd you know Sweet didn't leave?"

"The road goes down that draw over there." Charon jerked his head a half inch. "I was watching for dust. There wasn't any. There's a wide place under a cottonwood where the creek still has water in it this time of year. He's sitting there in the shade waiting for you."

"Maybe he's circling around on foot to get a shot at you. Maybe he thinks you've outlived your usefulness."

"Sweet isn't stupid. I took him hunting. He knows he wouldn't have a chance in a hundred to kill me at my game, on my own ground. Now you may have dropped off someone on your way up here, someone who's a lot better than Sweet. So I've been looking. Those cattle out there on that hillside in front of the house are three-quarters wild, and they're not edgy. Bchind thc house—that's a possibility, but there's a flock of pheasants up there. Saw 'em fly in before you drove up."

Tassone looked carefully around him, perhaps really seeing the setting for the first time. In a moment he said, "Cities aren't like this. Ain't no spooky cows or cowshit or pheasants. Think you can handle that?"

"The principles are the same."

The visitor crossed his legs and settled back into his chair. He took out a pack of cigarettes and lit one. "Got a little business proposition for you." An hour later he walked down the road toward the car where Sweet was waiting.

That was the last time Charon saw Sweet, the savings-and-loan man. Three years had passed since then, busy years.

This afternoon, when the plane landed, Henry Charon joined the throng in the aisle and eased his one soft bag from the overhead bin. As usual, the stewardess at the door of the plane gave him her mindless thank-you while her eyes automatically shifted to the person behind him. Anonymous as always, Henry Charon followed the striding lawyer into the National Airport concourse.

Taking his time, his eyes in constant motion, Charon moved with the crowd, not too fast, not too slow. He avoided the cab stand in front of the terminal and started for the buses, only to change his mind when he glimpsed the train at the Metro station a hundred yards away.

He studied a posted map of the system, then bought one at a kiosk. Soon he was in a window seat on the yellow train.

The second hotel he tried had a vacant single room. Charon registered under a false name and paid cash for a four-day stay. He didn't even have to show his false driver's license or credit card.

With his bag in his room and the room key in his pocket, Henry Charon set forth upon the streets. He wandered along looking at everything, reading street signs and occasionally referring to a map. After an hour of strolling he found himself in Lafayette Park, across the street from the White House.

Comfortable in spite of the sixty-degree temperature, he sat on a bench and watched the squirrels. One paused a few feet away and stared at him. "Sorry," he muttered with genuine regret. "Don't have a thing for you today."

After a few moments he strolled toward the south edge of the block-sized park.

Four portable billboards stood on the wide sidewalk facing the White House. ANTINUCLEAR PEACE VIGIL the signs proclaimed. Two aging hippies in sandals, one male, one female, attended the billboards.

Across the eight-lane boulevard, surrounded by lush grass and a ten-foot-high, black wrought-iron fence, stood the White House, like something from a set for *Gone With the Wind.* The incongruity was jarring amid the stone-and-steel office buildings that stretched away in all directions.

Along the sidewalk curb were bullet-shaped concrete barricades linked together at the top by a heavy chain. Henry Charon correctly assumed they had been erected to impede truck-bomb terrorists. Similar barricades were erected around the White House gates, to his left and right, down toward the corners.

Tourists crowded the sidewalk. They pointed cameras through the black fence and photographed each other with the White House in the background. Many of the tourists, at least half, appeared to be Japanese.

On the sidewalk, parked back-in against the fence, sat a security guard on his motorcycle, a Kawasaki CSR 350, doing paperwork. Charon walked closer and examined his uniform; black trousers with a blue stripe up each leg, white shirt, the ubiquitous portable radio transceiver, nightstick, and pistol. The shoulder patch on his shirt said U.S. PARK POLICE.

Another man standing beside Charon spoke to the guard: "Whatever happened to the Harleys?"

"We got them too," the guard responded, and didn't raise his eyes from his report.

Charon walked on, proceeding east, then turned at the corner by the Treasury building and walked south along the fence. Looking in at the mansion grounds he could see the guards standing at their little kiosks, the trees and flowers, the driveway that curved up the entrance. A black limo stood in the shade under the roof overhang, waiting for someone.

He strolled westward toward the vast expanse of grass that formed the Ellipse. Tourists hurried by him without so much as a glance. Never a smile or a head nod. The little man who wasn't there found a spot to sit and watch the people.

Inside the White House the attorney general was passing a few minutes with the President's chief of staff, William C. Dorfman, whom he detested.

Dorfman was a superb political operator, arrogant, condescending, sure of himself. An extraordinarily intelligent man, he had no patience for those with lesser gifts. The former governor of a Midwestern state, Dorfman had been a successful entrepreneur and college professor. He seemed to have a sixth sense about what argument would carry the most weight with his listeners. What Dorfman lacked, the attorney general firmly believed, was any sense of right and wrong. The political expedient of the moment always struck Dorfman as proper.

The real flaw in Dorfman's psyche, the attorney general mused, was the way he regarded people as merely members of groups, groups to be manipulated for his own purposes. Over at Justice the attorney general referred to Dorfman as "the Weathervane." He had some other, less complimentary epithets for the chief of staff, but these he used only in the presence of his wife, for the attorney general was an old-fashioned gentleman.

Others in Washington were less kind. Dorfman had racked up an impressive list of enemies in his two years in the White House. One of the more memorable remarks currently going around the cocktail-party circuit was one made by a senator who felt he had been double-crossed by the chief of staff: "Dorfman is a genius by birth, a liar by inclination, and a politician by choice."

Just now as he listened to Will Dorfman, the senator's remark crossed the attorney general's mind.

"What happens if this guy gets acquitted?" Dorfman asked, for the second time.

"He won't," the attorney general, Gideon Cohen, said curtly. He always found himself speaking curtly to Dorfman.

"There'll be a dozen retired crocks and out-of-work cleaning women on that jury, people who are such little warts they've never heard of Chano Aldana or the Medellín cartel, people who don't read the papers or watch TV. The defense lawyers won't let anyone on that jury who even knows where Colombia *is*. When the jurors finally figure out what the hell is going on, they're going to be scared pissless."

"The jury system has been around for centuries. They'll do their duty."

Dorfman snorted and repositioned his calendar on the desk in front of him. He glanced at the vase of fresh-cut flowers that were placed on his desk every morning, one of the White House perks, and helped himself to a handful of M&Ms in a vase within his reach. He didn't offer any to his visitor. "You really believe that crap?"

Cohen *did* believe in the jury system. He knew that the quiet dignity of the courtroom, the bearing of the judge, the seriousness of the proceedings, the possible consequences to the defendant—all that had an effect on the members of the jury, most of whom, it was true, were from modest walks of life. Yet the honest citizen who felt the weight of his responsibilities was the backbone of the system. And ten-cent sophisticates like Dorfman would never understand. Cohen looked pointedly at his watch.

Dorfman sneered and hid it behind his hand. Gideon Cohen was one of those born-to-money Harvard grads who had spent his adult life waltzing to the top of a big New York law firm, a guy who gave up eight or nine hundred thou a year to suffer nobly through a tour in the cabinet. He liked to stand around at parties and cluck about the financial sacrifices with his social equals. Cohen was a royal pain in a conservative's ass. Even worse, he was a snob. His whole attitude made it crystal clear that Dorfman couldn't have gotten a job polishing doorknobs at Cohen's New York firm.

When Cohen looked at his watch the third time, Dorfman rose and stepped toward the door to check with the secretary. As he passed Cohen, he farted.

Alone in the chief of staff's plush, spacious office, Gideon Cohen let his eyes glide across the three original Winslow Homer paintings on the wall and come to rest on the Frederick Remington bronze of a bronc rider about to become airborne, also an original. More perks, gaudy ones, just in case you failed to appreciate the exalted station of the man who parked his padded rump in the padded leather chair. The art belonged to the U.S. government, Cohen knew, and the top dozen or so White House staffers were allowed to choose what they wanted to gaze upon during their tour at the master's feet. Unfortunately the art had to go back to the museums when the voters or the President sent the apostles back to private life.

Ah, power, Cohen mused disgustedly, what a whore you are!

Behind him, he heard Dorfman call his name.

Three minutes later in the Oval Office Dorfman settled into one of the leather chairs as Cohen shook hands with the President. George Bush had on his Kennebunkport outfit this afternoon. He was leaving for Maine just as soon as he finished this meeting, which Cohen had pleaded for.

"The dope king again?" the President muttered as he dropped into a chair beside Cohen.

"Yessir. The drug cartels in Colombia are issuing death threats, as usual, and the Florida senators are in a panic."

"I just got off the phone with the governor down there. He doesn't want that trial in Florida, anywhere in Florida."

"You seen this morning's paper?"

George Bush winced. "Mergenthaler's on his high horse again."

Ottmar Mergenthaler's column this morning argued that since the drug crisis was a national crisis, the trial of Chano Aldana should be moved to Washington. He also implied, snidely, that the Bush administration was secretly less than enthusiastic about the war on drugs. "I detect the golden lips of Bob Cherry," Bush said. Cherry was the senior senator from Florida. No doubt he had been whispering his case to the columnist.

"I think we should bring Aldana here, to Washington," Cohen said. "We can blanket the trial with FBI personnel, convict this guy, and do it without anyone getting hurt."

Bush looked at his chief of staff. "Will?"

"Politically, it'll look good if we do it right here in Washington in front of God and everybody. It'll send a message to Peoria that we're really serious about this, regardless of Mergenthaler's columns. Stiffen some backbones in Colombia. *If*—and this is a damn big if—we get convictions."

"What about that, Gid?" the President asked, his gaze shifting to the attorney general. "If this guy beats the rap, it sure as hell better happen down in Florida."

"We can always fire the U.S. attorney down there if he blows it," Dorfman said blandly and smiled at Cohen.

"Chano Aldana is going to be convicted," Gideon Cohen stated forcefully. "A district jury convicted Rayful Edmonds." Young Rayful had led a crime syndicate that distributed up to two hundred kilos of crack cocaine a week in the Washington area, an estimated thirty percent of the business. "A jury'll convict Aldana. If it doesn't happen, you can fire your attorney general."

Dorfman kept his eyes on Cohen and nodded solemnly. "May have to," he muttered. "But what will a conviction get us? When Rayful went to jail the price of crack in the District didn't jump a dime. The stuff just kept coming in. People aren't stupid—they see that!"

"This drug business is another tar baby," the President said slowly, "like the damn abortion thing. It's political dynamite. The further out front I get on this the more people expect to see tangible results. You and Bennett keep wanting me to take big risks for tiny gains, yet everyone keeps telling me the drug problem is getting worse, not better. All we're doing is pissing on a forest fire." He sent his eyebrows up and down. "Failure is very expensive in politics, Gid."

"I understand, Mr. President. We've discussed—"

"What would we have to do to solve this drug mess, and I mean *solve* it?"

Gideon Cohen took a deep breath and exhaled slowly. "Repeal the Fourth Amendment or legalize dope. Those are the choices."

Dorfman leaped from his chair. *"For the love of—*are you out of your *mind?"* he roared. *"Jeez-us H.—"*

Bush waved his chief of staff into silence. "Will convicting Chano Aldana have *any* effect on the problem?"

"A diplomatic effect, yes. A moral effect, I hope. But—"

"Will convicting him have any direct effect at all on the amount of drugs that comes into the United States?" Dorfman demanded.

"Hell, no," Cohen shot back, relieved to have a target for his frustration. "Convicting a killer doesn't prevent murder. But you have to try killers because a civilized society cannot condone murder. You have to punish it whenever and wherever you can."

"This war on drugs has all the earmarks of a windmill crusade," Dorfman explained, back in his seat and now the soul of reason. "Repealing the Fourth Amendment, legalizing dope . . ." He shook his head slowly. "We have to take positive steps, that's true enough, but the President cannot appear as an ineffectual bumbler, an incompetent. That's a sin the voters won't forgive. Remember Jimmy Carter?" His voice turned hard: *"And he can't advocate some crackpot solution.* He'd be laughed out of office."

"I'm not asking for political hara-kiri," Cohen said wearily. "I just want to get this dope kingpin up here where we can try him with enough security so that we don't have any incidents. We need to ensure no one gets to the jurors. The jurors have to *feel* safe. We *will* get convictions."

"We'd better," Dorfman said caustically.

"Will, you've argued all along that what was needed here was more cops, more judges, and more prisons," Cohen said, letting a little of his anger leak out. " 'Leave the rehab programs and drug-prevention seminars to the Democrats,' you said. Okay, now we have to put Aldana in prison. This is where that policy road has taken us. We have no other options."

"I'm not suggesting we let him go," Dorfman snarled, his aggressive instincts fully aroused. "I'm wondering if you're the man to put him in the can."

The President waved his hands to cut them off and rose to his feet. "I don't fancy having to apologize to this asshole and buy him a plane ticket back to Medellín. Bring Aldana to Washington. But announce this as your decision, Gid. I've got a plane to catch." He paused at the door. "And Gid?"

"Yessir."

"Don't make any speeches about repealing the Fourth Amendment. Please."

Cohen nodded.

"Everybody's getting panicky. Ted Kennedy says cigarette smoking leads to drug abuse. That dingy congresswoman—Strader—wants to put a National Guardsman on every corner in Washington. Somebody else wants to put all the addicts in the army. A columnist out in Denver wants us to invade Colombia—I'm not kidding—as if Vietnam never happened." Bush opened the door and held it. "Maybe we should put all the addicts in the army and send *them* to Colombia."

Dorfman tittered.

"You're a good attorney general, Gid. I need you to keep thinking. Don't panic."

Cohen nodded again as the President went through the door and it closed behind him.

Henry Charon took twenty minutes to circle the White House grounds. On the west side of the executive mansion he found himself across the street from a gray stone mausoleum that his map labeled the Executive Office Building.

He was standing facing it with his hands in his pockets when he heard the sound of a helicopter. He turned. One was coming in from the southeast, lower and lower over the tops of the buildings, until it turned slightly and sank out of sight, hidden by the trees, on the grounds behind the White House.

Henry Charon retraced his steps south along the sidewalk, looking for a gap in the trees and shrubs where the helicopter would be visible. He could find no such gap. Finally he stopped and waited, listening to the faint tone of the idling jet engines. The sound had that distinctive whop-whop-whop as the downwash of the rotors rhythmically pulsed it.

The chopper had been on the ground for four and a half minutes by Charon's watch when the engine noise rose in pitch and volume. In a few seconds the machine became visible above the trees. The nose pitched down and the helicopter began to move forward. Now it laid over on its side slightly and veered right as it continued to climb, its engines apparently at full power. The mirage distortions that marked the hot jet exhausts were plainly visible.

The machine finished its turn to the southeast and continued to climb and accelerate. Finally it was hidden by one of the buildings over beyond the Treasury. Which one? Henry Charon consulted his map.

With his hands in his pockets, Charon walked past the White House on Constitution Avenue and proceeded east.

Six blocks north, in the Washington Post building on Fifteenth Street NW, Jack Yocke had asked to attend the afternoon story conference of editors. At the meeting an editor from each of the paper's main divisions—metro, national, foreign, sports, style—briefed the lead stories that his staff wanted run in tomorrow's paper. The *Post*'s executive or managing editor then picked the stories for the next day's front page.

Arranged on the table in front of every chair were stacks of legal-sized papers, "slug" sheets, containing brief paragraphs on each of the top stories for tomorrow's paper. On weekdays the *Post*'s executive editor, Ben Bradlee, routinely attended Page One meetings. Weekends, Yocke knew, Bradlee would escape to his Maryland west shore hideaway unless his wife, Sally, was throwing a dinner or the Redskins were playing at home.

Yocke took his seat and studied the slug sheets. The beltway killing yesterday afternoon was in there, as was last night's "stoop murder." Both stories had unusual twists. The beltway killing looked like a wire-service story from Los Angeles, the city of rage, yet it had happened here in Washington—Powerville U.S.A.—and the killer had used a rifle. The victim was one Walter P. Harrington, head cashier of Second Potomac Savings and Loan. The neighbors had told Yocke that Harrington was a prig, a martinet, married to an equally offensive wife, yet for all of that respected as an honest, hard-working citizen who kept to himself and never disturbed the neighborhood.

The stoop murder appeared to be a garden-variety mob rubout, but the victim, Judson Lincoln, apparently had not been associated with the mob in any way. Yocke had spent two hours this morning working the phones and hadn't heard a hint. Lincoln owned a string of ten check-cashing establishments scattered through the poorer sections of downtown D.C. He had been mentioned in stories in the *Post* at least seven times in the last twelve years, always as a prominent local businessman. Twice the *Post* had run his photo.

How would one handle that in a news story? *"Judson Lincoln, prominent District businessman who was not a member of any crime family, was professionally assassinated last night on the stoop of his mistress's town house as the lady looked on."* Great lead!

Black, honest, respected, sixty-two-year-old Judson Lincoln had enjoyed the company of young women with big tits. If that was his worst sin he was probably sitting on a cloud strumming a harp right now. Lincoln had just returned from the theater with one such woman when he was gunned down. Had his outraged wife arranged his murder?

Jack Yocke was musing on these mysteries when the framed lead press plate mounted on the wall, the *Post*'s very own trophy, captured his attention. It was Bradlee's favorite *Post* front page: NIXON RESIGNS.

Yesterday's news, Yocke sighed to himself as he surveyed the ranks of the fashionably disheveled men and women taking seats around the table. Most of them were young, in their late twenties or early thirties.

These aggressive, mortgaged-to-the-hilt graduates of prestigious colleges had replaced the overweight cigar chompers of yesteryear for whom murders were bigger news than presidential pontifications. Whether the new journalism was better was debatable, but one thing was certain: trendy cost more, a lot more. The new-age journalists of *The Washington Post*—always three words with the definite article capitalized, intoned the style manual—were paid about twice the real wages of the shiny-pants reporters of the manual typewriter era.

Some of this new breed dressed like fops—white collars atop striped shirts, with carefully uncoordinated padded coats and pleated trousers. How the old *front page*-style reporters would have hooted through their broken teeth at these dandies of the nineties!

And here was their leader, the deputy managing editor, Joseph Yangella, making his entrance. He was nattily dressed, fashionably graying, socially concerned, a man you would never see half potted at a prizefight with a floozie on his arm. He nodded right and left and settled into his seat at the head of the conference table. His shirtsleeves were rolled up and his tie was loosened, as usual. Why did he wear a tie, anyway? He got right to business.

"This Colombian doper—where is he going for trial? Ed?" Yangella looked over his glasses, which he habitually kept perched precariously on the end of his nose.

The national editor said, "We're getting all kinds of rumblings. Senator Cherry doesn't want him tried in Florida and is throwing his weight around. Justice isn't saying anything. The governor of Florida is having a fit. Nothing from the White House, although we hear the attorney general went over there about an hour ago."

"Any announcements coming?"

"Maybe later today. Nothing for sure."

"What's your lead right now?"

"Cherry and the governor."

The editor nodded. He perused the slug sheet. "Another airliner bombing in Colombia?"

"Yes," the foreign editor told him. "Seventy-six people dead, five of them Americans. The Medellín cartel is taking credit. Retaliation for the extradition of Aldana. It's the fifth or sixth one they've blown up in the last couple of years. They also blew up a bank yesterday and killed another judge. We've got some pictures."

The paper's pollster spoke. "We've got a poll conducted by a newspaper in Miami coming in over the wires. Seventy-three percent of those polled don't want Aldana tried in south Florida."

"Can we get a poll here in Washington?" Yangella asked him.

"Take some time."

The conversation moved to international affairs; political events in Germany, Moscow, and Budapest, and a flood in Bangladesh. They spent a minute discussing the efforts to rescue a child trapped in an abandoned well in Texas, a story that the TV networks were feasting on. Forty-five seconds were devoted to a new study on the reasons high schools gave diplomas to functional illiterates.

The managing editor didn't say a word or ask a question about Jack Yocke's murder stories. A murder is a murder is a murder, Yocke told himself. Unless you have the good fortune to be spectacularly butchered by a beautiful young woman from a filthy rich or politically prominent family, your demise is *not* going to make the front page of *The Washington Post*.

Joseph Yangella was clearing his throat to announce his decisions when the door opened and a woman from national stuck her head in.

"News conference at Justice in forty-five minutes. Rumor has it Cohen will announce that Aldana is being brought back to Washington for arraignment and trial."

Yangella nodded. The tousled head withdrew and the door closed softly.

"All right then," Yangella announced. "On the front page we'll go with the doper to Washington." He put a check mark beside each story as he announced it. "The poll in Miami, airliner bombing and violence in Colombia, flooding in Bangladesh, the kid in the well, illiterate graduates. Photos of the airliner bombing and the rescue team in Texas. Let's do it."

Everyone rose and strode purposefully for the door.

After dinner that evening Henry Charon bought copies of the *Post* and the *Washington Times* and took them to his room. It was after nine P.M. when he finished the papers. The assassin stood at the window a moment, looking at the lights of the city. He stretched, relieved himself in the bathroom, and put on a sweater and warm coat. The paper said the temperature might drop to forty tonight. He made sure the room door locked behind him on his way out.

CHAPTER THREE

* * * * * * * * *

Jack Yocke and his date could hear the voices through the door. When he knocked the door was immediately opened by a black-haired, gawky colt of a girl, about twelve years old or so. She smiled, flashing her braces, as she stood aside to allow them to pass.

"Hi," said Jack.

"Hi. I'm Amy. My folks are here somewhere. Drinks are in the kitchen." She spoke quickly, the words tumbling over each other.

"Jack Yocke." He stuck out his hand solemnly. "This is Tish Samuels."

The youngster shook hands with her eyes averted, blushing slightly. "Pleased to meet you," she murmured.

They found their hostess in the kitchen talking with several other women. When she turned to them, Yocke said, "Mrs. Grafton, I'm Jack Yocke, one of your students. This is Tish Samuels."

"I remember you, Mr. Yocke. You had such a terrible time with your pronunciation." She extended her hand to Tish. "Thanks for joining us. May I fix you a drink? Snacks are in the dining room."

"What a lovely apartment you have, Mrs. Grafton," Tish said.

"Call me Callie."

His duty done, Yocke left Tish to visit with the women and wandered into the dining area. He surveyed the crowd with a professional eye. His fellow students he knew, and their spouses and dates he quickly catalogued. But there were some other guests he didn't know. He was greeting people and reminding them of his name when he saw the man he wanted to meet lounging against a wall, beer in hand, listening to a shorter man wearing a beard. Jack Yocke nodded and smiled his way through the crowd.

The bearded man was monopolizing the conversation. Yocke caught snatches of it: ". . . The critical factor is that real communism has never been tried . . . commentators ignore . . . still viable as an ideal. . . ."

The trapped listener nodded occasionally, perfunctorily. Steel-rimmed glasses rode comfortably on a prominent nose set in a rather square face. His thinning, short hair was combed straight back. Just visible on his left temple was a jagged scar that had obviously been there for years. As his gaze swung across Yocke, who grinned politely, the reporter got a glimpse of gray eyes. Just now the man's features registered polite interest, although when his eyes scanned the crowd, the expression faded.

The reporter broke in, his hand out. "Jack Yocke."

"Jake Grafton."

Grafton was a trim six feet tall, with just the slightest hint of tummy sag. He looked to be in his early forties. According to the people Yocke talked to, this man was destined for high command in the U.S. Navy, assuming, of course, that he didn't stumble somewhere along the way. And Jack Yocke, future star journalist, needed access to those on their way to the high, windswept places.

"Our host," Yocke acknowledged, and turned to the other man.

"Wilson Conroy."

"Ah yes, Professor Conroy, Georgetown University. You're something of a celebrity."

The professor didn't seem overjoyed at that comment. He grunted something and took a sip of his drink, something clear in a tall glass.

"Political science, isn't it?" Yocke knew that it was. Conroy was a card-carrying communist with tenure on the Georgetown faculty. A couple of years ago the paper had a reporter attend several of his classes, during which Conroy vigorously championed the Stalinist viewpoint in a one-sided debate with his students, few of whom could defend themselves from the professor's carefully selected facts and acid tongue. The resulting story in the Sunday edition of the *Post* had ignited yet another public drive to have the professor fired. The encrusted layers had been thoroughly blasted from the pillars of academic freedom with columns, editorials, and a flood of letters to the editor, all of which sold a lot of newspapers but accomplished nothing else whatever. A half dozen congressmen had gotten into the act for the edification of the folks back home, on the off chance there might be a couple of votes lying around loose in their districts.

Conroy had relished the villain's role, reveled in the notoriety, right up until the fall of 1989, when communist governments in Eastern Europe had begun collapsing like houses of cards. Since then he had been keeping a low profile, refusing to grant interviews to the press.

"Yes. Political science." The academic's eyes flicked nervously over the crowd of people, who were chattering in the usual cocktail-party hubbub.

"Tell me, Professor, what do you make of the latest moves in the Soviet Politburo?"

The professor turned to face Yocke squarely. As he did Jake Grafton lightly touched Yocke's arm, then slid away from the wall and moved toward the snacks.

"They're abandoning the faith. They're abandoning their friends, those who have believed and sustained them."

"Then, in your opinion, communism hasn't failed?"

The professor's lips quivered. "It's a great tragedy for the human race. The communists have become greedy, sold their souls for dollars, sold their dream to the American financial swashbucklers and defrauders who have enslaved working people. . . ." He ranted on, becoming more and more embittered.

When he paused for breath, Yocke asked, "What if they're right and you're wrong?"

"*I'm* not wrong! We were *never* wrong!" Conroy's voice rose into a high quaver. "*I'm not wrong!*" He backed away from Yocke, his arms rigid at his sides. His empty glass fell unnoticed to the carpet. "We had a chance to change mankind for the *better*. We had a chance to build a true community where all men would be brothers, a world of workers free from exploitation by the strong, the greedy, the lazy, those who inherit wealth, those . . ."

All eyes were on him now. Other conversations had stopped. Conroy didn't notice. He was in full cry: ". . . the exploiters have triumphed! *This* is mankind's most shameful hour." His voice grew hoarse and spittle flew from his lips. "The communists have surrendered to the rich and powerful. They have sold us into *bondage,* into *slavery!"*

Then Callie Grafton was there, her hand on his shoulder, whispering in his ear. Wilson Conroy's eyes closed and his shoulders sagged. She led him gently from the silent room and the startled eyes.

Subdued conversations began again.

Jack Yocke stood there isolated, all eyes avoiding him. Tish Samuels was nowhere in sight. Suddenly he was desperately thirsty. He headed for the kitchen.

He was standing there by the sink working on a bourbon and water when Jake Grafton came in.

"What'd you say your name was?"

"Jack Yocke, Captain. Look, I owe you and your wife an apology. I didn't mean to set Conroy off."

"Umm." Jake opened the refrigerator and took out a bottle of beer. He twisted off the cap and took a sip. "What kind of work do you do?"

"I'm a reporter. *Washington Post.*"

Grafton nodded once and drank beer.

"Your wife is a fine teacher. I really enjoyed her course."

"She likes teaching."

"That comes through in the classroom."

"Heard anything this afternoon about that Colombian druggie, Aldana? Where is he going to end up?"

"Here in Washington. Justice announced it three or four hours ago." Jake Grafton sighed.

"Think there'll be trouble?"

"Wouldn't surprise me," Yocke's host said. "Seems every age has at least one Caligula, an absolute despot absolutely corrupted. Ours are criminal psychopaths, and we seem to have a lot more than one. I hear Chano Aldana has a net worth of four billion dollars. Awesome, isn't it?"

"Is the American government ready to endure the problems the Colombian government is having?"

Jake Grafton snorted. "My crystal ball is sorta cloudy just now. Why'd you take a Spanish class, anyway, Jack?"

"Thought it would help me on the job." That was true enough, as far as it went. Jack Yocke had taken the course so he could get bargaining chips to talk his way onto the foreign staff where reporters fluent in foreign languages had a leg up. Still, he wasn't about to pass up an opportunity to meet anybody who might help him later in his career, so he had come to the end-of-semester party to meet Jake Grafton. "Maybe I can get a jail-cell interview with Aldana."

That comment made Grafton shrug.

"I understand you're in the Navy?"

"Yeah."

"On the staff of the Joint Chiefs?"

Those gray eyes behind the steel-rimmed spectacles appraised Yocke's face carefully. "Uh-huh."

Yocke decided to try a shot in the dark. "What do you think will happen when they bring Aldana here for trial?"

Jake Grafton's face registered genuine amusement. "Enjoy the party, Jack," he said over his shoulder as he went through the door.

Oh well, Yocke reflected. Creation took God six days.

He heard someone knocking on the hall door and stepped to the kitchen door, where he could inspect the new arrival. The daughter, Amy, passed him and pulled the door open.

"Hey, beautiful." The man who entered was about thirty, five feet ten or so, with short brown hair and white, even teeth. He presented Amy with a box wrapped in Christmas paper. "For you, from some ardent admirers. Merry yo ho ho and all that good stuff."

The girl took the box and shook it enthusiastically.

"I wouldn't do that if I were you," the newcomer said seriously. "That thing breaks, the world as we know it will cease to exist. Time and space will warp, everything will be twisted and grossly deformed and sucked right in—rocks and dirt and cats and kids and everything." He made a slurping sound with his mouth. "The moon'll probably go too. Maybe a couple planets."

Smiling broadly, Amy shook the box vigorously one more time, then threw her arms around the man. "Oh, Toad! Thank you."

"It's from me *and* Rita." He ran his fingers through her hair and arranged a lock behind an ear.

"Thank her too."

"I will."

As Amy trotted away, Jack Yocke introduced himself.

"Name's Toad Tarkington," the newcomer informed him.

Another navy man, Jack Yocke thought with a flash of irritation, with another of those childish buddy-buddy nicknames. He wondered what they called Grafton. "Toad, eh? Bet your mother cringes when she hears that."

"She used to. The finer nuances, sometimes they escape her." Tarkington gestured helplessly and grinned.

Jack Yocke suddenly decided he didn't like the smooth, glib Mr. Tarkington. "Most civilians don't understand the subtleties of male bonding, do they? But I think it's quaint."

The grin disappeared from Tarkington's face. He surveyed Yocke with a raised eyebrow for two or three seconds, then said, "You look constipated."

Before he could reply, Jack Yocke found himself looking at Tarkington's back.

A half hour later he found Tish in a group on the balcony. The view was excellent this time of evening, with the lights of the city twinkling in the crisp air. Washington had enjoyed an unseasonably long fall, and although there had been several cold snaps, the temperature was still in the fifties this evening. And all these people were outside enjoying it, even if they did have to rub their arms occasionally or snuggle against their significant other. To the left one could catch a swatch of the Potomac and straight ahead the Washington Monument rose above the Reston skyline.

"Everybody, this is Jack Yocke," Tish told the five people gathered there.

They nodded politely, then one of Yocke's fellow Spanish students resumed a monologue Yocke's appearance had apparently interrupted. He was middle-aged and called himself Brother Harold. "Anyway, I decided, why all the fasting, chanting, special clothes, and mantras to memorize? If I could reduce meditation to the essentials, make it a sort of subliminal programming, then the balance, the transcendence, could be made available to a wider audience."

"You ready to leave?" Yocke whispered to his date.

"A minute," she whispered back, intent on Brother Harold's spiel.

Yocke tried to look interested. He had already heard this tale three times this fall. Unlike Jake Grafton or Wilson Conroy, Brother Harold thought it would be a very good thing for Yocke to do a story about him for the newspaper.

". . . So I introduced music. Not just any music of course, but carefully chosen music of the soul." He expounded a moment on the chants of ancient monks and echo chambers and the spheres of the brain, then concluded, "The goal was ecstasy through reverberation. And it works! I am *so* pleased. My followers have finally found quiescence and tranquility. The method is startlingly transformative."

Yocke concluded he had had enough. He slipped back through the sliding glass door and waited just inside. Toad Tarkington was standing alone against a wall with a beer bottle in his hand. He didn't even bother to look at Yocke. The reporter returned the compliment.

In a moment Tish joined him. "What is quiescence?" she asked as she slid the door closed behind her.

"Damned if I know. I bet Brother Harold doesn't know either. Let's say good-bye to the hostess and split."

"He's so sincere."

"Crackpots always are," Yocke muttered, remembering with distaste his scene with Conroy.

Callie Grafton was at the door saying good-bye to another couple, her daughter Amy beside her shifting from foot to foot. Callie was slightly above medium height with an erect, regal carriage. Tonight her hair was swept back and held with a clasp. Her eyes look tired, Jack Yocke thought as he thanked her for the party and the Spanish class.

"I hope Professor Conroy is all right, Mrs. Grafton. I didn't mean to upset him."

"He's lying down. This is a very trying time for him."

Yocke nodded, Tish squeezed her hand, and then they were out in the corridor walking for the elevator.

"I really like her," Tish said once the elevator doors had closed behind them. "We had a delightful talk."

"She has strange friends," Yocke remarked, meaning Wilson Conroy.

"Since the collapse of communism in Eastern Europe and the Soviet Union," Tish explained, "people have been laughing at Conroy. He never minded being hated, reviled—"

"Never minded? The poisonous little wart *loved* it!"

"—but the laughter is destroying him."

"So Mrs. Grafton feels sorry for him, eh?"

"No," Tish Samuels said patiently. "Pity would kill him. She's Conroy's friend because he has no others."

"Umph."

In the parking lot she asked, "Did you meet Toad Tarkington?"

"Uh-huh."

"He and I had a nice chat. His wife is out of town, so he came by himself. He's very nice."

"Navy, right?"

"Golly, I'm not sure. I didn't ask."

"The military is what's wrong with this town. Every other guy you meet is in the service."

"So?"

Yocke unlocked the car and helped her into the passenger seat.

"I don't like the military," he said when he was in the driver's seat. He stuck the key into the ignition and engaged the starter. "I don't like the simplistic way they look at the world, I don't like the rituals, the deference to seniority, the glorification of war and suffering and death. I don't like the demands they make on the public purse. The whole gig irritates me."

"Well," said Tish Samuels tentatively, "I'm sure that basically the people in the service are pretty much like the rest of us."

Yocke continued his train of thought, unwilling to let it lie. "The military is a fossil. Warriors are anachronisms in a world trying to feed five billion people. They cause more problems than they solve."

"Perhaps," said his date, looking out the window and apparently not interested in the reporter's profound opinions.

"Did you meet Mrs. Grafton's husband?"

"Oh, I said a few words to him. He seems very nice, in a serious sort of way."

"Want to go get a drink someplace?"

"Not tonight, thank you. I'd better be getting home. Maybe the next time."

"Sure." Jack Yocke flicked the car into gear and threaded his way out onto the street.

After he dropped Tish Samuels at her apartment building, Jack Yocke drove downtown to the office. As he had expected, Ottmar Mergenthaler was working late. The columnist was in his small glassed-in cubicle in the middle of the newsroom tapping away on the word processor. Yocke stuck his head in.

"Hey, Ott. How's it going?"

Mergenthaler sat back in his chair. "Pull up a chair, Jack." When the reporter was seated, the older man asked, "How did it go this evening?"

"Okay, I guess."

"Well, what do you think of him?" Mergenthaler had been the one who suggested he try to meet the husband of Callie Grafton, the Spanish instructor.

"I don't know. I asked him for a simple opinion and he grinned at me and walked away."

"Rome wasn't written in a day. It takes years to develop a good source."

Yocke worried a fingernail. "Grafton doesn't give a hoot in hell what anybody thinks, about him or about anything."

Mergenthaler laced his fingers behind his head. "Four people whom I highly respect have mentioned his name to me. One of them, a vice admiral who just retired, had the strongest opinion. He said, and I quote, 'Jake Grafton is the most talented, most promising officer in the armed forces today.'" Mergenthaler cocked an eyebrow and pursed his lips. "Another senior official put it a little differently. He said, 'Jake Grafton is a man of war.'"

Jack Yocke snorted. "We really need guys like that with peace breaking out all over."

"Are you a natural-born cynic, or are you trying to grow into one?"

"These military people—a damned clique of macho knotheads worshiping the phallic gun. Grafton is just like all of them—oh, he was pleasant enough—but I could feel it."

Mergenthaler looked amused. "My very young and inexperienced friend, if you have to like the people you write about, you are in the wrong line of work."

Yocke grinned. "What're you writing tonight?"

"Drugs again." Mergenthaler turned back to the screen and scrolled the document up. He tapped the cursor position keys aimlessly while he read. Yocke stood and read over his shoulder.

The column was an epitaph for three young black men, all of whom had died yesterday on the streets and sidewalks of Washington. All three had apparently been engaged in the crack trade. All three had been shot to death. All three had presumably been killed by other young black men also engaged in the crack business. Three murders was slightly above the daily average for the metropolitan area, but not significantly so.

Mergenthaler had obviously spent most of the day visiting the relatives of the dead men: the column contained descriptions of people and places he could not have acquired over the phone.

When Yocke resumed his seat, he said, "Ott, you're going to burn yourself out."

The older man spotted something in the document he wanted to change. He punched keys for a moment. When he finished he muttered, "Too sentimental?"

"Nobody cares about black crackheads. Nobody gives a damn if they go to prison or starve to death or slaughter each other. You know that, Ott."

"I'll have to work some more on this. My job is to make people give a damn."

Yocke left the columnist's cubicle and went to his desk out in the newsroom. He found a notebook to scribble in amid the loose paper on his desk and got on the phone to the Montgomery County police. Perhaps they had made some progress on the beltway killing.

Jack Yocke had two murders of his own to write about, whether anyone gave a damn about the victims or not.

* * *

After all the guests had left, Toad Tarkington was washing dishes in the Graftons' kitchen when Amy came in and posed self-consciously where he could see her. She had applied some eyeshadow and lipstick at some point in the evening, Toad noted with surprise. He consciously suppressed a grin. This past year she had been shooting up, developing in all the right places. She was only a few inches shorter than Callie.

"Little past your bedtime, isn't it?"

"Oh, Toad, don't be so parental. I'm a teenager now, you know."

"Almost."

"Near enough."

"Grab a towel and dry some of these things."

Amy did as requested.

"Nice party, huh?" she said as she finished the punch bowl and put it away.

"Yeah."

"Is Rita coming for Christmas?"

"I hope so." Rita, Toad's wife, was a navy test pilot. Just now she was out in Nevada testing the first of the Navy's new A-12 stealth attack planes. Both Toad and Rita held the rank of lieutenant. "Depends on the flight test schedule, of course," Toad added glumly.

"Do you love Rita?" Amy asked softly.

Toad Tarkington knew trouble when it slapped him in the face. His gaze ripped from the dishes and settled on the young girl leaning against the counter and facing him self-consciously, her weight balanced on one leg and her eyes demurely lowered.

He cleared his throat. "Why do you ask?"

"Well," she said softly, flashing her lashes, "you're only fifteen years older than I am, and I'll be eighteen in five years, and . . ." She ran out of steam.

Toad Tarkington got a nice chunk of his lower lip between his teeth and bit hard.

He took his hands from the water and dried them on a towel. "Listen, little one. You've still got a lot of growing left to do. You'll meet Mr. Right someday. Maybe in five years or when you're in college. You've got to take life at its natural pace. But you'll meet him. He's out there right now, hoping that someday he'll meet you. And when you finally find him he won't be fifteen years older than you are."

She examined his eyes.

A blush began at her neck and worked its way up her face as tears welled up. "You're laughing at me."

"No no no, Amy. I know what it cost you to bring this subject up." He reached out and cradled her cheek in his palm. "But I love Rita very much."

She bit the inside of her mouth, which made her lips contort.

"Believe me, the guy for you is out there. When you finally meet him, you'll know. And he'll know. He'll look straight into your heart and see the warm, wonderful human being there, and he'll fall madly in love with you. You wait and see."

"Wait? Life just seems so . . . so *forever!*" Her despair was palpable.

"Yeah," Toad said. "And teenagers live in the now. You'll be an adult the day you know in your gut that the future is as real as today is. Understand?"

He heard a noise. Jake Grafton was lounging against the doorjamb. Jake held out his hands. Amy took them.

He kissed her forehead. "I think it's time for you to hit the sack. Tell Toad good night."

She paused at the door and looked back. Her eyes were still shiny. "Good night, Toad."

"Good night, Amy Carol."

Both men stood silently until they heard Amy's bedroom door click shut.

"She's really growing fast," Toad said.

"Too fast," said Jake Grafton, and he hunted in the refrigerator for a beer, which he tossed to Toad, then took another for himself.

Ten minutes later Callie joined them in the living room. The men were deep into a discussion of the Gorbachev revolution and the centrifugal forces pulling the Soviet Union apart. "What will the world be like after the dust settles?" Callie asked. "Will the world be a safer place or less so?"

She received a carefully thought-out reply from Toad and a sincere "I don't know" from her husband.

She expected Jake's answer. Through the years she had found him a man ready to admit what he didn't know. One of his great strengths was a complete lack of pretense. After years of association with academics, Callie found Jake a breath of fresh air. He knew who he was and what he was, and to his everlasting credit he never tried to be anything else.

As she sat watching him tonight, a smile spread across her face.

"Not to change the subject, Captain," Toad Tarkington said, "but is it true you're now the senior officer in one of the Joint Staff divisions?"

"Alas, it's true," Jake admitted. "I get to decide who opens the mail and makes the coffee."

Toad chuckled. After almost two years in Washington, he knew only too well how close to the truth that comment was. "Well, you know that Rita is out in Nevada flying the first production A-12. She's going to be pretty busy with that for a year or so, and they have a Test Pilot School–graduate bombardier flying with her. So I'm sort of the gofer in the A-12 shop now."

Jake nodded and Callie said something polite.

"What I was thinking," Toad continued, "was that maybe I could get a transfer over to your shop. If I'm going to make coffee and run errands, why not over at your place? Maybe get an X in the joint staff tour box."

"Hmmm."

"What d'ya think, sir?"

"Well, you're too junior."

"Oh, Jake," Callie murmured. Toad flashed her a grin.

"Really, Callie, he is too junior. I don't think they have any billets for lieutenants on the Joint Staff. It's a *very* senior staff."

"Then it needs some younger people," she told her husband. "You make it sound like a retirement home, full of fuddy-duddies and senior golfers."

"I am *not* a fuddy-duddy," Jake Grafton told her archly.

"I know, dear. I didn't mean to imply that you were." She winked at Toad and he laughed.

The lieutenant rose from the couch, said his good-byes, and after promising to tell Rita the Graftons said hello, departed.

"Really, Jake," Callie said, "you should see if he could transfer to the Joint Staff."

"Be better for his career if he cut his shore tour short and went back to sea in an F-14 squadron."

"Toad knows that. He just thinks very highly of you and wants to work nearby. That's quite a compliment."

"I know that." A smile spread across Jake Grafton's face. "The ol' Horny Toad. He's a good kid."

Henry Charon stood leaning against an abandoned grocery store in northeast Washington and watched the black teenagers in the middle of the street hawk crack to the drivers of the vehicles streaming by. Some of the drivers stopped and made purchases, some didn't. The drivers were white and black, men and women, mostly young or middle-aged. Knots of young black men stood on the corners scrutinizing traffic, inspecting the pedestrians, and keeping a wary eye on Charon.

The wind whipped trash down the street and made the cold cut through Charon's clothes. Yet he was dressed more heavily than most of the crack dealers, who stayed in continual motion to keep warm. Somewhere a boom box was blasting hard rock.

He had been there no more than five minutes when a tall, skinny youngster detached himself from the group on the corner across the street and skipped through the cars toward him.

"Hey, man."

"Hey," said Henry Charon.

"Hey, man, you gonna buy this sidewalk?"

"Just watching."

"Want some product?"

Charon shook his head. Four of the teenagers on the corner were staring at him. One of them sat down by a garbage can and reached behind it, his eyes glued to Charon and his interrogator. Charon would have bet a thousand dollars against a nickel that there was a loaded weapon behind that garbage can.

"A fucking tourist!" the skinny kid said with disgust. "Take a hike, honkey. You don't wanta get caught under the wheels of commerce."

"I'm curious. How do you know I'm not a cop?"

"You no cop, man. You ain't got the look. You some little booger tourist from nowhere-ville. Now I'm tired of your jive, honkey. You got ten seconds to start hiking back to honkey-town or you'll have to carry your balls home in your hand. You dig?"

"I dig." Henry Charon turned and started walking.

The intersection two blocks south was covered with steel plates and timbers. Under the street, construction was continuing on a new subway tunnel.

Using his flashlight, Charon looked for the entrance. He found it, closed with a sheet of plywood. He had it off in seconds.

The interior resembled a wet, dark, dripping cavern. Henry Charon felt his way along, inspecting the overhead when he wasn't looking for a place to put his feet. The tunnel continued ahead and behind him as far as he could see.

He began walking south, stepping over construction material and dodging the occasional low-hanging electrical wire. He inspected the sides of the tunnel and the overhead, looking for the ventilator shafts he knew would have to be there. He found three.

It was warmer here than it had been on the street. There was no wind, though a match revealed the air was flowing gently back in the direction from which he had come. Actually quite pleasant. Charon unbuttoned his coat and continued walking.

In several places the workmen had rigged forms to pour the concrete floor. The precast concrete shells were already in place on the arched top and sides of the tunnel, probably installed as the tunnel was dug.

After what he judged to be four hundred yards or so of travel, he came to a giant enlarged cavern. His flashlight beam looked puny as it examined the pillars and construction debris. When finished, this would no doubt be a subway station. Another tunnel came in on a lower level. Charon descended a ladder and walked away in the new direction.

This was his third exploratory trip to Washington in the past four weeks and the second time he had been in these tunnels. If the construction crews were making progress, it was not readily visible to Charon's untutored eye.

Tassone had visited him a month ago at the ranch in New Mexico, and he had had a list. Six names. Six men in Washington he had wanted killed. Was it feasible? Would Charon be interested? Charon had looked at the list.

"George Bush?"

"Yeah."

"You're asking me to kill the President of the United States?"

"No. I'm asking you if it can be done. If you say yes, I'll ask you if you're interested. If you say yes, I'll ask you how much. If all those questions are decided to the satisfaction of everyone involved, then we will decide whether or not to proceed, and when."

"These other names—all of them?"

"As many as possible. Obviously, the more you get, the more we'll pay."

Charon had studied the names on the list, then watched as Tassone burned it and crumbled the ashes and dribbled them out onto the wind.

"I'll think about it."

So after three trips to Washington, what did he think?

It was feasible to kill the President, of course. The President was an elected officeholder and had to appear in public from time to time. The best personal security system in the world could not protect a working politician from a determined, committed assassin. All the security apparatus could do was minimize the possibility that an amateur might succeed and increase the level of difficulty for a professional.

The real problem would come afterward. Charon had no illusions on that score. Successful or not, the assassin would be the object of the most intensive manhunt in American history. Every hand would be against him. Anyone found to have knowingly aided the assassin would be ruthlessly destroyed—financially and professionally and in every other way. In addition, accused conspirators would face the death penalty if the government could get a conviction, and God knows, the prosecutors would pull out all the stops. Before the hit the assassin would be on his own. Afterward he would be a pariah.

For the assassin to walk away from the scene of the crime would not be too difficult, with some careful planning, but as the full investigative resources of the federal government were engaged, the net would become more and more difficult to evade. The longer the killer remained at large, the greater the efforts of the hunters.

Yes, it would be a hunt, a hunt for a rabid wolf.

As Henry Charon saw it, therein lay the challenge. He had spent his life stalking game in the wild mountain places and, these last few years, in the wild city places. Occasionally a deer or elk or cougar had successfully eluded him and those moments made the kills sweeter. After assassinating the President, he would be the quarry. If he could do the unexpected, stay one jump ahead of those who hunted him, the chase would be—ah, the chase would be sublime, his grandest adventure.

And if he lost and his hunters won, so be it. Nothing lives forever. For the mountain lion and the bull elk and Henry Charon, living was the challenge. Death will come for the quick and the bold, the slow and the careful, the wise and the foolish, each and every one.

Death is easy. Except for a moment or two of pain, death has no terrors for those who are willing to face life. Henry Charon's acceptance of the biologically inevitable was not an intellectual exercise for a philosophy class, but subconscious, ingrained. He had killed too often to fear it.

Now he reached that place in the tunnel he had found on his last visit. It was in a long, gentle curve, halfway up the wall. As he had been walking along he had momentarily felt a puff of cooler air. Investigation had revealed a narrow, oblong gap just wide enough for a wiry man to wriggle through. On the other side was an ancient basement, the dark home of rats and insects.

After checking the area with his flashlight, Henry Charon squirmed through the gaping crack, which was lined with stones at odd angles. He was now in a room with a dirt floor and walls of old brick. The ceiling was a concrete slab. Above that, Charon had concluded after an afternoon of discreet pacing, was dirt and an asphalt basketball court.

This basement was at least a century old. The house which had stood above it had apparently been demolished thirty or forty years ago during a spasm of enthusiasm for urban renewal. The ceiling slab had not been poured here: the edges were not mated to the brick walls in any way. No doubt the demolition contractor had thought it cheaper to just cover the hole rather than pay to haul in dirt to fill it.

There was no way out of this room except through the subway tunnel. That was the bad news. The good news was that the subway tunnel was the only entrance. A man would be reasonably safe here for a short while if he could get in without being observed.

Air entered this subterranean vault from several cracks in the brick walls and around the large stones that choked the opening through which coal had once probably been dumped into the basement. Charon suspected that nearby were other basements, other century-old ruins of nineteenth-century Washington, and the dark air passages were used by rats to go back and forth.

He checked the supplies he had brought here on two evenings last week, on his last trip to Washington. Canned food, a sterno stove, a first-aid kit, two gallons of water, three blankets, and two flashlights with extra D-cell batteries. It was all here, apparently undisturbed. He examined one of the blankets more carefully with his flashlight. A rat had apparently decided it would make a good nest. He shook out the blanket and refolded it.

He picked up a handful of dirt from the floor and sifted it through his fingers. It was dry, the consistency of dust. That was good. This would not be a safe place to be if water in any quantity ever came in.

Charon turned off the flashlight and sat in the darkness near the exit hole, listening. The sounds of traffic on the street twenty to thirty feet over his head were always there. Faint but audible. There was another sound too, of such low frequency as almost to be felt rather than heard. He eased his head out into the tunnel for a look, then crawled out. Now he heard it, a faint rumble. It seemed to be coming down the tunnel.

Standing in the subway tunnel he reinspected the hole with the flash. He wanted to leave no obvious evidence that anyone had been in there. Satisfied, he walked south as the rumbling noise faded again to silence. Not total silence, of course. He could still hear the street sounds from the world above.

If Tassone just wanted George Bush assassinated, that would be a large enough challenge to satisfy anyone, Henry Charon mused as he walked along. Make the hit, ride out the manhunt that would immediately follow, then leave Washington several weeks later for the ranch. Sit at the ranch for several years enduring the agony of waiting for the FBI to come driving up the road, and hoping they never came.

But Bush was merely the first name on the list. The other five, they would have to be killed after the presidential hit. That was the rub. The sequence was dictated by logic. If he first shot the Chief Justice of the Supreme Court, or the attorney general, the Secret Service would surround Bush with a security curtain that one man could not hope to penetrate. So Bush had to be the first target.

That sequence inevitably created an escape problem of extraordinary complexity. He had to move in spite of the dragnet and find his targets. And escape without revealing his identity. Again and again.

Could it be done? Could he do it?

He glimpsed light ahead and doused the flashlight. Two hundred yards of careful walking brought him to a steel mesh. Here the new tunnel joined an existing one. He stood in the darkness and waited.

Yes. Here comes the rumble again, much louder, swelling and growing, rushing toward him.

He stood watching as a subway train rushed by with a roar, the passengers plainly visible in the windows, standing, sitting, reading, talking to each other. And as fast as the train had come, it was gone, the sound fading.

Henry Charon extracted a subway map from his hip pocket and consulted it in the dim glow of the flashlight. He traced the lines and looked again at the layout of the system, committing the routes to memory. The avenues and streets and subway lines, they had to be as familiar to him as the ridges and mesas of the Sangre de Cristos.

With the map back in his pocket, he examined the steel fence carefully and the padlocked mesh door in the middle of it. He could cut that lock if he had to. A Yale. He would buy one just like it, just in case.

It felt strange here in this tunnel, walking through the darkness with just the glow of the flashlight and the smell of earth in his nostrils. In fifteen minutes he arrived at the cavern that would someday be a subway station and picked his way around and through the scaffolding. He found the opening to the outside world, kicked the plywood off, then reset it.

It was chilly on the street. After buttoning his coat, Henry Charon walked along absorbing the sights and sounds, looking, examining the terrain yet again, searching for cover, committing everything to memory.

Could it be done? Could *he* do it?

Even if he pulled it off, did everything absolutely right and fate had no nasty little surprises for him—like a cop at an unexpected place or a tourist snapping pictures at the wrong time—Tassone and his unknown masters were still the weak links.

Who did Tassone work for? How many people in Tassone's organization knew of the New Mexico hitter, Tassone's trips, the cash in the suitcases? Were any of these people government informers? Would they become so in the future? Were any of them alcoholics or drug addicts? Would someone whisper to a mistress, brag at a bar?

All who knew the identity of the assassin of the President of the United States were serious threats for as long as they lived. They would always carry this immense, valuable secret. If they were ever arrested or threatened, the immense, valuable secret could always be sold or traded.

The project tempted Henry Charon. The preparations, the anticipation that would grow and grow, the kill, the chase afterward, just thinking of these things made him feel vigorously alive, like the first glimpse of a bull elk against a far ridge on a clear, frosty morning. Yet the unknown, faceless ones could ruin him at any time. If he successfully escaped he would have to live with the possibility of betrayal all the rest of his life.

Yet you had to weigh everything, and the hunt was what really mattered.

Henry Charon walked on, thinking again of the hunt and how it would be.

CHAPTER FOUR

★ ★ ★ ★ ★ ★ ★ ★ ★

On Sunday, T. Jefferson Brody woke up alone in his king-sized bed in his five-bedroom, four-bathroom, $1.6 million mansion in Kenwood. After a long hot shower, he shaved and dressed in gray wool slacks and a tweed sports coat that had set him back half a grand.

Ten minutes later he eased the Mercedes from the three-car garage and thumbed the garage-door controller as he backed down the drive.

T. Jefferson Brody should have felt good this morning. Friday he had deposited another fat legal fee in his Washington bank and shuffled another equally fat fee off to the Netherlands Antilles on the first leg of an electronic journey to Switzerland. He had done some calculations on an envelope last night, then burned the envelope. The sums he had managed to squirrel away were significant in any man's league: he had over four million dollars in cash here in the States on which he had paid income taxes and six million in Switzerland on which he hadn't. That plus the house (half paid for) and the cars, antiques, and art (cash on the barrelhead) gave him a nice, tidy little fortune. T. Jefferson was doing all right for himself.

The fly in the wine of T. Jefferson Brody was that he wanted a lot more. He knew there was a lot more to be made, a whale of a lot more, and it just didn't seem that he was getting a share commensurate with his contribution. The things he did—the things only he could do—enabled his clients to make mountains of money, yet he was left with the crumbs that dribbled from their napkins. Just fees. Never a percentage of the action. Of course, lawyers traditionally have received fees for their services, but T. Jefferson Brody's services weren't traditional.

As he drove down Massachusetts Avenue into the District this morning for breakfast with the representative of his oldest, though certainly not richest, client, T. Jefferson tried to decide if he should announce a fee increase or something equally nebulous that would put more money into his pocket. He would wait, he decided, to hear what the client wanted.

These people were going to have to realize that T. Jefferson Brody was a very valuable asset to have in their huddle. T. Jefferson delivered.

Always. Money talks and bullshit walks. Somehow he would have to make that point. Professionally and unobtrusively, of course.

He checked his car with the valet at the Hay Adams Hotel and walked purposefully through the lobby to the elevator. Whenever Bernie Shapiro came to town he always stayed in the same suite, a huge corner job with an excellent view of Lafayette Park and the White House.

Bernie opened the door, grunted once, and closed it behind the visitor. "When's it gonna get cold down here?"

"Weird weather," T. Jefferson agreed as he took off his topcoat and laid it on a handy chair. "Maybe the climate is really getting warmer."

"Like hell. Nearly froze my ass off in New York these past two weeks."

Bernie Shapiro was a bear of a man. He had been fearsome in his youth; now he was merely fat. The years, however, had added no padding to his abrasive personality. He sank into an easy chair and relit the stump of cigar that protruded from his fleshy jowls. "Breakfast'll be here in a few minutes," he muttered as he eyed his visitor through the thick smoke.

The attorney found a chair and took in the luxurious room and the White House, just visible from this angle through the naked tree branches.

Classical music played on the radio beside the bed a tad too loud for comfortable conversation. This was a normal precaution. The music would vibrate the window glass and foil any parabolic mikes that might be pointed in this direction by inquisitive souls, such as FBI agents.

The men discussed the Giants' and Redskins' chances this year as they waited for breakfast to be delivered. The knock of the room-service waiter came precisely on the hour. After all, this *was* the Hay Adams.

When the white-jacketed waiter had wheeled the serving cart back into the hall and closed the door behind him, Bernie opened his briefcase and extracted a device artfully crafted to look like a portable radio. This device detected the electromagnetic field created by microphones. Bernie pulled out the antenna, then walked around the room, paying careful attention to the needle on the dial as he paused at light switches and electrical outlets, swept the antenna over the food and slowly down Brody's back and front. The operation took about two minutes. Finally satisfied, Bernie nodded toward the conference table laden with food as he collapsed the antenna and flipped switches.

The lawyer seated himself and poured a cup of coffee while Bernie put the device back in his briefcase. Only when both men were seated and had their food on their plates did the serious conversation begin.

"We've decided to expand our business. What with everybody making acquisitions and expanding their profit potential, it seemed like the thing to do."

"Absolutely," T. Jefferson agreed as he forked into the eggs benedict.

"We thought we would get into the check-cashing business at several likely places around the country. We've located a little business here in

Washington and want you to buy it for us. You'll do all the negotiating, set up some corporations, front the whole deal."

"Same as the DePaolo deal?"

"Pretty much."

"What's the name of the company you want to buy?"

"A to Z Checks. The owner ran into some trouble Friday evening and the business now belongs to his widow. I want you to make her an offer. Better wait until Tuesday. The funeral's tomorrow. The business is ten outlets. We'll pay a flat four hundred thousand, but if you can get it for less you keep the difference."

"Okay."

Bernie got to work on his sausage as Jefferson Brody turned the project over in his mind and decided it offered few problems. A couple of dummy corporations and some negotiating. Assignments of the leases on the outlets—he knew from experience that these storefront operations were always leased—and the usual business papers. All very straightforward.

"If the widow won't take our offer, you let me know."

"What's the business make in profit?"

"About a hundred grand a year."

"Your offer sounds reasonable. But if you don't mind my asking, why do you want this business?"

"That's the second half of the project. The crack business here in Washington is turning some hefty dollars. Six organizations here in the area have all the trade. Anyone else tries to get started, they shut them down. These organizations are all getting along and turning decent money, with the usual friction at street level for turf." Bernie waved that away as a problem not worthy of discussion. "The real problem is washing the dough after they got it. That's the service we'll provide. We'll take the cash and trade it for government checks—welfare, ADC, Social Security, and so on—and the usual private checks, deposit the checks in a business account, then run the money through dummy corporations which will feed it to legit businesses owned by us. Other real businesses with absolutely no connection to the first set will feed money back to our crack friends. They'll get a nice legit income from a corporation they own and nobody can ever prove a thing. I think they'll really like this operation when it's explained to them. We won't need you for that though."

"What will you charge for this service?"

"Twenty percent." Bernie grinned.

Brody felt his eyebrows struggling to rise. He made an effort to control his face.

"They're paying ten to fifteen percent now. So they'll be less than enthusiastic at first. They'll change their minds, though, and see the benefits of our proposal."

"Will ten outlets do enough business to handle the volume you'll need?"

"I doubt it," Bernie said. "We'll probably double the number of outlets within a month, then open other outlets in other cities. A to Z is going to enjoy an explosive expansion."

They discussed the intricacies of it. The key to staying in business was having a bulletproof cover story. "You'll need a bank, maybe two," Brody told his client as they pushed their plates toward the center of the table and poured coffee.

"Yeah. There's a savings and loan in Alexandria that should become available in the next week or so. The head cashier had a bad accident on the freeway Friday. Guy named Harrington." Bernie grinned. "Fridays are not good days around here, apparently."

The lawyer chuckled his agreement.

Bernie continued: "This Harrington was washing money for Freeman McNally." McNally was the largest crack dealer in Washington and also one of T. Jefferson Brody's clients. Bernie Shapiro may or may not have known that. Brody survived by *never, ever* mentioning one client's affairs to another client. He had absolutely no intention of breaking that rule now.

Bernie continued: "A guy on the inside figured out what Harrington was up to and talked to a guy who knew somebody. One thing led to another, and now we got a deal with this guy on the inside. Tomorrow or the day after the regulators will be called in. Three or four days after that, the place will probably be for sale cheap. You're going to buy it for us."

T. Jefferson Brody grinned this time. "Okay. But we'll need some front people for this one. Little tougher to buy an S&L."

"Our guy inside will get a piece, and he'll come up with three or four names. We put up all the money and he'll run it for us. You'll do the legal work, of course."

They discussed it for over an hour. When they had ironed out the details, T. Jefferson Brody thought it time to broach the subject of his fee. "Bernie, this new enterprise should be very profitable for you."

"Should be." Bernie lit a fresh cigar.

"I want to raise my fee."

Bernie puffed serenely on the cigar and stared through the smoke at the lawyer. "We pay you fifty a month, Tee."

"I know. And I do excellent work that enables you to make really major money. In good conscience, Bernie, I think my fee should be higher."

"You're a fixer," Bernie Shapiro said, his eyes on the attorney. "If we go down the tubes, you'll still be standing there high and dry. You take no risks, you invest no money, you're shielded by client confidentiality. Fifty a month is enough."

Brody tried to interrupt but Bernie raised his palm. "We never expected you to do our work exclusively. If we thought you'd violated a confidence, Tee, tried to shave a little for yourself from one of our deals, or played both ends against the middle, we'd find another lawyer. We'd even send flowers to your funeral. But you don't do things like that. So we pay you a fifty-thousand-dollar monthly retainer for whatever little chores you do, regardless."

T. Jefferson Brody opened his mouth, then closed it again.

Bernie Shapiro smiled. He had a good smile. "Think of it this way, Tee. You don't even have to go to the trouble of billing us. We send the check on the first of the month even if you spent the previous month on vacation in the Bahamas. Isn't that so?"

Brody nodded.

"Thanks for dropping by this morning, Tee. Tuesday you start with the widow." Bernie stood and held the lawyer's coat. "Stay in touch."

"Sure."

"Remember, Tee. Greed is bad for your soul."

As T. Jefferson Brody drove away from the Hay Adams in his Mercedes coupé, Henry Charon left his hotel, a significantly more modest establishment than the Hay Adams, and set forth upon the sidewalks. This morning his course took him toward the Supreme Court building, immediately behind the Capitol. He circled the building slowly, examined the tags on the parking spaces, and stood looking at buildings across Second Street. Then he wandered in that direction.

Assassinating people was exactly like hunting deer. The hunter's task was to place himself to take advantage of a momentary opportunity. The skill involved was to get to the right place at the right time with the right equipment and to make the shot when fate and circumstances offered.

He should have been a military sniper, Charon thought, not for the first time. He would have been good at the work and he would have enjoyed it. Yet snipers need wars to employ their skills. An assassin is in demand all the time.

He came back to the unsolved problem of potential informers in the organization or group that wanted to hire him. He had no idea who these people were, though he supposed that with a reasonable effort he could find out. If he found out, what then?

Perhaps the thing to do was to plan now for a permanent disappearance, a permanent change of identity. The drawback was time. He didn't have enough time to do it right. And if done incorrectly, such a move would be worse than doing nothing at all.

Afterward, could he devote six months to proper preparation, then vanish? Would he have six months?

Mulling these and similar questions, in the alley behind the buildings facing Second Street Henry Charon found a dumpster sitting directly beneath a fire escape. He moved the large metal trash box and pulled on rubber gloves. Apparently no one was watching. Vaulting to the top of the dumpster, he curled his fingers around the lowest rung of the ladder and pulled it down. With one last glance around, Charon was on his way up.

The building didn't even have a burglar alarm. It was old, with wooden-frame windows. He used a credit card on a latch and was inside in seconds. The elevator worked. He took it to the top floor. The offices on this floor were empty and dark this Sunday afternoon. Henry Charon went looking for the stairs.

The door to the roof had a lock that yielded to a set of picks. Charon stepped out on the roof and took in the scene at a glance. The view down into the Supreme Court parking lot was partially obscured by defoliated tree branches. That didn't bother him. He had made many a shot through much thicker brush and foliage and at much longer ranges. The Supreme Court building was about a hundred yards from here and the Capitol about five hundred. The adjacent buildings were of the same height as this one. An eighteen-inch-high combing provided cover around the edge of the flat roof. Excellent.

Thirty seconds after opening the door, Charon had it closed and locked. Back down the stairs he went, out through the top-floor office window to the fire escape, down the ladder to the top of the dumpster. He was walking briskly toward Constitution Avenue a minute and nine seconds after he closed the door on the roof.

Jack Yocke carefully proofed his follow-up story on Friday's beltway murder. He scrolled it slowly up the screen as he checked every word and comma.

The heart of the story was a speculation by a Montgomery County police lieutenant that some frustrated speeder might have potted Walter P. Harrington in a moment of rage because he was a sadistic jerk who always drove at fifty-five miles per hour in the fast lane. Yocke had dressed it up some for the *Post,* but that was the essence of the story. No new evidence. The bullet that killed Harrington had not been recovered. No witnesses to the killing had come forward. The widow was devastated. The funeral was Monday.

Off the record, the Montgomery County police had admitted that the killing would probably never be solved unless the killer got drunk and talked too much. Jack Yocke had passed that information to the editor so he would not expect follow-up stories.

As he punched keys to send the story of Walter P. Harrington on its electronic way, Yocke saw Ottmar Mergenthaler stroll through the newsroom on his way to his cubicle. Mergenthaler waved him over.

"Hey, Jack, you busy right now?"

"Nothing that can't wait."

"That Colombian drug kingpin is having a press conference. Want to go with me?"

"Sure."

"Gotta get a tape recorder, then we'll do it."

In the car Jack asked, "How'd you get this plum, anyway?"

Mergenthaler chuckled. "I know the lawyer representing Aldana. Guy name of Thanos Liarakos, big criminal defense mercenary. Known him for years. He always represents mob guys and dopers. They're the only crooks who can afford him. Gets one off the hook just often enough to be able to charge outrageously and still have all the work he can handle. Anyway, he called and said Aldana was demanding a jail-cell press conference with a network TV crew, but I could come if I wanted."

"What's he going to say?"

"Liarakos didn't know. He strongly advised Aldana against talking to the press, but the client insisted."

"There goes his claim that media hype has prejudiced possible jurors—prevented any possibility of a fair trial."

"Yep. Looks like Aldana isn't the type to take advice from lawyers, no matter what they cost to keep around."

"Has he really got a net worth of four billion dollars?"

"Who the hell knows? I'll bet even Aldana doesn't."

Four billion! What is that . . . ? *Four thousand million?* The sum was beyond comprehension. Oh, the government throws around numbers like that, but not individuals. Four billion was more than the gross national product of Iceland. You could buy Arkansas for that amount, own your own state. You could hire every whore in North and South America and keep them as your private harem in the state you owned on the Mississippi. And if the feds didn't like it, you could hire every lawyer in New York and Washington to raise hell in every court in America. "That's a lot of money," Jack Yocke muttered.

"Too much."

Yocke snorted. "That's heresy, Ott! There's no such thing. Bite your tongue."

There was a mob at the district jail. Reporters and cameramen crammed the entryway. After Yocke and Mergenthaler elbowed their way to the desk, they found the desk sergeant engaged in a shouting match with a local TV anchorman as the cameras rolled.

"You can't keep us out. We're the press!"

"I don't give a fuck who you are. The only people who get in are people on this list." The sergeant stabbed the sheet of paper on the counter in front of him with a rigid finger. "You ain't on it. Now get the hell outta here or we'll find a cell for you. And turn off that fucking spotlight!"

"This is *America!*"

"Read my lips, asshole! *Out!*"

"Mergenthaler, *Washington Post.*" The reporter slid his credentials across the dark wood at the sergeant, who consulted his list while the TV anchorman made yet another eloquent protest.

"You're on the list. Through that door over there."

"I have another guy with me from the *Post*."

Yocke displayed his credentials and was waved through as the sergeant addressed himself to the still spluttering TV man: "No. No! *No!* What part of no don't you understand?"

Two policemen searched them for weapons while a third checked Mergenthaler's tape recorder. Then they were led down a long corridor that had decades worth of dirt caked on its dark, once-green walls. Up a flight of ill-lit stairs, through another security checkpoint, through steel doors that slid open as they approached and closed behind them, and past rows of brimming cells. The occupants jeered and shouted obscenities.

The reporters were led through another steel door into a booking room of some sort where a camera crew was busy setting up lights and two cameras. This room had several steel doors besides the one they had entered. One was partially open and Yocke peeked. Beyond was a suite of four cells, padded, cells for psychos. Apparently the cops didn't want Aldana out in the multiple-occupancy cells with the common criminals.

The network correspondent, whom Yocke recognized but didn't know, nodded at Mergenthaler, then consulted a notebook while a woman worked on him from a portable makeup box. She combed his hair and squirted hairspray. One of the technicians tested a pin-on microphone as a uniformed cop watched without expression.

Mergenthaler found a spot where he could observe and not be caught by the cameras. Yocke leaned against the wall beside him.

The minutes passed. Five, then ten.

Occasionally someone coughed, but mostly they stood silently. Waiting.

What kind of man was this Aldana? Jack Yocke tried to picture the man he thought would appear, based upon what he knew about him. A thug, he decided. Some sort of hate-filled Latin American barrio bastard who thought Adolf Hitler was the prophet of how to win and rule in the coming chaos. Sounds like the title of a self-help best-seller. Yocke wondered if there was a big book in Chano Aldana's future.

A darkly handsome man in a gray suit came out of one of the doors. He squinted against the floodlights, then said hello to the TV talker and Mergenthaler.

"My client will be out in a moment. Here are the rules. He has a statement to make, then the TV people get five minutes to ask questions. After they finish, Mergenthaler gets five minutes."

"I don't want Mergenthaler here while we're filming," the correspondent said.

"When will you run your interview?" Thanos Liarakos asked.

"Tonight probably, and on the morning show tomorrow."

"I don't see any problem." The lawyer frowned. "He isn't going to scoop you. And you can film while he asks questions, if you wish."

No, the TV people weren't going to do that. Under no circumstances were they going to take the chance that Mergenthaler might ask more perceptive questions on camera than their man.

"Show business," Mergenthaler whispered sourly to Yocke. Speaking louder, he asked, "Mr. Liarakos, do you know what Aldana will say?"

"No."

"Has he discussed it with you?"

"No."

"Did you recommend to your client that he hold a press conference?"

"No comment."

"If the prosecutors ask the judge for a gag order, will you fight it?"

"I never speculate in that manner."

"Can Aldana get a fair trial here in Washington?"

"I don't think that he can get a fair trial anywhere in the United States."

"How much longer do we have to wait?" grumped the TV man.

"I have one question, Mr. Liarakos," Yocke said. "Jack Yocke of the *Post.*"

"He with you, Ott?"

"Yes."

"Okay. Shoot."

"Are you satisfied that your client has arranged to pay your fee, which reportedly is very high, with money that is not the proceeds of any criminal activity?"

Liarakos frowned. "No comment," he said crisply, and disappeared through one of the steel doors.

The TV man grinned broadly at Yocke. A trace of a smile flickered across Mergenthaler's lips.

Time passed slowly. The TV man kept glancing at his watch.

After seven minutes, the door opened and two uniformed cops came out, then two men Jack Yocke took to be U.S. marshals. Liarakos followed them, then a Latin-looking man of medium height wearing a trim mustache. Other cops and marshals followed, but this was the man who captured Yocke's attention.

As he arranged himself in the chair and the television lights came on, Yocke stared. The man was pleasantly plump, with full cheeks that would turn into saggy jowls in a few more years. He looked like a middle-aged banker who hadn't raised a sweat since his school days. He was clad in slacks and a short-sleeved white shirt, no tie. He blinked at the glare of the lights and looked around warily as a technician hooked up the lapel mike.

When the technician was out of the way and one of the marshals had been waved out of camera-shot, the correspondent began. "I understand you have a statement to make, Señor Aldana."

Aldana looked straight at the camera.

"I am Chano Aldana," he said with a noticeable Spanish accent. "I am your worst nightmare come to life. I am the faceless, starving masses whom you refused food. I am the slave you delivered in chains to the merciless altar of the moneylenders. I am the sick you refused to heal. I am the beggar you turned away from the feast. To me has been given the key to the bottomless pit. And I have opened it."

The network correspondent stood for several seconds with his mouth ajar, his face slack.

"Señor Aldana, are you guilty of the crimes of which you are accused?"

"You are the guilty ones. Not I."

"Are you the head of the Medellín cocaine-smuggling cartel?"

"I am a Third World businessman."

When it became obvious that was the whole answer, the correspondent persisted, "Are you a cocaine smuggler?"

"I have never smuggled cocaine."

"Your statement seems to imply that people working for you will cause violence if you are not released. Is that what you mean?"

"I meant what I said. Precisely. The people who know of my reputation will tell you that I am a man of my word."

When Mergenthaler's turn came and the TV lights were off, he asked, "What did you mean, 'To me has been given the key to the bottomless pit'?"

"I am He who was thrown out of Heaven. I am He you have kept away from the feast. *To me has been given the key to the pit and I have opened it.*"

"How about one straight answer. Are you or are you not involved in the cocaine-smuggling business?"

"I have never smuggled cocaine."

"Do you really have a net worth of four billion American dollars?"

"I am a wealthy man. I do not know just how wealthy."

"At last, a straight answer."

Aldana's upper lip curled into a sneer and his eyes narrowed. His gaze locked on the journalist, he rose from the chair. As the marshals led him through the door that led back to his cell, he kept his eyes on Mergenthaler until the door cut off his view.

"He's crazy as a bedbug," Yocke said in the car.

Ottmar Mergenthaler sat motionless behind the wheel, the ignition key in his hand. "Too bad Geraldo Rivera missed this one."

"He didn't scare you with that staring act, did he?"

Mergenthaler glanced at the younger man. "Yeah. He did."

The columnist examined the key and carefully placed it in the ignition switch. "He's insane and has armies of hired killers that have murdered hundreds of politicians, judges, and police in Colombia. They've blown up airliners, bombed department stores and newspapers, and assassinated dozens of journalists who refused to be quiet. They don't care who they kill. They truly don't."

The columnist started the car and engaged the transmission. "Yeah, Jack, that man scared me."

CHAPTER FIVE

★ ★ ★ ★ ★ ★ ★ ★ ★

An American's enthusiasm for law and order is directly proportional to the degree to which he believes his personal safety or his livelihood is threatened. When the perceived threat recedes, so does his willingness to be policed.

America is the most underpoliced nation on earth. The average American spends his life without any but casual contact with policemen—except for the ubiquitous traffic cops enforcing ridiculously low speed limits that Americans insist are necessary and yet almost universally ignore. Many law-abiding citizens have never in their lives spoken to a policeman, and the vast majority have never suffered the indignity of contact with policemen performing their duty.

No paramilitary police patrol American streets. No secret police monitor telephone conversations or scrutinize mail or hire neighbors to tattle. No policeman calls an American to account for slandering the government or the president or writing scurrilous letters to editors or politicians.

Regardless of the degree of his paranoia or hatred, an American will be left undisturbed unless and until his conduct crosses the threshold into violence, in which case he can expect to reside in a cell for a relatively short time, there to contemplate the error of his ways. No firing squad. No political prison. No gulag. Though he be mad as a March hare, no permanent commitment to an insane asylum. In America a man's right to hate his neighbor is protected as it is nowhere else on earth.

In spite of repeated influxes of immigrants from every hate-soaked, war-torn corner of the earth, America has institutionalized personal freedom. The courts have zealously fostered it, perhaps unintentionally, by acting vigorously and self-righteously on the oft-stated and highly dubious assumption that for every wrong there is a remedy. Not a remedy in the next life, but here, in America. Now! Never in all of the tragic, bloody course of human history has such a radical, illogical concept been routinely accepted and acted upon by so many supposedly rational beings.

So the social fabric remains intact. No group of any size sincerely believes no one will listen to its grievance. Everyone will listen. Newspa-

pers will spill ink, the idle sympathize and donate money, politicians orate, judges fashion a remedy.

And America will go on.

J ACK Yocke stared at the words on the screen as he worried a fingernail. This was America as he saw it, a deliciously mad, pragmatic place. Americans want justice, but not too much. They want order, but not too much. They want laws, but not too many. Now, into this cauldron of free spirits had been introduced Chano Aldana and his four billion dollars.

$4,000,000,000. The amount of murder, mayhem, treachery, and treason that four billion dollars would buy was almost beyond comprehension. And Aldana was just the man to make the purchase. What did he care if the foundations cracked and the house came down? He had his. And he had served notice.

"Your style is atrocious." Ott Megenthaler was reading over his shoulder.

"Not right for the *Post,* eh?"

"Definitely not."

"Aldana can't win."

"You know it and I know it, but apparently he doesn't."

"A little licentiousness, Americans enjoy that. A little illicit pleasure to apologize for on Sunday morning, what's the harm? But Aldana will sooner or later be crushed like a gnat if he tries to intimidate people here like he did in Colombia."

"No doubt Liarakos tried to tell him that."

"His best defense is to play the underdog. David versus Goliath."

"Chano Aldana *is* Goliath," the columnist said dryly and pulled a nearby chair around. "He made that pretty plain this afternoon."

"We're going to have to legalize dope, Ott. Right now nobody wants to make it legal, yet nobody wants to live in an America that is so well policed that it can't be sold."

"If more-efficient police are what it takes, I'm for it," Mergenthaler said.

"Aww, bullshit. You haven't thought this through. You despised J. Edgar Hoover. You thought the House Un-American Activities Committee was a cancer on the body politic." When Mergenthaler tried to reply, Yocke raised his voice and overrode him. *"I've* read some of your old columns. Don't try to change your spots now."

After making sure Yocke had really shut up, Mergenthaler said, "I've been to Holland and seen the kids lying in the public squares, whacked out on hash, scrambling their brains permanently while the police stand and watch, while the world walks around them. I've been to the Dutch morgues and seen the bodies. *I've been to the D.C. morgue and seen the bodies there too.* This shit ain't tobacco and it ain't liquor. Two crack joints will make an average person an addict. Legalize it? *No! A thousand times no."*

Jack Yocke threw up his hands. "Medellín had four thousand and fifteen murder victims delivered to the morgue in 1989. Those were the bodies they found. Medellín has a population of two million. That's a murder rate of over two hundred per hundred thousand people." Yocke's eyes narrowed. "Our rate here in the District is around eighteen or nineteen. That's four hundred and thirty-eight murders in 1989. When our murder rate is ten times worse than it is now, Ott—*ten times worse*—then I'll ask you how much sympathy you feel for all those addicts who knew better and took their first puff anyway."

"It won't get that bad here."

"You think the black militants and liberals who run this town are gonna fix things? You met Aldana this afternoon. Like hell it won't get that bad!"

"Didn't you just say that Aldana would get his sooner or later?"

"It isn't Aldana I'm worried about. It's all the other flies that kind of money will attract."

When Mergenthaler left and went back to his office, Jack Yocke tried to write some more and found he couldn't. He was fuming, irritable. His eye fell on the front page of today's paper with its photo of George Bush sailing off Kennebunkport, Maine. Bush was waving, wearing a wide grin. Jack Yocke threw the paper into the wastepaper basket.

Rock Creek Park is Washington's attempt at Central Park. Unlike that vast expanse of trees and grass in New York City, Rock Creek Park is not a pedestrian's paradise. Part of the reason is geography.

The park begins a dozen miles north of the Potomac River in Montgomery County, Maryland, as an undeveloped stretch along a modest creek meandering southward toward the river.

For several hundred yards after the creek flows under the eight-lane beltway, houses and yards come right to the edge of the water. The gentle trickle soon reaches the grounds of the Walter Reed Army Hospital, however, with its vast expanse of lawns. South of the hospital grounds the park is about a quarter mile wide for several miles. Here it is a pleasant oasis of trees and greenery on the steep banks of the creek ravine.

Crossing into the District, the green belt finally assumes parklike dimensions. For the next four miles the park is about a mile wide and provides a site for a golf course and numerous scenic stretches of two-lane blacktop that wind through the wooded, boulder-choked ravines of aptly named Rock Creek and its tributaries.

The park narrows at the National Zoological Park, which occupies its entire width. South of the zoo, the park along the creek drainage is only several hundred yards wide, merely the sides of the steep Rock Creek ravine, and is crisscrossed by bridges that carry the major streets and avenues of Washington.

Two miles south of the zoo the creek deposits its saline solution of street and lawn runoff into the Potomac. The creek mouth is directly across the Georgetown Channel from Theodore Roosevelt Island. The park there provides a modest accent of green near the water, a mere foreground for the vast urban skyline behind it.

For most of its length the park consists of uncomfortably steep, rock-strewn hillsides densely covered with hardwood trees. In spite of the mild autumn, by early December the trees had lost all their leaves and transformed themselves into a semi-opaque wilderness of gray branches and trunks that gently muffled some of the city noise.

Henry Charon automatically adjusted the placement of his feet to avoid fallen branches and loose rocks, yet the thick carpet of dead, dry leaves rustled loudly at every step. A good soaking rain, he knew, would leave the leaf carpet sodden and allow a man to walk silently across it. Not now, though.

Below him, on his right, cars hummed along Ross Drive, one of the scenic lanes along Rock Creek that functioned as an alternate commuter route during rush hour. Charon strode along the hillside in a tireless, swinging gait with his eyes moving. He paused occasionally to examine major outcrops of rock, then resumed his northward movements.

This type of terrain he knew well. It would be a wonderful area in which to hide, if he could find the right place. These sidewalk warriors would be on his turf if they hunted him here.

He consulted his map again, then changed course to top the ridge. This ridge wasn't high, only a hundred feet or so, but it was far too steep for casual urban walkers and hikers. Accustomed as he was to scrambling up slopes in the Rockies, Henry Charon didn't even draw a deep breath as he climbed to the top of the narrow ridgeline and paused to examine his surroundings.

Just before dusk he found it. He was exploring along the foot of an outcropping from the formation that formed the caprock of the ridge. A gap in the rock led into a small sheltered cave, more of an overhang, really. A large boulder obscured most of the opening. In the gloom he could see several pop cans and cigarette butts. The dirt of the floor was packed hard, no doubt from the feet of teenagers or derelicts. Many footprints and shoe marks. This place would do nicely, if he ever needed it.

He examined the place carefully, paying particular attention to the cracks and crevices that rose off to one side. He pulled some loose rock from one. Yes, he could put a gun and some other supplies in there and pile the rock back in, just in case.

Henry Charon left the cave and paused outside to examine the setting again. He was sure he could find it again. After a last look around in all directions, Henry Charon set off down the hillside.

About a half hour later Thanos Liarakos arrived at his home in Edgemoor and parked the Jag in the garage.

His wife, Elizabeth, was in the kitchen putting the finishing touches on the canapés. The guests were supposed to arrive at seven. She gave him a buss on the cheek as he poured himself a drink. "How'd it go today?"

"You wouldn't believe it. The man is certifiably insane. At the press conference he claimed he was the devil."

She looked at him to see if he was kidding. "An insanity defense?"

"I suggested it, and he didn't say anything one way or the other, until I mentioned the psychiatrists and psychologists, then he just said no. That's it, one word. 'No.' End of discussion."

"Your mother called this afternoon." Elizabeth had her back to him and was spreading cream cheese on the celery.

"Umph." Elizabeth's birthday had been last week. She had just turned thirty-nine. As he stared at her trim waistline and the way her buttocks shaped her dress, Liarakos decided she could pass for ten years younger.

"She just heard on the news that you're representing Aldana."

"And she was unhappy."

"She had a fit. Wanted to know how you could defend scum like that. 'All those years . . . my little boy . . . no honor.' It wasn't a pleasant conversation."

Liarakos turned his attention to the backyard. They had almost an acre here. The hired man had raked the leaves three times this fall but at least a bushel had collected on the top of the pool cover and in the hot tub. He would have to clean up the leaves again when he had time.

"I told her," Elizabeth was saying, "that every man is entitled to a defense, but you know her."

"Yeah."

"I tried to be nice to her, Thanos, I really did. But I am so sick of hearing her whine and bitch. Honest to God, I have completely had it with her ethics lectures."

"I know."

"Why don't you explain it to her one more time?" She turned to face him. "It's not fair that I have to be the one who keeps explaining the Constitution and the American legal system to her. When she starts that how-can-my-Thanos-do-this crap, I just cringe. She doesn't listen, she won't listen."

"I'll talk to her again."

"Promise?"

"Yeah, promise."

She turned back to the celery.

"Where are the girls?" he asked.

"Upstairs. They're going to be doing homework while the guests are here. And I bought them a new CD today. They're listening to that for the eleventh time."

Liarakos wandered into the living room. Elizabeth had the crystal out, the wine open, and the cheeses and crackers already arranged on the white damask tablecloth. At least she understood what he did professionally. She had been a new associate, a Harvard Law grad, when they started dating. Six months later they spent a long ski weekend in Aspen and returned home married. She had had to resign her position with the firm of course, but he had just made junior partner.

It had been rocky along the way, but they were still trying, still hanging in there.

His mind turned to his new client, turning over possible defense tactics, reviewing the charges yet again. Aldana's case was going to be difficult. The government had two turncoat witnesses and enough circumstantial evidence to sink the *Titanic*. Aldana's little press conference performance this afternoon hadn't helped.

He would tape the network news at six. Tomorrow he would put the associates to researching pretrial publicity issues. Perhaps the press conference hadn't precluded such a motion, considering the overwhelming publicity Aldana's extradition had received.

He checked his watch. The network evening news would come on in ten minutes. He should probably set up the VCR now.

When that chore was completed, he wandered back to the kitchen for another drink. "When did the maid leave?"

"About five. She helped me with all of this."

"You want me to help?"

"No. Go relax. I've got everything under control."

Everything under control. A defense lawyer never had everything under control. The concept was foreign to him. About all you could do was anticipate the thrusts and jabs of the prosecution and attempt to parry them. And have a few surprises of your own up your sleeve. The name of the game was damage control.

How could he control the damage the government witnesses would do? And the client, Aldana? Could he be controlled? Would he listen to good advice? Liarakos snorted. He already knew the answer to that. Oh well, it was Aldana's ass on the line, not his. Still, he hated to lose. He never fought gracefully in a losing cause, which was why his defense team was bringing in two million dollars a year in fees to the firm.

He snapped the television on in the living room and stood watching it as Elizabeth set the last of the hors d'oeuvres on the table.

Aldana's press conference was the lead story. "Come watch this, Elizabeth."

The anchor said Aldana's statement spoke for itself. He fell silent and looked off to one side, at the monitor no doubt, waiting. Aldana came on the screen. As his voice filled the living room— *"To me has been given the key . . ."*—Liarakos heard his wife's sharp intake of breath. "My God!"

"He has an effect, doesn't he?"

After the questions, the network replayed the statement three times. The consensus of the "experts"—a lawyer, a psychiatrist, and a college instructor in South American voodoo culture—was that Aldana was a criminal megalomaniac.

The phone rang and at the same time the door chimes sounded. As Elizabeth went to the front door to admit the guests, Liarakos went to the study to take the call. The firm's senior partner was on the line:

"I just saw our newest, most famous client on the news."

"Yeah, I watched it too."

"Thanos, you've got to figure out a way to shut him up. In one performance he managed to convince half the people in America that he's guilty as hell. And that was the half that was undecided."

"I strongly urged him not—"

"Thanos, he's one man. Our firm has fifty-two partners and one hundred twelve associates who represent over a dozen Fortune five hundred companies and about a hundred fifty smaller ones. The heart of our business is regulatory matters and commercial litigation. Now it's one thing to represent run-of-the-mill criminal defendants, but it's quite another to represent a man who's out to prove he's the Antichrist, beyond a reasonable doubt."

"He's innocent until proven guilty."

"You know that and I know that, but the general public may not. I'm laying it right on the line, Thanos. We have never told you whom you could or couldn't represent. But this firm is not going to bankrupt itself for the privilege of representing the most notorious criminal since Al Capone. Now you shut that man up or tell him he'll have to get another lawyer. Have I made myself clear?"

"You have, Harvey."

"Stop by my office tomorrow." The connection broke.

Thanos Liarakos sat for a moment with the telephone receiver in his hand, then slowly lowered it onto its cradle.

Harvey Brewster was something of an ass. If he thought the firm could get rid of Chano Aldana by just throwing his file at him and filing a notice with the clerk of the court, he was in for a rude surprise. The judge would not let Liarakos or the firm out of the case unless and until another competent, experienced attorney had agreed to represent Aldana and not delay the proceedings. The pressure on the judge to proceed expeditiously would be excruciating, and the judge had the tools to transfer that pressure squarely onto counsel for both sides.

Liarakos knew the judge would not hesitate to use his authority. Liarakos knew the judge. Gardner Snyder was in his early seventies and had been on the bench for over thirty years. He was the frostiest curmudgeon wearing a judicial robe that Liarakos had ever run into. No doubt that was why the Justice Department had maneuvered so adroitly to ensure that this case went onto Snyder's calendar.

Perhaps tomorrow the prosecutor would move for an order gagging both sides. Liarakos suspected that just now the prosecutor's phone was also ringing. Perhaps he should make the motion himself. It was indisputable that Aldana would have to be silenced one way or the other or the man wouldn't get a fair trial.

The door opened. Elizabeth's head appeared. "Thanos, come visit with our guests."

The guests were buzzing about Aldana's news conference. Those who hadn't seen the news show were being briefed by those who had. Liarakos was bombarded with questions, all of which he shrugged off with a smile. The smile was an effort.

He had finished his third drink of the evening and was telling himself he didn't need and probably couldn't handle a fourth, when he saw Elizabeth motioning to him from the kitchen.

"Your mother's on the phone. She's really revved."

"I'll take it in the study."

Jefferson Brody and a woman Liarakos knew only vaguely were in a serious discussion in the study, but he made his excuses and closed the door firmly behind them.

"Hi, Mom."

"Thanos, Thanos, what have you done?"

"Well, I—"

She wasn't interested in his answer. She steamrollered on: "I saw that horrible man—*your client*—on the news this evening. I meant to call you immediately but my friends have been on the phone for over an hour. I called you as soon as I had a chance."

"Mom, I'm a lawyer. I—"

"You don't have to make a living representing dope-peddling scum like that! My God, your father and I scrimped and saved and did without to put you through college and law school so you could represent filth like Alda . . . Alda-something. Have you no honor? Have you no morals? What kind of man are you, Thanos?"

"Mom, I'm a lawyer—no, *let me finish!* I'm a lawyer and this man is entitled to be represented by a lawyer no matter what crimes he is accused of."

"But he is *guilty!*"

"He isn't guilty until a jury says he is. And guilty or not, he must have a lawyer."

"I hope to God you lose and this man pays for his crimes, Thanos. He has murdered and assassinated and bribed and done God knows what-all and he must be put somewhere so he can't keep hurting innocent people.

Thousands of innocent people. Thanos, you pervert your talents and your religion by helping such a man."

"Mom, I'm not going to keep arguing this."

"He says he has the key to hell. And he *does.* You are helping this scum stay in business. You are helping him murder innocent people. How in the name of your dead father do you sleep nights?"

"I've heard all of this I'm going to listen to."

"No, you haven't! You are going to listen to your mother who loves you and wants to save your soul. You are going to stop helping these people. Thanos! My Thanos. You are breaking my heart."

"Mom, we have a houseful of guests. I'm not going to insult them by staying here in the study listening to you rant about something you don't understand. Don't you have any faith in me?"

"Faith in you? When you prostitute yourself for criminals such as Aldana? You make me nauseous." She slammed her phone down.

Is there anybody who didn't watch the news tonight?

His baseball glove was lying on the table. He picked it up and kneaded the soft leather. He smacked the pocket with his fist. Damn! Damn, damn, damn.

He turned off the lights and sat in the darkness. After a moment he loosened his tie and stretched out on the couch. The hum of voices through the door, the gentle background of the furnace fans, the noises reached him and he listened for a while, then didn't listen. The noises became background, like an evening crowd in the grandstand at Tinker Field in Orlando, buzzing and sighing in rhythm with the game.

The crowds were never large, maybe fifteen hundred people on a good evening. But all the hot, muggy evenings were very good, regardless of how many people came to watch. The fastballs only came in about eighty miles per hour, plenty fast if you were forty-one years old and trying to get the bat around on one of them. On those all-too-rare occasions when you slapped the ball with good wood you strained every tendon charging for first. Occasionally you even surprised yourself and beat the throw.

That summer now seemed like a dream time. Liarakos could still smell the sweat, still feel the earth under his spikes, still see the ball leave the bat and float toward him as he charged it. Even then he knew he was living a fantasy, the sublime pinnacle of his life. The sun and the sweat and the laughter of his teammates . . .

Someone was shaking him. "Daddy. Wake up. Daddy."

The lights were on. "Huh?"

It was Susanna, his twelve-year-old. "Daddy, it's Mommy. She's locked herself in the upstairs bathroom and won't come out."

Thanos Liarakos uncoiled and rushed from the room. Through the living room and the guests staring, up the stairs two at a time with Susanna in her nightie running behind him, trying to keep up.

He tried the handle on the door. Locked! He pounded on the door with his fists. "Elizabeth? *Elizabeth, can you hear me?"*

Nothing.

Not again! Please God, not again!

"Elizabeth, if you don't open this door *now,* I'm going to break it down."

Susanna and her younger sister were standing there in the hallway, watching. They were sobbing.

"You girls go to your room. Do as I say." They went.

He kicked at the door. The girls were standing in their doorway, watching and crying. He braced himself against the wall and smashed at the door with his right foot. It splintered. Another kick and the lock gave.

She was on the floor. A trace of white powder around her nostrils. Some powder on the counter. A rolled-up dollar bill clutched in her hand. Her eyes unfocused, the pupils huge. Her heart going like a racehorse.

Damn!

"Where did you get it, Elizabeth? Who gave you the cocaine?"

He shook her vigorously. Her eyes swam.

"Can you hear me, woman? *Who gave you the coke?"*

"Jeff, uhh, Jeffer . . ."

He lowered her to the floor and went to the girls' bedroom. "Susanna, call an ambulance. Dial nine-one-one. Your mother's sick."

The child was crying freely. He held her at arm's length and stared into her face. "Can you do this?"

She nodded and wiped at her tears.

"Good girl. Dial nine-one-one and give them our address and tell them to send an ambulance."

Down the hall past the bathroom to the staircase, and down them two at a time. T. Jefferson Brody was standing by the far wall.

Brody put up his hands as Liarakos charged at him. "Now, Thanos—"

"Get outta my house, you son of a bitch." He hit him with all he had. Brody went down and two men grabbed Liarakos' arms.

"Out! All you people get out!" He jerked his arms free. "Party's over. Everybody get the fuck outta my house."

He gestured toward Brody, who was sitting on the floor rubbing his jaw. "Drag this piece of dog shit out with you or I'll kill him."

CHAPTER SIX

★ ★ ★ ★ ★ ★ ★ ★

AT six o'clock the alarm rang beside Thanos Liarakos' bed. He silenced it and rolled out. He had been asleep less than an hour. He had gotten home from the hospital at three a.m., checked on the kids and the maid, who had graciously agreed to return and spend the night when he called her at midnight. The lady and the kids were all asleep in the same bed. Tired as he was, Liarakos couldn't sleep. The last time he remembered glancing at the clock it had been almost five a.m.

He showered and shaved and dressed. In the kitchen he wrote a note for the kids:

> *Your Mom is okay. She is in the hospital and was asleep when I left her. You may stay home from school with Marla today if you wish.*
> *I love you both,*
> *Dad*

When he backed the car out of the garage there was a television reporter and a cameraman at the end of the driveway, on the sidewalk. They shouted questions at him as he backed down the drive right at them. Two cameramen. One refused to get out of the way. Liarakos kept the car creeping backward. The reporter, a woman, held a microphone against the driver's window glass and shouted: "Is Aldana threatening Americans? Is he sane? How much money has he paid you?"

She expected no answers in this theater of the absurd, Liarakos knew. Asking rhetorical questions was the whole show. *This* was award-winning television journalism.

The rear bumper lightly contacted the camera tripod. Then the man moved.

Liarakos kept the car drifting backward into the street, flipped the transmission into drive, and accelerated away.

The morning was overcast and gloomy. A wind drove the dry brown leaves along the streets in waves. Here and there whirlwinds built little columns of leaves that spun crazily for a few seconds in the gray half light, then flowed on.

His wife was still asleep. The blinds were closed and the lights off in her private room. Still wearing his topcoat, Thanos Liarakos sank into the padded visitor's chair.

In a few moments his breathing rhythm matched hers. He felt himself relaxing and drifting and didn't fight it.

He had been in his late thirties when he realized that he could see his entire life, all of it, as if he were a detached observer and his life were a play that he had seen several times before. The whole of it was being acted out before him daily, scene by scene. Yet he knew how it had been and how it would have to be.

Staring at his face in the mirror as he shaved every morning, he could see how the lines would deepen, how the jowls would continue to sag, how the hair would gray and thin. He stared at a face not young and soon to be old.

In nursing homes, he knew, a portion of the daily routine for the elderly is reminiscence therapy. The staff encourages the fragile people waiting to die to look back, to savor the events in their life as if they were great feats woven into a tapestry to instruct generations yet unborn.

Thanos Liarakos was seeing it as it would be, looking back while he was still living it. All his achievements and accomplishments that he had previously thought so important shrank mercilessly from the vantage of this curious double perspective. Court victories lost their sweetness and disasters lost their sting. He had found a way to live with life, or perhaps a merciful God had given him the way. Whichever. Only the perspective mattered.

Drifting now, half asleep, Liarakos swirled the colored glass inside his kaleidoscope of past and future, looking for the pattern. His father had stepped off the boat from Greece with fifty dollars in his pocket and one extra shirt, and parlayed that into five submarine sandwich shops which had sent three sons through college. His mother had raised the sons while his father worked twelve to fifteen hours a day. Those bittersweet days were irretrievably gone. They were as far from the present as the day Odysseus sacked the stronghold on the proud height of Troy. Yet when he talked to his mother he was listening to a voice from the past that would soon be lost to him. So soon, so soon, he would be standing by her grave and his father's grave, remembering, feeling the life escaping like a handful of sand flowing through his fingers. So he tolerated her diatribes and cherished her.

His daughters—they were his offerings to the human race, to the future and its infinite potential, to God and whatever great and incomprehensible thing He had in mind for the human species. The girls were not special, not gifted—they were just people. They and their children would work and love and marry and have children, long after Thanos Liarakos and the Greek of the sandwich shop were dust. So he loved them desperately.

Elizabeth. Ahh, gentle Elizabeth, with your mother's heart and your empty desires and your cravings . . .

You love a woman for many reasons. A goddess she seems when you are young. But finally you see she is of common clay, the same as you, with faults and fears and vain, foolish dreams and petty vices. So you cherish her, love her even more. As she ages you cling closer and closer, holding tighter and tighter. She becomes the female half of you. The roughening of her skin, the engraved lines on her face, the thickening waistline and the sagging breasts, none of it matters a damn. You love her for what she is not as much as for what she is.

Elizabeth, your vices aren't so petty. You are selling your soul for that white powder. It will lay you in your grave, devastate your husband who loves you, deprive two girls of the mother that you promised to be when you gave them life.

Two nurses entered the room and flipped on the light over the bed. Thanos Liarakos came fully awake and squinted at the two white-clad figures bending over Elizabeth. They pried open her eyes and checked her pulse. The stouter nurse rigged a blood-pressure cuff. Elizabeth groaned but said nothing. She was still intoxicated.

"Lucky," one of them muttered as she checked the IV drip. "She was lucky this time."

Liarakos looked at his watch. Almost eight o'clock. The sounds of the staff chattering in the corridors and moving tray carts and equipment came through the open door. He levered himself out of the chair and stood swaying while his heart compensated for the sudden change of position.

He was still standing at the foot of the bed when the nurses bustled out.

She looked old. With no makeup and her hair a mess, Elizabeth looked finished with life. No more warm moments with the children, no more sensuous I-love-yous, no more evenings with the fire crackling and the children laughing. She looked used up. Burned out.

Thanos Liarakos rubbed his face and wondered why he wasn't crying. Ah, it was that crazy double perspective. He had lived this play before.

But he should be crying. He really should. This was the place he was *supposed* to cry.

The lead headline in this morning's *Post* was THE KEY TO HELL. The bold black letters spanned the width of the top of page one. The editor had run a photo of Aldana getting off the plane at Andrews Air Force Base wearing handcuffs and a fierce scowl. Ottmar Mergenthaler and Jack Yocke had shared the byline on the story. Beside the story was Mergenthaler's column.

Jack Yocke read the four inches of Ott's column that was on the front page and flipped to page A-12 for the rest of it. The federal government and the American people, Mergenthaler said, shouldn't let themselves be intimidated by Chano Aldana, who was obviously going to try the same tactics here that he had used with mixed success in Colombia. If he thought the American people would respond like frightened sheep to terrorism and extortion, Aldana didn't understand the American people.

Yocke snorted and tossed the paper on his desk. Maybe he should give Ott a soapbox for Christmas.

His phone rang. "Jack, there's a reporter from a Dallas paper on the line. He wants to talk to you about your interview yesterday with Aldana."

"I don't answer questions. I ask them."

"Does that mean no?"

"Yep."

Yocke tucked a notebook and pencils in his jacket pocket as he stirred through his message slips and the unopened mail. He would have to return these calls later, maybe this evening. With his coat over his arm, he went looking for his editor. Maybe he could go down to the courthouse with the rest of the newsroom crew and mill around smartly while Aldana was arraigned.

In a dingy office two doors from the courtroom, Thanos Liarakos arranged his fanny in a chair across a desk from the U.S. attorney for the District, William L. Bader.

Bader was known as an aggressive prosecutor who meticulously prepared his cases. Rumor with the hard tang of truth had it that Bader had judicial ambitions. Liarakos didn't hold that against him. Bader was a damn good lawyer.

"I dropped in to have a little chat about the shenanigans your people used to get my client on Judge Snyder's calendar."

"What shenanigans?" Bader's eyebrows rose a sixteenth of an inch.

"You can wipe off the innocent look. You're wasting it on me. The people in the clerk's office have whispered in the wrong places."

"So you'd rather be in front of Maximum John or Hanging Jack?"

"Well, you know how these things are. My client might have lucked out with Judge Worth if the deck hadn't been so neatly stacked against him." Judge Worth had the reputation, probably exaggerated, of bending over backward to help defense counsel and screwing the prosecution at every opportunity.

"So why are you in here complaining? The hearing in front of the magistrate starts in twenty minutes. Complain to her."

"I don't think opening this can of worms will do you any good in the newspapers, Will. People might get the idea the government is conducting a vendetta against Aldana, trying to make him a scapegoat. I thought you might do something for me, and I'll live with Judge Snyder."

"What?"

"Make a motion for a gag order. Both sides. Including the defendant."

Bader's eyes went to a copy of the *Post* on the corner of the desk. He spent several seconds looking at it. Then he sat back in his chair and rubbed his nose. It was a big nose, but it was well arranged in a large, square, craggy face.

"You want a trial or a circus?" Liarakos asked.

"That fool is putting the noose around his own neck. I don't give a damn if he holds press conferences twice a day and threatens to butcher everybody east of Pittsburgh."

"You don't know how that will cut and neither do I," Thanos Liarakos shot back. "What we *both* know is that we're officers of the court. Let's have a fair trial and not let this deteriorate into some kind of Geraldo Rivera spectacular."

Bader snorted derisively.

"We gotta stopper this asshole before he poisons the well," Liarakos said softly. "What if no one with an IQ above fifty is willing to serve on the jury? What if one or two jurors become afraid to convict him?"

"I'll worry about that when and if it happens. He's *your* client, dammit! You want him quiet, *you* shut him up."

"Gimme a fucking break, Will."

Bader's lips twisted and he massaged an eyebrow. He was, Liarakos suspected, trying to decide how Judge Snyder would view the prosecutor's failure to ask for a gag order if the defendant kept grabbing headlines with veiled threats. Thanos Liarakos sensed that he had won. He sat back in his chair and crossed his legs.

"All right, all right."

Bader called for a secretary and dictated the motion. When he finished, he asked Liarakos, "Is that satisfactory to you?"

The defense lawyer suggested a change that strengthened the requested order. He cited a case from memory. Will Bader nodded and waved the secretary toward a typewriter.

"I might as well tell you now," Bader said, "while you're in a good mood and feeling full of bonhomie—I'm filing a motion today to seize all of Aldana's assets. Everything he has, including the money he used to pay your fee, is proceeds of criminal activity. Every dime."

Both men were well aware of the implications of such a motion. If he were stripped of all his assets, an accused individual could no longer pay his attorney's fee. Of course, the court could then appoint an attorney to represent him, but the defense that could then be mounted was severely restricted by the limited funds that were, by law, available from the government to pay defense counsel. In effect, by confiscating the defendant's assets in a civil action the government could greatly increase its odds of ultimately convicting the defendant in the criminal case, where the burden of proof was so much higher. These motions were fair, the judges reasoned, because in good conscience a criminal should not be allowed to use the proceeds of his crime to avoid being punished for committing it.

Critics—mainly defense attorneys—argued that the government had the cart before the horse: stripping assets from a defendant before he had been convicted of anything seemed to shrink the presumption of innocence to the vanishing point. The problem was that the profits of crime were real—you could touch the money—but the presumption of innocence was a legal fiction, and ninety-nine percent of the time it was just that, fiction. The defendant was guilty and everybody knew it except the jurors. So the government grabbed the bucks.

Liarakos, of course, had been expecting just such a motion. The only question was when. The arguments pro and con he knew well, for he had fought these motions in other cases. Some he won, some he lost.

He cleared his throat. "I might as well tell you now, my client has engaged another firm to represent him in any civil confiscation action. Off the record, no doubt you'll get some assets. But you'll not get them all."

"Every little bit helps," Bader said grinning. "What with the deficit and all, it's nice to see guys like Aldana contributing their mite. We'll be serving interrogatories next week, and maybe depositions the following week?"

"Not up to me. Serve them on him and he'll send them to the firm he's hired."

If Chano Aldana thought he had problems now, Liarakos told himself, wait until he read the interrogatories. Any answer he supplied could be used against him in the criminal trial. Most of these asset confiscation actions went uncontested for this very good reason. Regardless of how the criminal action went, Aldana was going to return to Colombia a much poorer man.

Which somehow didn't break Liarakos' heart.

Jack Yocke stood against the back wall of the courtroom shoulder to shoulder with three dozen other reporters and made notes on his steno pad. "Courtroom packed . . . crowd hushed, expectant . . ."

Defense attorney Thanos Liarakos' assistant, Judith Lewis, was already at the defense table, which was marked with a small sign. To her far right, with an empty chair between them, sat a man in a brown sports coat and slacks. Yocke murmured to the man beside him and pointed.

"The interpreter."

At the prosecutor's table sat another woman, whom Yocke assumed was an assistant. He whispered another question to the man beside him. Wilda Rodriguez-Herrera. The man spelled the name as Yocke wrote it down. Why is it, the *Post* reporter wondered, that most high-powered lawyers these days have female factotums? Both women were in their middle-to-late twenties or perhaps early thirties—it was impossible to tell at this distance—and were dressed for success in conservative getups that must have set each of them back a week's pay. Yocke jotted another note.

Aldana entered in company with two U.S. marshals. He was wearing a dark suit and a deep maroon tie. His hands were cuffed in front of him. As one of the marshals took the cuffs off, Aldana looked quickly around the room, scanning each face. Every eye in the room was on him. The room was so quiet Yocke could hear the clink of metal as the cuffs were removed from Aldana's wrists.

The defendant sat down at the defense table between Judith Lewis and the interpreter. One of the marshals took a chair immediately behind him, inside the barricade, while the other moved to a chair against the wall where he could watch the defendant and the crowd without turning his head.

Lewis whispered something to Aldana. He made no reply, didn't look at her, kept his face impassive. Now the interpreter whispered in his ear. Aldana replied, a few phrases only, and didn't look at him. He surveyed the bailiff, who averted his eyes; then Aldana turned his head, leaned forward slightly in his chair, and stared for several seconds at Assistant Prosecutor Rodriguez-Herrera, who was busy with a sheet of paper that lay on the table in front of her.

Now his eye caught the *Post* courtroom artist in the far corner, who was studying him through a pair of opera glasses mounted on a tripod. For the first time Aldana's features moved—the upper lip rose into a slight sneer and his eyes became mere slits.

The moment passed and the face resumed its impassive calm. Aldana looked back toward the front of the room, at the magistrate's bench with the flags behind it. He leaned back in his chair, sat loosely, comfortably, staring at the flags. He crossed his legs. In a moment he uncrossed them.

He's nervous, Yocke decided, and scribbled some more in his notebook. He's trying not to show it, but he is nervous. Maybe he's human after all.

Minutes passed. Coughs and hacks and muttered comments from the audience. Aldana poured himself a cup of water from the pitcher on the table and spilled some. He ignored the spill. After several sips he placed the cup on the table in front of him and didn't touch it again.

As he stared at Aldana, Jack Yocke reviewed what he had heard about the defendant. A barrio brat from Medellín, Chano Aldana reputedly had worked his way to the top of the local cocaine industry by outthinking and murdering his rivals. He was smarter than the average sewer rat and twice as ruthless. Rumor had it he had personally executed over two dozen men and had ordered the murders of hundreds more by name, including a candidate for president of Colombia. A vicious enemy of the law-and-order forces battling the cartels for control of Colombia, he had ordered airliners and department stores bombed, judges murdered, and policemen tortured.

Yet this monster had a human side: he liked soccer and controlled several teams in the central Colombian league. Referees and star players on rival teams had been assassinated on his order. Finally the government had suspended league play because of organized crime's corrosive influence on the games.

The last two years Aldana had allegedly spent hiding somewhere in the Amazon. He had been captured by the Colombian government when he decided in a weak moment to visit a prostitute of whom he was fond. Somehow he had survived the ensuing shootout, although six of his bodyguards hadn't. Sewer rat's luck.

By all accounts Aldana was an amazing man, a Latin Al Capone with several of Hitler's worst traits thrown in for seasoning. Yet staring at this slightly overweight, middle-aged Latin male with the black curly hair and the modest thin mustache, Jack Yocke found this tale of unadulterated evil hard to believe. It was incredible, really. Even Aldana's performance at yesterday's news conference couldn't overcome one's natural inclination to accept the man as a fellow human being. Yocke tried to picture him eating snake and monkey meat in the jungle—and gave up.

U.S. Attorney William Bader had a herculean task ahead of him to convince twelve working-class Americans that Chano Aldana was *el padrino,* the godfather.

Yocke was furiously scribbling notes when the door to the hallway opened and a man entered, a man wearing a naval officer's blue uniform. Captain Jake Grafton. His ribbons and wings made a splotch of color on his left breast. Those and the four gold rings on each sleeve looked strangely out of place among all these civilians.

Jack Yocke stared as Grafton surveyed the seating arrangements, apparently concluded the place was full, and took up a station against the wall, near the door. His eyes met those of the reporter. He nodded once, then his gaze settled on Chano Aldana, who had turned to examine the newcomer. Aldana turned back toward the bench.

Several of the spectators looked the captain over, whispering back and forth, and finally dismissed him.

Jake Grafton? Why is he here? Yocke scribbled down the name in his notebook and put three question marks after it.

A few minutes later the door behind the bench opened and Bader came in, followed by Thanos Liarakos. Bader glanced at Aldana and the audience and sat down beside Rodriguez-Herrera.

Judith Lewis moved to the chair at the far left of her table and Liarakos took the one she had vacated. He spoke to the defendant, got something in reply, then spoke to Lewis.

He looks tired, Yocke thought, and studied the attorney. Dark, trim, of medium height with black hair streaked with gray at the temples,

Liarakos habitually wore thousand-dollar tailor-made wool suits. He was wearing one today, if Yocke's eyes could be trusted. Liarakos normally looked every inch the successful criminal lawyer. Yet Mergenthaler had said that Liarakos had spent the summer of 1989 playing baseball in a professional senior league in Florida. At the age of forty-one he had tried out for a team composed almost exclusively of former major leaguers and made it. Jack Yocke didn't know exactly what to make of that.

This morning, the reporter thought, the honest, sincere face that juries loved looked softer, less on stage. Then the explanation occurred to him—there was no jury.

"All rise," the bailiff announced. The lawyers rose respectfully as the audience shuffled noisily to its feet. Aldana hesitated a second, and Liarakos pulled almost imperceptibly on his sleeve.

The magistrate, enshrouded in her judicial robe, entered and took her seat behind the raised bench.

The bailiff chanted the incomprehensible incantation that opened every court session and ended with a curt "Be seated."

Jack Yocke kept his attention on the defendant. Aldana was leaning forward in his chair staring at the magistrate, a fiftyish woman with her hair pulled back severely, wearing a stylish pair of large glasses. He didn't take his eyes off her as she read the indictment handed down by a grand jury in Miami several years ago and the interpreter spoke in a low tone in his ear. Yocke could just hear the rat-a-tat-tat of the Spanish, although he couldn't make out the words.

"How do you plead?"

Liarakos half rose from his chair. "Not guilty, your honor."

The magistrate ordered a not guilty plea entered in the record, then addressed the prosecutor. "I understand you have a preliminary motion in this matter, Mr. Bader?"

"Yes, your honor. May I approach the bench?"

She nodded and he walked up and handed the clerk a paper, which the clerk stamped and passed to the magistrate while Bader handed a copy to Liarakos.

"The prosecution is asking the court for a gag order in this case, your honor. The order is to apply to attorneys for both sides and the defendant."

"Any argument, Mr. Liarakos?"

"No, your honor. We will have some motions of our own, and I understand you have set a date next week to hear them?"

"That's correct." She gave him the date and time. "Without argument, Mr. Bader, your motion is granted." She consulted the proposed order. After a moment, she read, "'Counsel for the government and the defendant, and the defendant, are enjoined from discussing this case, the facts, legal theories, possible witnesses, testimony to be introduced at trial, and any and all other matters connected therewith with the press or any of the representatives thereof. They shall not do, say, or write anything for publication or broadcast that might in any way prejudice possible jurors or interfere with the orderly administration of justice.' Is there a motion for bail, Mr. Liarakos?"

"Not today, your honor."

"Mr. Bader?"

"We have filed a motion, your honor, to confiscate the defendant's assets as proceeds of criminal activity." The courtroom buzzed and the magistrate looked stern. She raised her gavel but the noise ceased before she could tap the anvil. Bader continued: "We'd like you to set a date for a hearing."

The attorneys and the magistrate discussed the scheduling and checked their calendars and settled on a Monday in January.

"This matter is adjourned until next Thursday." The magistrate rose from the bench as the bailiff intoned, "All rise," and the reporters gathered their coats for the dash to the phones.

As the marshals put the cuffs on him, Aldana got in a heated discussion with his attorney. Yocke edged as close as he could.

"Why didn't you argue against this?"

Liarakos spoke too softly to hear, although Yocke tried.

"But she can't make me be silent!"

More whispers.

"No one can gag me up. No one." His voice was loud, but the sharp edge of command was there too. The crowd stopped dead, captivated by this drama. "That woman can't gag me up while they send me up the railroad for a crime of which I am not guilty. This is *supposed* to be America! Not the Germany of the Nazis or the Russia of the Stalinistas."

"This is not the time or place—"

"Are you *my* lawyer or *their* lawyer?" The voice was a brutal snarl.

"Shut the fuck up." Although Liarakos' voice was low, it cut like a whip.

The lawyer turned to the nearest marshal. "Clear these people out of here, please, and give me a moment alone with my client. You may wait in the hallway. Ms. Lewis will knock on the door when we need you."

"Everybody out." The crowd began to move.

Just before he went through the door, Jack Yocke glanced back at Chano Aldana. The defendant was glaring at Liarakos, his face dark with fury, his lips pressed together. His body was tense, coiled.

In the hallway Yocke sprinted to catch up with Jake Grafton. "Captain, wait! Please! Jack Yocke of the *Post*. I was at your party the—"

"I remember you, Jack." Grafton had his dark bridge coat over his arm and held his white hat with the scrambled eggs on the bill in his left hand. Yocke glanced at his chest to see if the blue-and-white ribbon of the Congressional Medal of Honor was displayed there. It wasn't. Maybe Mergenthaler was correct: he had said that Grafton never wore the decoration he received several years ago for ramming El Hakim's plane with his F-14 over the Med.

"I'm curious, Captain. You were the last man in town I expected to see here today. Why'd you come?"

"Wanted to get a look at Aldana."

"Officially?"

For a fraction of a second Grafton looked annoyed. "What's an official look?"

"I mean is this personal or does the Joint Staff have some interest in Aldana?"

"No comment."

"Aw, come on, Captain! Gimme a break. Why is the military interested in Chano Aldana?"

A grin spread slowly across the captain's face. He settled his white hat on his head, nodded, and turned away.

Jack Yocke watched him go, then remembered he needed to find a phone.

"You should have seen him come unglued, Ott. That man is something else!"

"Jack, you need to stop using those banal phrases. People will get the idea you're a semiliterate bum."

"I'm telling you, Ott, you should have seen him! Oh, he never really lost his temper. He didn't actually threaten Liarakos, but that look! This man *could* order the murder of hundreds of people. He could kill them himself. I was ten feet from him and I could literally feel the energy."

"Maybe you should write a letter to Shirley MacLaine."

"Listen to me, Ott. Aldana is *criminally insane.*"

"He's behind bars and guarded night and day. What should we do about it?"

Yocke lost his temper. "Okay, go ahead and snicker like a retarded hyena. I'm telling you we've got a rattlesnake in our pocket and the pocket is cloth. Dammit, Aldana scared the hell out of me!"

"He scared the hell out of me too," Ott admitted.

The telephone rang. Yocke reached for it without looking.

It was his editor. "Jack, the feds just closed a savings and loan over in Maryland. Please go up there and interview everyone you can lay hands on. Try to find some depositors this time."

"You want some brain surgeon who'll miss his ski Christmas in Aspen?"

"I was hoping that with some diligent effort you might find some little old white-haired lady who's got five bucks in her purse and no access to her checking account."

"What's the name of this place?"

"Second Potomac Savings and Loan."

Where had he heard that name before? Yocke asked himself as he pocketed his notebook and checked his pocket pencil supply. Oh yes, that Harrington guy who was killed on the beltway—he'd worked there, hadn't he?

The wind made the bare tree limbs wave somberly back and forth under the gray sky. Sitting under an ancient oak just inside the tree line, Henry Charon listened intently to the gentle rattling and tapping as the limbs high above him softly impacted those of other trees. The noise of traffic speeding by on the interstate eighty yards away muffled all the lesser forest noises, the rustle of the leaves, the sound of a chipmunk searching the leaf carpet for its dinner, the chirping of the birds.

The hunter tried to ignore the drone of the cars and trucks. He paid close attention to the gusts and swirls of the wind, subconsciously calculating the direction and velocity.

The rest area in front of him was almost empty. At the far end sat a ten-year-old pickup with Pennsylvania plates and sporting a camper on the back. The driver was apparently asleep inside. Closer, facing the highway, sat the rental car that Charon had driven to this rest stop halfway between Baltimore and Philadelphia. He had rented it using one of his fake driver's licenses and a real Visa card in that name.

A station wagon chock-full of kids and pillows and suitcases came off the highway and pulled to a stop in front of the rest rooms. Youngsters piled out and ran for the little brick building. New Jersey tags. Three minutes later the station wagon accelerated past the pickup toward the on-ramp.

Henry Charon adjusted the collar and fastened the top button on his coat. The wind had a chill to it, no doubt due to its moisture content. Yet it didn't smell of snow.

What if snow came while he were still in Washington? How would that affect his plans?

Charon was still considering it when another car came off the interstate and proceeded slowly through the parking area. One man at the wheel. Tassone. He drove slowly through the lot, looked over the rental car, and braked to a stop beside the pickup. After a moment Tassone's car, a sedan, backed the hundred feet to the rest room building, where he turned off the ignition and got out.

Tassone glanced around as he walked toward the rest rooms. In a few moments he came out and strolled over to where Charon was sitting.

"Hey." Tassone lowered himself to the ground and leaned back against a tree trunk six feet or so from Charon. "How's everything?"

"Fine," Charon said.

"Gonna snow," Tassone said as he pulled his coat collar higher and jabbed his hands into his pockets.

"I doubt it."

Tassone wiggled around, trying to find a soft spot for his bottom. "Wanta sit in the car?"

"This is fine."

"What d'ya think about the job?"

"You'll have to make a list."

Tassone fumbled inside his coat for a pencil. From an inside jacket pocket he produced a small spiral notepad. "Shoot."

Charon began to recite. He had not committed the items to paper since the possession of such a list would inevitably be incriminating. Tassone could write it down in his own handwriting and take the risk of the list being discovered on his person. Charon could still deny everything.

It took five minutes for Tassone to list all the items. Charon had him read the list back, then gave him two more items, with careful descriptions.

Tassone looked over the list carefully and asked a few questions, then stored the notebook in his pocket.

"So it's feasible?" he asked the hunter.

"It can be done."

"When?"

"When could you deliver everything on the list?"

"Take about a week, I think. Some of these things will take some work and some serious money. I'll call you."

"No, I'll call you. A week from today, at precisely this time." Both men glanced at their watches.

"Okay."

"No names."

"Of course. You'll do it then?"

"How many people know about me, counting yourself as one?"

"Two."

"Only two?"

"That's right."

Something was stirring in the leaves behind them. Henry Charon came erect in one easy motion and, with a tree for cover, stood looking carefully in that direction. Then he saw it, a flash of brown. A red squirrel.

"Ten million, cash, in advance."

Tassone whistled. "I—"

"That's for the first name on your list. One million for each of the others, if and when. No guarantees on any of them. You pay a million for each one I get. Take it or leave it."

"You want the bread sent to Switzerland or what?"

"Cash. In my hands. Used twenties and fifties. No sequential numbers."

"Okay."

"You have the authority to make this commitment?"

Now Tassone stood. "You ain't going to pop anybody until you get paid, are you?"

"No."

"Well, I'm telling you you'll get paid. How long before you get started?"

"A week or ten days after I get the stuff on that list. Two or three weeks would be better."

"Better for you. Not for me. We want you started as soon as possible."

"Let's see how you do getting the equipment I requested."

"Okay," said Tassone, and dusted off his trousers. "Okay. I'll call you in a week."

When Jake Grafton returned to his office in the Pentagon, there was a message waiting. The chairman wanted to see him. He called the chairman's office and reached an aide. They agreed he could probably get in to see the general in fifteen minutes or so.

This would be only the fourth occasion on which Jake had met General Hayden Land. For most of the thousand officers on the Joint Staff, a meeting with the senior officer in the American military, even with all the Joint Chiefs present, was a rare occurrence. As he walked out of the office this morning the other six officers in the antidrug section appeared and formed a line of sideboys at the door that Jake would have to walk through. They did some pushing and shoving, then came to rigid attention and saluted with mighty flourishes as Jake walked between the rows.

"You guys!"

The other naval officer in the antidrug section whistled, imitating a boatswain's pipe.

"Carry on," said Jake Grafton with a wide grin and headed for the corridor.

Grafton was the senior officer in the group, which spent its time doing the staff work required to allow the Joint Chiefs to make informed decisions about military cooperation with antidrug law-enforcement efforts. When Jake reported to the Joint Staff a year ago he came to this billet for the simple reason that the O-6 who held it was completing his tour and leaving. Grafton had no special training for the job—indeed, he spent the first two months simply trying to understand what it was the military was doing to assist the various law-enforcement agencies—but no matter. Learning on the job went with the uniform. And this past year the job had grown by leaps and bounds as an increasingly alarmed public demanded every federal resource be harnessed to combat the narco-terrorists, and the reluctant Joint Chiefs had finally turned to face the pressure. So Jake Grafton had been busy.

The first black man to hold the top job in the military, General Hayden Land was reputed to be as sharp as they come, an extraordinarily fast study on the intricacies of military policy. He was also, rumor said, very politically astute. He had come to his current post from the National Security Council where he had personally witnessed the meshing of politics and national security issues and the resultant effects on the military.

As he walked out of the Joint Staff spaces just ten minutes after he had entered, Jake was again hailed by name by Mr. James, the portly door attendant who had been greeting members of the Joint Staff for over twenty years. He seemed to know everyone's name—quite a feat considering that there were 1,600 officers on the Joint Staff—and shook hands right and left when they streamed past him into the secure spaces in the morning. "Short day, eh, Captain Grafton?"

"Some people have all the luck," Jake told him.

The foyer of General Land's E-Ring office was decorated with original paintings that depicted black American servicemen in action. As the aide informed the general that he was there, Grafton examined them again. One was of union soldiers in the crater at Petersburg, another was of cavalrymen fighting Indians on the western plains, and a third was of Army Air Corps pilots manning fighters during World War II.

"He'll see you now," the aide said, and walked for the door. That was when Jake's eye was captured by the painting of a black sailor defiantly firing a machine gun at attacking Japanese planes. Dorrie Miller aboard U.S.S. *West Virginia* at Pearl Harbor.

"I like the general's taste in art," he muttered to the aide as he passed into the chairman's office.

"Captain Grafton, sir," the aide said to the general behind the desk, then stood to one side. The general carried his fifty or so years well, Jake thought as he scanned the square figure, the short hair, the immaculate uniform with four silver stars on each shoulder strap.

"Come in, Captain, and find a chair. I called down to your office this morning to suggest you go see Aldana, and they said you had already left."

"Yessir, I went over there." Jake sank into a chair with the general's gaze upon him. "Just curious, I guess," Jake added. "The prosecution asked for a gag order and got it. That might help keep the lid on, at least for a little while."

General Land turned his gaze toward the window, which looked out across the Pentagon parking lots at the skyline of Arlington. "You really think it'll come out?"

"If only American soldiers knew, sir, I'd be more hopeful. They know what classified information is. But with all those Colombian cops and Justice Department lawyers in on it, there's just no way. The press is going to get this and probably pretty soon. Who knows? Aldana's lawyer,

Liarakos, may want to make a motion to have the court consider the legality of the arrest. I'm not a lawyer and I don't know any to ask, but Liarakos looks like the type of guy who will throw every stone he can lay hands on."

"Oh, but surely it's got to be legal," the general said. "The attorney general is the one who requested our help."

"All I'm saying, sir, is that Liarakos may raise the issue with the court. In fact, the press may have already caught the rumblings of this. This past weekend a reporter, one of my wife's language students, was at a party at my house. He saw me today in court and buttonholed me afterward."

"Reporter for whom?"

"The Washington Post, sir."

Land grinned. "God," he said, "I feel like Dick Nixon. Think Deep Throat's been whispering?"

Jake laughed. "I don't think Gideon Cohen is going to have a heart attack if he reads in the newspapers that American Special Forces troops captured Aldana with the cooperation of Colombian police. I told him that it would come out eventually and he shrugged it off. He knows."

"What about this Aldana?"

"A psychopath."

"Umm. When he was captured he told the major leading the raid he was going to see them all dead." General Land showed his teeth. It was not a nice smile. "I was against us getting into this mess. The military has no business in law enforcement. Won't work, can't work, isn't good for the military or the country. But when I heard that scum threatened our men, my doubts got smaller. Maybe Cohen's right. Maybe we need to go in there and kick some ass."

"General, if you want my opinion, you were right the first time. These cartel criminals have bribed, threatened, bullied, and occasionally subverted the Colombian authorities. They haven't gotten to our men yet, but now they're going to try. We're not set up to investigate our own people. We take any eighteen-year-olds who can pass the written test and the physical and turn them into soldiers, sailors, and marines. Background checks and loyalty investigations are messes we shouldn't get ourselves into."

"We may have to," General Land said. "The world's changing and we may have to change with it."

CHAPTER SEVEN

* * * * * * * * *

WHEN the attorney general walked into William C. Dorfman's White House office, the morning paper was on the desk, open and folded, displaying Mergenthaler's column. Gideon Cohen sighed and sat while he waited for the chief of staff to finish a telephone call.

"No, we are not going to release a text of the indictment. It's sealed. And no, we are not going to ask Mexico to hand over any of its citizens. We have no extradition treaty with Mexico."

He listened for several seconds, then spat into the phone, "Fuck no!" and slammed it down.

"That bubble-brain wants to know if we are really offering rewards for these guys"—Dorfman stabbed the newspaper with a rigid finger—"and paying bounty hunters to bring them to the U.S. for trial."

Cohen pursed his lips and crossed his legs. Ottmar Mergenthaler's column in the *Post* this morning had revealed, for the first time, that a federal grand jury in Los Angeles had handed down a secret indictment several weeks ago bringing charges against nineteen former and present members of the Mexican government for drug smuggling and complicity in the kidnapping and murder of U.S. Drug Enforcement Administration undercover agent Enrique Camarena, whose body had been discovered near Guadalajara in March 1985, over five years ago. One of those indicted was the former director of the Mexican Federal Judicial Police—the Mexican equivalent of the FBI—and another was his brother, the former head of the Mexican government's antidrug unit. And one of those indicted was a medical doctor who had been arrested just yesterday in El Paso. It seemed that several unknown men had accompanied the good doctor on a plane trip from Mexico, turned him over to waiting federal agents, then immediately reboarded the plane for the flight back to Mexico.

"Are you going to pay bounties?"

"Why not? It's perfectly legal to pay rewards to people who deliver fugitives to lawful authority. That principle has been firmly embedded in the common law for hundreds of years."

"Oh, spare me the lecture. What in hell are you trying to do, anyway?"

Two years ago Cohen would have bristled. Not anymore. "Enforce the law," he said mildly. "That's still one of the goals of this administration, isn't it?"

Dorfman sat back in his chair and stared at Gideon Cohen. Dorfman's eyes looked owlish when magnified by his hornrim glasses. "It won't be news to you that I don't like you."

"Do you mean that personally or professionally?" Cohen asked, and tried to look interested.

Dorfman continued as if he hadn't heard. "I've suggested to the President that he ask for your resignation. In my opinion you are not loyal to this administration. You don't seem to appreciate the political realities that the President has to face every day, for every decision. With you every decision is black or white."

"Frankly, Dorfman, I really don't give a damn about your opinion. Are you informing me officially that the President wants my resignation?"

The chief of staff took his time answering. He played with a pen on the table, scrutinized a coffee cup, examined the framed photograph of his family that sat on his desk. "No," he said when he had squeezed all the juice from the moment that it could conceivably yield, "I'm not. I'm just letting you know where you stand."

"Thanks." The disgust Cohen felt showed on his face. Dorfman's petty grandstanding was so typical of the man.

Dorfman and Cohen went into the Oval Office as a Boy Scout troop came out. The official photographer was still there, snapping pictures of the President behind his desk. This morning, Cohen thought, George Bush looked more harried than usual. He obviously was not paying much attention to the photographer's directions.

"Come on over here, Gid. Let's get some of the two of us."

When the photo session was over, the photographer closed the door behind him on the way out. Dorfman flopped the morning paper on Bush's desk.

"Where did Mergenthaler get this information?" the President asked curtly.

"I don't know."

"This administration has more leaks than an antique rowboat. Anybody who's caught chopping any more holes in the bottom without the permission of a cabinet officer is to be fired on the spot."

"If we catch anyone."

Bush nodded, his mind already on something else. In the age of telephones leaks were an inevitable fact of government life, although that didn't make them any easier to swallow. Still, the Bush White House had been remarkably tight under Dorfman's iron hand.

"When's the Mexican ambassador coming over?" the President asked his chief of staff.

"Two-thirty."

"What should I tell him about this indictment?" he asked Cohen. "And this bounty business?"

"That we have good solid evidence against these nineteen individuals. Tell him we want Mexico to sign an extradition treaty."

Dorfman exploded. *"They will never—"*

Bush chopped him off. "Mergenthaler says the DEA wants to kidnap a couple of these men and bring them here for trial."

"That's accurate. The whole column is accurate. The way the DEA presented it to me, they want to escort one or two of these men into United States territory and arrest them here."

President Bush picked up the paper and let it fall to the desk. He pushed his chair back and sat staring at Gideon Cohen. "No."

"Yes."

"No, and that's final. The Mexicans owe us 50 *billion* dollars." He repeated the figure sourly. "Nine years into the longest economic expansion in American history and we're in debt to our eyes. Trillions of dollars in federal debt, savings-and-loan fraud, farm credit disasters, credit card debt at an all-time high, the junk bond market ready to implode, and the Third World tottering on the brink of bankruptcy—no, no, they're beyond that—they went beyond the brink years ago and are dancing as fast as they can on thin air. They're paying the interest on old loans, *in exactly the same way that the federal government finances the federal deficit.* The same kind of funny-money shenanigans that sank the American S-and-L industry. It's fraud. Outright, government-approved fraud. And now, on top of everything, the Soviet Union wants foreign aid. I feel like a poor man with twelve sick kids and one aspirin."

"How do we know Mexico would default?"

"That is precisely what they would do. Try to imagine the howl that would go up if agents for the Mexican government kidnapped a few prominent citizens here in the United States and dragged them off to Mexico City for trial. Half of Texas would grab the ol' thirty-thirties and head for Nuevo Laredo to teach the chili peppers some manners."

Dorfman added, "I can name a dozen senators who would demand a declaration of war."

"We'll never get the money back regardless," the attorney general pointed out with impeccable logic.

"I'm not going to argue, Gid." This said, the President continued anyway: "Right now foreign investors are financing about thirty percent of the federal deficit by buying Treasury bonds. If Mexico defaults on its foreign debt, the rest of Latin America probably will too. The American banking system will then collapse unless the federal government bails it out, which it will be forced to do since all deposits are insured by the government up to a hundred thousand dollars. The only way to bail out the banks will be with more bonds, and to sell more bonds interest rates *must* rise. This will only work for a short period, then the government *must* raise taxes, which will suck even more money from consumers' pockets. The net effect of all this will be to send the economy of the United States—and the rest of the world—into a deep recession, further decreasing the nation's ability to service existing debt. Get the picture?"

"And if the Fed lowers interest rates drastically to save the economy, the Japanese and Europeans will stop buying bonds."

"You got it."

Cohen ran his fingers through what was left of his hair. He was reminded of a remark by a Soviet politician: "The Soviet Union is on the edge of the abyss." Here in the Oval Office he was hearing a different version of the same thing. Only this time it was the United States. Gideon Cohen shivered involuntarily.

"We'd have to devalue the dollar," Cohen said slowly.

George Bush flipped his hand in acknowledgment.

"So why not devalue right now and go after these dope smugglers who are murdering us with slow poison?"

A sneer crossed Dorfman's face as the President rubbed his eyes with the heels of his hands. "Get serious," Dorfman muttered.

The President said, "Congress would never approve it. If I even publicly suggested devaluing the currency, you wouldn't see another Republican in this office in your lifetime. For God's sake, Gid, I didn't run for this job just so I could become the most hated man in America. I'm *supposed* to be doing what the people want. That's what I'm trying to do. Surely you see that?"

"Mr. President, your good faith has never been in question. Not with me, at least. My point is that the American people want an effective solution to this dope business. A lot of past and present Mexican government officials—including cops, especially cops—are in it up to their eyes. We're not talking about just looking the other way while a load of marijuana goes by—we're talking about the torture and murder of U.S. law-enforcement officers by Mexican police officials. *The voters in this country want it stopped!*"

"The voters have got long shopping lists, and they elect congressmen to get the goods for them. They elected me to mind the store. The American people aren't stupid: they know that government can't be all things to all people. I'm supposed to do what's in the best interests of the United States as a nation, as an ongoing concern. *And I will!*"

"Mr. President, I'm saying that drugs are our number-one domestic problem. Mexico is a large part of that problem. We can't ignore that simple, fundamental fact."

"Mexico, land of *la mordida,* the bite," Bush said, the fatigue evident in his voice. "Everybody who's ever been there has had to bribe some petty functionary or other. Five bucks here, a ten-spot there. And no doubt big bribes are taken for big favors. I recall one time when Barbara and I—"

"Are you implying that there's no drug corruption here?" Cohen asked ingenuously. "In America?"

The President and the chief of staff looked at each other.

"What are you saying?" Dorfman asked.

"Mexicans are no different from anybody else. The amounts of money that are right there for the taking—it's a rare man who can say no. The DEA has been swarming over Mexico for years, so we have a pretty good feel for who, when, and how much. We're years behind here."

"The FBI is working on cases against highly placed American officials? Not just county sheriffs and border patrolmen?"

Cohen nodded.

Dorfman sighed. "That really wouldn't be so bad," he told the President. "Exposing bad apples is good politics."

"There are exceptions to that rule. This will probably be one of them." Cohen leaned forward in his seat and spoke to the President. "A fistful of indictments against some highly placed officials, very high. Think about it. Dorfman can manage the PR impact until hell won't have it, but the 'war on drugs' is going to look like those little red, white, and blue WIN buttons—all show and no attempt to tackle the underlying problems, the *real* problems. We're going to get it all thrown back in our faces unless we take effective steps to meet the drug problem head-on."

The President got out of his chair and stepped to the window behind him. He stood looking out into the Rose Garden. "We aren't just sitting on our thumbs. I approved the bounty on that Mexican doctor. I approved the use of U.S. soldiers to arrest Aldana. That hasn't come out yet but it will. When it does the hue and cry will be something to hear. I don't give a damn what anybody says, we're doing a lot, all we can, and the voters will see that."

Cohen spoke. "Mr. President, I'm not questioning your commitment. But the public doesn't see enough of it. What the public sees is slogans and presentations to sixth-graders. 'Just say no' is an obscene joke. Hell, the mayor of Washington couldn't say no. The chief of the Mexican federal police couldn't say no. The president of Panama couldn't say no. Professional athletes and movie stars can't say no. Cops can't say no. Congressmen can't say no. *That list is going to grow like a hothouse tomato in radioactive soil irrigated with steroids.*"

"Who?" George Bush asked.

"I haven't asked," Cohen replied. "I don't want to know."

"You don't?" The President turned slightly and looked at Cohen with raised eyebrows.

"It's come to that," the attorney general said woodenly. "If I don't know I can't be accused of tipping anyone off, of inadvertently or intentionally warning a suspect under investigation. You don't want to know either. Believe me, some of them will find out one way or another that they are under suspicion and try to throw their weight around. It's human nature."

With the possible exception of journalism students in a university somewhere, no one reads every single word in any edition of *The Washington Post*. Even if the classified ads were ignored and one were a fast reader, reading all the stories would take hours. Your twenty-five cents usually buys you two and a quarter pounds of paper, ten or more sections full of news, features, articles, and ads aimed at different tastes and interests. Statecraft, politics, murders, rapes, disasters, business, sports, science, gardening, celebrity gossip and gushings, book reviews, movie hype, music tripe, opinions from every hue of the political spectrum, television listings—the entire world was captured every day on thirty-six ounces of newsprint. Or as much of the world as any civilized being at the very center of the universe—Washington—could possibly care to learn about.

Jack Yocke had a secret ambition to be the first human to read the whole thing. He had it on his list for some morning when he was in bed with the flu. But not today. Sitting at his desk he flipped through the paper scanning the headlines and speed reading the stories that looked interesting.

The Soviets' formal request for foreign aid from the United States was the hottest topic of the day. Senators and representatives were having a field day, as were most of the political columnists. No one denied that the Soviets needed real money—all they could get—but the hard fact mentioned only by the hopelessly practical was that the United States government had no money to give. The cookie jar was empty. There weren't even any crumbs.

Most pundits and politicians were making lists of things the Soviets would have to do to qualify for American largess, confidently assuming that if America wanted to badly enough, some largess could be found somewhere. After all, do we really need a military in this brave new world? Surely the nations now receiving foreign aid, together with welfare recipients and Social Security retirees, would be willing to share their mite with the Russians, for the greater good.

In any event, to qualify for the American dole the Soviets would need to free the Baltic states, release all their remaining political prisoners, and open borders for U.S. trade and investment. Of course the Russians would also have to permanently cease all financial and military aid to Cuba and Libya and Vietnam and Afghanistan and Angola and every other Third World manure pile where the godless commies had opposed the holy forces of capitalism and democracy. They would also have to disband the KGB and the GRU, quit spying on the U.S. and everybody else. And—this almost didn't need to be mentioned—while they were at it the Russians would have to disband the entire Soviet military and sell their ships, tanks, and artillery for scrap. If they did *all* this, well, they would certainly be entitled to some bucks if and when we found some.

Today Jack Yocke scanned the wish lists and moved on. He found a couple of interesting columns by two pundits who had solved the foreign aid issue yesterday. The price of coca leaves in Bolivia and Peru was down from one hundred U.S. dollars to just ten dollars per hundred-weight. One columnist opined that this fact meant that George Bush was winning the war on drugs. Another, who had probably stayed awake during his freshman economics class, thought the price drop meant that Bolivian and Peruvian farmers had a bumper crop this year and all the millions spent on eradication efforts had been wasted.

Jack Yocke checked his Rolodex. He found the number he wanted under a code he had made up himself. He called it.

"Yeah, man."

"Hey, this is Jack Yocke. How's it going?"

"Too smooth, dude. What's on your mind?"

"You seen this morning's paper?"

"I never read that honkey shit. You know that."

"Question. What's the street price doing right now?"

"What d'ya mean?"

"Is it going up or down?"

"Steady, man. Five bucks a pop. Some talk about dropping it to four, but nobody wants to do that. Not as much juice for everybody, you know?"

"Any supply problems?"

"Not that I heard."

"Thanks."

"Be cool, dude."

The man that Yocke had been talking to, Harrison Ronald Ford—he had taken to using his full name since that actor became popular—cradled the telephone and went back to his coffee.

The newspaper that he had just told Yocke he never read was spread on the kitchen table in front of him. The story he had been reading when the phone rang had Yocke's byline. Second Potomac Savings and Loan taken over by the feds, the headline shouted. Recently murdered cashier Walter P. Harrington apparently involved in money laundering, according to an unnamed source. Second Potomac officials aghast. Massive violations of record-keeping requirements. The rank-and-file staff knew something fishy was going on, but no one wanted to speak out and risk his job and pension rights. So now they had neither.

Harrison Ronald poured himself another cup of coffee and lit another cigarette. He glanced out the dirty window at the building across the alley, then resumed his seat at the kitchen table and flipped to the comics.

After he scanned them and grinned at "Cathy," he picked up a pencil and began the crossword puzzle.

Harrison Ronald liked crossword puzzles. He had discovered long ago that he could think about other things while he filled in the little squares. Today he had much to think about.

At the head of his list was Freeman McNally. He knew that McNally had been laundering money through Harrington's S-and-L. What would McNally do now? McNally's operation was taking in almost three million cash a week. About a fourth of that amount went to the West Coast to pay for new raw product, and a big chunk went to salaries and payoffs and other expenses. Still the operation produced a million a week pure profit—a little over four million a month—cash that Freeman McNally had to somehow turn into legitimate funds that he and his immediate cronies could spend and squirrel away.

It was certainly a pleasant problem, but a problem nonetheless. It would be interesting to hear Freeman's solution.

In the year that Harrison Ronald had spent working for the organization he had acquired a tremendous respect for Freeman McNally. A sixth-grade dropout, McNally had common sense, superior intelligence, and a cat's ability to land on his feet when the unexpected occurred, as it did with a frequency that would have appalled any legitimate business-man.

Many of McNally's troubles were caused by the people who worked for him: they got greedy, they became addicted, they liked to strut their stuff in front of the wrong people, they became convinced of their own personal invulnerability. McNally was a natural leader. His judgments were hard to fault. Those people that he concluded were a danger disappeared, quickly and forever. Those errant souls whom he believed trainable he corrected and trusted.

Like every crack dealer, McNally was in a never-ending battle to protect his turf, the street corners and houses where his street dealers sold his product. This was combat and McNally had a natural aptitude for it. He was ruthless efficiency incarnate.

And like every crack dealer, McNally was in a cash-and-carry business that demanded constant vigilance against cheaters and thieves. Here too McNally excelled, but he had been blessed with a generous dollop of paranoia and a natural talent for larceny. To Harrison Ronald's personal knowledge, poorly advised optimists had attempted to swindle Freeman McNally on two occasions. Several of these foolish individuals had received bullets in the brain as souvenirs of their adventure and one had been dismembered with a chain saw while still alive.

But although Freeman McNally had many attributes in common with other successful crack-ring leaders, he was also unique. McNally intui-tively understood that the most serious threat to the health of his enterprise was the authorities—the police, the DEA, the FBI. So he had systematically set about reducing that threat to an acceptable level. He found politicians, cops and drug enforcement agents who could be bought and he bought them.

Consequently Harrison Ronald Ford was in Washington undercover instead of riding around Evansville, Indiana, in a patrol car. He wasn't known as Harrison Ronald Ford here though, but as Sammy Z.

Mother of Galahad, 23 Across. Six letters, the last of which is an E.

Ford had arrived in Washington a year ago and rented this shithole to live in. After two weeks of hanging around bars, he got a job as a lookout for one of McNally's distributors. He had been doing that for about a month when who should come strolling down the street one rainy Thursday night but his high school baseball buddy from Evansville, Jack Yocke.

He had leveled with Yocke—he had no choice: Yocke knew he was a cop—and the reporter apparently had kept the secret. Ten months had passed, Harrison Ronald was still alive, with all his arms and legs firmly attached, and he was now personally running errands and delivering product for Freeman.

He was close. Very close. He knew the names of two of the local cops on Freeman's list and one of the politicians, but he had no evidence that would stand up in court.

It would come. Sooner or later he would get the evidence. If he lived long enough.

Elaine. Elaine was the mother of Galahad.

If that fox Freeman McNally didn't catch on.

Damn that Yocke anyway. Why did that white boy have to pick today to call? Oh well, if worse came to worst, Jack Yocke would write him one hell of an obituary.

The late Judson Lincoln had lived in a modest three-story town house in a fashionably chic neighborhood a mile or so northeast of the White House. T. Jefferson Brody wheeled his Mercedes into a vacant parking place a block past the Lincoln residence and walked back.

He was expected. He had telephoned the widow this morning and informed her of his interest in discussing the purchase of the business that had belonged to her deceased husband. She had apparently called her attorney, then called him back and proposed this meeting at two p.m.

Mrs. Lincoln had sounded calm enough on the phone this morning, but that was certainly nothing to bank upon. This would in all likelihood be a tense afternoon with the sniveling widow, probably some brainless, ill-mannered brats, and for sure, one overpaid fat lawyer anxious to split hairs and niggle ad nauseam over contractual phrasing. Looming like a thunderstorm on the horizon would be the question of who had killed

Judson Lincoln, prominent black businessman and civic pillar to whom we point with pride. And police. They would be in constant contact with the widow, asking every question they thought they could get away with.

Oh well, T. Jefferson could handle it.

After pushing the doorbell, Brody adjusted the twenty-dollar royal-blue silk hanky in his breast pocket. He hoped he wouldn't need to offer it as a repository for the contents of the widow's nose, but. . . . He straightened his tie and made sure his suit jacket was properly buttoned and hanging correctly under his knee-length mohair topcoat.

The door was opened by a black woman in a maid outfit that was complete right down to the little white apron. He handed her his card and said, "To see Mrs. Lincoln, please."

"I'll take your coat, sir." When Brody had shed the garment, the maid said, "This way, sir."

She led Brody fifteen feet down the hallway to the study.

Mrs. Lincoln was a tall woman with chiseled features and a magnificent figure. Her waist, Brody noted appreciatively, wouldn't go over twenty-two inches. Her bust, he estimated, would tape almost twice that. Judson Lincoln must have been out of his mind to go chasing floozies with this magnificent piece waiting for him at home!

Then she smiled.

T. Jefferson Brody felt his knees get watery.

"I'm Deborah Lincoln, Mr. Brody. This is my attorney, Jeremiah Jones."

For the first time Brody glanced at the attorney. He was about twenty-five with slicked-back hair, miserable teeth, and a weasel smile. "Yes, yes, Mr. Brody. Deborah has told me of your client's interest in her husband's business. Such a tragedy that took him from her so early in life."

As Brody feasted his eyes upon the widow, it occurred to him that she seemed to be weathering her husband's unfortunate demise very well. Just now she made eye contact with Jones and they both smiled slightly. She turned back to Brody and, it seemed to him, made a real effort to arrange her face.

"A tragedy," Brody agreed after another look at gigolo Jones. "Ahem, well, life must go on. Sorry to disturb you so soon after . . . ah, but my clients are anxious that I speak to you about their interest in your husband's business before you . . . ah, before you . . ."

The beautiful Deborah Lincoln took her attorney's hand and squeezed it as she gazed raptly at Brody.

". . . They want to buy the business," Brody finished lamely, his thoughts galloping.

Yes, indeed, Deborah Lincoln. Yes, indeed, you need a man to comfort you in your hour of need. But why this pimp in mufti? Why not T. Jefferson Brody?

"I have an excellent offer to lay before you." Brody gave the widow Lincoln his most honest, sincere smile.

Negotiations with Deborah Lincoln and attorney Jones took all of an hour. Brody offered $350,000, the attorney demanded $450,000. After some genteel give-and-take, Mrs. Lincoln graciously agreed to compromise at $400,000. Her attorney held her hand and looked into her eyes and tried to persuade her to demand more, but her mind was made up.

"Four hundred thousand is fair," she said. "That's about what Judson thought the business was worth."

She gave Jones a gentle grin and squeezed his hand. When they weren't looking his way, T. Jefferson Brody rolled his eyes heavenward.

It was agreed that tomorrow afternoon Mrs. Lincoln and Mr. Jones would come to Brody's office to look over the lease assignments, bill of sale, and other documents. Brody would have the check ready.

After shaking hands all around, Brody was escorted from the room by the maid, who helped him with his coat and held the door for him.

Down on the sidewalk, with the door firmly closed behind him, Jefferson Brody permitted himself a big smile as he walked toward his car.

The door was opened by a young woman with a scarf around her head. "Yes."

"I understand you have an apartment for rent?" Henry Charon raised his eyebrows hopefully.

"Yes. Come in, come in. It's too cold out there. What is it, forty-five degrees?"

"Nearer fifty, I think."

"It's upstairs. A bedroom, bath, living room, and kitchenette. Fairly nice."

They were standing in the hallway now. The New Hampshire Avenue building was old but fairly clean. The woman wore huge glasses in brown, hornrim frames, but the optical correction in the glass was so large that her eyes were comically enlarged. Charon found himself staring at those brown eyes, fascinated. She focused on one thing, then another, and he could plainly see every twitch of the muscles around her eyes.

"I'd like to see the apartment, please."

"The rent's nine hundred a month," she apologized. She had a pleasant voice and spoke clearly, articulating every word precisely. "Really obscene, I know, but what can we do?"

Charon grimaced for her benefit, then said, "I'd like to see it."

Her eyes reflected her empathy, then she turned and made for the stairs. "Just moving to town?"

"That's right."

"Oh, you'll like Washington. It's so vibrant, so exciting! All the great ideas are here. This is such an intellectually stimulating city!"

The apartment was on the third floor. The living room faced the street, but the bedroom looked down on an alley that ran alongside the building. The grillwork of a fire escape was visible out the bedroom window, and he unlocked the sash, raised it, and stuck his head out. The fire escape went all the way to the roof.

He closed the window as his guide explained about the heat. Forced-air gas, no individual thermostats, temperature kept at sixty-five all winter.

"You must come look at the kitchen." She led him on. "It's small but intimate and reasonably equipped. Perfect for meals for two, but you could do food for four quite easily, six or eight in a pinch."

"Very nice," Henry Charon said, and opened the refrigerator and looked inside to humor her. "Very nice."

She showed him the bathroom. Adequate hot water, he was assured.

"The neighbors?" he asked when they were standing in the living room.

"Well," she said, lowering her voice as if to tell a secret. "Everyone who lives here is so very nice. Two doctoral students—I'm one of those—a Library of Congress researcher, a paralegal, a free-lance writer, and a public-interest attorney. Oh, and one librarian."

"Ummm."

"This is the only vacancy we've had in over a year. We've had five inquiries, but the landlord insisted on a hundred and fifty a month rent increase, which just puts it out of so many persons' reach."

"I can believe it."

"The previous tenant died of AIDS." She looked wistfully around the room, then turned those huge eyes on Charon. He stared into them. "It was so tragic. He suffered so. His friend just couldn't afford to keep the apartment after he passed away."

"I see."

"What kind of work do you do?"

"Consulting, mostly. Government stuff."

He began asking questions just to hear her voice and watch the expressions in her eyes. She was studying political science, hoped to teach in a private university, got a break on her rent to manage the building, the neighborhood was quiet with only reasonable traffic, she had lived here for two years and grown up in Newton, Massachusetts, the corner grocery on the next street over was excellent. Her name was Grisella Clifton.

"Well," Henry Charon sighed at last, reluctant to end the conversation. "You've sold me. I'll take it."

A half hour later she walked out the door with him. She paused by her car, a weathered VW bug. "I'm delighted you'll be living here with us, Mr. Tackett."

Henry Charon nodded and watched her maneuver the Volkswagen from its parking place. She kept both hands firmly on the wheel and leaned toward it until the moving plastic threatened to graze her nose. On the back of the car were a variety of bumper stickers: ONE WOMAN FOR PEACE, CHILDCARE BEFORE WARFARE, THIS CAR IS A NUCLEAR FREE ZONE.

On Wednesday afternoon Jefferson Brody concluded that Jeremiah Jones wasn't much of a lawyer. While Mrs. Lincoln examined the original oil paintings on the paneled mahogany and the bronze nude that Brody had paid eleven thousand dollars for, Jones looked over the legal documents, asked two stupid questions, and flipped through the two full pages of representations and warranties that Mrs. Lincoln was asked to make as seller of the business without taking the time to read them carefully. Jones was a sheep, Brody decided. A black sheep, he chuckled to himself, pleased at his own wit.

Mrs. Lincoln signed the documents while Brody's secretary watched. Then the secretary notarized the documents, carefully sealed them, and separated them into piles, one pile for Mrs. Lincoln and one for Brody's clients, whose identities were, of course, still undisclosed. The documents merely transferred the business to the ABC Corporation, which was precisely one day old.

"You understand, I'm sure," Brody commented to Jones, "why my clients have not given me the authority to reveal their identities."

"Perfectly," Jones said with a wave of his hand. "Happens all the time."

Brody produced the cashier's check of a New York bank in the amount of four hundred thousand dollars. After Jones had examined it, it went to Mrs. Lincoln, who merely glanced at it and folded it for her purse.

Jones glanced at his watch and stood. "I'd better run. I have an appointment at my office and I think I'm going to be late. Deborah, can you get home in a taxi?"

"Of course, Jeremiah. Oh, why don't you take this check and have your secretary deposit it for me? Could you do that?"

"If you'll make out a deposit slip."

"Won't take a minute." Mrs. Lincoln got out her checkbook, carefully tore a deposit slip from the back, and noted the check number on it. Then she turned the check over and endorsed it. This didn't take thirty seconds. She handed both pieces of paper to Jones. "Thank you so much."

"Of course. I'll call you."

Jones shook hands with Brody and left.

"Well, Mr. Brody, I've taken up enough of your time," Deborah Lincoln said. "I'll ask your secretary to call me a taxi."

T. Jefferson stood. "I've enjoyed meeting you, Mrs. Lincoln."

"Please call me Deborah."

"Deborah. It's such a shame that the tragedy to your husband . . . I hope the police weren't too rough."

"Oh," she said with a slight grimace, "they certainly weren't pleasant. Almost suggested I'd hired it done. They said it was a professional killing." She tried to grin. "It certainly didn't help that Judson was killed on the stoop of his bimbo's house, if you know what I mean."

"I understand," Brody said gravely and reached for her hand. She let him take it.

"You know, I'm not sure how to say this, but I have the feeling that things will go well for you from now on."

"Well, I hope so. With the business sold and all. That certainly is a load off my mind. I know nothing at all of Judson's business, Mr.—"

"Jefferson, please."

"Jefferson, and your people paid what the business was worth, I believe." She took her hand back and looked again at the paintings and the sculpture. "Such a nice office."

"What say—how about I buy you dinner? Could I do that for you?"

She looked at him with surprise. "Why, Mr.—Jefferson. So nice of you to ask. Why, yes, I'd like that."

Brody looked at his watch, a Rolex. "Almost four o'clock. I think we've done enough business for today. Perhaps we might go to a little place I know for drinks, then dinner afterward, when we're hungry?"

"You're very thoughtful."

The evening turned out to be one of the most pleasant that T. Jefferson Brody could remember. The beautiful black woman with the striking figure was a gifted conversationalist, Brody concluded, a woman who knew how to put a man at ease. She kept him talking about his favorite subject—T. Jefferson Brody—and drew from him a highly modified version of his life story. Professional triumphs, wealthy clients, vacations in Europe and the Caribbean—with a few drinks in him Brody waxed expansive. As he told it his life was a triumphant march ever deeper into the palace of wealth and privilege. He savored every step because he had earned it.

After dinner—chateaubriand for two of course—and a $250 bottle of twelve-year-old French wine, Jefferson Brody seated the widow Lincoln and her magnificent rack of tits in his Mercedes and drove her to his humble $1.6 million abode in Kenwood.

He led her through the house pronouncing the brand names of his possessions as if they were the names of wild and dangerous game he had stalked and vanquished in darkest Africa while armed only with a spear. Majolica plates from Rosselli, trompe-l'oeil paneling, Italian leather sofas and chairs, Jesurum lace tablecloth and bed linen, two original Chippendale chairs, Fabergé eggs—they were trophies, in a way, and it would not be overstatement to say that he loved them.

After the tour, he led her back to the den where he fixed drinks. She had a vodka tonic and he made himself a scotch and soda. With the lights dimmed and the strains of a Dvorak CD floating from the Klipsch speakers, T. Jefferson Brody ran his fingertips along the widow's thigh and kissed her willing lips.

Three sips of scotch and three minutes later he went quietly to sleep. The remains of his drink spilled down his trouser leg and onto the Kashan carpet.

Mrs. Lincoln managed to lever herself out from under Brody's bulk and find a light switch. She refastened her brassiere and straightened her clothes, then made a telephone call.

When Jefferson Brody awoke sunlight was streaming through the window. He squinted mightily against the light and rashly tried to move, which almost tore his head in half. His head was pounding like a bass drum, the worst hangover of his life.

"My God . . ."

His memory was a jumble. Deborah Lincoln, with the sublime tits . . . she was in—no, she was here. Here! In his house. They were kissing and he had his hand . . . and nothing! There was nothing else. His mind was empty. That was all he could remember.

What time is it?

He felt for his watch. Not on his wrist.

The *Rolex! Not on his wrist!*

T. Jefferson Brody pried his eyes open, gritting his teeth against the pain in his head. His watch was missing. He looked around. The TV and VCR were gone. Where the Klipsch speakers had stood only bare wires remained. His wallet lay in the middle of the carpet, empty. *Oh God . . .*

He staggered into the dining room. The doors to the china cabinet were ajar, and the cabinet was bare! The Spode china, the silver and crystal—*gone!*

"I've been robbed!" he croaked. *"God fucking damn, I've been robbed!"*

He lurched into the living room. The Fabergé eggs, the engravings, everything small enough to carry, all gone!

The police! He would call the police. He made for the kitchen and the phone on the counter.

A newspaper was arranged over the phone. He tossed it aside and picked up the receiver while he tried to focus on the buttons.

Something red on the newspaper caught his eye. A big red circle around a photo, a photo of a fat, frumpy black woman. The circle—it was *lipstick!* He bent to stare at the paper. Yesterday's *Post.* The picture caption: "Mrs. Judson Lincoln, at National Airport after her husband's funeral, reflected on the many civic contributions to the citizens of Washington made by the late Mr. Lincoln, a District native."

"Lemme get this straight, Tee. You paid this woman you thought was Mrs. Lincoln four hundred grand. You took her to dinner. She slipped you a Mickey last night and cleaned out your house?"

"Yeah, Bernie. The papers she signed are worthless. Forgeries. I don't know who the hell she is, but I'm sitting here looking at a photo of Mrs. Judson Lincoln in yesterday's paper, and the broad who signed the papers and took the money ain't her."

"Did she have nice tits, Tee?"

"Yeah, but—"

Bernie Shapiro had a high-pitched, nasal he-he-he laugh that was truly nauseating if you were suffering from the aftereffects of a Mickey Finn. Brody held the telephone well away from his ear. Shapiro giggled and snorted until he choked.

"Listen, Bernie," Brody protested when Shapiro stopped coughing, "this isn't so damned funny. She's got your money!"

"Oh, no, Tee. She's got four hundred grand of *your* money! We gave you *our* four hundred Gs to buy that goddamn check cashing company, and you had better do just precisely that with it. You got forty-eight hours, Tee. I expect to see documents transferring title to that business on my desk within forty-eight hours, and they goddamn well better be signed by the real, bona fide, genuine Mrs. Judson widow Lincoln. Are you on my wavelength?"

"Yeah, Bernie. But it would sure be nice if you helped me catch up with this black bitch and get the money back."

"You haven't called the cops, have you?"

"No. Thought I oughta talk to you first."

"Well, you finally did something right. I'll think about helping you catch up with the broad, Tee, but in the meantime you had better get cracking on the Lincoln deal. I'm not going to tell you again."

"Sure. Sure, Bernie."

"Tell me what this woman looked like."

Brody did so.

"This lawyer with her, what'd he look like?"

Brody described Jeremiah Jones right down to his shoelaces and bad teeth.

"I'll think about it, Tee, maybe ask around. But you got forty-eight hours."

"Yeah."

"Don't do nothing stupid." The connection broke.

Jefferson Brody cradled the receiver and picked up the ice bag, which he held carefully against his forehead. It helped a little. Maybe he should take three more aspirins.

He needed to lie down for a few hours. That was it. Get his feet up.

But first he wandered through the house, cataloguing yet again all the things that were missing. If he ever caught up with that cunt, he'd kill her. Maybe after he'd closed the Lincoln deal he could talk Bernie into putting a contract on her black ass.

In the hallway, as he passed the door to the garage, a sense of foreboding came over T. Jefferson Brody. He opened the door and peered into the garage. Empty. Hadn't he parked the Mercedes in here last night? Or had he left it in the driveway?

He hit the button to open the garage door. The door rose slowly, majestically, revealing an empty driveway.

Oh no! She'd stolen the damned car too!

CHAPTER EIGHT

★ ★ ★ ★ ★ ★ ★ ★ ★

"WHY? Tell me why."

"Because I wanted it," Elizabeth snarled. "Is that too difficult for you to understand?"

Thanos Liarakos pinched his nose and stroked an eyebrow. His associates had seen him do this many times in the courtroom, and they knew it was an unconscious mannerism to handle stress. If his wife knew the significance of the gesture, she ignored it now. She hugged her knees and stared at the hospital's stenciled name on the sheets.

After a moment he said, "That stuff will kill you."

She sneered.

"What am I supposed to say to you? Should I talk about the kids? Should I tell you how much I love you? Should I tell you once again that you're playing Russian roulette? And you are going to *lose.*"

"I'm not one of your half-witted jurors. Spare me the eloquence."

"You're prostituting your soul for this white powder, Elizabeth. Prostituting your dignity. Your intelligence. Your humanity. You are! You're trading everything that makes life worth living for a few minutes of feeling good. God, you are a fool."

"If that's the way you feel, why don't you get out of here? I'm not going to sit quietly while you call me a whore. You bastard!"

"What *do* you want, Elizabeth?"

She glared at him and wrapped her arms around her chest.

"Do you want to come home?"

She said nothing.

"I'm going to lay it out for you in black and white. You're a cocaine addict. When they discharge you in a few days you're going back to that clinic. I've already made the phone calls and sent them a check." This would be her third trip. "You are going to sign yourself in and stay until you are cured, finally, once and for all. You are going to learn to live without cocaine for the rest of your life. *Then* you may come home."

"Jesus, you make it sound like I've got a nasty virus or a pesky little venereal disease. 'When the pus in your vagina drys up—'"

"You *can* kick it, Elizabeth."

"You're so goddamn certain! *I'm* the one that's in here living it. What if I *can't?*"

"If you *don't,* I'll file for a divorce. I'll ask for custody and I'll get it. You can whore and steal and do whatever else you have to to maintain your addiction, and when the people from the morgue call, the kids and I will see that you get a Christian burial and a nice little marble slab. Every year on Mother's Day we'll put flowers on your grave."

Tears ran down Elizabeth's face. "Maybe I should just kill myself and get it over with," she said softly. But too late. Her husband missed this histrionic fillip. He was already halfway through the door.

Before she could say anything else he disappeared down the corridor.

Henry Charon was at the apartment on New Hampshire Avenue at nine a.m. when the truck from the furniture rental company came. Grisella Clifton wasn't home, and Charon felt vaguely put out. He showed the truck crew where to put the bed, the couch, the dresser, the chairs, and the television, then tipped the driver and his helper a ten-spot each.

At eleven o'clock he was at the apartment he'd rented in Georgetown when the truck from the furniture rental company in Arlington arrived, A-to-Z Rentals. The deliverymen had the furniture inside and arranged by eleven-forty. He tipped both those men and locked the door behind him as he left.

At one he was at the apartment near Lafayette Circle. The telephone company installation person—a woman—showed up a half hour late. She apologized and Charon waved it aside. She had almost finished when the furniture arrived, this time from a rental company in Chevy Chase.

At four p.m. he bought a car from an elderly lady living in Bethesda. He had called five people with cars for sale in the classified section of the newspaper and settled on her because she sounded like an elderly recluse.

She was. Even better, she peered at him myopically. At her daughter's insistence, she explained at length while he nodded understandingly, she was giving up the car, a seven-year-old Chevrolet two-door sedan, brown. The plates were valid for three more months. He paid her cash and drove it straight to a Sears auto service center where he had the oil and plugs changed, the radiator serviced, all the belts and hoses replaced, and a new battery and new tires installed. While he was waiting he ate a hamburger in the mall.

As he strolled through the evening crowd toward the auto service center at the north end of the mall, he passed an electronics store. In he went. Fifteen minutes later he came out with a police band radio scanner.

That evening at the Lafayette Circle apartment he read the instruction book and played with the dials and switches. The radio worked well whether plugged into the wall socket or on its rechargeable batteries. He stretched out on the bed and listened to the dispatcher and the officers on the street. They routinely used two-digit codes to shorten the transmissions. Tomorrow he would go to the library and try to find a list of the codes. And he would visit more electronics stores and buy more scanners, but only one at each store.

Tomorrow the telephone people were installing phones in the other two apartments. And tomorrow he would have to shop for food and first-aid supplies. Then tomorrow night he would begin moving food, water, and medical supplies to the subway hideout.

Maybe the following night he could put some dried beef and bandages in the cave in Rock Creek Park.

So much to do and so little time.

As he listened to the scanner he mentally went through the checklist one more time.

The real problem was afterward, after the hunt. He did not yet have a solution and he began to worry about it again. The FBI would have his fingerprints—that was inevitable. Henry Charon had no illusions. The fact that the fingerprints the FBI acquired would match not a single set of the tens of millions they had on file would eventually cause the agents to look in the right places. They would have plenty of time—all they needed, in spite of exhortations by politicians and outraged pundits— and the cooperation of every law-enforcement officer in the nation.

Eventually, inevitably, the net would pull him in. Unless he was not there. Or unless the FBI stopped looking because they thought they already had their man. The false clues would not have to hold up forever; indeed, every day that passed would allow the real trail to get colder and colder. A month or so would probably be sufficient.

Why not a red herring?

At three the following afternoon Jack Yocke was finishing a story on the collapse of Second Potomac Savings and Loan. His editor had told him earlier to keep the story tight: space was going to be at a premium in tomorrow's paper. The Soviets had just announced an immediate cessation of foreign aid to Cuba and Libya. Both nations would be permitted to continue to purchase goods from the Soviet Union but only at world market prices, with hard currency.

Yocke hung up the telephone without looking and kept right on tapping on the computer keyboard. The authorities were fully satisfied that the late Walter P. Harrington had been using Second Potomac to launder money for the crack trade. Local crack money or from somewhere else? No one was saying, not even off the record.

And someone had used a high-powered rifle to blow his head off while he drove the left lane of the Beltway at fifty-five miles per hour—his widow fervently insisted that he *always* drove fifty-five.

It certainly had not been a motorist enraged over Harrington's highway manners. Not using a rifle.

Money, money, money. Hadn't the other man killed the evening Harrington died also had something to do with money? Didn't he own some kind of check-cashing business?

The phone rang.

Still tapping the Second Potomac story, Yocke cradled the receiver against his shoulder and cheek. "Yocke."

"Jack, there's been a shooting at the day-care center in the Shiloh Baptist Church, next door to the Jefferson projects. About thirty minutes or so ago. Would you run over there? I'm also sending a photographer."

"Yo."

Yocke looked over his story, pushed RECORD, and then left the terminal to turn itself off.

The Jefferson projects was not the worst public housing project in the city, nor was it the best. It was simply average. Ninety-eight percent black and Hispanic, the tenants existed in a netherworld of poverty and squalor where the crack trade boomed twenty-four hours a day and men sneaked in and out to avoid jeopardizing their girlfriends' welfare eligibility.

All the legitimate merchants in a five-block radius of the projects had long ago gone out of business, except for one sixty-year-old Armenian grocer who had been robbed forty-two times in the last sixty months, a record even for Washington. Yocke had done a story on him six months or so ago. He had been robbed four times since then.

"One of these crackheads is going to kill you some night," Yocke had told the grocer.

"Where am I gonna go? Answer me that. I grew up in the house across the street. I've never lived anywhere else. The grocery business is the only trade I know. And they never steal over a day's receipts."

"Some strung-out kid is going to smear your brains all over the back counter."

"It's sorta like a tax, y'know? That's the way I look at it. The scumbags take my money at gunpoint and buy crack. The city takes my money legally and pays the mayor a salary he doesn't earn and he uses it to buy crack. The feds take my money legally and pay welfare to that crowd in the projects and they let their kids starve while they spend the money on crack. What the hell's the difference?"

Still pondering the crack tax, Yocke slowed the pool car as he went by the Armenian's corner grocery and looked in. The old man was bagging groceries for an elderly black lady.

He parked the car two blocks from the project and walked. As he rounded a corner, there they were, long three-story gray buildings, four to a block, decaying without grace under a cold gray sky.

Something about the scene jarred him. Oh yeah, the place was deserted. The teenage boys who manned the sidewalks and sold crack to the white people who drove in from the suburbs were gone. The cops were here.

Yocke veered onto a sidewalk between the buildings and strode along purposefully, his steps echoing on the cinderblock walls and the gray, vacant windows.

White man, white man, the echos said, over and over. White man, white man . . .

The church was across the street from the projects, on the western edge. Police cars in front, lights flashing. An ambulance. One cop keeping an eye on the vehicles.

Yocke showed the cop his ID. "Understand there's been a shooting?"

The cop was a black man in his fifties with a pot gut. The strap that held his pistol in its holster was unlatched. The gun could be drawn in a clean, crisp motion. The cop jerked his thumb over his shoulder and grunted.

"Can I go in?"

"After they bring the body out. Be another ten minutes or so."

Yocke got out his notebook and pencil. "Who is it?"

"Was."

"Yeah."

"The woman who ran the day care. I don't know her name."

"What happened?"

"Well, near as I can figure, from what I've heard, a couple squad cars stopped over on Grant." Grant was the street bordering the west side of the projects. "The dealers ran through the projects. A cop chased one guy. He went charging into the church, through the day-care center toward the playground door, and when the victim didn't get out of his way fast enough, he drilled her. One shot. Right through the heart."

The radio transceiver on the cop's belt holster crackled into life. He held it to his ear with his left hand. His right remained near his gun butt.

Other cops were searching the abandoned buildings and tenements to the west of the church. The cryptic transmissions floated from the radios of the parked cruisers.

When the radio fell momentarily silent, Yocke asked the patrolman, "Where were the kids when the shooting occurred?"

"Where the hell do you think? Right there. They saw the whole thing."

"When?"

"About two-forty or so."

"You haven't got the killer yet?"

The cop spit on the sidewalk. "Not yet."

"Description?"

"Black male, about eighteen or so, five feet ten to six feet, maybe a hundred fifty or sixty. Medium-length hair. Was wearing a red ball-cap, black leather coat, white running shoes. That's the description from the cop chasing him. All the kids say is that he had a big gun."

Big gun, Yocke scribbled. Yeah, any pistol vomiting bullets into real people, with real blood flying, it's a big gun when you remember it. Big as your nightmares, big as evil personified, big as sudden death.

"How old are the kids?"

"Youngest's a few weeks. Oldest is almost six."

"Name of the cop chasing the shooter?"

"Ask the lieutenant."

"Why was the cop chasing the shooter?"

"Ask the lieutenant."

"Is there anything else you can tell me?"

"Your newspaper sucks."

Yocke put the notebook in his pocket and rolled his collar upright. The wind was picking up. Dirt and trash swirled around the cars and funneled between the barracks of the projects. A chilly wind.

"May rain," the cop said when he saw Yocke looking at the gray sky.

"Might."

"Been a dry fall. We need the rain."

"How many years you been on the force?"

"Too fucking many."

The minutes passed. Yocke fought the chill wind as the police radio told its story of futility. The man who had done the shooting was nowhere to be found.

The *Post* photographer showed up. He burned film as Yorke shivered.

Finally, after twenty minutes, the ambulance crew brought the body out on a wheeled stretcher covered with a white sheet, which was strapped down to keep it from blowing away. It went into the vehicle and the crew followed. One man got in the driver's seat, turned off the flashing overhead lights, and drove away.

"You can go in now," the cop beside Yocke told him.

The church foyer was dirty and dark and needed paint. The sounds of children sobbing were plainly audible.

On the wall a small announcement board gave the title of this Sunday's sermon: "The Christian's Choice in Today's World." Beneath the sermon board was a faded poster with a girl's picture: "Missing since 4/21/88. Black female, 13, five feet two." Her name was there, what she had been wearing that evening nineteen months ago, a phone number to call.

A stairway led up to the left. To the sanctuary, probably. Yocke continued along the hallway, toward the sobbing. At the end of the hall the door stood open.

A young woman had the children huddled around her. About a dozen of them. God, they're so small! Talking softly among themselves were three policemen in uniform, two in plainclothes. Two lab technicians were repacking their cases. And curiously, no one stood on or near the ubiquitous chalk outline on the floor.

The *Post* photographer, Harold Dorgan, followed Yocke in. He began taking pictures of the children and the young woman trying to comfort them.

The lieutenant was in his forties. His shirt was dirty and he needed a shave. He also needed a breath freshener, Yocke soon discovered. After Dorgan had taken a dozen pictures, the lieutenant told him that was enough and shooed him out.

The victim's name was Jane Wilkens. Age thirty-six. Unmarried. Mother of three children. Killed by one .357-inch-diameter slug that had gone through her entire body, including her heart, and buried itself in the wall near the rear door. Wilkens had started shouting as the gunman burst through the door with the pistol in his hand. As he came at her he pointed the weapon and fired one shot from a distance of perhaps five feet. She was still falling when he ran by her. He jerked open the door to the playground and ran out.

No one saw which way he went after he went through the door. The playground was surrounded by a five-foot-high fence that an agile man could vault anywhere he wished.

The pistol had not been found, so searching officers had been advised to proceed with caution. "Maybe a thirty-eight Special," the lieutenant said, "but more likely a three fifty-seven Magnum. Damn bullet went through plaster, a layer of drywall, and shattered a concrete block. Almost went through it."

"A cop was chasing this guy," Yocke murmured.

"Yeah. Patrolman Harry Phelps."

"Why?"

"Because he ran."

"What do you mean?"

"I mean a couple cruisers pulled up over on Grant and a bunch of those kids took off like jackrabbits. Officer Phelps ran after this guy. The suspect pulled a weapon, looked back over his shoulder several times at the officer, and charged into this church. Officer Phelps kept coming, heard the shot, and stopped by the victim to administer first aid. She lived for about fifteen seconds after he reached her."

"So Jane Wilkens would still be alive if Phelps had not elected to chase this guy?"

"Whatever you're implying, I don't like it," the lieutenant snarled. "And I don't like your face. Phelps—Officer Phelps—was doing his job. We're trying to police this shithole, Mr. *Washington* fucking *Post!*"

"Yeah, but—"

"Get outta my face!"

"Listen. I—"

"Out! This is a crime scene. Out!"

Jack Yocke went.

Dorgan was sitting on the curb in front of the church. Yocke sat down beside him. The overweight cop attending the door ignored them.

"What d'ya think?" Dorgan said.

"I don't think. I gave that up years ago."

"I'm going to walk over to Grant and snap a few, then head back downtown. I think I got some good shots of the kids. Really tough on them to see that."

"Yeah."

"Try not to get mugged." With that Dorgan rose, adjusted his camera bags, and trudged away. Yocke watched him go.

The curb was cold on his fanny. He stood and dusted his seat, then walked back and forth on the sidewalk.

After a while the kids came out. Each of them was carrying a little brown paper bag. Yocke watched them disappear into the projects.

A few minutes later the cops began dribbling out. When the lieutenant came out he ignored Yocke and climbed into the passenger seat of a cruiser. The uniformed officer with him got behind the wheel.

Yocke saw the man coming a block away. With his hands in his jacket pockets, his head up, he walked rapidly in this direction.

He's coming here, Yocke decided, and watched him come. About forty-five, he had short gray hair. His chocolate skin was stretched tight over his cheekbones and jaw.

The man looked at the cop and Yocke and went up the three steps and through the door without pausing.

Yocke leaned on the little railing that protected what had once been grass. The temperature had dropped at least five degrees and the sky was grayer. He was wondering whether he should return to the office or try to get back inside when a drop of rain struck him.

He set off through the projects, back toward the car. Droplets of rain raised little puffs of dirt beside the empty sidewalks. He met a policeman coming the other way. The officer had his pistol in his right hand, down by his leg, and was talking on his hand-held radio. He ignored Yocke.

The pool car was still intact. All four wheels still attached, the windshield unbroken, the doors still locked and closed. Another miracle.

Yocke drove slowly through the projects as rain spattered the wind-shield. On impulse, he went back to the church and parked in front.

All the cops were gone.

Yocke locked the car and went inside.

In the foyer he paused and listened. The door to the day-care center was still open and he could hear voices. He walked toward it.

The young woman who had comforted the children was crying on the shoulder of the man Yocke had seen enter, the man with the gray hair and the skin stretched tight across his face.

"You a reporter?" the man asked.

"Yes." Yocke looked at the children's chairs, decided they were too small, and lowered himself into a cross-legged position on the floor.

"I want you to write this down. Write it down and write it good. It's all the writing that Jane is ever gonna get."

Yocke got out the notebook.

"Jane Wilkens was the mother of my children. Had two kids by her. We never lived together. Asked her to marry me years ago but she wouldn't. She knew I used to be on heroin and if I lived around these damn projects, I'd go off the wagon. But she couldn't live anywhere else. This was where her work was, these kids. These kids were her work. She was trying to save some of them.

"She grew up in the Jefferson projects, but got herself out. Got an education. Got a scholarship to George Washington and got a degree in biology. Went to Pennsylvania and got a masters. She worked for a couple years as a microbiologist, then gave it up and came back here to this church to run the day care. Work with the kids."

"Why?"

"You been in those projects? Really looked? Try to imagine living in there. No privacy, walls paper thin, kids abused and hungry, trash everywhere, light bulbs out, doors kicked in, liquor sales out of one apartment and crack out of another, the white women from the suburbs buying theirs down on the streets, the smell of shit and piss and filth and hopelessness. Yeah, it stinks. It gets in your nose so bad you'll never get it out. I smelled it again coming down the street this evening.

"So the kids are growing up in this manure pile, growing up like little rats, without love, without food, without anybody to hug them. Jane wanted to give them what their mamas couldn't. She wanted to give them a little love. Maybe save a couple. Can't save 'em all, but maybe save a few. Their mamas—all strung out, head nursing, whoring, whatever will turn a dollar to get the stuff from the number-one man."

"She took two kids to the emergency room last week," the young woman said. "One was starving to death even though she was eating— eating here, anyway—and the other had a bacterial infection of the lungs. Jane did things like that all the time."

The man shook his head, faintly irritated. "But Jane never tried to shut down the trade," he said slowly, "never interfered with anybody's addiction, never passed judgment, never talked to the police. She just tried to save the kids. The kids . . ."

"What's your name?"

"Name's Tom Shannon. I work for the city. Drive a street sweeper. I'm president of a chapter of Narcotics Anonymous. Biggest chapter in the city. Me, I try to do what I can to help the people who want to help themselves. I tried to get a chapter started over here in the Jeffersons, but there wasn't no interest. You gotta want to help yourself.

"Maybe that's what's wrong. Jane was trying to save a few little kids and I was trying to save the grownups that wanta save themselves, and nobody was doing anything for all these people who are locked in the cycle. Nobody was attacking the trade. So the trade killed Jane."

"A man killed Jane."

"No, the crack trade killed her. That guy who pulled the trigger, he was an addict and a dealer. He had it on him. So he ran from the cops. And he shot Jane because she was standing in front of him screaming. No other reason. She was just there. All the people who are making money from the crack business killed her as sure as if they pulled the trigger. They don't give a damn who they hurt. They don't give a damn if the world blows up, as long as they get theirs. *They* killed Jane."

The young woman was sitting by herself now, drying her eyes, listening to Tom Shannon. He was looking straight into Yocke's eyes.

"Now I'm telling you and you can write it any way you want, but I'm not going to be a victim anymore. Jane was a victim and I was a victim. No more! *I'm not going to be a victim anymore!*"

CHAPTER NINE

* * * * * * * * *

"B ERNIE, this is Jefferson Brody. I got it! The widow signed."

"Glad to hear it, Tee."

"She was reluctant but—"

"Yeah. Ya did good. I thought you would. That's what I told the guys. Tee screwed the pooch but he'll make it good. Wait and see."

"I appreciate—"

"Send me the papers. I'll be talking to you in a few days."

"Bernie, have you found that woman? I'd—"

"Working on that, Tee. I'll be in touch."

The phone went dead on T. Jefferson Brody. He cradled the receiver and sat staring at the dark cherry paneling on his office walls. He had had to pay Mrs. Lincoln $450,000 for the check-cashing business, but now didn't seem to be the time to lay that on Bernie. Although Bernie was a good client, he had his rough edges.

The black bitch with the big tits who had conned him and robbed him—she was going to pay. T. Jefferson Brody intended to teach her a lesson she would never forget. And that little weasel ambulance chaser who helped her. He rubbed his hands together as he contemplated his revenge.

But that would have to wait.

He buzzed his secretary on the intercom. "Hilda, get me Senator Cherry's office, please."

"Yes, Mr. Brody."

Thanos Liarakos completed the paperwork at the hospital's administration office, then took the suitcase to his wife's room on the third floor and helped her select an outfit from it. She made only one or two swipes at her hair with a comb and didn't bother with makeup or lipstick, although they were in the case. Liarakos said nothing. She was dressed and nervously pacing the room when a nurse arrived with a wheelchair for the grand exit.

"Where are we going?" Elizabeth asked, finally, when they were in the car.

As if she didn't know. Liarakos muttered, "To the airport."

"You mean we're not even going by the house so I can say good-bye to the children?"

"Oh, can it, Elizabeth! You talked to them this morning on the telephone and they're both in school right now."

"Well, I just wanted to see my home again for a few minutes. And I need some other outfits."

"I packed exactly the outfits you told me to pack."

"I forgot a few."

"You're going to the clinic *now. Right fucking now!*"

"You are a bastard."

He pulled over to the curb. The driver behind honked and gestured as he went by. Liarakos paid no attention.

"You can get out here or you can go to the clinic. Your choice."

"I don't have any money."

He put the transmission in park and stared out the window.

"Oh, Thanos, you know how much I love you. You know how much I love the children. I'll leave the stuff alone. I *promise!* Tell you what, darling. Let's go home and put on some soft music and I'll put on that gorgeous negligée you got me for my birthday. I'll show you just how much I love you." She caressed his arm, then his hair. "Darling, it'll be just like it was when we were first married, on those Sunday mornings when there were just the two of us. Oh, Than—"

"You don't know what this costs me, Elizabeth. You really don't."

"Darling, I—"

"You don't have *any* idea!" He pushed her hands away.

"You don't love *me,*" she snarled, "You're just thinking of your precious law practice, what your boss might think. Well, by God, I—"

Liarakos reached across her and opened the passenger door.

"Out."

She began crying.

He sat watching the traffic flow by, his face averted, his right hand on the wheel and his right shoulder up.

She was still sobbing uncontrollably when a police cruiser pulled up alongside. The officer twirled his finger. Liarakos rolled down his window. "Move it, Mac."

He pulled the lever down into drive and got the car into motion. Beside him Elizabeth blew her nose on tissues and continued to sob.

Traffic on the expressway to Dulles rolled along at slightly illegal speeds all the way to the airport. Liarakos parked and got the suitcase out of the trunk. He came around the car and opened the door for Elizabeth. She made a production out of blowing her nose one last time and stuffing the tissue paper into the trash bag hanging from the cigarette lighter.

He took her arm and guided her toward the terminal.

"I've got five dollars and seventy-two cents in my purse."

"You don't need money at the clinic."

"But what if I want to get my hair done somewhere else? And I may need to take a taxi to the clinic."

"They'll meet you at the airport. They have all the other times. Remember?"

"But Thanos, what if they don't? I'll be stranded. Give me a hundred to cover incidentals."

"Elizabeth, for Christ's sake! You're just making it harder on both of us."

"*You* have no idea how difficult this is for *me*. That's the problem. You only think of yourself. If you love me, think about *me!* I'm your *wife,* or have you forgotten?"

"I haven't forgotten."

He gave the ticket to the agent and checked the bag. "Window seat, please."

"Just Mrs. Liarakos?"

"Yes."

The agent gave them the gate number. "Boarding in fifteen minutes."

"Thanks."

They waited near the gate. Liarakos stood by the windows where he could see the shuttle buses going back and forth to the airplanes. Elizabeth walked away and found a seat by herself.

He watched her reflection in the glass. Every movement she made was like something from an old memory that you remember with pain. In the past when she had a moment she would remove her compact from her purse and check her reflection, touch up her hair, see that her eye shadow and lipstick were just so. Not today. She just sat there with her purse in her lap, her hands resting upon it, while she idly scanned people coming and going and sitting and reading.

When they called the plane Liarakos escorted her to the gate agent and handed him the ticket. He leaned toward her and whispered in her ear. "Get well."

She glanced at him, her face neutral, then went through the door into the shuttle bus.

He went back to the glass and watched her through the bus windows. She didn't look back at him. She sat staring straight ahead. She was still sitting like that when the passenger door closed and the bus pulled away.

That evening Captain Jake Grafton informed his wife that Lieutenant Toad Tarkington was getting orders to the staff of the Joint Chiefs, just as he desired.

"That's very nice," Callie told Jake. "Did you have to twist many arms to make it happen?"

"A couple."

"Does Toad know yet?"

"Not yet. I think they'll tell him in a day or two."

"You'll never guess who stopped me after class today to chat."

Jake Grafton made an uninterested noise, then decided to humor her and take a stab at it. "That commie professor, ol' what's-his-name."

"No. It was that *Washington Post* reporter, Jack Yocke. He thanked me for the party and . . ."

Jake went back to today's newspaper think-piece on Soviet internal politics. For generations the forces at work inside the Communist Party had been Soviet state secrets and the subject of classified intelligence summaries that circulated inside the U.S. military. Those summaries had been mere guesses made by analysts based on poor, fragmentary information. Now the Soviets were baring all with an abandon that would make even Donald Trump blush.

As he mused on this curious miracle, Jake Grafton became aware of a questioning tone in his wife's voice, which had risen in pitch. "Say again, dear?"

"I said, Jack suggested you and he have breakfast some morning. Would you like to do that?"

"No."

The captain scanned the column to find his place.

"Well, why not?"

He lowered the paper and scrutinized his wife, who was poised with a ladle in one hand, looking at him with one eyebrow raised aloft. He had never been able to figure out how she got one eyebrow up but not the other. He had tried it a few times in the privacy of the bathroom with no success.

"We are not friends or social acquaintances. We haven't said two dozen words to each other. And I have no desire to know him better."

"Jack is a brilliant, socially concerned journalist whom you should take the trouble to get to know. He's written an excellent book that you would enjoy and find informative: *The Politics of Poverty.*"

"He wants to pump me on what's going on inside the Pentagon. And there's absolutely nothing I can tell him. It'd be a waste of time for both of us."

"Jake . . ."

"Callie, I don't *like* the guy. I'm not about to waste an hour listening to him try to pump me. No."

She sighed and went back to stirring the chili. Jake rustled the newspaper and raised it ostentatiously.

"I've been reading his book," she said, undaunted. "He gave me a copy."

"I saw it on the nightstand."

"It's excellent. Well written, lots of insights that—"

"If I ever become CNO and get an overpowering itch to leak something to the newspapers, Jack Yocke will be the first guy I call. I promise."

Callie changed the subject. Her husband grunted once or twice, then she abandoned conversation. Jake didn't notice. He was engrossed in an account of Fidel Castro's latest speech, in which the dictator announced that the rice and meat ration of the Cuban people had been cut in half. Again. To two ounces of meat and a pound of rice per week. In addition, Cuba would henceforth purchase its oil from Mexico, not the Soviet Union, and it would cost more, a lot more. This meant more sacrifices, which Castro was confident the Cuban people would take in stride. The Cuban comrades had been betrayed by their Soviet brothers in socialism, but *viva la Revolución!*

The socially concerned journalist of whom Callie spoke was thinking impure thoughts. He had picked up Tish Samuels at the apartment that she shared with a mousy girlfriend and they had gone to a postwedding party at the home of a fellow reporter who had eloped several weeks ago with an oral surgeon. Earlier in the evening Yocke had been miserable company, but now, several drinks and two hours later, he was feeling fairly chipper and more sociable. Perhaps it was the cheerful bonhomie of his colleagues, who were ribbing the newlyweds unmercifully. Whatever, in spite of himself Jack Yocke had absorbed some of the glow.

Just now he stood half listening to one of the sports columnists expound on the coming NFL playoffs while he watched Tish Samuels on the other side of the room. She had glanced this way several times and was aware of his scrutiny.

The next time she looked, he gave her a wide grin. She returned it. He raised his glass at her and took a sip. She gestured with her glass in reply and nodded.

Yes indeed, in spite of everything, life goes stumbling on. And Jack Yocke did like life.

So he sipped his drink and listened to the sportswriter and assessed Tish's womanly charms as she moved along talking to everyone. She was a tall woman, but she certainly had it in all the right places. Jack Yocke took a deep breath and exhaled slowly as he waited for her to turn his way again.

The sportswriter rambled on. The most interesting events in the world were happening in the NFL. *This* was the Redskins' year. Hallelujah!

Tish turned. She smiled broadly and blew him a kiss. Jack Yocke grinned foolishly, exposing every tooth in his head.

An hour later in the car, she hummed softly while he kissed her. He kissed her again and she returned it with a fervor that he found most pleasant.

Finally, reluctantly, he inserted the key in the ignition and brought the engine to life. "Where to?" he asked.

"Your place?"

"Got a roommate too. He's home tonight."

"The bookstore."

He put the car in motion. In the empty parking lot in front of the strip shopping center, he parked and sat staring at the blank windows.

"Come on," Tish said, reaching for the door handle. "Let's."

Jack Yocke dug in the glove box and pulled out something red and frilly. "Would you wear these?" he asked hesitantly.

There were two of them. She held the soft cloth up so the light caught it. "What are these? *Garters?"*

"Yeah." He shrugged and grinned hopefully.

His grin was sort of cute, in a pathetic sort of way, Tish decided. "A little kink, eh?"

"Well, they're just—"

"You're kidding, right?"

"No, I just thought . . ."

"Garters." She sighed. "Jesus, I haven't worn garters since the senior prom." She took a good look at his face. "Oh, all right, you pervert."

She fumbled for the seat belt release. He reached down to help. She pushed his hands away. "I'm not going to put them on here in the car, for Christ's sake!"

"I—"

"Oh, shut up! Garters!"

Really, Tish thought as she walked toward the door of the bookstore, feeling in her purse for her keys. Is this my fate at thirty-one? Sex with oversized adolescent boys whose ideas of erotica came straight from a whorehouse?

"Are there no men left?" she murmured.

Jack Yocke missed that comment. He was furtively scanning the parking lot.

If he weren't so good-looking and so thoroughly nice . . .

She opened the door and held it for him, then relocked it. The only light in the store was that coming through the display windows from the big lights in the parking area. She walked by the light switches without touching them and led the way between the book racks toward the little office by the back door. Behind her she heard Yocke stumble over something.

The second time he stumbled she heard books fall. She took his hand and led him around the racks to the office. Yocke helped her with her coat. The scruffy couch held a half dozen cartons of books, which they set on the floor.

As they undressed in the darkness, she couldn't resist. "Why garters?"

"You don't have to wear them if you don't want to."

"Then why'd you ask?"

"Well—"

He touched her bare skin and all her doubts dissolved.

Afterward, with him on top and panting, she said, "We forgot the garters."

He caressed her thighs. "It doesn't matter."

"You're a pretty good lover, y'know. For a pervert."

He kissed her.

"Really, be honest about the garters. I want to know."

"You mean that?"

"Yes."

"Well, I've found that women sometimes change their minds. Yet if I give them something innocuous to think about, it takes their minds off sex and I get laid more often."

"Oooh . . . youuu . . ."

"Now admit it, you were so busy thinking about the garters that you forgot to have second thoughts. Isn't that so?"

Tish bucked once and pushed and he flopped off onto the floor with a thud. She closed the office door and flipped on the lights. It took several seconds for her eyes to adjust. Yocke was on his back amid the boxes, looking a little dazed.

She found the garters and pulled them on. Then she stood beside him on one leg and used the other foot to rub his chest and stomach.

"Do you like?"

"Gawd almighty," Jack Yocke said.

Evansville, Indiana, patrolman Harrison Ronald Ford, alias Sammy Z, watched the fat white man stroll down the sidewalk looking neither left nor right. Watching him, you would have thought he owned the sidewalk and all the houses and was out collecting rent. Everything about him said he was *the man.*

Harrison Ronald shifted his buttocks on the cold concrete stoop where he was perched and watched the man check house numbers. When he arrived in the dim glow of the nearby streetlight, he glanced at Ford, then started up the steps on which Ford was sitting.

"Going somewhere, Fatty?"

"Got an appointment."

"Great. I'll bet you got a name too."

"Tony Anselmo."

"Why don't you wait down there on the sidewalk and I'll check inside. Okay?"

As Anselmo retreated to the sidewalk, Harrison Ronald checked the street again. No traffic. No one in the parked cars. No strollers or tourists other than the guards posted on each of the corners. Although the guards weren't armed, each of them was within ten feet of a concealed Uzi. Except for the guards, this appeared to be a typical lower-middle-class black neighborhood. No crack was sold here.

Everything appeared normal to Ford's practiced eyes.

Harrison rapped on the door and disappeared through it when it opened.

Inside the hallway sat another guard with an Uzi on his lap. He nodded as Harrison walked by. The second man locked and bolted the door behind him.

Freeman McNally was in the kitchen eating cake, drinking milk, and reading a newspaper. He was twenty pounds or so overweight and had a hairline in full retreat. Still, encased within the fat was muscle. When he moved he was light on his feet. As Ford entered he looked up from the paper.

"Guy named Tony Anselmo says he has an appointment."

"What's he look like?"

"Fat honkey, about fifty or so. Prosperous."

"Let him in. After you frisk him, go on back out front."

"Sure, Freeman."

Out on the sidewalk, Ford said, "They heard of you. Go on in." He followed Anselmo up the stairs.

Inside, the guard with the Uzi centered it on Anselmo's ample middle. "Against the wall and spread 'em."

Ford quickly patted him down, checked his belt front and back, his crotch, and his ankles. "You do that like a cop," Anselmo rumbled.

"He's clean," Ford told the guard, then went back out onto the stoop and resumed his seat.

Harrison Ronald had heard of Fat Tony Anselmo. Sitting on the stoop smoking a cigarette and listening to the noises of the city at night, he tried to recall what he had read in the police intelligence briefing books. Anselmo was a soldier for a New York crime family, the Zubin Costello outfit. Bernie Shapiro was one of the three or four key lieutenants, and Anselmo was supposed to work for him. Suspected of a dozen or so hits in his younger days, Tony Anselmo had once plea-bargained a murder charge down to carrying a concealed weapon and was back on the street after six months in the can. That was the only time he had ever been in jail.

It would have been nice, Ford mused, if Freeman had invited him to remain. Sooner or later, if he lived long enough, but not yet.

As he sat on the stoop smoking, Ford speculated on whether Anselmo had asked for this meeting or Freeman had. And he formed various tentative hypotheses about the business being discussed. Certainly not the purchase of raw product: Freeman got all he could handle from the West Coast.

Money, Ford decided. They were probably doing a deal to wash or invest money. Ford assumed the Costello family had a lot of experience in both activities.

Or perhaps bribery of public officials. That was certainly a possibility.

When the glowing tip of the cigarette reached the filter, Ford lit another one from the stub. He automatically checked the street-corner guards yet again, then watched the smoke swirl on the gentle breeze.

Cold. Tonight was going to be cold. Harrison Ronald turned up the collar of his leather jacket and glanced at his watch.

"Why a bookstore?" Jack Yocke asked.

He and Tish were lying on the couch in the bookstore office in the darkness with Yocke's coat thrown over them. She was still wearing the garters.

"It sounds silly now," she said. "But I had to make a living at something, and I like books, so I drove around until I found a spot without a bookstore for two miles in any direction, and I rented that spot."

"Sensible approach."

"I thought I was very conservative. I love books. I was so certain the store would be a surefire hit. Ha! I'm barely eating. Still, two years in the business and I'm current on all my bills. That's something."

"Indeed it is. A lot of people can't say that."

"Now tell me, why a newspaper?"

"Oh, amazingly enough, in spite of the hours, in spite of the deadlines and the editors, I thought I'd like it. Talk about optimism! Sometimes I feel like a mortician. Or a minister. All the shattered lives. I spend my days galloping from tragedy to tragedy. 'Who what when where why, ma'am, and can you spell the perpetrator's name one more time?' I see as much blood as an ambulance driver. I ask the kinds of questions the morticians and chaplains don't have to ask. 'Why do you think your husband stabbed you, Ms. Butcher?' 'What did the gunman say before he shot you, Mr. Target?' 'After he raped, mutilated, and murdered her, why do you keep insisting he's such a good boy, Mrs. Spock?'"

"It must be challenging."

"It would be," Jack Yocke agreed, "if you had enough time to do it right, to write it right. You never do. You look at the blood—when you can get to the scene before they cart out the bodies—telephone everyone you can think of, then write six hundred words for the first edition which the editor chops in half or doesn't like at all. Then wait, wait, check, check. Up one blind alley after another. Finally you get a good story, only to get buried under a human wave attack of other reporters as some editor finally decides that there really is a good story here on Yocke's supposed beat but Yocke can't cover it all by himself."

"So why do you do it?"

"I don't know." He really didn't. At night he went home to his apartment either completely drained or completely frustrated. The stories, when he got some, were never good enough. The black ink on the newsprint never captured the insanity, the fear, the terror, the grief, the desperation of the people who live the lives that make police news. The waste, the future smeared all over the floor—he could never get that into the stories.

"People just read the paper while they drink their morning coffee," he told her, "then throw it away. Or wrap the garbage in it. Or use it to line the cat box. Then, hi-ho, off to work or aerobics class or luncheon at the club."

"What else could you do?"

"I've never been able to think of anything. And this police beat can't last forever."

She got up off the couch and turned on the light. She took off the garters as he watched and handed them to him. Then she began putting on her clothes.

"Get dressed and run me home. I have to get a little sleep, then be down here scrubbed and cheerful to open this place at nine. That's when the little old ladies like to come in to see if we have any new 'spicy' books."

"'Spicy'?"

"Bodice rippers. Soft-core porn. That's what pays the rent around here."

"You're kidding."

"I wish I were. I sold three Amy Tans last year and just one Fay Weldon. It's enough to make you cry."

"Maybe you need a better location."

"What I need is to write a sizzling world-class fuck book, one so hot it'll melt an old maid's panties." She eyed him as she buttoned her blouse. "That's what I'm scribbling on. You want to see it?"

"Sure."

Tish opened the desk drawer and pulled it out. She had about a hundred pages of manuscript that she had whacked out on the old typewriter on the corner of the desk. He flipped through the pages, scanning.

"The rule is no four-letter words. His cock is always his love member."

"Looks fine to me," Yocke said, and handed it back. He bent down to retrieve his trousers.

When he straightened up she was reading carefully. After a moment she tossed the pile of paper back in the drawer. "It's shit, I know, but that's what sells. And goddamn, if shit sells, that's what I'm going to write."

Twenty minutes later, in front of her apartment building, she said, "Don't get out. I can make it to the door."

He bussed her on the cheek.

"Are you going to call me again, or was this just a one-night stand?"

"I'll call you."

"Promise?"

"Yeah."

After he drove away he felt grubby. Oh well, what's one more lie in a world full of them.

Harrison Ronald—Sammy Z—got off work at five a.m. One of his colleagues dropped him at the apartment house he called home. He went upstairs and made a pot of coffee. Then, at the kitchen table, he tackled the crossword puzzle in the early edition of the *Post*.

After Tony Anselmo left Freeman, Sammy Z and one of the other lieutenants were sent to a crack lab in a sleazy motel on New York Avenue. There they picked up a bundle, watched the chemists at work, and flirted with a saucy nineteen-year-old with strawberry-sized nipples —and an aversion to brassieres—while they waited for their escort car to arrive. When it did and the three gunmen it contained had leered over the upthrust nipples, the group set out to deliver the crack to street rings at two locations. There the distributors had turned over the night's receipts, about sixty grand by the looks of it. And Freeman was currently selling at eleven locations in the metro area!

Sammy Z drove the money to Freeman's brother in a little house he was using for three or four nights. The elder McNally was the treasurer and accountant and payroll man. His office changed regularly and randomly. Freeman always knew, and he gave Sammy the location as he walked out the door.

Delivering dope or money was tricky. The lieutenant rode in the backseat of the car with the Uzi loaded and ready on his lap. The guard car behind always contained two or three men also armed with Uzis and pistols. The lead driver kept the two-car motorcade well within the speed limit, obeyed all the traffic laws, and never sped up to make it through a yellow light. The routes were agreed on in advance and snaked through the city without pattern. The same vehicle was never used two nights in a row.

The whole operation reminded Harrison Ronald of those old black-and-white *Untouchables* TV shows, with Al Capone and Frank Nitty delivering beer in Chicago and all the hoods packing Thompson subma-chine guns. Big guns and big bucks. White hoods and white cops—well, maybe things are a little different today.

The sky was graying nicely through the dirty kitchen window when Harrison Ronald finished the crossword puzzle and his third cup of coffee simultaneously. He turned off the coffeepot, got a conservative cloth coat out of the closet, and locked the door behind him.

Right now he was driving a fifteen-year-old, rusted-out Chrysler that belonged to Freeman McNally. It had once been royal blue. Now it was just dirty and dark. The seats were trashed. Damage to the left front fender and hood had been repaired with a sledgehammer by an ignorant enthusiast. The windshield was chipped and cracked. The only feature that might capture the eye of a careful observer was the new Michelin radials, mounted backward to hide the manufacturer's name on the sidewalls. All in all, the car looked like a typical D.C. heap.

As an observer might suspect, the Chrysler was difficult to start—damn near impossible on cold mornings. This particular December morning Harrison Ronald ground and ground with the starter while he played with the manual choke.

Eventually the engine fired. It strangled when he pushed the choke off too soon. With a sigh he engaged the starter again. Finally, with coaxing, the engine rumbled to life and gave signs of sustained combustion.

Still, she idled rough and spewed a gray haze that was visible in the rear-view mirror. That, however, was because the original six-cylinder mill had been replaced with a huge old V-8 hemi that had been breathed upon by someone who knew exactly what he was about. Under the crinkled hood was a work of art, complete with racing cams, valves, and pistons, hogged-out valve ports, a high-capacity fuel pump, and a four-barrel carb. To handle the extra power the go-fast man had added a four-speed transmission and beefed up the suspension and brakes. This car could lay rubber for two hundred feet.

When the engine had warmed and the idle smoothed somewhat, Harrison Ronald slipped the clutch to get out of the parking place.

He couldn't resist: he goosed it once on the street and the tires howled and smoked. With a little paint and bodywork, he told himself, this would be a *nice* car.

He checked his rearview mirrors constantly and darted through lights as they turned red. Finally satisfied that no one was following, he headed for the beltway. Rush-hour traffic was still flowing into the city, so the trip outbound was unimpeded. Once on the beltway, he followed the signs for I-95 south, toward Richmond.

The morning was gray and windy. The rain of a few days ago had soaked into the thirsty earth and settled the dust. Still, as dry as the fall had been, the earth needed more.

He exited the interstate at Fredericksburg. Five minutes later he drove past the office of a motel and went around to the back side, which faced a hill, and parked.

Harrison Ronald stood in the nearly empty lot and stretched. He should have been in bed two hours ago. Get a good job, his grandmother had said, something regular, with a future.

He knocked on the door of room 212.

"Just a minute."

The door opened. "Come on in."

The white man was tall and lean, with a prominent Adam's apple and a nose to match. He grinned and shook Ford's hand. His name was Thomas F. Hooper. Special Agent Hooper was in charge of the FBI's drug enforcement division. Hooper had recruited Ford from the Evansville police department. A little temporary undercover work, he said, that will do wonders for your police career. Both lies, he now cheerfully acknowledged.

"Want some breakfast?"

"I could eat something."

"Great. Freddy's over at McDonald's getting a bagful. He'll be back in a bit."

Ford fell into a chair and stretched out full-length.

"So how's it going?"

"Freeman's a busy fellow. Making money like he owned the mint."

Hooper got a cassette recorder from his leather valise and plugged it into the socket under the desk. He dictated his name and the date and Ford's name, then played it back to make sure it was working.

Harrison Ronald watched this operation with heavy eyelids.

"You're tired."

"Amen."

"Coffee will perk you up. You want to start now?"

"Okay."

It had been a week since Ford had talked to Hooper. So Ford covered the past week minute by minute—names, descriptions, addresses, drug quantities, estimated amounts of money, everything Ford could recall. He had taken no notes, written nothing down: that would have been too dangerous. Still, after eight months, he knew exactly what Hooper and the Justice Department wanted, so it flowed forth without prompting.

Freddy, Hooper's assistant, came in ten minutes after they started. Ford kept on talking as the men shared coffee and breakfast biscuits stuffed with eggs, cheese, and sausage.

Ford talked for almost an hour. When he finished Hooper had questions, lots of them. That went on for another hour with only two short pauses to change cassettes. When they were through Hooper knew what Ford had observed this past week almost as well as Ford did.

Finally Hooper said, "So what do you think?"

Harrison Ronald held out his coffee cup for a refill, which Freddy provided from a thermos. "I think there's too much crack in the city. They can't move the stuff fast enough. And I think Freeman is getting, or is about to get, a lot of pressure from the Costello mob to wash his money with them, probably at a higher cost. Somebody removed Walter Harrington and Second Potomac from the game. Freeman and his fellow dealers got some problems."

"What do you think Freeman'll do?"

"I don't know. I haven't been able to get a hint. I do know this: the guy is sharp as a razor. He didn't get where he is by letting people cut themselves in on his action, by taking less and liking it. I think Freeman might fight back. He's definitely the man for it."

Freddy disagreed. He was in his late forties, also white, and had chased dopers since he joined the FBI. "I think Freeman and the others will cut back on the amount of coke they're bringing in. They have to do that or expand the market by fighting each other. They all have a real good thing here and they've made a lot of money. A *lot* of money. They won't be able to retire and live the good life if they get into heavy ordnance."

"There's no love lost between the big hitters," Harrison Ronald objected.

"Business is business and money is money," Freddy said.

"What do you guys want me to do if the shooting starts?"

"Run like hell," Hooper muttered.

"For Christ's sake, don't kill any civilians," Freddy added.

"Cut and run?"

"Yep," said Hooper. "You're no good to anybody if you're dead."

"Do you guys have enough?"

"We got enough to lock up Freeman for thirty years, and most of the people he works for."

"And the cops and politicians on the take?"

Hooper turned off the recorder and removed the cassette. He marked it with a pen from his shirt pocket.

"And the cops and politicians?" Ford prompted.

"You got a lot. More than we hoped for. But if someone puts you in the cemetery we got nothing. Oh, we know a ton, but we won't have a witness to get it into evidence."

"I don't think I'll get into the inner circle anytime soon. Freeman's got four lieutenants, and two of them are his brothers. They're all million-aires many times over and each of them would go to the grave for Freeman McNally."

"Maybe that can be arranged," Freddy said.

"What d'ya mean by that?"

"Nothing to worry about. Gimme some particulars on each one." Freddy pulled out a pencil and a pocket notebook.

"Now wait just a fucking minute! We're cops. I'm not going to ice any of these guys, except in self-defense."

"We're not asking you to kill anybody and we're sure as hell not going to. Jesus! This isn't Argentina! But maybe we can get one of these guys off the street for a while and leave a vacancy at the trough for you."

The undercover officer talked for ten minutes. He told them everything he knew; the names of the wives, the mistresses, the kids, what they ate, what they laughed at, how they liked their liquor, and how often they used their own products.

In the silence that followed his recitation, Hooper asked, "How's that car running?"

"Real sweet." Ford smiled faintly. "You gotta go for a ride sometime. It's the hottest thing I ever sat in."

"Stay alive, Harrison. Please."

"I'll do my best." Harrison Ronald's smile broadened into a grin. "That's a promise."

"You can quit anytime, you know."

"Yeah."

"I mean it. We've got a lot more than we ever thought we'd get. If you want to go back to Evansville, just say so and you'll be on your way today."

"I'll stick a while longer. I confess, I'm curious about Tony Anselmo and how he fits in."

"Curiosity has killed a lot of cops."

"I know that."

On the way back to Washington the thought occurred to him, not for the first time, that he should have stayed in the Marines. At the age of twenty, after two years of college, he had joined the Corps. He had done a four-year hitch, the last two on Okinawa where he had been an instructor in unarmed combat. He had grown to love the Corps. But his girl was in Indiana and she wouldn't leave. So he took his discharge and went home and took the test for the police while he was trying to talk her into marrying him.

He got accepted by the police the afternoon before she ditched him. The oldest story in the world. She had dated other men while he was gone. He was a great guy but she wasn't in love. She hoped they'd always be friends.

He had learned a lot in the Corps, things that would keep him alive now, like managing stress and self-confidence. And unarmed combat. As a rule street gangs didn't contain experts at fighting with their hands. Oh, occasionally you ran into a karate guy who thought he was pretty tough. But while he was getting ready to give you one of those lethal kicks, you went for him in an aggressive, brutally violent way and broke his leg, then crushed his windpipe. And these Uzi toters never practiced with their weapons. Murder was their game, not combat.

He thought about murder for a while. His murder.

When this was over, he might go back to the Corps. Why not?

CHAPTER TEN

* * * * * * * *

JAKE Grafton had no more than walked through the door Wednesday evening when the telephone rang. Callie answered it. After exchanging pleasant greetings with whomever was on the other end, she offered the instrument to Jake. "It's for you."

"Hello."

"Captain Grafton, this is Jack Yocke, *Washington Post.*"

"Hi."

"Sorry to bother you at home, but we just got a story from a stringer in South America that perhaps you can help me with. It seems that the U.S. Army sent some people to Colombia and they shot it out with Chano Aldana's bodyguards and arrested him. Apparently there were some Colombian police along, but the word we get is that it was a U.S. Army operation all the way."

"Why do you think I can help you with that story?" Callie was standing there watching him, futilely trying to push her hair back off her forehead. She must really like this jerk, though Jake hadn't the foggiest idea why.

"I've been doing some checking," Yocke said, "since I saw you at Aldana's arraignment. Apparently you're the senior officer in the antidrug operations section of the Joint Staff. So this little matter had to cross your desk."

"You haven't answered my question, Mr. Yocke. Why do you think I can help you with your story?"

"You're saying you won't?"

"Mr. Yocke, I drink coffee in the morning and go to lunch every day. Everything else I do at my office is classified. I cannot help you." Callie frowned. Jake turned his back on her. "I suggest you try the Pentagon's public information office."

"Do you have that number handy, Captain?"

"Try the phone book." Jake cradled the receiver without saying good-bye.

"Jake, that was rude."

"Oh, Callie!"

"Well, it was."

"That damned kid calls me at home and asks me to give him classified information? Bullshit! You tell him the next time he's conjugating some verbs for you that he had better never pull this stunt on me again or I'll rearrange his nose the next time I meet him."

"I'm sure he didn't know the information was classified," Callie said, but she was talking to herself. Her husband was on his way to the bedroom.

Well, she told herself, Jake was right. A reporter should know better. Yocke's young. He'll learn. And fast, if he spends much time around Jake.

That evening when Harrison Ronald arrived at Freeman McNally's house for work, Ike Randolph met him at the door.

"Freeman wants to see you."

Ike grinned. It was more of a sneer, Harrison thought, and he had seen it before, whenever someone was about to lose a pound of flesh. Ike enjoyed the smell of fear.

In spite of himself, Harrison Ronald felt his heart accelerate. For some reason his armpits were instantly wet.

Ike patted him down. That was routine, but this evening Ike was more thorough than usual—on purpose, no doubt.

Ike Randolph, convicted armed robber, convicted child rapist—you had to have the milk of human kindness oozing from your pores to like Ike. He had, Harrison knew, grown up in the same cesspool that spawned Freeman. Mom McNally had fed them both and paid bail when they got arrested for shoplifting and, later, stripping cars. She hadn't had the money to bail them out when they were caught mugging tourists. Ike had had the gun and taken the felony fall; Freeman had pleaded guilty to a misdemeanor. Yet after his plea Freeman spent ten more days in jail while Ike walked on probation. The two of them still liked to laugh about that when they were drinking.

Several years later a judge decided to let Ike do a little time after a six-year-old girl required surgery on her vagina and uterus following Ike's attentions. He had had a couple of minor possession convictions since—nothing serious.

This evening Ike gave Harrison a little shove after he finished frisking him.

"Hey!"

"Shut up, motherfuck! Go on. Freeman's waiting."

McNally was sitting on a sofa in the living room at the back of the house. Both his brothers were there too. Ike closed the door behind them.

"Called you this morning," Freeman said.

Harrison Ronald concentrated on managing his face. Look innocent!

"Where were you?"

"Out. I do that every now and then."

"Don't gimme no sass, Z. I don't take sass from nobody."

"Hey, Freeman. I just went out to get some tail."

"What's her name?" This from the eldest of the brothers, Ruben. He was the accountant.

"You don't know her."

Freeman stood up and approached Ford, who was still trying to decide if he should break McNally's arm and use him for a shield when Freeman slapped him. "You weren't at your pad last Wednesday either. You're gonna tell me the truth, bro, or I'm gonna unscrew your head and shit in it. *What's her name?"*

This appeared to be an excellent time to look scared, and Harrison did so. It was ridiculously easy. The fear was boiling. "Her name's Ruthola and she's married. We got this little thing going. I sneak over on Wednesday morning when the kid's at day care. Honest, Freeman, it's just a piece of ass."

Freeman grunted and examined Ford's eyes. Ford forced himself to meet his gaze. McNally's deep brown eyes looked almost black. The urge to attack was almost overpowering: Harrison flexed his hands as he fought it back.

"Call her."

"Christ, her ol' man might be home."

"So this'll be the end of a good thing. A piece of ass ain't worth your life, is it?"

"Not to me."

"Call her."

Freeman McNally picked up the phone on the table by the couch and motioned to the one on the other side of the room. Ford lifted the indicated instrument from its cradle and dialed.

It rang on the other end. Once. Twice. Three times. Harrison held his breath.

"Hello." It was a woman's voice.

"Ruthola, this is Sammy."

Silence. At that instant Harrison Ronald Ford knew he was a dead man. A chill surged through him. Then her voice came in a hiss. "Why'd you call? You *promised* you wouldn't!"

"Hey, babe, I won't be able to make it next week. Gonna be out of town. Just wanted you to know."

"Oh, honey, don't call me when he's *home!"* The words just poured out. "You *promised!* Call me tomorrow at ten, lover." She hung up.

Harrison Ronald cradled the phone. He felt a powerful urge to urinate.

Freeman snickered once. He rubbed his fingers through his hair while everyone in the room watched. "She a nice piece?" he said, finally, the corners of his lips twitching perceptibly.

Harrison tried to shrug nonchalantly. The shrug was more of a nervous jerk.

"Where's her ol' man work?"

Ford's stomach was threatening to heave. This, he decided, would be a good place for the truth. He got it out: "He's FBI."

They stared at him with their mouths open, frozen. Harrison tried another grin, which came out, he thought, like a clown leering.

"You *stupid*—" Ike roared from behind him. "*Of all the*—"

Freeman giggled. Then he laughed. The others began laughing. The laughter rose to a roar. Freeman McNally held his sides and pounded his thigh.

Harrison turned slowly. Even Ike was laughing. Harrison Ronald joined in. The relief was so great he felt a twinge of hysteria. The tears rolled down his cheeks as his diaphragm flapped uncontrollably.

Eight months ago, when Hooper had told him that someday he might need an alibi and introduced him to Ruthola, he hadn't anticipated it would be like this, hadn't understood that he would be so taut he almost twanged.

Ruthola Barnes, wife of Special Agent Ziggy Barnes, she had known. "I've done this before," she told him then. "Trust me. Just say you're Sammy and talk to me like we just got out of bed, like we're both still naked and standing in the kitchen making coffee. I'll do the rest."

That was eight months ago. He hadn't seen her since. Yet when he needed her, she was there.

Ah, Ziggy Barnes, you are a lucky, lucky man.

The key to success for a trial lawyer lies in preparation, and no one did it better than Thanos Liarakos. Thursday morning he began to submerge himself in the reams and reams of witness interrogation transcripts that were spewing from the prosecutor's office just as fast as the folks over there could run an industrial-size copy machine.

There were going to be a lot of transcripts, tens of thousands of pages, the prosecutor had told the judge. The people answering the questions were drug dealers, wholesalers, smugglers—pilots, guards, boat crewmen, drivers, lookouts, and soon—people from every nook and cranny of the drug business. At some point in their interrogation by police or FBI or DEA they were asked where they got the drug, when, how much, and of course, from whom.

Liarakos' associates had spent the last two days going over this pile and placing small squares of yellow sticky paper at every passage that they thought might be of interest. The difficulty, of course, was that at this stage of trial preparation the prosecutor still had not decided on a list of witnesses. So a lot of the material being read by the defense attorneys would be superfluous, unless Liarakos wanted to try to subpoena a witness himself and introduce testimony he hoped would be exculpatory.

Exculpatory, a nifty little word that meant confuse the hell out of the jurors.

Confusion and deceit were at the very heart of the trial process. The theory that comfortable law professors and appellate judges liked to cite stated that in the thrust and parry of adversarial combat—somehow, for reasons only a psychiatrist would find of interest, these legal thinkers still believed in medieval trial by combat—the truth would be revealed. Revealed to whom was a question never addressed. Perhaps it was best for everyone that the philosophical questions were left to mystics and the tactics and ethics to the trial lawyers. "The American legal system isn't going to be reformed anytime soon, so we're stuck with it"—Thanos Liarakos had made this remark on several occasions to young associates appalled at their first journey into the morass.

The meat of the defense lawyer's job was to ensure that the truth revealed in the courtroom melodrama was in the best interests of his client. Thanos Liarakos was very good at that.

He had already come to the conclusion that the point of his attack had to be on the jury's perception of Chano Aldana. He had assumed all along that the prosecution had sufficient evidence to convince any twelve men and women that Chano Aldana was imbedded to his eyes in the drug-smuggling business. Yet there was more to it than that. The whole thrust of the government's case was that Aldana was the kingpin of the entire Medellín cartel, some Latin American ogre who bought men's souls and terrorized and murdered those he couldn't buy. Liarakos wanted the jury to believe that the prosecutor, William C. Bader, had to prove that Aldana *was* the devil incarnate or they could not convict.

Everything Liarakos did or said at trial would be designed to force the jury to the question, Is Chano Aldana the personification of evil? Is this man sitting here with us today Adolf Hitler's insane bastard? Is this slightly overweight gentleman in the sports coat from Sears the spiritual heir of Ivan the Terrible? If Liarakos could induce the jury to raise the bar high enough, the prosecutor's evidence would fall short.

Liarakos' primary asset was Aldana himself. He looked so average, so normal. He would be dressed appropriately. He would smile in the right places and look sad in the right places. And regardless of the testimony of the prosecution's witnesses, Chano Aldana would continue to look like an underdog. Even the sheer weight and number of the prosecution's witnesses would be turned against the government—Liarakos would ask, After all these years, after all the money spent and hundreds—nay, thousands—of people questioned, is this *all* the government has? *Is this all?*

The difficulty was going to be controlling Aldana. He appeared to be pathologically adverse to taking direction from anyone and he had all the charm of a rabid dog. Yet there must be a way. . . .

He was musing along these lines when Judith Lewis, his chief assistant, brought in another stack of transcripts festooned with yellow stickies.

She put the pile on his credenza, then sat down. When Liarakos looked up, she said, "I don't think they've got it."

"Explain."

"If this sample of transcripts is representative of the government's evidence, they don't have enough to get a conviction. Most of this stuff is inadmissible hearsay. They might get it into evidence if we were stupid enough to make Aldana's character an issue, but not otherwise. In this whole pile there is not one possible witness who had direct contact with Aldana."

"They must have better stuff. They just haven't given it to us yet."

"No, sir. I'll bet you any sum I can raise they don't have it." She swallowed hard. "Chano Aldana is going to walk."

Liarakos examined her face carefully. "That's our job, Judith. We're *trying* to get him acquitted."

"But he's guilty!"

"Who says?"

"Oh, don't give me that crap. He's guilty as Cain." She crossed her legs and turned her head toward the window.

"He isn't guilty until the jury says he is."

"You can believe that if it makes you feel any better, but I don't. He's taken credit for arranging the murders of at least three Colombian presidential candidates. I spent thirty minutes with the man yesterday." She sat silently for a moment recalling the meeting, then shuddered. "He did it," she said. "He had them killed, like they were cockroaches."

"Colombia didn't choose to try him for murder, Judith. Colombia extradicted him to the United States. We're not defending him from a murder charge."

"Colombia *couldn't* try him. Get serious! In 1985 forty-five leftist guerrillas drove an armored car into the basement of the Colombian Palace of Justice. They held the place for a day and executed all the justices. Aldana hired them. Over a hundred people died—were murdered—that day. Try Aldana in Colombia? My God, wake up! Listen to yourself!"

"Judith, you don't *know* he did that! We're lawyers. Even if he committed a thousand crimes, he isn't *guilty* until a jury convicts him."

"Semantics," Judith Lewis muttered contemptuously. "I spent my childhood learning the difference between good and bad, and now, all grown up and wearing two-hundred-dollar dresses, with an expensive education, I sit here listening to you argue that evil is all in the label. *Bullshit! Fucking bullshit!* I *know* Chano Aldana is guilty as charged on every count in the American indictment, and on probably another two thousand counts that haven't been charged. He is a dope smuggler, a terrorist, an extortionist, a man killer, a murderer of women and unborn babies. He deserves to roast in the hottest fire in hell."

"Only if the government can prove it," Thanos Liarakos pleaded. "Only if the jury *says* the government proved it."

"The government hasn't got it."

"Then they shouldn't have indicted him."

"I quit," she said simply.

She walked for the door, opened it, and passed through. She left the door standing open.

Liarakos sat for a moment thinking about what she had just said. Then he went after her. She was in her office putting on her coat. "Ms. Lewis, would you come back to my office, please, and discuss this matter further?"

Wearing her coat, she followed him past the secretary's workstation and, when he stood aside, preceded him into his office. He closed the door and faced her.

"What do you mean you quit?"

"I quit. That's plain English. It's exactly what I mean."

"Do you mean you wish to work on some other case or perhaps for another partner?"

"No. I mean I quit this firm. I quit the legal profession. *I quit!* I am through trying to be a lawyer. I don't have the stomach for it."

She brushed past him. She paused at the door. "You can mail my last check to the Salvation Army. There's nothing in my office I want to come back for."

"Take a few days off and think this over. You spent three years in law school and three years in practice. That's six years of your life."

"No. I know you're doing what you think is right. But I don't think it's right. I don't *want* to think it's right."

"Judith—"

"No, Mr. Liarakos. I'm not going to squander another minute of my life arguing about a dope dealer's constitutional rights. I'm not going to touch another dollar earned by helping a dope dealer escape justice. No."

This time when she left he didn't go after her.

He sat in his chair and stared at the transcripts.

A ball glove wrapped around a scruffy baseball lay on the credenza. He pulled on the glove and tossed the ball into it. The impact of the ball meeting the leather made a satisfying "thock" which tingled his hand. The thumb of the glove was sweat stained. He had habitually raked it across his forehead to wipe away the perspiration. He did that now, enjoying the cool smoothness of the leather, then placed the glove back on the polished mahogany.

He kept a bottle of old scotch in the bottom drawer of his desk. He got it out and poured a shot into an empty coffee cup.

He was pouring a second when the phone rang.

"Yes."

"There's a lady on the phone calling from California. She won't give her name. Says it's a personal matter."

"My wife?"

"No, sir. I know her voice."

"I'll take the call."

The phone clicked.

"Hello," he said. "This is Thanos Liarakos."

"Mr. Liarakos, this is Karen Allison with the California Clinic?"

"Yes."

"Your wife apparently left the clinic during the night, Mr. Liarakos. We can't find her on the grounds. She took her suitcase with her."

"Yes," he said.

"I'm sorry, Mr. Liarakos. We did what we could."

"Yes," he said, and gently cradled the telephone.

On Friday morning Henry Charon drove to Baltimore to find a pay telephone. He parked at a mall and located a bank of three phones near the men's room. Since he was early, he ate lunch in the food court, lingered over coffee, then strolled the mall from end to end. Finally, with five minutes to go, he walked to the pay phones and waited. A woman was busy explaining to her husband why the new sheets on sale were a bargain. She hung up a minute before the hour and walked away briskly, apparently the winner of the budget battle. She had glanced at Charon once, for no more than a second, and had not looked at him again.

Charon dialed. The number he was calling, according to Tassone, was a pay phone in Pittsburgh. The area code—412—was right, anyway. Charon had checked. When the operator came on the line he fed in quarters from a ten-dollar roll.

Tassone answered on the second ring. "Yes."

"You got my shipment?"

"Yes. Where and when?"

"Truck stop at Breezewood, Pennsylvania. Tomorrow at three."

"Got it." The connection broke.

Charon walked out of the mall and got in the car. Before he started it he carefully studied a map, then folded it neatly and stuck it above the visor.

Four hours later in Philadelphia he bought a ticket for tomorrow's seven-fourteen bus to Pittsburgh. He ate dinner in a fast-food restaurant, then drove around north Philly until he found a cheap motel, where he paid cash.

He was up at five a.m. He parked the car at a twenty-four-hour garage a half block from the bus station and was in the waiting room thirty minutes early.

The bus left right on the minute. Charon's luggage consisted only of a backpack, which rested on the seat beside him. There were eleven passengers. Charon sat near the back of the bus where the driver couldn't see him in his mirror.

Two seats forward, on the other side of the aisle, sat a couple that lit a marijuana cigarette thirty minutes into the trip, just after the bus had reached cruising speed on the Pennsylvania Turnpike. The odor was sickly sweet and heavy. Charon cracked his window and waited for the driver to see the obvious smoke cloud and stop the bus. The bus never stopped. After a second cigarette the man and woman drifted off to sleep.

Henry Charon watched the countryside pass and wondered what it would be like to hunt it.

Four people got off the bus at Harrisburg and three got on. The couple across the aisle lit more marijuana. One of the new passengers cursed, which drew laughter from the smokers. The bus driver ignored the whole affair.

The driver pulled into the bus parking area at the Breezewood truck stop a little after noon. He announced a thirty-minute lunch stop, then darted down the stairs and headed for the restaurant. Most of the passengers trailed after him.

Taking his backpack, Henry Charon went to the men's room in the truckers' section of the building. He found a stall, dropped his trousers, and settled in. When he came out an hour later the bus was gone.

Charon bought a newspaper, then went into the restaurant and asked for a menu and a booth by the windows.

Senator Bob Cherry had the reputation of being an old-time politician. Now in his early seventies, he had been a U.S. naval aviator during World War II and had shot down seven Japanese planes. After the war and law school, Bob Cherry had gone into politics. He had served four years in the Florida legislature, four years in the United States House of Representatives, and then run for the Senate. He had been there ever since.

Tall, gaunt, with piercing eyes and a gravel voice, he mastered the rules of the world's most exclusive gentlemen's club and set out to make it his own. He had. He had passed up chances to run for majority leader and whip: he preferred to lend his support to others, more ambitious than he and perhaps less wise, and use his influence to dictate who sat on the various committees that accomplished the work of the Senate. As chairman of the Government Oversight Committee and patron of the party leaders the power he wielded was enormous. Cabinet officers invited him to breakfast, presidents invited him to lunch, and every socialite in Washington invited him to dinner. When Bob Cherry wanted something, he usually got it.

His wife had died ten years ago, and ever since he had had a succession of tall, shapely secretaries. Each lasted about two years. His current helper was approximately twenty-six and was a former Miss Georgia.

Today, at lunch, T. Jefferson Brody had trouble keeping his eyes off her. He wasn't trying very hard. He knew Bob Cherry well enough to know that the old goat got a kick out of younger men drooling down the cleavage of the sweet piece who was screwing him afternoon and night. So T. Jefferson Brody, diplomat that he was, ogled Miss Tina Jordan appreciatively. When she walked across the dining room on her way to the ladies', he made a point of admiring her shapely ass as it swayed deliciously from side to side.

Brody sighed wistfully. "She's something else."

"That she is," Bob Cherry agreed with a tight grin. "What's on your mind, Jefferson?"

Brody took a check from his inside jacket pocket and passed it to the senator. It was for five thousand dollars. "A donation to your voter-registration PAC."

Cherry stared at the check. "The FM Development Corporation. Never heard of 'em."

"They're nationwide. Build shopping centers and stuff all over. They've contributed to your PAC before."

"Oh. Forgot. And they say the memory is the first thing to go." Cherry folded the check and slipped it into a pocket. "Well, thank you and FM Development. Any donation on behalf of good government is deeply appreciated."

"What's the government going to do about foreign aid to Russia?"

Cherry took a sip of his wine, then said, "Probably arrange tax credits for corporations that do joint ventures with the Soviets. Something like that. American business could teach the Russians a lot, provide capital, management expertise, inventory control, and so on. Our companies wouldn't have to make much of a profit, if any, with tax credits as an incentive. It might work pretty well." He went on, detailing some of the proposals.

Jefferson Brody didn't pay much attention. He was thinking about PACs—political action committees. PACS were a glaring loophole that had survived the latest get-naked-and-honest bloodletting over election reform. Members of Congress could have private war chests with which they could pretty much do as they pleased as long as the money wasn't spent for direct reelection efforts. So the war chests were for voter-registration efforts, political education of constituents, presidential exploratory efforts, that kind of thing.

The niftiest thing about the noncampaign PACs though, and Brody felt his chest expand as he contemplated the genius of the guy who had thought of this, was that the elected person could put wife, son, daughter, and two or three girlfriends on the PAC payroll, thereby supplementing the family income. He could also use the donated loot to pay his own expenses if those expenses were related, in even a vague, hazy way, to the purposes of the PAC.

Consequently congressional PACs were slush funds, pure and simple. In private the politicians scrambled desperately to avoid the hardship of trying to make ends meet on a salary four times larger than the average American's, while in public they orated endlessly about all they had done to improve the lot of those said average working stiffs. Harsh and heavy, they told their constituents, were the burdens of public service.

Not that T. Jefferson Brody was put off by the hypocrisy of many politicians—Brody would have recoiled in horror at the mere thought of trying to survive on ninety thousand dollars a year. On the contrary, their greed was a real plus. Some needy soul on Capitol Hill always had a hand out. And T. Jefferson Brody was making a fine living counseling clients to fill those empty palms.

As Miss Tina Jordan returned from the powder room, Brody glanced at his watch. He had a dinner engagement this evening with another senator, Hiram Duquesne, who wanted a campaign contribution. Hiram was one of those lucky dogs who had gotten into office before January 8, 1980, so by law when he retired he could pocket all the campaign contributions he had received over the years and hadn't spent. Needless to say, with the most recent election only six weeks past and Duquesne once again a winner, he was still soliciting. Luckily FM Development had a campaign contribution PAC to help those pre-1980 incumbents, the Hiram Duquesnes of the world, who wanted their golden years to be truly golden.

Bob Cherry was in that blessed group, too, Brody remembered with a start. No doubt he would have Miss Jordan call him next week and remind him of that fact. Brody had that to look forward to. He glanced again at his watch. He was going to have to get back to the office and transfer some funds before he delivered Duquesne's check.

Still, he didn't want to rush Bob Cherry and his piece. He suggested dessert and Cherry accepted. Miss Jordan sipped a cup of cappuccino while the senator ate cheesecake and Brody admired the scenery.

When the luncheon bill came, Brody expertly palmed it. Cherry pretended he hadn't seen it.

After an hour Henry Charon got up, paid his bill at the truck stop's restaurant—it was a *lot* less than Brody had just put on his gold plastic—and went to the gift shop–convenience store. He spent twenty minutes there, then another twenty in the men's room. By a quarter to three he was once again seated in a booth by the windows in the restaurant. So at five minutes before three p.m. he saw the van pull in and Tassone get out. He stood beside the truck and pulled off a pair of driving gloves while he looked around. He stuck the gloves in his pocket and walked toward the building.

Tassone came into the restaurant right on the hour. He looked around casually and came over to Charon's booth in the corner.

"Hi."

"Want some coffee?" Charon muttered.

"Yeah." When the waitress came over Tassone ordered.

"It's all there."

"All of it?"

"Everything."

Henry Charon nodded and again scanned the parking area.

"So how many people know about this?" Charon asked after Tassone's coffee came and the waitress departed.

"Well, it took some doing to get what you wanted. Obviously, the people that supplied it know I took delivery. But they aren't going to be shooting their mouths off. Most of this stuff is hot and they were paid well."

"Who else?"

"The guy fronting the dough. He knows."

"And all the people working for him?"

"Don't make me laugh. He and I know, but nobody else. And believe me, I'm not about to tell you who he is. Another thing, after you get the bread, you won't see me again. If you're entitled to any more money under our deal, someone else will deliver it."

"I don't want to see you again."

"You might as well know this too: Tassone ain't my real name."

A flicker of a grin crossed Charon's lips. He watched the other man sip his coffee.

Charon passed a yellow slip of paper across the table. "You'll need this to get the truck back. Wednesday of next week. At a garage in Philadelphia." He gave Tassone the address.

"The money? When and where."

"My place in New Mexico. A week from today. Just you."

"I understand." Tassone sighed. "You really think you can do this?"

"Yeah."

"When? My guy wants to know."

"When I'm ready. Not before." Tassone started to speak but Charon continued: "He won't have to wait too long."

The truck wore Pennsylvania commercial plates. Charon drove out of the parking area and followed the signs toward I-70 east. The truck was new—only 326 miles on the odometer—and almost full of gas. Charon wore his own driving gloves. Twenty-five miles after leaving Breezewood he crossed into Maryland.

He kept the truck at fifty-five miles per hour where he could. Laboring up the low mountain east of Hagerstown the best he could do was thirty-five in the right-hand lane. Crossing the crest he kept the transmission in third gear to keep the brakes from overheating.

At Frederick he took I-270 toward Washington. Traffic was light and he rolled right along in the right lane.

The storage place he had rented was in northeast Washington. Charon's worst moment came as he backed the truck between the narrow buildings and nicked the corner of one. He inspected the damage—negligible, thank God—and tried it again. This time he got the truck right up to the open garage door of the storage bin he had rented last week.

The extra key on the ring fit the lock on the back of the truck. Charon unloaded the vehicle carefully but quickly. It wasn't until he had the garage door down that he stood and took inventory.

Four handguns, rifles, ammo, medical supplies, food, canned water, clothes, and those green boxes with U.S. Army stenciled all over them. Charon opened each box and inspected the contents. He went through all the other items, examining everything.

Thirty minutes later he got into the truck and maneuvered it carefully out of the alley between the storage buildings.

It was going well, he decided. Everything was there, just as it should be. Getting everything done in time and in sequence, that was the difficulty. Still, it was do-able. Now to get this truck to Philly and pick up the car.

Henry Charon grinned as he came off the entrance ramp onto I-95 north. This was going to be his best hunt ever.

CHAPTER ELEVEN

★ ★ ★ ★ ★ ★ ★ ★ ★ ★

JACK Yocke was pecking randomly and morosely on his computer keyboard when Ott Mergenthaler walked by, then sat on the edge of the desk as he played with a piece of paper. "I read your story," Ott said, "on the Jane Wilkens murder over in the Jefferson projects."

"Umph."

"It's good, real good."

"They aren't going to run it now. Going to save it for some Sunday when they need some filler. If they run it at all."

"It's still a good story."

"Too many murder stories are bad for a paper, y'know? The matrons in Bethesda don't want to read that crap. The White House and political reporters take all the space anyhow. What could possibly be more important than Senator Horsebutt's carefully staffed and massaged opinion about what the Soviets ought to do to qualify for American foreign aid?"

"So what are you working on today?"

"Oh, just trying to get someone in the police or the DEA or the FBI or the Federal Home Loan Bank Board to say that there is a connection between the Harrington murder—he was the cashier at Second Potomac S and L—and the Judson Lincoln murder. Lincoln ran a chain of check-cashing outlets here in the metro area. Apparently they've just been sold to some outfit nobody ever heard of."

"What makes you think the killings are connected?"

"The men were shot about four hours apart, apparently by professionals. Both were in finance. Harrington, at least, was laundering money for someone. Coincidence, maybe, but I got this feeling."

"What do the pros say?"

"They aren't saying anything. Absolutely nothing. They just listen and grunt 'no comment.'"

"So what else is new?"

"The world just keeps on turning."

"That's page one news."

"This rag needs some real reporters. Not blood-and-guts guys like me, but some dirt sniffers who will get the *real* news, like who Senator Horsebutt is fucking on Tuesday nights and an opinion from his doctor on how he manages. Perhaps a think-piece listing the names and vital statistics and track records of all of America's top bimbos. Why are we scribbling stories about problems at the sewage farm when we could be picking on rich and famous assholes and selling a lot more papers?"

"Lighten up. And quit feeling sorry for yourself."

"I'm maudlin, I know." Yocke stretched and grinned. "But self-pity soothes a tortured soul, Ott. You ought to try it sometime."

"I gave it up when I quit smoking."

"What windmill are you tilting at today?"

"I don't see my columns quite that way, Sancho. My literary efforts, short and sweet as they are, are really the beating heart of this newspaper that you so irreverently called a rag, the newspaper that pays your generous and unearned salary, by the way."

Ott hoisted his cheeks off the desk. He tossed the paper he was holding in Yocke's lap and walked away. Yocke unfolded it. On the sheet was Ott Mergenthaler's column for tomorrow's paper, printed in three columns.

Unnamed sources in the Justice Department were quoted as saying that the evidence against Chano Aldana was weak. An acquittal was a definite possibility. Ott chided, gently and eruditely, as was his style, the prosecutors and Justice Department officials who had induced a grand jury to indict on weak, hearsay evidence. He also carved off a polite piece of the administration officials who had moved heaven and earth to extradict a man from Colombia that they probably couldn't convict.

Yocke refolded the paper and tossed it on top of one of his piles.

Mergenthaler's column in the *Post* the following morning should have caused a two-kiloton explosion in William C. Dorfman's office, but amazingly, no one on the White House staff saw it that morning. No staffer had time to read anything in the newspaper until early afternoon, because at seven a.m. a thunderbolt arrived from Havana: another Cuban revolution was in full swing.

The evening before in Havana army troops had fired upon a mass rally of over forty thousand people protesting the government's food rationing policies. Some reports said over a hundred people had been killed and several hundred wounded: the casualty figures varied wildly from source to source. This morning half the army was locked in combat with troops loyal to Castro. A group of students had seized Radio Havana and were proclaiming a democracy.

The *Washington Post* staff, with better sources than the White House or the State Department, knew about the revolution at six-thirty a.m., only an hour after the students went on Radio Havana chanting, "*Comunismo está muerto.*" Communism is dead.

Jack Yocke heard the news at eight-oh-five at police headquarters. He charged out of the building and headed for the *Post*.

Breaking into a conference of editors in the newsroom, he blurted, "I speak Spanish." None of the editors discussing how to cover the Cuba story seemed to hear him. He danced from foot to foot. This was his break, the one he had been waiting for. He *knew!*

He scurried off to find Ottmar Mergenthaler. The columnist was not at his desk. There he was, coming out of Bradlee's office. Yocke intercepted him.

"Ott, I got to talk to you. You gotta help me. I gotta go to Cuba."

"Sure, Jack. Sure."

"I speak Spanish. I've been taking a class. *You're not listening, Ott!* I write good blood-and-guts. *Great* blood-and-guts. I've paid my dues covering cops. I deserve a shot. Ott, you ancient idiot, *I speak Spanish!"*

"I'm listening, Jack. But I just write columns around here."

"Be a pal. Go in and see Bradlee. Hell, call Donnie Graham if you have to. But get me to fucking Cuba!"

Mergenthaler stopped, took a deep breath, and rolled his eyes. Then he turned around and walked back toward Bradlee's office. "Wait here, goddammit!" he growled when Yocke tagged along immediately behind him, threatening to step on his heels.

Ooooh boy, what a break this would be, Jack Yocke told himself as he waited. His big assets were that he was young, single, low salaried, and spoke Spanish . . . sort of. Callie Grafton would probably give him a C for his first semester. No reason to burden Ott or Bradlee with those trivial details, of course. As far as they were concerned he had no nervous family to bug the editors if he went and might even speak a little Spanish, like he claimed.

Every writer needs a war, at least one good one, to get famous in a hurry. You mix the blood and shit and booze together and anoint yourself and then, by God, you're Ernest Hemingway.

There are just so damn few good wars anymore! A revolution in Cuba wouldn't be a zinger like Korea or Vietnam, but Castro wouldn't go quietly, without a fight. Whatever happened, it would be better than covering cops. Jack Yocke assured himself of that. He had the talent to make it something big if he got the chance.

Two minutes later Ott returned.

"Okay, Ben is going to talk to foreign. Better get your passport in case they decide to request a visa for you. But you'd be helping out the regulars. Remember that, Junior."

Yocke grabbed the older man by his ears, pulled his head down and kissed him soundly on his tan, bald pate.

"Thanks, Ott," Yocke called as he trotted away. "I owe you."

That day Jack Yocke took the problems as they came. He encountered the first one when he got back to his apartment to throw some clothes in a bag.

What do you take to a revolution? Some underwear, sure. A suit and tie? Well, maybe. Why not? Tennis shoes would be good, some slacks and pullover shirts. Cuba's in the tropics, right? But it might get chilly at night this time of year. Maybe a sweater or sweatshirt. Socks. He wadded all this stuff into a soft, fake-leather vinyl bag and tossed in a razor and toothbrush and toothpaste.

Cuba. In Latin America. Cuba's bacteria have undoubtedly been recycled through fifty generations of immune natives and have probably grown virulent enough to disembowel a gringo, like the bacteria the Mexicans are so proud of. Yocke added all the antidiarrhea medicine in his bathroom to the bag.

His passport was in the top left drawer of his dresser, under the hankies. He didn't bother packing any hankies.

With the encased laptop computer that he had signed for from the *Post* dangling from a strap over his shoulder and the fake-leather bag banging against his leg, he hailed a cab—hey, he was on the expense account—and rode with nervous anticipation back to the *Post*. He kept the cab waiting while he trotted into the building and rode up to the travel office.

Trying very hard to conceal his nervousness, he stood in line until he had his tickets and money. They were *really* going to let him go!

He didn't feel safe until he was on his way to the airport. Then he sat back and grinned broadly. This was his chance! All the writing he had ever done had been mere preparation for this story. And he felt confident. He was *ready*.

After he had checked his bag at the ticket counter and gotten his seat assignment, Jack Yocke wandered into a newsstand and bought a carton of Marlboros. He took the cigarette packs out of the carton and stuffed them around the computer inside its case. Fortunately there was room. Then he went to the bar and watched the latest news on the Cable News Network.

While Yocke was sipping coffee from a paper cup, one of the CNN White House correspondents assured the audience that President Bush was closely monitoring the situation in Cuba.

That statement had been given out by the White House press flacks upon the order of William C. Dorfman.

Actually the President was at that very moment discussing with Dorfman and the chairman of the national Republican party a matter more weighty than a revolution in Cuba. The American people had recently elected a larger Democratic House and Senate majority, and two of the loyal Republican congressmen who would be unemployed in January wanted government jobs.

Dorfman suggested ambassadorships: he named several possible small nations in sub-Sahara Africa. The national chairman thought the two

Republican legislators might prefer to be assistant secretaries of something or other. "Who the hell wants to go to equatorial Africa?"

The men in the Oval Office had their feet up and were in no hurry. Dorfman had canceled most of the President's regular schedule today so he would have plenty of time to closely monitor the Cuban thing.

At noon the President went down to the White House situation room for a briefing. He was back at twelve-fifteen and when lunch was brought in turned on the television to see what the media were saying. Various loyal army units in the provinces had capitulated to mobs that had besieged their barracks shouting for food. Fidel Castro had appeared on Havana television—the show ran thirty seconds of poor-quality tape—and blamed the "riots" by "counterrevolutionaries" on Yankee imperialists. He announced that the traitors who had seized Radio Havana that morning had been captured and shot.

"There's no organized opposition," Bush informed his guests. "The lid just blew off."

CNN then ran a story about several dozen major corporations buying up huge tracts in West Virginia to open landfills for the entire eastern seaboard's garbage. The President watched while he ate a BLT on whole wheat with a double shot of mayo. The governor of West Virginia, a Democrat, was outraged, but the yokels in the legislature refused to forbid landfills or even regulate them. Apparently a lot of West Virginians thought their children and grandchildren wouldn't mind living on top of New York City's garbage and drinking the effluvia in their water so long as they got jobs driving the bulldozers.

"Makes you wonder about democracy, doesn't it?" the national chairman muttered. "If the Russians and Cubans only knew."

Bush finished off the last bite of the BLT and jabbed the remote control, turning off the television. He asked the national chairman what the Democrats thought about foreign aid to the Soviets.

They were deep into that subject when an aide motioned Dorfman from the room and showed him Mergenthaler's column.

Dorfman ate three Rolaids as he read. When he finished he snapped, "Get Cohen on the phone," and went to his office to take the call.

"I'm calling about Mergenthaler's column, Gid."

"What about it?" Cohen was equally brusque.

"Somebody over in your empire told him you guys can't convict Aldana."

"That's somebody's opinion. I don't know whose. It isn't mine."

"You gonna call a press conference and deny it?"

"Deny what?"

Dorfman held the phone away from his ear and looked at it distastefully. If the man was as stupid as he sounded, he wasn't qualified to prosecute a traffic ticket.

"Are you or are you not going to convict Chano Aldana?"

"I'm not a psychic."

"You want me to tell the President that?"

"If the President wants to talk to me about the case against Aldana, I'll be delighted to brief him. We have evidence. Mountains of it. We're still sifting through it page by page. We think Aldana's guilty and we'll try to prove it."

"The President will want you to say that in a press release."

"Have you talked to him about it?"

"Not yet, but—"

"If the President wants a press release, we'll do one. I don't advise it. If we start issuing press releases to deny leaks we're going to be as busy as the sorcerer's apprentice. Call me back when you find out the President's decision." The attorney general hung up.

The President did want a press release. Dorfman had his youngest, most junior aide call the attorney general and deliver the message.

When Jack Yocke had collected his bag from the luggage carousel at Miami airport, he found a pay phone with a Miami telephone directory still attached. He looked up an address, then hailed a cab in front of the terminal.

2422 South Davis was smack in the middle of the Cuban section of town. The business signs were in Spanish. Latin rhythms floated from passing cars. Yocke paid the cab driver and stood on the sidewalk for a moment watching the passing swarms of humanity.

The storefronts looked Mexican. Maybe that's what Cuba looks like, sort of Matamoros East without the tourists, whores, and sex shows.

The black lettering on the glass of the door between a dress store and what he took to be a laundry had been painted freehand by someone in a hurry. CUBA LIBRE, it said, like the rum drink. "Free Cuba."

Jack Yocke opened the door and went inside. He walked along a hall, then began climbing a flight of stairs. The worn steps creaked as they took his weight. At the top of the stairs was another door, one with no glass. He tried the knob. It turned.

The small office was empty. Two closed doors against the back wall presumably led to offices that overlooked the back alley. He could hear people, men and women, arguing in Spanish behind one of the doors. Yocke took a seat and arranged his bag and computer on the chair beside him.

He crossed his legs and tried to figure out what the conversation was about. No soap. These people didn't speak Spanish like Mrs. Grafton. They should have taken her course.

The phone rang. And rang. And rang, while the argument continued unabated.

It stopped, finally. Shortly thereafter a woman opened the door and started. "Who are you?"

"Name's Jack Yocke. You the receptionist?"

"How long have you been sitting here?" She had a definite accent and her skin was a warm brown.

"Just a couple of minutes." About fifteen, actually. "Your door was unlocked and . . . I hope you don't mind."

"We're closed."

A man came from the inside of the office and stood in the doorway looking at Yocke. "I don't know him," he told the woman. His accent was less pronounced than the woman's, but noticeable. He was a slight man without a trace of excess flesh. His skin stretched tightly across his face; his eyes were deeply set.

Yocke took out his wallet and removed his press card. He handed it to the woman and smiled broadly. "Jack Yocke, *Washington Post.*"

The man snatched the card and looked at it incredulously. "You, reporter?"

"Yes. I—"

"Out! Take your card." The man threw it at him. "Beat it! Scram! Right now, *hombre.*"

Yocke pocketed the card. He slowly arranged the strap of the computer case over his shoulder and hefted the vinyl bag. "Could I get your name for my story? I don't know much Spanish, but I know *bote* and *viaje por mar* and a couple more words. I know that Santa Clara is a city in Cuba. And I can add two and two."

"Tienes las orejas grandes y la mala lengua."

"Yep. Big ears and a bad mouth. That's me."

They stared at him openmouthed. The phone started ringing again. They let it ring.

"What you want?" Back to English.

"Same as you. To go to Cuba."

"Why?"

"I'm a reporter. They're having a revolution." Jack Yocke grinned.

The phone was still ringing. The man and woman looked at each other.

"No," she said.

"Sí." The man stood partially aside. "Come in."

"Why don't you answer your phone?"

"Reporters." He spit out the word. "They have treated us as cracked pots—that is the words, no?—for years, ignored us, and now they drive us *loco.* 'A story, *now* give us a story! Tell us of Cuba and Fidel.' *Now* you want to spill on us some of the ink you use for your football and your stories of foolish rich men and silly women with the big tits, eh? Truly, *señor,* yours is a miserable profession."

There were two other men in the room. Cubans. In their thirties, lean and wiry, they were sitting in straight-backed chairs and they didn't rise. They did, however, scrutinize Yocke's face with the coldest stares he could remember.

The cadaverous man who had admitted him closed the door carefully and said, "But first let's establish just what your real profession is, *señor.*"

Yocke turned to face him. "What do you think my profession might be, if I'm not a reporter?"

The man went behind the desk and opened a drawer. He extracted a large revolver and pointed it straight at Yocke. "Oh, let me think. What a puzzle! Can you help me?"

The revolver looked like as big as a cannon. The black hole in the muzzle looked large enough to drive a car through. Jack Yocke grinned nervously. No one else smiled.

"Perhaps you are of Fidel. Perhaps you are CIA. Those possibilities leap immediately to my mind. Sit!"

Yocke sat.

"Now. Put that thing over your shoulder on the floor there beside you. Place your hands on the table in front of you, *señor,* and remain still as the most dead man you ever saw, or *Holy Mother!* I will make you very very dead very very quickly."

The two spectators came over and, carefully staying out of the possible line of fire, emptied Yocke's pockets, turning them inside out. The contents they put on the desk.

"Stand in the corner, *señor,* facing the wall."

Jack Yocke obeyed.

He heard the door open, then fifteen seconds later close again. He heard the sounds of zippers being opened. His computer case. Maybe his suitbag.

"You could call my editor at the *Post* and ask him what I look like."

"I know I look like a fool, *señor.* For that I blame my father. But a fool I am not. If you are a *Fidelista* or a CIA, you have a wonderful cover. I expect no less. *Por favor, señor,* do not twitch like that! The noise of this pistol is distressing in such a small room."

After several minutes the cadaverous man, who was the only one who had spoken, told Yocke, "Turn around."

The reporter did so. The contents of his wallet were spread all over the desk. One of the Cubans was punching the buttons of the computer, slowly, randomly, absorbed, while he watched the screen. The third man was pawing through Yocke's clothes and underwear, which were piled on the floor.

With his gun just under his right hand, the man at the desk was ripping open cigarette packs. He crumbled the cigarettes into piles of tobacco and paper and randomly ripped apart filters with his fingernails. It took two more minutes. Satisfied at last, he raked the mess into a trash can beside the desk. Most of it went into the trash, anyway: the rest went onto the wooden floor.

Now the man wiped his hands together to get rid of the tobacco crumbs, then picked up the revolver. He pointed it at the reporter's belly button.

"*Ahora bien,* we will come to Jesus, as you say. The truth."

"My name is Jack Yocke. I'm a reporter for the *Washington Post.* I left Washington this morning to go to Cuba. I figured that none of the other correspondents trying to get there would think of going over to Cuba with the exiles. So I flew into Miami Airport and looked in the telephone book. I looked under 'Cuba' and found an address for Cuba Libre. I hailed a taxi. Here I am. That's the truth."

The man stared. The other two finished their explorations and joined in the scrutiny.

"We don't have time for your games. We have things to do."

"Take me with you to Cuba, please. I'm asking you as nice and polite as I know how."

"What makes you think we are going to Cuba?"

"Please, mister, don't jerk my chain! Some of the Cubans *must* be going! If you guys aren't, who is? I need to get to Cuba one way or the other. What the hell you want me to do—hire an airplane and parachute out of it? Goddammit, my paper wants stories from Cuba and sent *me* to get them. I won't write a story about you or mention your names without your approval. Is that what you're worried about? You can be a confidential source. I'm just asking for your help. But with or without you, I'm going to Cuba."

The three men glanced at each other. Nothing was said.

After several seconds, the man behind the desk put the pistol back in the drawer and gestured. "Your things." He shook his head. "Only in America . . ."

His name was Hector Santana. He didn't introduce the other two, but Yocke later learned their names: Jesús Ruiz and Tomás García. The three conferred briefly in whispers in the far corner, then Santana faced him again.

"You must understand the danger. There is much danger. We will go by boat. We will have to avoid your Coast Guard, which will be alert for boats going to Cuba, and we will have to avoid the Cuban Navy, which will be even more alert. If we are caught by the Americans, we will be in serious trouble. If we are caught by the Cubans, we will be dead."

"I understand. I want to go."

"You say it so easily, so lightly. A ride in a pedal-boat on a park lake! You would risk your life for your employer's sake, to write a story for a newspaper?"

"Well, it does sound sort of stupid, when you put it like that. But yes, I—"

"You are a *fool.*"

"You'll be just as dead as I."

"Ahh, but we are fighting for our country. For *Cuba*. You, you risk your life for money, for glory. And those things they are as nothing. They are as smoke. You are a very great fool."

"You've told me the risks. You've given me your opinion. I still want to go if you'll take me."

Santana shrugged grandly. "You must stay with us and make no calls. You may telephone anyone anywhere, if the telephones work, when we get to Havana. Not before."

"That's reasonable. Sure."

"And we, of course, accept your offer of professional secrecy. No stories about us. No names. Ever. You must swear it."

"I swear. When do we get to Havana?"

Around midnight the three men, with Jack Yocke wedged in the backseat, drove through a steady rain to a marina. Yocke never knew where the marina was because the Cubans made him wear a blindfold. He was led from the car to a slick gangplank which he stumbled up carrying the computer. Only when he was in a little cabin below decks was he allowed to remove the blindfold. His escort tossed the vinyl bag on the deck, then left, closing the door behind him.

The engine on the boat was already running, a muffled throbbing that pulsated the deck and bulkheads. After sitting in the darkness a few minutes Yocke tried the door latch. Locked. There was a tiny porthole, but the view was only of black water and shimmering lights.

Within minutes the boat got under way. The deck tilted and the vibration changed and the noise level rose. Yocke checked his watch: twelve forty-six a.m.

Yocke tried to decide how large the boat was. It wasn't little, he concluded. But it wasn't a ship. It turned too quickly. He stretched out on the couch bunk in the darkness and tried to sleep.

After a half hour or so the motion of the vessel changed. She began to roll and pitch with authority. Sometime later the motion changed again as the growl of the engine rose. Now the motion was more vigorous, the roll and pitch moments sharper and quicker.

The day had been a long one. Jack Yocke slept.

He awoke sometime later. The vessel was pounding in the sea, the engines throbbing heavily. They were pushing her hard. He wedged himself into the bunk and in minutes was again asleep.

Hector Santana shook him awake at five a.m. "You may come up on deck now."

The boat was still pitching enthusiastically. Worse than when he went to sleep, but not as badly as it had several hours ago. Above the engine noise Yocke asked, "Where are we?"

"Just off Andros Island."

"Are we in the Gulf Stream?"

"We've crossed it. The ride was much worse."

On deck the only illumination was from several little red lights above the chart and binnacle in front of the helmsman. The rain had stopped. The boat appeared to be a giant cabin cruiser. This high above the water the motion was even more pronounced. Yocke found a handhold.

A ghostly white wake stretched away behind the boat straight as a highway into the vast, total darkness. Not a star or other light in the entire visible universe.

He could hear a radio, the announcer speaking in Spanish. When his eyes became better adjusted, he could just make out the figures of four or five men huddled around it.

"How goes the revolution?"

"Fighting in the cities. Much of the army is still loyal to Fidel."

"Where will we land?"

"Caibarién."

"When?"

"Tomorrow morning, before dawn."

"How fast are we going?"

"Twenty-eight knots."

After a few moments, Yocke asked, "This your boat?"

"Belongs to a friend."

"Nice of him to let you use it like this."

"He will report it stolen this evening."

"Why are you going to Cuba?"

"It's my country."

Yocke eased himself to another handhold. His eyes were fairly well adjusted now and he could just make out Santana's face. "Uh-uh. Nope. Yesterday evening I told you why I wanted to go, but you didn't bother to tell me why you and your friends were going. And I didn't ask."

"We noted the omission. Very good manners for a reporter. Tomás thought too good. I said no. He is *diplomático,* I said. Finally Tomás agreed."

"Perhaps you can tell me now."

"Maybe later. We'll see. If you're still alive." With that Santana went below.

CHAPTER TWELVE

* * * * * * * * *

AT dawn the blackness faded to slate gray. A gray, indefinite sky above a gray sea. Visibility about a mile in fog. There were no other vessels to be seen, no land, nothing but gray in every direction.

The helmsman slowed the boat to two or three knots and it began to roll and pitch sloppily. On the low fantail, behind the raised bridge, the other passengers baited fishing rods with small fish and rigged them to troll. One man went up on the high fish platform. Jack Yocke had no desire to join him. The motion of the boat would be much worse there.

Sandwiches and coffee were brought up from below. Yocke had had two bites before he realized he had made a mistake. He puked over the rail and the wind sprayed some of it over the men sitting on the fantail watching the fishing rods. They were angry at first, then they laughed.

"Go below and lie down," Santana told him.

Yocke was back on deck in two minutes, heaving again. The motion of the boat was impossible to endure in the confined spaces below.

He ended up lying on the deck forward, crawling to the rail to puke, then lying on his back waiting.

Hours passed. He was reduced to dry heaves.

Oh God, he was sick. Every now and then he could hear the Cubans on the bridge laughing. He didn't care. He didn't care if he died here and now. Nothing was worth this.

Once he heard a plane. A jet. Oh, to be up there, sitting in a comfortable, stable seat, one that didn't bob and roll and go endlessly up and down, up and down. . . .

Since there was absolutely nothing in his stomach at this stage, he merely curled into the fetal position and retched until he gagged, then retched some more.

He resolved never again to travel by water, anywhere. To never again set foot on boat, ship, ferry, scow, schooner, sloop, anything that floated. If he couldn't go by air or rail, he wouldn't go.

When Jack Yocke finally felt better it was after twelve o'clock on his watch. He sat and stared at the sea. The visibility had improved—maybe three or four miles—and the clouds were broken, with sunlight shining through in places, making the sea a brilliant blue. The sunlight on the sea hurt his eyes. He got up and staggered along the deck edge, holding on like grim death, to the bridge area. How had he managed to get to the forward deck when he was so sick?

"Drink this. It's water," Santana said, and he obeyed.

His stomach was still queasy, but nowhere near as bad as it had been.

For the first time he seriously examined his companions, of whom five were visible above decks. Santana, the two from yesterday—Jesús Ruiz and Tomás García—and two more whose names he never learned. Ruiz was the helmsman while García spent his time listening to a shortwave radio. Yocke got a chance to observe García closely for several minutes, and he seemed to be monitoring the VHF band.

Santana saw him looking over García's shoulder. "That jet two hours ago was U.S. Coast Guard. They saw us with their radar but never got a visual identification. They reported our position, course, and speed to their headquarters in Miami, which presumably passed it to the two cutters that are somewhere out here."

"Where?"

"I wish I knew."

"Did we change course after the jet passed?"

"Yes. We are now headed northeast, toward Andros Island."

"What are we worried about? We're just out here fishing."

"Fishing," Santana agreed. Automatically he checked the rods and the angle of the lines.

"No luck, huh?" Yocke said, also looking.

"We had a tuna strike this morning, while you were sick. I had them take the baits off. We are just trolling bare hooks."

"Maybe we should try to catch something."

"We don't have the fuel to waste on a fight. And the fish would be killed for no reason. That," Hector Santana added with a glance at the reporter, "would be a sin."

Jack Yocke listened to the news, sometimes in Spanish, sometimes in English from a U.S. station, and watched the men. He avoided drawing them into conversation, and none of them except Santana approached him to talk.

All afternoon the Cubans huddled near the radio and chafed, each man in his own way. The revolution was in full swing, people they knew and cared deeply for were risking everything, including their lives, yet here they sat on a fifty-foot boat on a vast, empty sea, going nowhere at three knots.

Yocke was as impatient as the rest. He reminded himself that his interest was strictly professional. Well, sporting too, in that he was rooting hard for the underdogs, yet somehow this thought tweaked from him a pang of guilt, which annoyed him. It wasn't his fault he wasn't a

Cuban or that Cuba had become a poor, starving bucolic workers' paradise under the magnificent benevolence of the "maximum leader." For thirty-one years Fidel Castro had been the Cuban saint, a sugarcane version of George Washington, Marx, Lenin, Stalin, and St. Paul, togged out in army fatigues and spouting revolutionary bullshit that the vast majority of Cubans believed or at least tolerated. It wasn't until the Soviets had cut them off the dole and starvation threatened that the Cuban people had finally held up a yardstick to see how tall Fidel really was.

Yocke vomited again in late afternoon, but afterward the queasiness seemed to leave him. Weak and dehydrated, he still felt better.

As evening came the visibility lifted significantly. Just before dark Yocke could see land off to the northeast and east, a dark line on the horizon perhaps ten miles away. It was difficult to judge and he didn't ask. As the light faded the two men on the fantail reeled in the fishing lines and stowed the rods.

When the night enclosed them completely and the only lights in the universe were the red glow from the binnacle and chart table, Santana spoke to the helmsman. He spun the wheel and pushed the twin throttles forward. The fantail descended and the bow rose as the screws bit into the sea.

With Santana bending over the chart and Ruiz at the helm, the boat glided through the night. García played with the Loran and the other two acted as lookouts.

Yocke stood on the left rear corner of the bridge, out of whispered earshot and out of the way, and watched. He was the first to see the weak flashes of light off in the darkness a little to the left of their course, and pointed them out to Santana.

Ruiz cut the throttle. The boat rose and fell gently on the swell, enveloped by darkness. Santana pointed a flashlight with a cone of paper taped around the head in the direction of the first light and keyed it several times. At the answering light, Ruiz advanced the throttles.

After five minutes or so and another hurried conference over the chart, the Cubans killed the engine. One man went forward to lower the anchor.

Rocking in the night, they waited. Jack Yocke could just faintly hear breakers crashing on a beach. Or perhaps against rocks.

Santana came over for a moment beside him. "Be very quiet. Stay here on the bridge," he whispered. "If there is any trouble, lie down and do not move." To reinforce his message, he tapped the reporter's arm gently with a revolver.

Yocke looked. García came up from below decks with a rifle of some kind. He moved forward of the bridge. The man on the fantail also had a rifle or perhaps a submachine gun. It was very difficult for Yocke to see clearly in the haphazard starlight coming through gaps in the cloud cover overhead.

Twenty minutes passed. Thirty. Ruiz muttered something in Spanish to Santana about the time.

Yocke didn't realize they had company until the other boat bumped against theirs. Other men came aboard. After a quick conference on the fantail, everyone except Ruiz went to the fantail to help.

The job took about fifteen minutes, as close as Yocke could tell. Box after heavy box was handed from the smaller boat to this one, then carefully carried below. Over thirty boxes, perhaps three dozen.

Then the other boat was pushed away into the darkness. Ruiz started his engines, waited just a moment to ensure that the other boat would drift clear, then engaged the screws and advanced the throttles. He brought them up slowly and steadily as the speed built until the two throttles were against the forward stops and the bow was leaping off swells and whacking into others. Yocke found a hand-hold.

After a while Santana and the others came up from below and stood joking and laughing on the bridge. They were in a jovial mood. They passed a bottle around, then Santana brought it over to where Yocke sat and offered him a swig.

Yocke declined. "My stomach."

"I understand. Perhaps when we reach Cuba."

"What do you guys have in those boxes?"

"You don't really want to know. You're just an uninvited hitchhiker, remember?"

"Amazing how your accent goes and comes."

"Accents are useful. They are like clothes. One dresses the part. Always."

"Watching you load those boxes, I finally realized how big a fool I've been."

Santana tilted the bottle. He wiped his mouth on his sleeve. "Well, perhaps. If so, that is progress. Most fools live their entire lives without ever knowing wisdom." He belched. "I think there's one swallow left. You never know, it might be your very last."

Yocke took the bottle and drained it. The rum burned all the way down. He wound up and threw the bottle as far out into the wake as he could. He didn't see it splash.

"None of us ever know, do we?"

"That is right," Santana agreed cheerfully enough and left him to examine the chart and fiddle with the Loran and confer in a low voice with Ruiz and García.

In a few minutes García made himself comfortable across from Yocke. He still had the rifle. He rested it across his knees.

The hours passed. Sometimes the ride would grow rougher or smoother for a time, but the throttles stayed against the stops. Ruiz worked the helm only to hold his course. He did have to work at it. After a few hours

Santana relieved him and he went below. García smoked cigarettes and never moved.

When Ruiz came back on deck at midnight, Yocke asked Santana if he could go below and get his gear. Santana got it for him.

Yocke donned a sweatshirt and pulled a sweater over it. Using the vinyl bag for a pillow, he stretched out on the deck.

When he awoke he was aware that the boat was not rolling as before. She was now moving directly across the swells and pitching heavily, the engine still at full cry.

All the men were on deck, looking away to port. Yocke joined them and peered into the darkness. Beside him García pointed.

A white masthead light was just visible, another light under it. "Cuban patrol boat."

"Has he seen us?"

"*Sí.* I think so."

Yocke moved over to where Santana stood, beside the helmsman. He was looking at the chart.

"Where are we?"

"Here." Santana jabbed with his finger. The spot he indicated was ten miles or so north of the Cuban coast. "The patrol boat has us on radar."

"You could run east away from him."

"No. We have been picking up radar signals from the east. There is a patrol boat over there too, though farther away. We were trying to go between them."

"You have a radar detector?"

"Yes. One of your American ones for detecting police radar. We have modified it to receive different frequencies. It works quite well."

"So what are you going to do?" Yocke looked again at the lights on the horizon. Was the Cuban boat visibly closer or was that his imagination?

"We can try for shallow water. We don't have many options."

"You could turn around and go north."

Santana was looking at the chart.

"Surely that's better than getting killed?"

"Go sit down. Stay out of the way."

Yocke didn't have to be told twice.

After a quick conference around the helm, everyone except Santana went below. He took the wheel.

Yocke was watching the lights, which were truly closer, when he saw the flash. Santana saw it too and spun the wheel. The nose of the boat slewed to port. Yocke heard the rumble as the shot went over and, after a moment, the splash. Then, finally, he heard the boom of the shot.

Santana spun the wheel again, turning starboard, then steadied up after thirty degrees or so of heading change. The next shot was short, though much closer.

The stars seemed to be brighter. Yocke checked his watch. A few minutes after five a.m. He looked down toward the south. Lights. Towns, perhaps. Or villages. Cuba. God, it would be a long swim! And sharks—these waters were full of sharks.

He was thinking of sharks and wondering about the current when he saw the third flash. The gunboat was definitely closer.

This time the shot fell just in front of the bow.

"The next one'll be the charm," Yocke said loudly enough for Santana to hear.

"Pray," was the response.

The other Cubans rushed up from below. Two of them went forward and two settled on the port side of the bridge. They each had a dark pipe on their shoulder, something like a World War II bazooka.

"Get over here, Yocke! By me!" Santana ordered.

"Ready?" Santana shouted.

"Sí. Adelante!"

Santana spun the wheel and the boat heeled to starboard as her nose came port. She had completed forty-five degrees or so of heading change when the gunboat fired again. Santana held in his turn until he was heading only ten or fifteen degrees south of the gunboat, running toward her at full throttle. "Not yet," he shouted.

The swells were smaller and farther apart here in the lee of Cuba and the boat rode more steadily on the step.

Jack Yocke peered through the bridge glass trying to estimate the distance. Ahead of him, on the deck, the two men lay prone, on their elbows, each with a tube across his shoulder and pointed toward the charging gunboat.

The gunboat fired again. Santana swerved port, bringing the gunboat dead onto the nose. Just when Yocke concluded the Cuban Navy had again missed, the platform above the bridge exploded, showering the fantail with debris.

Santana chopped the throttle and slammed the transmission into neutral.

"They're gonna hit us with the next one," Yocke shouted.

"Everybody down. Take cover!"

"They'll kill us," Yocke shouted at Santana, infuriated at the man's composure.

"They're not in range yet."

"Oh, damn," Yocke muttered, and got facedown on the floor.

The seconds passed. Miraculously, the next explosion didn't come. Yocke lay on his belly waiting, sweating profusely, and when it finally seemed that the shooting was over, he got up on his knee for a look. The gunboat was closer, much closer.

Another flash. This time the bridge glass to Yocke's right exploded. He felt the sting of something hitting his face and instinctively raised his arm.

"Fire!" Santana shouted.

One of the men behind fired first. A whooshing crack and a great flash of light and the rocket shot forward, illuminating the surface of the black sea with the fire from its exhaust.

Then the man beside him fired. Another report and flash.

The men up forward fired no more than a second apart.

Half blinded by the flashes, Jack Yocke tried to look anyway.

One of the missiles hit a swell and detonated. Well short.

Another hit the gunboat with a flash. A second impacted almost in the same place. The fourth must have missed.

Yocke turned. The two men behind him were going down the ladder, heading below. Santana shoved the transmission lever forward and firewalled the throttle. As the stern bit into the sea he cranked the helm over.

In thirty seconds they were back, carrying more rocket launchers.

They squatted and waited.

The gunboat was obviously hit badly. Her bow turned northward and the smear of fire was visible.

Santana veered off to the south, to pass under the gunboat's stern, perhaps a quarter mile away, Yocke guessed.

As they approached to almost abeam, tracers reached from the gunboat. The man behind Yocke fired another missile. This one impacted the Cuban gunboat just above the waterline.

Then they were by, the distance increasing.

"What the fuck are those things?" Yocke asked.

"LAW rockets." Yocke had heard of these, though he had never seen one. Light antitank weapons.

"How many you got down there?"

"Not as many as we started with."

"Where'd you get 'em?"

"You never stop asking fool questions, do you?"

"Sorry."

The gunboat was on fire, dead in the water, rapidly falling astern when Yocke saw her last. His face was stinging. It was blood.

The back end of the port side of the bridge was a mess. The shell had blown out the window and passed through the supporting structure that held up the roof. Luckily the stuff offered too little resistance to activate the fuse or everyone on the bridge would have been cut to bits by the shrapnel of the exploding warhead. And the fiberglass had been cooked by the exhaust of the missiles getting under way.

To hell with these idiots!

Jack Yocke went below and found the cabin he had slept in leaving Miami and turned on the light. He was shaking like a leaf. He sat on the bunk and tried to get his breathing under control while blood dripped off his chin onto his shirt and trousers.

Ten minutes later he was looking in the mirror above the washbasin and using a towel to extract the glass shards from the cuts in his face when Hector Santana came in.

"How do you feel?"

"You want the truth or some macho bullshit from a B movie?"

"Whatever pleases you."

"I damn near shit myself."

Santana grinned. The grin looked wicked on that tight, death's-head face.

Yocke averted his eyes and concentrated on raking a glass splinter from a cut over his eye. When he got it out, he said, "Why'd you let me come along?"

"Tomás and Jesús wanted to kill you in Miami. You were obviously a plant. Even if you were a reporter, you might talk, talk far too much, much too soon. I don't like to kill unless it is required. So we brought you."

"A great bunch of guys you are! What would you have done earlier this evening if you had run into a U.S. Coast Guard cutter? After you picked up the weapons?"

"Probably scuttled."

"My ass! You'd have shot it out."

"Think what you like."

"If we had survived that encounter, you would have killed me."

Santana shrugged. "A lot of time, effort, and money went into acquiring these weapons. Three men lost their lives. We desperately need these weapons to fight the *Fidelistas*. Much is at stake. Many lives. Yet you came to our office and stuck your nose in where it didn't belong. You wanted a free ride to the revolution, as if a revolution against Castro would be some kind of a Cuban circus that you had improvidently forgotten to buy a ticket for. You wanted to sneak in under the tent flap!"

Santana snorted. "You Americans! You persist in thinking the world is a comfortable little place, full of comfortable, reasonable people, despite all the evidence to the contrary. If only everyone would buy a Sunday edition of the *Post* and read it carefully, perhaps write a thoughtful, well-crafted letter to the editor, then everything would be *okay.*"

Hector Santana sucked in a bushel of air and sighed audibly. "Have a *nice* day," he said over his shoulder as he went through the door.

Jack Yocke stared at his face in the mirror. Blood was still trickling from several of the deeper cuts.

The boat glided gently through the shallow waters of an inlet behind an island as the daylight came. The remains of the fishing tower above the bridge listed at a crazy angle. The back end of the bridge didn't look any better in the gray half light of dawn than it had an hour ago. The plexiglass fragments were charred a sooty black.

As Yocke watched, Santana ran the boat into a cut on the bank sheltered by several trees. A half dozen men came aboard and carried the LAW rockets, still in their olive-drab boxes stenciled U.S. ARMY, over a plank to a truck barely visible amid the vegetation.

When the job was complete, the men piled into the truck and drove away. Everyone went with them except Santana. He stood on the bridge with Yocke. "Well," he said, "that's done."

"What next?"

"Unless you're in the mood for a swim, I suggest you go ashore. Better take your stuff with you. Oh, and take my bag from the galley ashore with you. And this." Santana drew his revolver from his waistband and tossed it at the reporter, who barely caught it.

With Yocke standing on sand trying to readjust his muscles to the absence of motion, Santana maneuvered the boat from the cut and slowly eased her several hundred yards out into the inlet, where he killed the engine. He went forward and heaved the anchor overboard.

He worked on the boat for ten or fifteen minutes while Yocke sat on the vinyl suitbag watching. The quiet was uncomfortable after two nights and a day listening to the engines. Yocke could hear birds singing somewhere and the slap-slap of water lapping at the shore, but that was about it. No engine noise, no jets overhead, no barely audible radio or television babble. Just the chee-cheeing of the birds and the water.

The pistol felt strange in his hand. Yocke examined it. A Smith & Wesson .357. It wasn't a new gun or even in very good condition. He could see bare metal in places where the blueing was gone. But the thing that struck Jack Yocke was the weight. This thing was heavier than he thought it would be. He knew very little about firearms and had handled them on only a few occasions. Looking into the chambers from the front, he could see the bullets. Shiny little pills of instant death. Ugliness. Everything he didn't like about the world and the people in it was right here in his hand.

He carefully laid the pistol on top of the computer case and wiped his hands in the sand.

Santana came off the boat in a clean dive and began swimming. The sun was up now and the water was a pale, sandy blue. The man swam efficiently, without wasted effort.

He was standing beside Yocke taking off his wet clothes when a dull "crump" reached them and the remains of the fish tower toppled slowly into the water. Ten seconds later another explosion, more powerful but still strangely muffled.

Santana stripped to the skin and opened his bag. He had his underwear and trousers on when he next looked at the boat. She was down visibly at the head and listing.

"How deep's the water there?"

"Sixty or seventy feet, maybe. That's the channel."

"Clear as this water is, she'll be visible from the air."

"No one will look from the air for a few days. Then it won't matter. We'll be in Havana."

"Or dead," Jack Yocke added.

"You are very intuitive. Your grasp of the situation is really remarkable."

"Fuck you very much."

The forward deck was completely awash when Santana stood and dusted the sand from his trousers. He tucked the revolver into his waistline and let the loose shirt hang over it. "Come on," he said, slung his bag over his shoulder and began walking as Yocke hurried to pick up his gear.

From a low dune a hundred yards or so inland Yocke paused and looked back at the inlet in time to see the water close over the bridge of the boat. Hector Santana kept walking. He didn't bother to look.

"Campaigning with Cortés," Jack Yocke muttered under his breath. He shifted the computer strap to ease the strain on his shoulder and hefted the vinyl suitcase. "Or perhaps, *Walking Across Cuba* by Jack Yocke, ace reporter and world-class idiot."

An hour passed as they walked. Yocke got thirsty and said so. Santana didn't say a word.

They were on a dirt road leading through sugarcane fields. The cane was knee high or so and green, rippling from air currents that never seemed to reach the two hikers. Away off to the south, the direction they were walking, Yocke could see clouds building over low hills or perhaps mountains. "Are there mountains in Cuba?" he asked.

They passed several empty shacks. One had an ancient, skinny chicken wandering aimlessly in the yard. No other living thing in sight.

"Where is everybody?" he asked. "Maybe we ought to look around for some water, huh? I'll bet they got a well or something." Santana kept walking without replying. "What's wrong with that idea, Jack?" Yocke muttered loud enough for the Cuban to hear.

"Hey, Hector," Jack Yocke said five minutes later. "Wanta tell me where we're going? If we're going to walk clear to Havana maybe I should lighten the load. What d'ya think?"

When Santana didn't reply, Yocke stepped near his ear and yelled, *"Hey, asshole!"*

"Did it ever occur to you," Santana said patiently, "that if we are stopped by Cuban troops, the less you know the better? For you, for me, for everyone?"

They walked for another hour. A small group of shacks came into sight and Santana headed for them. He went into the yard and motioned for Yocke to stay. Then he went up to a porch and looked through the screen. "María? Carlos?"

Santana went inside. Yocke sat on his vinyl bag and took his shoes off and massaged his feet. A skinny chicken came over to watch. Does Cuba have any chickens that aren't skinny?

An old car, almost obscured by grass and weeds, sat rotting in a shed beside the house. Yocke went over and examined the car as murmurs of Spanish came through the window. An ancient Chevrolet sedan. Forty years old if it was a day. There wasn't enough paint even to tell what the original color had been. The back window was missing. Several chickens had obviously been raising their families on the rear seat.

At least he wasn't seasick. That was something. He was hungry enough to eat one of those scrawny chickens raw. He was watching one and trying to decide if he could catch it when Santana and a young woman came out of the house. The woman stood by Yocke as Santana went over to the car, got in, and ground on the engine.

Amazingly enough, a puff of blue smoke came out from under the car and the engine caught.

Santana backed the car into the yard. The woman opened the rear door and raked the chicken shit and straw out onto the ground. Santana got out of the car, leaving the engine running. "This is it. This is our transportation to Havana."

"You gotta be shitting me!"

"Put your stuff in the trunk."

"Can I have some water?"

"In the house. They don't have any food, so don't ask."

The young woman took him inside. There was an old woman in a rocker, and she nodded at him. His escort dipped him a glass of water from a pail that sat in the kitchen. He drained it and she gave him another.

"You speak English?"

"A little," she said.

"What's your name?"

"María."

"You know Santana?"

"Who?"

Yocke jerked his head toward the yard. "Santana."

"Oh. Pablo." She smiled. "He's my brother."

Yocke handed back the glass. "Thanks. *Gracias.*"

"De nada."

Santana was waiting in the car. Yocke walked around and opened the front seat passenger door. "You ride in back," Santana told him. "María's coming with us."

Yocke dusted the rear seat as best he could and sat. The odor of chicken shit wouldn't be too bad at speed if they kept the windows down. María came out of the house with three or four plastic jugs filled with water. She put them in the trunk and climbed in beside her brother.

As they rolled out of the farmyard, Yocke could hear the transmission grinding. Or the differential. Perhaps both. "This thing'll never make it to Havana."

"Beats walking," Santana said.

They had gone just a mile or so when they came to a two-lane asphalt road running east and west. Santana turned right, west.

For the first few hours the car made good time, rolling along at twenty-five or thirty miles per hour, Yocke estimated. The speedometer needle never moved off the peg. The few vehicles on the road were all westbound. The flatbeds of cane trucks were packed with people, the old cars similarly stuffed and riding on their frames. Occasional knots of people walked west alongside the road.

Cane fields swept away to the horizon to the north and south across the flat, rolling fields, under a bright sun. Here and there shacks near the roads stood deserted and empty, with not even a chicken or pig in sight.

After two hours they came to a town. It was a real town, with streets and throngs of people in the streets. The car took an hour to creep through as Santana leaned out and shouted to knots of people in doorways, huddled around radios, *"Que pasa?"*

"The prisons have been emptied," Santana told Jack Yocke at one point. "The guards refused to fire on the people, who liberated the prisoners."

On the west side of town the road was jammed with walking people: men, women, children, the elderly, the lame. The western pilgrimage grew denser at every crossroads, every village.

The Chevy proceeded little faster than the walking people, who gently parted in front of it to let it past and closed in again behind, like water in the wake of a boat's passage.

The radiator boiled over around noon. The three of them piled out and sat beside the car in a little shady strip as the human stream trudged by. Some of the people carried chickens and ducks with their feet tied together. Every now and then a man passed with a pig arranged around his shoulders.

Yocke mopped his face with his shirttail and relieved himself beside the road. Everyone else was doing likewise. There was no embarrassment: there was nowhere else to do it. He stood there with his back to the road looking out across the miles of growing cane and breathing deeply of the sweet odor, and made a wet spot on the red earth.

An army truck came by, also headed west. In addition to the troops packed willy-nilly in the back, civilians had clambered aboard, poultry, kids, and all. Yocke thought the truck looked like Noah's ark as it slowly breasted the human sea, trailing diesel fumes. He caught a glimpse of a goat amid the people and protruding rifles.

Eventually the steam from the Chevy's tired engine subsided. Water from bottles in the trunk was added, the worn-out radiator cap was replaced and carefully wired down, then Santana got behind the wheel and cranked the engine. It caught. For Santana's benefit, Yocke raised his hands in thanksgiving, then took his place amid the chicken dung.

In late afternoon the radiator failed catastrophically. Clouds of steam billowed from around the hood.

They pushed the car off the road, into the cane, and took what they could carry from the car. Yocke had to have the computer. He took the toothbrush and razor from the vinyl bag and put them in his pockets. His passport and money were already in his pocket. He changed shirts and socks. The rest of it he left.

As Yocke stood on the road beside the car waiting for the others, another army truck approached. A young woman sat on the left front fender facing forward with her blouse open breast-feeding a baby, her long, dark hair streaming gently in the shifting air currents. Her attention was concentrated on the child. She appeared golden in the evening sunlight. Yocke stood transfixed until the truck was far up the road and the young madonna no longer visible.

His companions were already walking westward with the throng. Jack Yocke eased the strap of the computer on his shoulder and set off after them.

At dusk, with the sunset still glowing ahead of them, they came to a burned-out Soviet-made armored personnel carrier—APC—sitting fifty feet or so off the road in a drainage ditch. Jack Yocke walked over to look.

A missile had punched a neat hole in the side armor; explosion and fire had done the rest. Burned, mutilated bodies lay everywhere, perhaps a dozen. Several reasonably intact bodies lay on the side of the ditch. These men had been shot by someone who had gotten behind them. The holes in their backs were neat and precise. Very military. The bodies had begun to bloat, stretching the clothing on the corpses drum-head tight.

One of the men was very young, just a boy really. He had been dead a while, perhaps since this morning. Flies crawled around his mouth and eyes and ears. A shift in the breeze gave Yocke a full dose of the stench.

He staggered out of the ditch retching.

Santana and the young woman were waiting for him. Together they rejoined the human river flowing westward in the gathering dusk.

They reached the outskirts of Havana about nine p.m.

The streets were packed. People everywhere. Water could be had but no food. Those who had poultry or the carcasses of dogs built a fire out of anything that would burn and roasted them. The smoke wafted through the streets and between the buildings: the shadows it cast under the flickering streetlights played wildly over the crowd. Some people were drunk, shouting and singing and scuffling.

Government warehouses had been looted earlier in the afternoon, Santana learned, but the food had been eaten by those who carried it off. *Mañana,* tomorrow, the Yankees would send food. That was the rumor, oft-repeated, as hungry children wailed endlessly.

Castro was being held by the revolutionary committee, according to the radios, which were being played at maximum volume from every window. Fidel and his brother and the top government officials would be shot tomorrow in the Plaza de Revolución. *Viva Cuba! Cuba Libre!*

People stretched out in the street to sleep. Whole families. The crowd swirled and eddied and flowed around them, flowed toward the center of the city and the government offices around the Plaza de Revolución. Yocke followed Hector Santana and his sister.

The American was exhausted. The endless walking, the lack of sleep and food—these things had taken their toll. He wanted to slump down on the first vacant stretch of pavement he came to and sleep forever.

On he trudged, following Santana, following the crowd through the smoke and noise and dim lights.

When he reached the plaza he stopped and gaped. It was huge, covering several acres, and was packed with people. There wasn't room to lie down. People stood shoulder to shoulder, more people in one place than Jack Yocke had ever seen in his lifetime. The crowd was alive, buzzing endlessly with thousands of conversations. As he stood and looked in awe, chants broke out. "Cu-ba, Cu-ba, Cu-ba," over and over, growing as tens of thousands of voices picked it up. The sound had a low, pulsating thud to it that seemed to make the building walls shake.

Then Yocke realized he had lost Santana. He didn't care. He had to sleep.

He turned and retraced his steps, away from the plaza. Several blocks away he found an alley. It was full of sleeping people. He felt his way in, found a spot, and lay down. The chanting wasn't as loud here, two blocks from the square, but it was clear, distinctive, sublime. "Cu-ba, Cu-ba," repeated endlessly, like a religious chant.

Jack Yocke drifted into sleep thinking about dead soldiers and madonnas on army trucks and listening to that relentless sound.

They shot Castro around ten o'clock the next morning. He was shot first. The dictator was led out onto the platform where he had harangued his fellow countrymen for thirty-one years. Behind him were arrayed his lieutenants. All had their hands tied in front of them.

Yocke listened as a speaker read the charges over a microphone that blasted his voice to every corner of the square. Yocke understood little of it, not that it mattered. He elbowed and shoved and fought his way through the crowd, trying to get closer.

Ten men and women were selected from the crowd and allowed to climb up to the platform. Castro was led to a wall and faced around at the volunteers, who were lined up and given assault rifles by soldiers who stood beside them.

The speaker was still reading when someone opened fire. Three or four shots, ripping out. Castro went down.

He was assisted to his feet. The speaker stopped talking.

Someone shouted an order and all ten rifles fired raggedly.

The dictator toppled and lay still.

The soldiers took back their rifles and the members of the firing squad were sent back into the crowd. More leaped forward, too many. Ten men and women were selected and the rest herded back, forcibly, as three of the dictator's comrades were led over to stand beside his body. A jagged fusillade felled all three.

The scene was repeated four more times. Then a man with a pistol walked along and fired a bullet downward into each head. After six shots he had to stop and reload. Then six more. And finally four more.

"Viva Cuba! Viva Cuba! Viva Cuba!"

For the first time since the drama began, the reporter tore his gaze from the platform and looked at the faces of the people around him. They were weeping. Men, women, children—on every face were tears. Whether they were weeping for what they had lost or what they had gained, Jack Yocke didn't know.

About two that afternoon he was wandering along a mile or so from the square, by the front of a large luxury hotel on a decently wide street that had obviously been built in the bad old days B.F.—Before Fidel—when he heard his name called.

"Jack Yocke! *Hey, Jack! Up here!*"

He elevated his gaze. On a third-floor balcony, gesturing madly, stood Ottmar Mergenthaler. "Jesus Christ, Jack! Where the hell you been?"

CHAPTER THIRTEEN

★ ★ ★ ★ ★ ★ ★ ★ ★ ★ ★

THREE hours into his first day as a junior—*very* junior—weenie on the Joint Staff of the JCS, Lieutenant Toad Tarkington was wondering if perhaps Captain Grafton hadn't been right. Maybe he should have asked to have his shore tour cut short and gone back to sea. Sitting at a borrowed desk in an anonymous room without windows deep in the Pentagon, Toad was working his way through a giant hardbound manual of rules and regulations that he was supposed to be reading carefully, embedding permanently in the gray matter. He glanced surreptitiously around the large office to see if there was a single other O-3 in sight.

He was going to be the coffee and paperclips guy. He knew it in his bones. Rumor had it there were other peasants with railroad tracks on the staff, although he hadn't yet seen a live one.

At the next desk over a female navy lieutenant commander was giving him the eye. Uh-oh! He turned the page he had been praying over for five minutes and examined the title of the next directive in the book. Something about uniforms, shiny shoes, and all that. He initialed it in the stamped box provided, sneaked a glance at the lieutenant commander— she was still looking—and pretended to read.

Without moving his head he checked his watch. Ten thirty-two. Oh, my God! He would be dead of boredom by lunchtime. If his heart stopped right now he would not fall over, he would just remain frozen here staring at this page until his uniform rotted off or they decided to buy new desks and move this one out. Maybe some of these other people sitting here at the other twenty-seven desks were already dead and nobody knew. Perhaps he should get a mirror and check all the bodies for signs of respiration. Maybe—the telephone buzzed softly. His first call!

He grabbed it and almost fumbled the receiver onto the floor.

"Lieutenant Tarkington, sir."

"Is this Robert Tarkington?" A woman's voice.

"Yes it is."

"Mr. Tarkington, this is Nurse Hilda Hamhocker, at the Center for Disease Control?"

He glanced around to see if anyone was eavesdropping. Not noticeably so, anyway. "Yes."

"I'm calling to ask if you have known a woman named Rita Moravia?"

"Let's see. Rita Moravia . . . a short, squatty woman with a Marine Corps tattoo and a big wart right on the end of her nose? I do believe I know her, yes."

"I mean, have you *known* her? In the biblical sense, Mr. Tarkington. You see, she's one of our clients and has given your name as an 'intimate' partner."

The lieutenant commander was all ears, surveying him from beneath a droopy bang.

"That list of partners is modestly short, I trust."

"Oh, no. Tragically long, Mr. Tarkington. Voluminous. Like the Manhattan telephone directory. We've been calling for three months and we're only now getting to the Ts."

"Yes. I have *known* her, Nurse Hamhocker."

"Would you like to know Miss Moravia again, Mr. Tarkington?"

"Well, yes, this very minute would be just perfect. Right here on my clean borrowed desk while everyone watches. But you see, the dear little diseased squatty person is never around. Not *ever!*"

"Oh, my poor, poor Horny Toad. It's that bad, is it?"

"Yes, Rita, it's that bad. Are you ever coming home?"

"Christmas leave starts in a week, lover. I'll be coming into National on United." She gave him the flight number and time. "Meet me, will you?"

"Plan on getting known again in the parking lot."

"If you'll make that a backseat, I'll say yes."

"Okay, the backseat."

"I'll hold you to that, Toad. 'Bye."

" 'Bye, babe." He cradled the instrument and took a deep breath.

The lieutenant commander arched an eyebrow and raked her errant bang back into place. Then she concentrated on the document on the desk in front of her.

Toad took another deep breath, sighed, and resumed his study of the read-and-initial book. Ten minutes later he found a memo that he read with dismay. "Staff is reminded," the document said—rather too officially and formally for Toad's taste—"that classified information shall not be discussed over unsecure telephones. [Numerous cites.] To ensure compliance with this regulation, all telephones in the staff spaces are continuously monitored while in use and the conversations taped by the communications security group."

"Stepped in it again, Toad-man," he muttered.

His stupor had returned and was threatening to become terminal ennui when Captain Jake Grafton entered the room, scanned it once, and headed in Toad's direction. Toad stood as the captain walked over and pulled a chair around. As usual, both officers wore their blue uniforms. But, Toad noticed with a pang, the two gold stripes around each of his sleeves contrasted sharply with the four on each of the captain's.

"Sit, for heaven's sake. If you pop up every time a senior officer comes around in this place, you'll wear out your shoes."

"Yessir." Toad put his bottom back into his chair.

"Howzit goin'?"

"Just about finished the read-and-initial book." Toad sighed. "What do you do around here, anyway?"

"I'm not sure. Seems to change every other week. Right now I'm doing analyses of counternarcotics operations from information sent over by the FBI and DEA. What can the military do to help and how much will it cost? That kind of thing. Keeps me jumping."

"Sounds sexy."

"Today it is. And it has absolutely nothing to do with training troops and aircrews or sustaining combat readiness."

"Exciting, too, eh?"

Jake Grafton gave Tarkington a skeptical look.

"Well, at least we're pentaguys," Toad said earnestly, "ready to help chart the future of mankind, along with a thousand or so equally dedicated and talented Joint Staff souls. Makes me tingle."

"Pentaguys?"

"I just made that up. Like it?" The lieutenant's innocent face broke into a grin, which caused his cheeks to dimple and exposed a set of perfect teeth. Deep creases radiated from the corners of his eyes.

The captain grinned back. He had known Tarkington for several years; one of Toad's most endearing qualities was his absolute refusal to take anything seriously. This trait, the captain well knew, was rare among career officers, who learned early on that literally everything was *very important.* In the highly competitive world of the peacetime military, an officer's ranking among his peers might turn on something as trivial as how often he got a haircut, how he handled himself at social functions, the neatness of his handwriting. For lack of a neat signature a fitness report was a notch lower than it might have been, so a choice assignment went to someone else, a promotion didn't materialize. . . . There was an acronym popular now in the Navy that seemed to Jake to perfectly capture the insanity of the system: WETSU—We Eat This Shit Up. One battleship captain that Jake knew had even adopted WETSU as the ship's motto.

Toad Tarkington seemed oblivious to the rat race going on around him. One day it would probably dawn on him that he was a rodent in the maze with everyone else, but that realization hadn't hit him yet. Jake fervently hoped it never would.

"So what am I gonna be doing around here to thwart the forces of evil?" Toad asked.

"Officially you're one of thirty junior officer interns. For a while, at least, you'll be in my shop assisting me."

"How about them apples!" Toad's eyebrows waggled. "I'll start by drafting up a memo for you to fire off to the Joint Chiefs: 'Shape up or ship out!' Don't worry, I'll make it more diplomatic than that, take the edge off, pad it and grease it. Then memos for the FBI and DEA. We'll—"

"We'll start in the morning at oh-seven-thirty," Jake said, rising from his chair. He looked around again, taking it all in. "What do you think of this place, anyway?"

"All these different kinds of uniforms, it looks like a bus drivers' convention." Toad lowered his voice. "Don't you think the Air Farce folks look like they work for Greyhound?"

"I'll give you the same advice my daddy gave me, Tarkington, when he put me on a bus and sent me off to the service. Keep your mouth shut and your bowels open, and you'll do okay." Jake Grafton walked away.

Toad grinned broadly and settled back into his chair.

"I couldn't help overhearing your insensitive remark, Lieutenant," the lieutenant commander at the desk across the aisle informed him.

Toad swiveled. The lieutenant commander reminded him of his third-grade teacher, that time she caught him throwing spitballs. She had that look.

"I'm sorry, ma'am."

"Our friends in the Air Force are very proud of their uniform."

"Yes, ma'am. No offense intended."

"Who was that captain?"

"Captain Grafton, ma'am."

"He was very informal with you, Lieutenant." The way she said "lieutenant" made it sound like the lowest rank in the Guatemalan National Guard. "Here at Joint Staff we're much more formal."

"I'm sure." Toad tried out a smile.

"This is a *military* organization."

"I'll try to remember," Toad assured her, and stalked off toward the men's head.

Henry Charon eased the car to a stop in front of the abandoned farmhouse and killed the engine. He rolled down his window and sat looking at the overgrown fields and the stark leafless trees beyond.

The dismal gray sky seemed to rest right on the treetops. The crisp air smelled of snow.

He had followed the dirt road for four miles, just a rut through the forest, and made it through a mudhole that he had explored with a stick before he tried it. There were tire tracks that he thought were at least a month old, left by deer hunters. Nothing fresh. That was why he had selected this dirt road after he had examined three others.

He was deep in the Monongahela National Forest, four hours west of Washington in the West Virginia mountains. Henry Charon took a deep deep breath and smiled. It was gorgeous here.

He pulled on his coat and hat and locked the car, then walked back along the road in the direction from which he had come. He inspected the remnants of an apple orchard and the brush that had grown up on a two-acre plot that had once been a garden.

When he had walked about a mile, he left the road and began climbing the hillside. He proceeded slowly, taking his time, pausing frequently to listen and look. He moved like a shadow through the gray trees, climbing steadily to the top of the ridge, then along it with the abandoned farm, which was somewhere below him on his left. He intended to circle the farm to ensure there were no people nearby. If there were he would hear or see enough to warn him of their presence.

As he moved Henry Charon examined the trees, noting the places where deer had browsed, feeling the pellet droppings and estimating their age. This was his first outing in the hardwood forests of the eastern United States. He felt like a youngster again, exploring and greeting new things with delight. He saw where the chipmunks had opened their acorns and he spent five minutes watching a squirrel watching him. He examined a groundhog hole and ran his fingers along the scars in a young sapling that a buck had used to rub the velvet from his antlers earlier this autumn. He heard a woodpecker drumming and detoured for a hundred yards to glimpse it.

He had been in the fourth grade when he found a biography of Daniel Boone in the school library. The book had fascinated him and, he admitted now to himself as he glided silently through the forest, changed his life. The years Boone spent alone in Kentucky hunting wild game for furs and food and avoiding hostile Indians had seemed to young Henry Charon to be the ultimate in adventure. And now, at last, he was in the type of forest Boone had known so well. True, it wasn't the virgin forest of two hundred and fifty years ago, but still . . .

He was thinking of Boone and the hunting years when he saw the doe. She was browsing and had her back to him. He froze. Something, instinct perhaps, made her turn her head and swivel her large ears for any sound that should not have been there.

Henry Charon stood immobile. The deer's eyes and brain were alert to movement, so Charon held every muscle in his body absolutely still. He even held his breath.

The gentle wind was from the northwest, carrying his scent away from her as she sampled the breeze. Satisfied at last, she resumed her browsing.

Slowly, ever so slowly, he stepped closer. He froze whenever her head position would allow his movement to be picked up by her peripheral vision.

He was only twenty-five feet or so from her when she finally saw him.

She had moved unexpectedly. Now she stood stock still, tense, ready to flee, her ears bent toward him to catch the slightest sound.

Henry Charon remained motionless.

She relaxed slightly and started toward him, her ears still attuned, her eyes fixed on him.

Surprised, he moved a hand.

The deer paused, wary, then kept coming.

Someone tamed her, he thought. *She's tame!*

The doe came to him and sniffed his hands. He presented them for her inspection, then scratched between her ears.

Her coat was stiff and thick to his touch. He stroked her and felt it. He spoke to her and watched her ears move to catch the sound of his voice.

The memory must have been strong. She seemed unafraid.

The moment bothered him, somehow. Man had changed the natural order of things and Henry Charon knew that this change was not for the better. For her own safety the doe should flee man. Yet he had not the heart to frighten her. He petted her and spoke softly to her as if she could understand, then watched in silence when she finally walked away.

The doe paused and looked back, then trotted off into the trees. She was soon lost from sight. Thirty seconds later he could no longer hear her feet among the leaves that carpeted the ground.

An hour later he arrived back at his car. He opened the trunk and got some targets, which he posted on the wall of the ramshackle farmhouse.

The pistols were first. All 9 mm, he fired them two-handed at the target at a distance of ten paces. There were four pistols, all identical Smith & Wesson automatics. He fired a clipful through each. One seemed to have a noticeably heavier trigger pull than the others, and he set it aside. When he finished, he carefully retrieved all the spent brass. If he missed one it was no big deal, but he didn't want to leave forty shells scattered about.

After he posted a fresh target, he took the three rifles and moved off to fifty yards.

The rifles were Winchester Model 70s in .30-06, with 3×9 variable scopes. He squeezed off three rounds from the first rifle, checked the target with the binoculars, and adjusted the scope. All three bullets in his third string formed a group that could be covered with a dime. Charon carefully placed every spent cartridge in his pocket.

After repeating the process with the second and third rifle he moved back to one hundred yards. He fired three, checked the target, fired again.

The final group from each rifle formed a small, nickel-sized group about one inch above his point of aim. This with factory ammunition.

Satisfied, he wiped the weapons carefully and stored each in a soft guncase and repacked them in the trunk of the car.

The final item he carried several hundred yards up the hill. Then he came back to the car and backed it down the road past the first bend.

From the floor of the backseat he took several old newspapers. He retrieved the targets from the wall of the house and added them to the newspapers.

On the side of the other hill, high up near the tree line, was a fairly prominent outcropping of rock. Standing on the rock and using the binoculars, he could just make out the item he had left amid the trees and leaves on the other side of the little valley. At least three hundred yards, he decided. Closer to four hundred.

He used the targets and wadded up sheets of newsprint to build a small fire. To this he added sticks and twigs and a relatively dry piece of a dead limb. Then he walked back across the valley.

The weapon was in an olive-drab tube. Ridiculously simple instructions were printed on the tube in yellow stenciled letters. He followed them. Tube on right shoulder, eyepiece open, power on, crosshairs on the rock outcropping—listen for the tone. There it is! Heat source acquired.

Charon squeezed the trigger.

The missile left in a flash and roar. Loud but not terribly so. It shot across the valley trailing fire and exploded above the rock ledge, seemingly right in the fire.

Carrying the now empty tube, Henry Charon walked back across the valley. The weapon had gone right through the fire and exploded against the base of a tree on the other side. The shrapnel had sprayed everywhere. The bark of the trees was severely flayed: one small wrist-thick tree trunk had been completely severed by flying shrapnel. The tree the missile had impacted was severely damaged. No doubt it and several other trees would eventually die.

Satisfactory. Quite satisfactory. The other two missiles should work equally well.

He put the remnants of the fire completely out, scattered the charred wood, and dumped dirt on the site where it had been.

Fifteen minutes later Henry Charon started the car. The empty cartridges and spent missile launcher were all in the trunk. He had found a likely spot to bury them on the way in, about two miles back. There was enough daylight left.

Smiling, thinking about the doe, Henry Charon slipped the transmission into drive and turned the car around.

CHAPTER FOURTEEN

* * * * * * * * * * *

HARRISON Ronald Ford drove McNally's old Chrysler that evening.
Pure luck, he later decided. He picked up the guard at a Seven-Eleven at
nine o'clock that night and together they drove to the old Sanitary Bakery
warehouse on Fourth Street NE, on the edge of the railyard. The guard
didn't say much—he never did. About twenty-five or so, he called
himself Tooley.

The window openings in the lower two levels of the ancient bakery
warehouse were blocked up with concrete blocks. The windows in the
upper levels showed the ravages of rocks and wind. A high chain-link
fence surrounded the property out to the Fourth Street NE sidewalk and
the dirt street that ran along the north side. Inside the fence were about a
dozen garbage trucks. Watching through the wire as Ford rumbled by
were two Dobermans.

He pulled into the parking area on the south side of the building and
walked toward the only door, which had steel bars welded over it, as
Tooley trailed along. Two other cars sat in the empty lot.

Ford opened the door. Tooley never opened doors, preferring to let the
driver do it. He was being paid to look tough and shoot, if necessary, and
that was all he was going to do.

Ike Randolph was there supervising the cutting and packaging operation, as usual. McNally had used this warehouse for only three days now,
and in a few more, anytime the whim struck him, he would change to
another location. Not that Freeman was or had ever been within a mile of
the building. That's what he hired Ike and the others for. If the cops
raided the place, the hired help could take the fall.

"Okay," Ike said and spread out a large map of the city. "Here's the
route tonight and where to take the stuff. Pay attention." He traced the
route he wanted Harrison Ronald to follow as Tooley and one of the guys
from the chase car watched over his shoulder. Two deliveries. When Ike
finished, Harrison then traced the route, calling out streets and turns,
proving that he knew it.

"You got it."

The gunnies from the chase car said little. In their early twenties, wearing expensive, trendy clothes, they looked, Harrison thought, exactly like what they were, drug guys with more money than they knew how to spend. Which was precisely the impression they hoped to create. In the world of the inner city these young men had spent their lives in, the druggies had the bucks and the choice ass—they had the *status.* Tonight, as usual, these two young gunnies stood around looking tough and with it.

The little sweet piece was also there, and Harrison Ronald flirted with her to keep up appearances. She flirted right back as Tooley watched, looking bored.

"She's a hooker, man," he told Harrison as they walked through the empty lower floor of the warehouse toward the entrance. Harrison carried the stuff in a plain brown grocery bag. "Uses so much of that shit she's cutting, Freeman *charges* her to work here."

"So what's your bitch, Tooley? She won't go down on you?"

"Stick it in that, Z, and it'll rot right off. You won't have nothing left to piss through but some grotty ol' pubic hair."

The guard at the door handed Tooley and the chase car crew Browning 9-mm automatics. As Harrison watched, Tooley popped the clip out, inspected it, then slid it home. He cocked the weapon, pulled back the slide just enough to glimpse brass, then lowered the hammer and put the pistol in his coat pocket. The other two men did the same, their evening ritual.

Now the guard handed Tooley an Uzi. He inspected the clip to ensure it was fully loaded, then pulled the bolt back into the cocked and ready position and engaged the safety. Then he reached for the grocery sack the guard offered him and inserted the weapon in it. After checking their Uzis, the two gunmen put them under their coats and walked to their car as the guard watched through the one dirty window. Satisfied, he opened the door again and motioned to Tooley and Harrison Ronald.

Tooley got into the backseat of the Chrysler while Harrison Ronald slid behind the wheel and put the dope on the floor on the passenger's side.

Two youngsters about ten years old were playing basketball on the street. The hoop was mounted on a backboard on a pole right by the edge of the pavement. They stood aside while Harrison eased the car past them and headed north, toward Rhode Island Avenue. The chase car, a dark Pontiac Trans-Am, followed four car lengths behind.

Ford glanced in the rearview mirror. Tooley had the Uzi out and was examining the safety.

"Put that fucking thing down where nobody can see it."

"Just drive, mother."

"And point it in some other direction."

Tooley grinned. He didn't have a nice grin. He kept the gun aimed in the center of Ford's back. "I told you to drive, motherfuck."

At Rhode Island the light was red. Waiting, Ford checked the rearview mirror. Tooley was just sitting back there, watching the back of Ford's head, with his hand on the trigger and the gun pointed at Ford's back.

"Turn right here," he said.

"You heard Ike."

"Little change of plan." He prodded Harrison in the back of the neck with the barrel of the submachine gun.

The light turned green.

"Now! Turn right."

Ford kept his feet on the brake and clutch and sat staring into the rearview mirror, trying to read what was in Tooley's face.

"Do it, Z, or I'll blow your fucking brains right out the front windshield." Tooley jabbed him with the barrel, hard.

Ford cranked the wheel and turned right.

"Now what?"

"Just do like I tell you."

"Freeman'll kill you. Slow."

"Who's gonna tell him, man? You?"

"He'll find out. He always does."

"Your problem is your mouth. I've got a cure for that. Turn left up ahead on Thirteenth." Tooley glanced behind to see if the Trans-Am was following. It was.

As they went around the corner, Tooley looked over his shoulder again to check the chase car. As he did so Harrison Ronald stiffened, rose, and half twisted in his seat. He used the bottom of his hand in a swinging backhand chopping motion that caught Tooley in the throat.

The gunman gagged, then choked. The Uzi fell to the floor as he clawed at his throat. Harrison applied the brakes moderately and brought the Chrysler to a swift halt. Then he turned and chopped again with all his strength at the hands around Tooley's neck. His larynx crushed, the gunman collapsed.

The rear window and front windows both popped as a bullet punched a neat hole in them and left them crazed, with radiating and circular cracks.

Harrison Ronald Ford popped the clutch and slammed the accelerator down, both in one fluid motion.

The tires squawled and smoke poured from the rear wheel wells as the big engine revved and Ford tried to keep the steering wheel centered.

He cranked it over and slid around the first corner, braking hard, then jamming on the gas halfway through the turn. The engine snarled and responded with neck-snapping power.

The Trans-Am stayed with him. Several more shots. Another bullet punched glass. In the backseat Tooley was still struggling to breathe, the tendons in his neck standing out like cords, his feet kicking spasmodically.

Ford took another right, then shot across oncoming traffic in a sweeping left turn, still accelerating, onto Rhode Island northeast-bound.

The fat was in the fire now. The two men in the chase car had to kill him. If they didn't, Freeman McNally would kill *them,* just as surely as the sun would rise tomorrow.

Fifty, sixty, seventy . . . he stayed on the gas and weaved around slower traffic. The engine was willing and the tires gripped well. The Pontiac was behind, still coming.

What to do? Think. Swerve to avoid a VW turning left, straight through a red light with horn blazing. Eighty . . . He backed off the gas, afraid to go faster.

Cops—where are the fucking traffic cops with their fucking speed guns and ticket books?

He was going to get the green light at South Dakota Avenue. Amen. At the last instant he slammed on the brakes and swerved right and went around the corner on two wheels.

Back on the gas. Around a truck, brakes on hard for a sedan just piddling, skidding some, then clear and in the right lane and back on the throttle.

They were still following. Flashes from the passenger side. Another bullet punched through the glass and he felt several more thump into the bodywork.

He was up to ninety approaching Bladensburg, crowding the centerline. Another green light. Hallelujah! Feathering the brake he dropped to about fifty and used the whole street to make the sweeping right onto Bladensburg southwest-bound.

Now he was heading into the heart of the city, toward the Capitol, which was still four miles or so ahead. The Capitol area would be crawling with tourists and cops. Right now Harrison Ronald wanted to see the flashing lights of a police cruiser more than he wanted anything else.

As he sawed at the wheel and tapped the brakes and swerved to avoid traffic, he realized he would never outrun the car behind. In spite of his car's capabilities, the gunmen in the Trans-Am had the telling advantage. Harrison Ronald was trying to keep from killing pedestrians and motorists while the men behind didn't care. They had bet their lives when they decided to rip off Freeman McNally. If some little old lady got run over, that was her tough luck.

Harrison Ronald held his horn down. He slammed the accelerator to the floor and went through a yellow light at the New York Avenue intersection at seventy-five.

The headlights of the dark Trans-Am were almost fifty yards back. In the rearview mirror he saw someone pull into the intersection in front of the speeding Pontiac and get lightly clipped. The left front fender of the Trans-Am disintegrated, the man at the wheel fought desperately to hold it on the road, and the black car kept coming.

With horn braying and the big hemi engine throbbing, Harrison Ronald straddled the painted centerline. He used his left foot to flash the low and high beams up and down.

His luck couldn't hold. It didn't. A yellow light ahead. It would be red when he got there.

He slowed. The Trans-Am grew larger in the rearview mirror.

More bullets spanged into the Chrysler. One buried itself in the dashboard.

He picked a gap between the cars crossing in front of him and aimed the Chrysler for the gap. Now—clutch out and on the throttle, skidding some, going through, pedal to the floor.

He checked the mirror. With luck the Trans-Am would hit somebody or stop to avoid a collision.

No luck. The Pontiac shot a gap and kept coming, but too far back to shoot.

Now he was on Maryland Avenue, a boulevard that went straight as an arrow toward the Capitol building. The lighted dome rose straight ahead above the trees.

The four lanes were crowded. Harrison Ronald straddled the median, which scraped the bottom side of the Chrysler, a ripping, grinding sound that sounded loud even above the engine noise. Something came off the car. The muffler and tailpipe. He ran over three traffic signs but had to swerve from the median to avoid the lightpoles.

Avoiding one lightpole his wheel clipped the curb and the Chrysler swapped ends and skidded backwards, straight into a delivery truck.

The engine was still running. He had trouble getting the shift lever into first but he made it, and with the wheel cranked over, did a wheel-spinning 180 and got under way as the Trans-Am came thundering down on him with the guy leaning out of the passenger window spraying lead.

Several cars crashed together getting out of the way. One car ran through a parking lot and buried itself in a plate-glass window.

Ahead was a park, one of those blocks from which the major avenues in the city radiated. Harrison Ronald went through it. If he didn't the Trans-Am might gain more ground than he could afford to lose.

The front end parted with mother earth as it bucked the curb, but the rear wheels impacting the obstruction brought the nose down with a crash that jammed the front bumper into the concrete in a shower of sparks.

Luckily the park was deserted on a December night. He braked hard and slid around the statue in the center and jam accelerated. The dome of the Capitol was dead ahead.

The front wheels were vibrating badly now and he gripped the steering wheel tightly to hold on.

A skidding right turn, doing about sixty or seventy, onto Constitution Avenue westbound. Okay, goddammit, where are the cops?

Almost on cue he heard a siren over the unmuffled roar of the engine. Yet the Trans-Am was gaining.

The Mall—he would go across the grass of the Mall. Everybody and their brother would see them. Even as he considered it another burst of bullets came through the car.

Something stung his ear.

He swung right, hard, the car skidding out of control. It used the whole road and then some, bouncing off parked vehicles, but he ended up headed north on First.

The damned Pontiac was still with him.

He swung left onto D Street. Aha! Ahead on the left was the Labor Department building and the ramp that went under it down onto I-395. If he could make that turn and get down onto the freeway . . .

A semitractor crept around the corner and filled the street. He slammed on the brakes. Skidding again. Off the brakes, just by the truck on the right, slamming over parking meters, then hard right, down a couple blocks, left, on the gas.

The Pontiac was gaining. Hadn't they had enough? The siren—was it closer?

Ahead was the mall on the south side of the National Collection of Fine Arts. He went for it.

And a bus.

A huge bus, coming from right to left. He braked hard. Another bus following. He could make the gap. He shot through.

Behind him he heard tires squealing, then the sound of a crash.

Harrison Ronald applied the brakes firmly. He avoided some drunks and trash cans, then turned left on Ninth, joining with traffic.

In the rear seat Tooley looked very very dead. His lips and tongue were swollen, protruding, as were his eyes, which were focused on nothing at all.

Sometime during the chase one or more of the bags holding the cocaine had split, and the white powder was all over the passenger seat floor.

Harrison Ronald got out a hanky and wiped the stick shift knob, the light switch, the dashboard, the mirror, the steering wheel. Jesus, his prints were all over this car. Still . . .

He turned some corners and pulled into the first vacant spot by the curb he came to. He wiped the door lever and took a last wipe of the wheel. Then he switched the ignition off and got out. Pocketing the key, he took two seconds to rub the handkerchief over the outside door handle, then walked away. On the sidewalk he took the car key off the ring which also contained the key to his apartment. After wiping it with the cloth, he dropped the car key into the first trash barrel he came to.

Three blocks later he found a pay phone that still worked. He dialed

911 and reported the car stolen. When the dispatcher asked his name, he hung up.

The wailing of the sirens echoed from the buildings and seemed to come from every direction. There was blood on his cheek and his left ear was burning fiercely. His left arm was burning too. Blood there on his jacket.

The second number Harrison Ronald Ford dialed was the home phone of FBI Special Agent Thomas F. Hooper. "We have to talk. Now. A difficulty has arisen."

Harrison Ronald Ford was sitting on the steps on the south side of the Lincoln Memorial when Hooper came around the corner and slowly climbed up toward him. The spot Ford had selected was in the shadow, out of the spotlights that illuminated the columns around him.

"You okay?"

"Fucking arm feels like it's on fire."

The undercover man had removed his undershirt in a subway restroom and torn it into strips. He had his shirt and jacket unbuttoned now and sat holding one of the folded cotton strips against the groove in his left tricep.

"How bad is it?"

"Just a crease. Hurts like hell, though."

"Want to go to a doctor?"

"Nah. After a while I gotta go see Freeman and they'll do the doctoring there." Bullet wounds treated by a doctor had to be reported to police, so Ford didn't want to try and explain to Freeman how he had gotten away with a stunt like that.

In the dim light Hooper inspected Ford's face, then used one of the pieces of tee-shirt to swab the wound.

"You were lucky."

"That's true."

"You're gonna run out of luck."

"Has to happen."

"Why don't you quit now. We'll bust McNally, go with what we have."

Harrison sat in silence, thinking about it. Fifty feet away a couple held each other close and sat looking at the lights of the city. From where they sat, off to the left, they could see the white obelisk of the Washington Monument against the black sky. "How many casualties?"

"Ten dead, apparently. Plus that guy you killed in the car."

"He was going to kill me when we got to where he wanted to go."

"I understand. It was justified."

"I had to do it."

"I understand! Christ, don't sweat it. He was a shithead. He had it coming."

Harrison removed the makeshift bandage from his arm and held it out where he could see it. Fresh blood. He was still bleeding. He refolded it and ran it back inside his shirt.

"I didn't know what to do. There're never any cops around when you

"All out on the freeway writing speeding tickets," Hooper agreed. After a few moments, he asked, "Who's the Chrysler registered to?"

"Some derelict. The address on the registration certificate is a vacant lot. Freeman McNally owns it but you'll never prove it. And my prints are all over it."

"Any of his prints on it?"

"Not to my knowledge."

"Too bad."

Yeah, it was all too bad. Eleven people dead! Holy shit!

"C'mon. You've done enough. Let me take you to the doctor. We'll do a taped debrief tomorrow and I'll have you on the plane to Evansville tomorrow evening."

"Got a cigarette?"

"No."

"Reach inside my coat here and get one and light it for me, will ya?"

Hooper did so.

"Y'know," Harrison Ronald said after a bit, "I think this little deal is gonna get me in tight with Freeman. Somebody tried to rip him off. He's gonna be curious as a cat about what I know and then he's going after somebody."

"What do you know?"

"Nothing. Absolutely nothing."

"Maybe we could dream up something for you to know."

"Too dangerous, man. He'd check it out. If it doesn't check out, I'm dead. Just like that. Lying to Freeman McNally is like playing Russian roulette. You tell one and stop breathing while you wait to see if your brains are flying out the side of your head."

"There's got to be a profit in this for us someplace," Hooper said.

"A few more days. You'll see. Just a few more days." Harrison Ronald sighed. "C'mon, help me up. My ass is frozen and my legs are getting stiff. I gotta go see Freeman."

"What if he decides that you might have been in it with the others and it just got fucked up?"

"There's that," Harrison Ronald said sourly. "But you didn't have to say it, man."

"There's no telling," Hooper insisted. "It could go down like that."

"If it does, it's been nice knowing you."

"What about a wire? You could wear a wire. We could wait just a block away."

"You gotta be shitting me!"

Hooper sat back down and watched Ford go down the steps and turn east to go around the front of the Memorial. It was too late for the subway so he had some walking to do. Maybe he would call Freeman from someplace.

Hooper felt cold. The steps were cold and the air was cold and he was cold. He pulled his coat tightly around him and sat looking at the lights of Arlington.

CHAPTER FIFTEEN

★ ★ ★ ★ ★ ★ ★ ★ ★ ★

ELEVEN DEAD IN DRUG CHASE, the morning headline screamed.

In the backseat of his limo on the way to his office, White House chief of staff William C. Dorfman read the story with a growing sense of horror. Six passengers on a bus had been killed and five injured—three critically—at ten-eighteen p.m. last night when a 1988 Pontiac Trans-Am slammed into a busload of Japanese museum directors and their families on the street near the National Collection of Fine Arts. The Japanese had just attended a reception at the museum and were returning to their hotel when the Pontiac smashed into the side of the bus. Witnesses estimated the car was traveling at seventy miles per hour just prior to impact. The two men in the automobile had died instantly. Two Uzi submachine guns were found in the wreckage.

A husband and wife from Silver Spring died five or six minutes earlier when the same vehicle, chasing an older four-door sedan, precipitated a head-on collision at an intersection on Bladensburg Road. The driver of a large truck belonging to a wholesale grocer had swerved to avoid the Pontiac and had struck the car driven by the Maryland couple.

Finally, if all that weren't enough, the body of a black man in his midtwenties had been found in a bullet-riddled Chrysler abandoned on H Street, three blocks from the White House. Police believed this to be the car the Pontiac had chased. Ten pounds of cocaine and crack had been recovered from the car, which had also contained an Uzi submachine gun.

The story contained accounts by three or four witnesses who told of the passenger in the Pontiac blazing away with an automatic weapon at the Chrysler as it tore down Bladensburg Road and Maryland Avenue at speeds of up to ninety miles per hour. Eight vehicles had been reported with bullet damage and police expected to learn of more.

Two photos accompanied the story. One was of the Chrysler shot full of holes and the other was of a Japanese woman in a kimono drenched with blood being assisted toward an ambulance.

Before he finished the story, Dorfman snapped on the limo's small television. The morning show on the channel that came up was running footage of the wrecked bus with the nearly unrecognizable remains of the Pontiac buried in its side. Shots of ambulance attendants leading away crying, bleeding victims followed.

Oh, my God! Why did that woman have to be wearing a kimono?

As if the savings-and-loan insider fraud debacle and the crises in the Baltic republics and Cuba weren't enough! And to make life at the top truly perfect, George Bush had a press conference scheduled for this afternoon. *God!* The reporters would be in a feeding frenzy.

Dorfman turned down the sound on the television and dialed the car telephone.

"Why wasn't I informed of this bus incident last night?" he roared at the hapless aide who answered. He ignored the aide's spluttering. He knew the answer. Procedure dictated that the chief of staff be informed immediately of national security crises and international incidents, and a car-bus wreck had not fit neatly into either category. Still, he had to do something to blow off steam and the aide was an inviting target. The little wart never went beyond his instructions, never showed an ounce of initiative.

I'm going to have to get out of this fucking business before I have a heart attack, Dorfman told himself. I'm thirty pounds overweight and take those damn blood pressure pills and this shit is going to kill me. Sooner rather than later.

When he charged into his office, an aide started talking before Dorfman could open his mouth. "The Japanese ambassador wants an audience with the President. This morning."

"Get the Mouth in here." That was the White House press secretary. "And where's that memo Gid Cohen sent over here last week? The one that lists all the antidrug initiatives he recommends?"

Thirty seconds later the memo from Cohen was on his desk. Let's see, the AG wants to change the currency to make hoards worthless—we can do that. It'll piss off the bankers and change-machine manufacturers and little ol' ladies with mattresses full of the stuff, but . . . He wants special courts and more federal judges and prosecutors to handle drug cases: okay, bite the bullet and do it. He wants to fund a nationwide drug rehab program: we'll need hard dollar info on that. He wants to fold the DEA in with the FBI and make one superagency. Christ, that will drive the Democrats bonkers.

A national ID card? Dorfman wrote no and underlined it. More prisons, mandatory sentencing for drug crimes, changes in the rules of criminal procedure, a revision of the bail laws, an increased role for the military in interdicting smuggling . . .

Dorfman kept reading, marking yes, no, and maybe. When he had originally received this memo he glanced at it and discarded it as yet another example of Cohen's lack of sensitivity to political reality. Well, he told himself now, reality was changing fast.

When the press secretary came in, Dorfman didn't bother to look up. "What're you going to say about the bus deal?"

"That the President will have a statement at his news conference. The government offers its condolences on behalf of the American people to the citizens of Japan who lost relatives last night. A quote from the President that says this accident was a tragedy."

"Let me see the quote." Dorfman scanned the paper, then passed it back. "Okay. What is the President going to say at the news conference?"

"I've got two speechwriters working on it. Have something for you in about an hour."

"Go. Do it."

Two minutes later, with Cohen's memo in hand, William C. Dorfman headed for the Oval Office to see the President.

The secretary in his outer office called after him: "The attorney general's on the phone. He wants to come over and see the President. He has the director of the FBI with him."

"Okay."

Dorfman and Bush had framed a strategy to respond to the public relations crisis posed by the death of six Japanese VIPs and were fleshing it out when the attorney general and the director of the FBI were shown into the Oval Office fifteen minutes later.

"What do you have on this bus thing?" President Bush asked the FBI director.

"For public consumption, we're working on it, following every lead. Doing autopsies on the people in the cars. When we know who they are, we'll work backward. For you only, one of our undercover agents was driving the car being chased. He was delivering ten pounds of coke and crack for Freeman McNally's drug syndicate when the people who were supposed to be guarding the shipment tried to rip him off. Those were the three men who died, two in the Pontiac and one in the Chrysler."

Dorfman couldn't believe his ears. He goggled. "Say again. The part about the undercover agent."

"Our man was driving the Chrysler."

"FBI?"

"One of our undercover people, temporarily on loan to the FBI from his regular police job."

"A cop drove like a freaked-out maniac through the heart of downtown Washington and got *eleven people killed?*"

"What the hell do you think he ought to have done?" the director demanded. "Let them shoot him?"

"Well, Jesus, I think you ought to ask the Japanese ambassador that question. Maybe he can give you an answer. One escapes me just now."

George Bush broke in. "Our guy okay?"

"Got grazed by two bullets. But he's okay. Shook as hell."

"You got enough to arrest Freeman McNally?"

"No, sir," said Gideon Cohen. "We don't. Oh, we have it chapter and verse from the undercover man, but we're going to need more than just the testimony of one man. And most of his testimony will be hearsay. He's had little personal contact with McNally."

"When?"

"Soon. But not yet."

"The press is gonna crucify us," Dorfman muttered.

"Had to happen sooner or later," Gideon Cohen remarked to no one in particular.

"Explain."

"We've got over four hundred murders a year here in the District, something like eighty percent of them drug related. It was just a matter of time before some tourists or political bigwigs got caught in a crossfire."

"I don't buy that. This drug chase in the downtown sounds like sloppy police work to me. Where were the uniformed police while these people were playing Al Capone and Dutch Schultz on Constitution Avenue?"

Cohen sneered. "Jesus, Dorfman, get real! If four hundred middle-class white people had been slaughtered last year in Howard County, there'd have been a mass march on Washington before the Fourth of July. They'd have dragged you politics-as-usual guys out of the Capitol kicking and screaming and hung the whole damn crowd."

"I think we're wasting our time pointing fingers at the cops," George Bush said dryly and adjusted the trousers of his eight-hundred-dollar suit. "The Japanese ambassador is coming over in a little while to hand me my head on a plate. The country is in an uproar. So what was politically impossible last week is possible now. That's all any politician can ever try to do, Gid—the possible. I'm not the Pied Piper. I can't take them where they don't want to go. And I'm not apologizing for that. I'm not Jesus Christ either."

Bush picked up Cohen's wish list from his desk. "A federal ID card for every man, woman, and child in the country? That'll never wash. The Supreme Court says they can burn the flag as political protest. They'll be using these cards for toilet paper."

"That'd be nice to have, but—"

"A national, mandatory drug rehab program? For an estimated ten billion per year? Where are we going to get the money? For another federal bureaucracy that will be so big and bloated it won't help anybody."

"It would—"

"And an overhaul of the criminal justice system," the President continued. "'Streamline and eliminate delay' you say. The procedures of the criminal justice system, obsolete and inefficient though they are, are mandated by the Bill of Rights according to the nine wise men on the Supreme Court. We'd need a constitutional convention to revise the Bill of Rights. Despite widely held opinions to the contrary, I am not damn fool enough to advocate opening that Pandora's box."

Cohen said nothing.

"Some of this stuff we can do. I've marked the items. Now, Gid, you and Bill and the secretary of the Treasury get together and come up with specifics. You've got two hours. We'll get the Senate and House leadership over here and brief them, then we'll go to the press conference and see if I can get through that with a whole hide. I don't suppose they'll have many questions about Cuba or Lithuania or foreign aid to the Soviets, all subjects I've spent two days reviewing." He threw up his hands. "In the meantime the Japanese ambassador, one of the best friends America has in the Japanese government, wants to tell me what he thinks of American law enforcement. Mr. FBI Director, you can sit here with me and sweat through that."

This morning in his Pentagon cubicle Captain Jake Grafton read with professional interest the stories in the *Washington Times* and the *Post* about the chase and spectacular accident of the previous evening. As the senior officer in the Joint Staff counternarcotics section, he routinely read the papers to learn what the public press had to say about the drug problem. The press, he knew, defined the issues for the electorate, which in turn set the priorities for the politicians. The issues with which the government sought to grapple were those nebulous perceptions created by the passing of selected raw facts through these imperfect double filters: any public servant who failed to understand this basic truth was doomed to frustrated ineffectiveness. Despite the fact that he had spent his professional life in a military organization solving simpler, more clearly defined problems, Jake Grafton, farmer's son and history major, instinctively understood how things worked in a democracy.

At a cubicle behind him, Jake could hear one of his colleagues, an air force lieutenant colonel, explaining the operation of the computer terminals to Toad Tarkington. A terminal rested on every desk. Tarkington seemed to be soaking up the procedures with nonchalant ease. Jake glanced at the dark screen on his own desk and smiled wryly. He had struggled like Hercules to acquire computer literacy while Tarkington seemed to pick it up as naturally as breathing.

Beside the front-page story in the *Post* about the car-bus crash was another story that the captain read with interest. By Jack Yocke, datelined Havana, Cuba, it was, the tag line promised, the first in a five-part series.

The story was about a rural family and its trek to the capital to personally witness the downfall of Castro. Why they came, what they saw and ate, where they slept, what they wanted for themselves and their children, these were the strands that Yocke wove. The story was raw, powerful, and Jake Grafton was impressed. Perhaps there was more to Jack Yocke than—

The telephone interrupted his perusal of the paper. He folded it and laid it on his desk.

"Captain, would you come to my office, please."

Four minutes later he stood in front of his boss, a two-star army general. When he had first reported to the Joint Staff Jake had studied the organization chart carefully and, after counting, concluded that there were fifty-seven flag officers between him and the chairman of the Joint Chiefs, a four-star army general. Major General Franks was the fifty-seventh down from the top. Jake Grafton had already discovered how short that distance really was.

"Captain, would you go to the chairman's office on the E-Ring. He is going over to the White House in a few minutes and he wants the senior officer in the counternarcotics section to accompany him."

"Yes, sir," Jake Grafton said, and made his exit. He didn't ask General Franks what this was about because Franks probably didn't know.

Leaving the Joint Staff spaces, Jake Grafton was hailed by the door attendant. Jake returned Mr. James' greeting with a preoccupied smile.

Hayden Land was brusque this morning. "They're in a snit over at the White House. Dorfman ordered me to appear. Ordered me! That man has the personality of a cliff ape."

The general's aide accompanied Hayden Land and Jake to the White House. As they rode through the streets in the chairman's limo, General Land briefed both the junior officers: "The President is going to announce new initiatives to combat the drug business. The White House staff have two proposals that affect the military. They want to increase the number of army teams patrolling the Mexican border, and they want a carrier battle group put into the eastern Caribbean or the Gulf of Mexico."

"The Caribbean?" Jake Grafton echoed, his surprise evident.

"The idea is that the carrier's aircraft can help intercept and track suspicious air and surface traffic."

"We do that now with air force AWACS planes, sir. Nothing moves over the gulf that we don't know about. And to put a carrier in there will mean that it will have to be diverted from someplace else, probably the Med. We'll only have one boat in the Med."

"I talked to CNO about it this morning," General Land said. "Those were the points he made. All you have to do today is listen. I just thought that seeing it and hearing it firsthand would help you do the staff work to make it happen if the President orders it, which he probably will. His staff believes that the incident last night with the busload of Japanese tourists requires an immediate response. Apparently they've sold that to the President."

"Yessir," Jake Grafton said and took off his white cover for a moment to run his fingers through his thinning hair. "I don't think a carrier in the Gulf of Mexico is going to help them grab one more pound of cocaine than we are getting now. But putting a boat down there for any extended period of time will have a negative effect on our combat capability in the Med. It'll cut it in half."

The aide spoke for the first time. "Sir, I understand there's also a proposal to authorize the Air Force and Navy to shoot down planes that refuse to obey the instructions of interceptors?"

General Land nodded.

"That's been around a while," Jake said. "The general aviation pilots' organizations have squealed loudly. God only knows what some doctor putting along in his Skyhawk will do when he meets an F-16 up close and personal for the first time. Cessnas and Pipers going down in flames over the Florida beaches will make great television."

"The doctors and dentists had better find someplace else to fly," General Land said in a tone that ended the conversation. "This drug mess just went from boiling to superheated. The administration is going to whale away with everything they can lay their hands on. Anybody that doesn't want to be hurt had better get the hell out of the way."

That comment seemed to capture the essence of the atmosphere at the White House. Jake stood against the wall and obeyed General Land's order: he kept his mouth firmly shut. He listened to William C. Dorfman brief the senators and congressmen on the initiatives ordered by the President, and he watched the President explain his reasoning to the senior officials.

"Gentlemen, the American people have had enough. I've had enough. We're going to put a stop to this drug business. We can't allow it to continue."

Senator Hiram Duquesne spoke up: "Mr. President, everyone's mad right now, but sooner or later they're going to sober up. I'm not about to sit silently and watch the rights of American citizens trampled by cops and soldiers on a witch hunt."

"We're not hunting witches, Hiram," the President said. "We're hunting drug smugglers and drug dealers."

A few smiles greeted this remark, but no chuckles.

"How long is this state of emergency going to last?" Duquesne pressed. Jake Grafton had met Senator Duquesne before, a year ago when he was working on the A-12 project. Apparently Duquesne hadn't mellowed any these past twelve months.

"I haven't declared a state of emergency."

"Call it what you like," Hiram Duquesne shot back. "How long?"

"Until we get results."

"It's going to cost a lot of money to change the currency," another senator pointed out. "You going to want to do it again next year?"

"I don't know."

"This marriage of the FBI and DEA," said Senator Bob Cherry. "I think that'll go over like a lead brick with Congress. The last thing this country needs is a bigger, more powerful police bureaucracy."

"It's efficiency I'm after."

Bob Cherry raised his eyebrows. "You won't get it with that move. More layers of paper pushers means less efficiency, not more. All you get when you add bureaucrats is more inertia. And a big police bureaucracy that can't be stopped is the last thing this country need or wants."

"I want to try it," the President insisted.

"Good luck," Cherry said.

"I need you on this, Bob. I'm asking for bipartisan support. I'm asking for your help."

"Mr. President, we in Congress are getting just as much, if not more, heat about that incident last night than you are. People want to know why tourists should have to run the risk of being slaughtered in the streets just to visit the capital of this country. My office this morning was a madhouse. We had to take the phones off the hooks. But Congress is not going to be stampeded. I can promise you this: we'll immediately look at your proposals, and those that have a chance of working we'll approve. Speedily. Those that don't . . ." He shrugged.

That evening at dinner Jake Grafton told his wife about his day.

"On television one of the commentators said the President has panicked," Callie told him.

Jake snorted. "And last year they said he was timid. The poor devil gets it from every side."

"Will these proposals work? Can the drug crisis be solved?"

The captain took his time answering. "There aren't any easy solutions. There are a lot of little things that will each have some effect on the problem. But there are no easy, simple, grand solutions just lying around waiting to be discovered. None."

"You're saying drugs are here to stay."

"At some level, yes. We humans have learned to live with alcohol and tobacco and prostitution—we're going to have to learn to live with dope."

"Even if it ruins people's lives?" Amy asked.

Jake Grafton chewed a bite of ham while he thought about that one. "A lot of things can ruin lives. People get so fat their hearts give out. They literally eat themselves to death. Should we have a law that regulates how much you can eat?"

"Drugs are different," Amy said.

"Indeed they are," Callie said, and gave her husband a sidelong glance with an eyebrow ominously arched.

Jake Grafton wisely changed the subject.

Later Callie said, "Did you read that terrific article in today's paper that Jack Yocke wrote about Cuba?"

"Yeah."

"I'm inviting him and his girlfriend over for dinner Saturday night, if he's back from Cuba. I'll call him tomorrow at the paper."

"Oh."

"Now, Jake, don't start that. I had him in class all semester and he is a bright young man with a lot of talent. You should take the time to get to know him."

"Doesn't look like I'm getting an option."

"Now dear, you know better than that."

"Okay, okay. Invite him over. If you think he's a nice guy, I'm sure he is. After all, look how right you were about me."

"Maybe you should reevaluate, Callie," Amy said tartly, and went off to her bedroom to do her homework.

CHAPTER SIXTEEN

★ ★ ★ ★ ★ ★ ★ ★ ★ ★ ★

THE wind was out of the northwest at fifteen or twenty knots. Small flakes of snow were driven almost horizontally in against the sage and juniper that covered the sloping sides of the arroyo. Higher up on the hillsides the pines showed a tinge of white, but the dirt road leading down the arroyo was still free from accumulation.

From a window in his living room, Henry Charon scanned the scene yet again.

The snow would accumulate as the day wore on and deepen significantly during the night. How much depended only on the amount of moisture left in the clouds coming down from the San Juans. The air was certainly cold enough. It leaked around the doorsill and the edges of the window and felt cold on his face.

Charon inserted another chunk of piñon in the wood stove. Then he went into the bedroom and got out the old .45 Colt automatic he kept in the drawer by the dresser and checked to ensure it was loaded, with a cartridge in the chamber. It was. He shoved it between his belt and the small of his back and pulled the bulky sweatshirt down so it couldn't be seen. Then he went back into the living room.

He liked sitting in the old easy chair here by the stove, with the window on his right. From it he could see the barn and the road, and against the sky, several tall hills. The mountains that were normally visible were obscured by clouds this morning.

Really, when you thought about it, it was a shame that life doesn't go on forever. To sit here and watch the winters, to spend the summer evenings on the porch listening to the meadowlarks and crickets, to step out in the morning with a rifle under your arm and walk off up the trail looking for deer and elk as the sky was shot with fire by the rising sun, he had done that all his life and it was very pleasant.

Very pleasant.

But this other hunt would be a real challenge, in a way that hunting deer and elk and bear had long ceased to be. And he would have to pay his dues. He had learned that in life. This might well be the last morning he was ever going to sit here feeding logs into the stove and watching the snow come down. So he let his eyes travel across the juniper and pines and took it all in, one more time.

About ten or so he saw the car coming up the road. The snow was beginning to stick. He pulled on his coat and went out onto the porch.

"Hey," Tassone said as he climbed out from behind the wheel.

"Come on in."

"Got some stuff here in the trunk. Help me with it."

There was a suitcase and two army duffel bags. They left the suitcase and carried the duffel bags inside. The bags were green, with U.S. ARMY stenciled on them, and they sported padlocks.

Inside, with the door closed, Tassone shivered involuntarily. "Getting cold out there."

"Winter's here."

Tassone tossed Charon a key ring and went to stand with his backside toward the stove.

Charon used the key on the padlocks of the duffel bags. Each was full of money, bundles of twenties and fifties.

"Five million in each bag," Tassone said. "Count it if you want."

Henry Charon felt deep into each bag, ensuring it was full of money. "No need for that, I think."

"It's a lot of money."

"You want the job?"

"No, thanks. I want to keep on living. My life's worth more than that."

"I hope to keep on living too."

Tassone nodded and looked around the room, taking it all in. Charon replaced the padlocks and put the duffel bags in the bedroom. When he came back Tassone had his coat off and was in the easy chair.

"I got coffee if you want it."

"Yeah. I'll take a cup. Black."

They both got a cup of coffee and sat listening to the wind. The snow continued to fall.

"What you gonna do? Afterward, I mean."

Henry Charon thought a moment. "Live here, I hope. I like it here."

"Lonely, I bet."

Henry Charon shrugged. He had never thought so.

They drank their coffee in silence. After a bit Charon added a log to the stove.

"What do you think about the other names on the list?"

"I'll do what I can. I told you that."

"A million each. I'll wait two or three months, then come up here with the money. If you aren't here, you want me to leave it?"

"Yeah," said Henry Charon, thinking about it. "Yeah. That would be good. I'll get here sometime." He hoped. "Leave the money under the porch. It's dry there. It'll be okay."

"There's going to be a couple other hit teams in Washington while you're there."

"You never told me that before."

"Didn't know before. I'm telling you now. You can back out if you want."

"I don't want out. But that does change things, of course."

"I know."

Change things! Henry Charon stared out the window at the snow. My God! They'll be searching every nook and cranny. Still, if he could evade long enough, one of the teams might get caught. This might be the red herring he had been thinking about.

"Well," Tassone said, draining his cup and setting it on the windowsill. "I don't want to get snowed in here. Got a flight from Albuquerque this evening. I'd better get going." He stood and put on his coat.

"Be careful going down. The road will be slick in places."

"Yeah. It was starting to get that way coming up."

"Keep to the high side and take it easy."

Charon followed Tassone out on the porch and stood watching him as he walked for the car. Then he put his right hand under his sweatshirt behind his back and drew the automatic from his belt. He leveled it, holding it with both hands.

As Tassone reached for the car door Charon shot him, once.

The big slug sent Tassone sprawling in the mud.

With the pistol ready, Charon went down the three steps and walked over to the man on the ground.

Tassone was looking up at him, bewilderment on his face. "Why?" Then all his muscles relaxed and he stopped breathing.

Charon put the muzzle of the pistol against the man's forehead and felt for a pulse in his neck. He felt a flutter, then it ceased. The bullet had hit him under the left shoulder blade and exited from the front of his chest.

The assassin carefully lowered the hammer of the weapon and replaced it between his belt and the small of his back. Then he went back inside to get his coat and hat and gloves.

Why? Because Tassone was the only link between whoever was paying the freight and Henry Charon. With him gone, the evidentiary link could never be completed. He had to die, the fool. And he *had* been a fool. The FBI would inevitably pick up the trail of the Stinger missiles and the guns. And that trail would lead to Tassone, who was now a dead end. Why, indeed!

He had shot Tassone in the front yard because he didn't want any blood or bullet holes in the house. The rain and snow would take care of any blood outside.

Charon fished Tassone's wallet from a pocket and took it inside to the kitchen table. There was very little there. A little over three hundred dollars in bills, some credit cards and a Texas driver's license for Anthony Tassone. Nothing else.

He carefully fed the credit cards and driver's license into the stove. Even the money. The wallet he put into his pocket.

Outside he pulled the pickup around and placed the body in the bed. He got the suitcase from the trunk and inspected the car carefully. As he suspected, it was a rental from one of the agencies at the Albuquerque airport. He would drive it down there himself tomorrow and park it at the rental car return and drop the paperwork and keys in the express return slot. At that moment Tassone would cease to exist. Then Charon would board the plane to Washington.

There was a candy wrapper on the floor of the car, and Charon pocketed that too.

The contents of the suitcase were as innocuous as the wallet. Several changes of clothing, toilet articles, and a paperback novel by Judith Krantz. He put everything back and tossed it into the bed of the truck.

It took him twenty minutes to travel the five miles up the mountainside to the old mine. He had the pickup in four-wheel drive, but still he took it slow and easy. The higher he climbed on the mountain the worse the snow was and the poorer the road. Tomorrow he might not even have been able to get the truck up here.

Visibility was poor at the mine, less than a hundred yards. The delapidated, weather-beaten boards and timbers that formed a shack around the shaft were half rotted, about to fall down. The mine had been abandoned in the late fifties. Henry Charon walked up on the hill, then around the mountain, then back down the road. Fifteen minutes later, satisfied that no one was around, he pulled the corpse out of the pickup and dragged it across to the mine shaft and dropped it in. The suitcase followed.

He then tied a rope around the front bumper of the pickup and lowered that into the shaft. He got a reel of coated wire from the tool chest behind the truck cab, and unwound a hundred feet or so and lowered that down the shaft. Finally, he put a flashlight, four sticks of dynamite, and a blasting cap into his pocket, took a last look around, and, using the rope, lowered himself down the shaft.

He worked quickly. He dragged the body fifty feet down one of the two drifts that led off from the bottom, then brought the suitcase and put it beside the body. He left the wallet and candy wrapper.

The dynamite he wedged between the rock wall and a six-by-six oak timber that helped hold up a weak place in the roof. He stripped the insulation from the wire he had lowered into the shaft and twisted the raw wire to the blasting cap, which he then inserted into one of the dynamite sticks. With the dynamite packed into place with dirt and small rocks, he took a last look around with the flashlight.

Had he forgotten anything?

The keys to the rental car. They were in his pocket. Okay.

Charon was not even breathing hard when he got to the surface. He pulled the rope out of the hole.

He had a little wind-up detonator in his toolbox. He attached the wire to the terminals, wound it up, and let it go. A dull thud that he could feel with his feet followed. Using his flashlight, he looked down into the shaft. It was all dust, impossible to see the bottom.

He got back into the pickup and started the engine. He turned the heater up. The visibility had deteriorated to less than a hundred feet. About four inches or so of snow on the ground.

Tassone was going to be missed, of course, but Charon thought that whoever wanted George Bush killed ten million dollars worth was not going to miss his messenger boy very much. And Charon would try to get as many of the other people on the list as he could. Of course, Tassone wasn't around to deliver additional money, and Charon didn't know who to go to to get paid, but so be it. Somebody was going to get his money's worth and that would be all that mattered.

And ten million was enough. More than enough. It was more money than Henry Charon could spend in two lifetimes.

Fifteen minutes later Charon tried to pull the wire up out of the shaft. It wouldn't come. Probably a rock lying on it. He dropped the rope back into the shaft and went back down. The dust had almost completely settled. The flashlight's beam revealed that the drift tunnel was blocked, with a huge slab pinning the detonator wire. Charon cut the wire, then came back up the rope hand over hand.

He coiled the rope and wire and stowed everything. Going down the mountain the pickup truck slid once, but he got it stopped in time. It took most of an hour to get back to the house. Only an inch of snow on the ground there.

Inside the cabin he threw another log in the stove and washed the cup Tassone had used and put it back in the cabinet. Henry Charon made a fresh pot of coffee. After it had dripped through, he poured some into his cup and stretched out in the easy chair.

"Your ten o'clock appointment is here, Mr. Brody."

The lawyer reached for the intercom button. "Send him in."

T. Jefferson Brody walked over to the door and met Freeman McNally coming through. Brody carefully closed the door and shook Freeman's hand, then pointed to the red leather client's chair. "Good to see you."

"Yeah, Tee. Howzit goin'?"

"Pretty good." Brody went around his desk and arranged himself in his eighteen-hundred-dollar custom-made swivel chair. "How's business?"

"Oh, you know," McNally said and made a vague gesture. "Always problems. Nothing ever goes right."

"That's true."

"You been watching the TV the last couple days?"

"You mean that car-bus crash? Yeah, I heard about that."

"One of my drivers. Some of our guards tried to rip off his load. He was lucky he wasn't killed."

"A lot of heat," Brody said, referring to the President's press conference and the announced government initiatives. The papers were full of it.

"Yeah. That's why I came to see you. Some of those things The Man wants to do are going to hurt. I think it's time we called in some of those markers for donations we been making to those senators and congressmen."

"I was wondering when you might want to do that."

"Now is when. Putting the DEA and FBI together is not going to help us businessmen. Yeah, like they say on TV, it'll take 'em forever to decide to do anything, but someday they'll know too much. I mean, it'll all go into the same paper mill and eventually something will pop out that's damn bad for me."

"What else?"

"Well, this new money proposal. Now that will hurt. I got about ten million in cash on hand to run my business on a day-to-day basis."

"I understand."

"Seems to me this whole thing is sorta antiblack, y'know? The black people don't use whitey's banks and they're the ones who'll lose the most. Shit, all the white guys got theirs in checking and investments and all that. It's the black women and poor families who keep theirs in cookie jars and stuffed in mattresses. Damn banks charge big fees these days for checking accounts unless you got a white man's balance."

"That's a good argument. I'll use that."

"Yeah. And this bail reform business. That's antiblack too. Whites got houses and expensive cars and all to post as bail. Black man's gotta go buy a bail bond. That takes cash."

Freeman had two or three other points to make, then Brody asked, "Who tried to rip you off the other night?"

"I don't know for sure, but I think Willie Teal's behind it. He's been getting his stuff through Cuba and that's dried up on him. So I think he put the word out he'd pay top dollar for supplies, and that sorta tempted my guys. No way to know for sure, though, as the three dips that tried to rip me all got killed."

"Saved you some trouble," Brody noted and smiled.

"It wouldn't have been no trouble. You gotta make folks want to be honest or you're outta business. That's part of it."

The buzzing of the intercom caused T. Jefferson Brody to raise a finger at his client. "Yes."

"Senator Cherry's on the phone, sir."

Brody looked at Freeman. "You'll get a kick out of this." He punched buttons for the speaker phone. "Yes."

"Bob Cherry. How's it going, Jefferson?" The sound was quite good, although a little tinny.

"Just fine, Senator. And you?"

"Well, I've been going over my reelection finances with my campaign chairman—you know I'm up for reelection in two years?"

"Yessir. I thought that was the date."

"Anyway, those PACs that you represent have been so generous in the past, I was hoping that one or two of them might make a contribution to my reelection campaign."

"Sir, I'll have to talk to my clients, but I'm optimistic. They've always believed that someone must pay for good government." Brody winked broadly at Freeman McNally, who grinned.

"I wish more people felt that way. Talk to you soon."

When the phone was back on the cradle, Brody smiled at Freeman McNally and explained. McNally threw back his head and laughed. "They just call you up and ask for money?"

"You got it."

"If I could do that, I could retire from business. You know, hire a few people to work the phones and generally take life easy."

"Well, you're not in Congress."

"Yeah. My business is a little more direct. Tell me, is Willie Teal one of your clients?" All trace of humor was gone from his face now.

"No."

"I'm glad to hear that. How about Bernie Shapiro?"

"Wellll . . . I'll be straight with you, Freeman. My rule is to never discuss my clients' identities or business with anybody. Ever. You know that."

Freeman McNally stood and walked around the room, looking at this and that. "You got a lot of nice stuff here," he said softly.

T. Jefferson Brody made a modest gesture, which McNally missed.

McNally spoke with his back to the lawyer. "Bernie Shapiro is in with the Costello family. They're moving in on the laundry business. Gonna cost me. And I don't like to pay more money for the same service."

Brody said nothing.

McNally came over to the desk and sat on the corner of it, where he could look down on T. Jefferson Brody. "Tee, I give you some advice. You're a good lawyer for what I need done. You know people and can get in places I can't get into. But if I ever hear, ever, ever, ever hear that you told anybody about my business without me giving you the okay, you'll be dead two hours after I hear it." He lowered his face to look straight into Brody's eyes. "You understand?"

"Freeman, I'm a lawyer. Everything you say to me is privileged."

"You understand me, Tee?"

"Yes." Brody's tongue was thick and he had trouble getting the words out.

"Good." Freeman got up and walked over to the window. He pulled back the drapes and looked out.

After ten or fifteen seconds Brody decided to try to get back to business. He had been successfully handling scum like McNally for ten years now, and though there were rough moments, you couldn't let them think you were scared. "Are you and Shapiro going to do business?"

"I dunno. Not if I can help it. I think that asshole killed the guy who was washing my dough. And I think he killed the guy who owned the check-cashing business. Guy named Lincoln. Shapiro paid off a broad, a grifter named Sweet Cherry Lane who was servicing the guy, and she set him up."

Bells began to ring for T. Jefferson Brody. "What does this Lane woman look like?" he asked softly.

Freeman turned away from the window. He came back and dropped into the client chair. "Sorta chocolate, huge, firm tits, tiny waist, tall and regal. A real prime piece of pussy, I hear tell."

"If someone wanted this bitch taught a lesson, could you do a favor like that?"

A slow grin spread across Freeman's face. "Lay it out, Tee."

"She robbed me, Freeman." Brody swallowed and took a deep breath. "Honest. Stole my car and watch and a bunch of shit right out of my house—and she stole the $400,000 that Shapiro paid for that check cashing business."

"Naw."

"Yes. The goddamn cunt pretended to be the widow, signed everything, took the check, slipped me a Mickey and cleaned me out."

"What the fuck kind of lawyer are you, Tee? You didn't even ask to see some ID before you gave her four hundred Gs?"

"Hey," Brody snarled. "The bitch conned me. Now I want to slice some off her. Will you help me?"

The grin on Freeman McNally's face faded in the face of the lawyer's fury. He stood. "I'll think about it, Tee. In the meantime, you get busy on those senators and congressmen. I've paid a lot of good money to those people, now I want something. You get it. Then we'll talk."

He paused at the door and spoke without looking at Brody. "I try to never get personal. With me it's all business. That way everybody knows where they stand. When you get personal you make mistakes, take stupid risks. It's not good." He shook his head. "Not good." Then he went out.

Brody stared at the door and chewed on his lower lip.

Ott Mergenthaler returned from lunch at two-thirty in the afternoon with a smile on his face and a spring in his walk. Jack Yocke couldn't resist. "Back to the old grind, eh, Ott?"

Mergenthaler grinned and dropped into a chair that Yocke hooked around with his foot. "Well, Jack, when you're the most famous columnist writing in English and you've been in the outback for a week or so, the movers and shakers are just dying to unburden themselves of nifty secrets and juicy tidbits. They can only carry that stuff so long without relief and then they get constipated."

"A tube steak on the sidewalk?"

"A really fine fettucine alfredo and a clear, dry Chianti." Ott kissed his fingertips.

"Who was the mover and shaker, or is that a secret?"

"Read my column tomorrow. But if you can't wait that long, it was Bob Cherry."

"Cuba, right? Did you tell him to read my stuff?"

"That car-bus wreck and the Bush initiatives. God, what a mess! Half the country is screaming that Bush is overreacting and the other half is screaming that he hasn't done enough. He's getting it both ways, coming and going. Why any sane man gets into politics, I'll never know."

"Any line on who the ten pounds of dope belonged to?"

"No, but funny thing. Cherry implied that the government knows all about it."

"What do you mean?"

"Well, he's on the Oversight Committee and presumably has been briefed, and he just shrugged off the question of how the investigation is going. Muttered something like, 'That's not an issue.'"

"What d'ya mean, that's not an issue? They know and aren't telling?"

"Yeah. Precisely." Ott Mergenthaler raised his eyebrows. "Normally you gotta watch Cherry like a hawk. He likes to pretend he knows everything, has a finger in every pie. Sometimes he does, sometimes he doesn't. Now at lunch today he didn't say so directly, but he left me and the other two reporters with the impression that the feds had a man on the inside. And he *knew* that was the impression he was creating and he could see by our reaction that we thought this was very important."

"On the inside. Undercover?"

Mergenthaler nodded.

"You're not going to print that, are you?"

"I have to. Two other reporters were there." He named them. "They'll use it. You can bet the ranch on that."

"You can't attribute this to Cherry."

"That's right. But this is an answer of sorts to a legit question. What is the federal government doing to bring to justice the people who indirectly caused eleven deaths in the heart of Washington? Cherry's answer—that's a nonquestion."

"And if Cherry has said that to three reporters, who else has he said it to?"

"Precisely. Hell, knowing Cherry, he's . . . And I know him. What I can't figure out is, did he spill the beans on his own hook or was he told to?"

"If you knew that," Jack Yocke mused, "you might get a better idea of whether or not it's true."

"Wonder what the government's told the Japs."

"Call the Japanese ambassador and ask."

"I'll do that." Mergenthaler made a small ceremony of maneuvering himself out of the chair and strolling off toward his office.

Jack Yocke watched him go, then jerked the Rolodex around and flipped through it. He found the number he wanted and dialed.

One ring. Two. Three. C'mon, answer the damn phone!

"Sammy."

"Jack Yocke. You alone?"

"Just me and Jesus."

"Your phone tapped?"

"How the fuck would I know, man?"

"Ah, what an affable, genial guy you are. Okay, Mr. Laid Back Bro, a U.S. senator just hinted to one of our columnists that the government knows all there is to know about that car-bus wreck. Our guy was left with the clear impression that the feds got somebody undercover."

"Give me that again, slower."

Yocke repeated his message.

"That's all?"

"Isn't that enough?"

"Who was the senator?"

"Bob Cherry."

"Thanks, man."

"It'll be in tomorrow's paper. Just thought you'd like to know."

"Thanks."

Harrison Ronald Ford hung up the phone and went back to his crossword puzzle. He stared at it without seeing the words. Then he went over to the sink and vomited into it.

It's out! The word's out. *Hooper*—that *asshole!*

His stomach tied itself into a knot and he heaved again.

He turned on the water to flush the mess down the drain. Saliva was still dripping from his mouth.

He heaved again, dry this time. He looked at the telephone on the table, tempted. No way! That fucker McNally had too goddamn many people on his payroll.

When the retching stopped, he grabbed his coat and slammed the door behind him.

"Hooper, you fucking *shithead! What're you trying to do to me?*" Harrison Ronald roared the words into the telephone.

"Calm down. What're you talking about?"

Ford repeated his conversation of six minutes ago with Jack Yocke.

"Gimme your number. I'll call you back in eight or ten minutes."

"This is a fucking pay phone, you shithead! Nobody can call this fucking number because Marion fucking Barry doesn't want fucking dope peddlers taking orders on this fucking phone."

"So call me back in ten minutes."

"In ten minutes I may well be as dead as Ma Bell, you blithering shithead. If I don't call the funeral will be on Wednesday. Closed casket!"

He slammed the phone onto its hook and looked around to see who had been listening to his shouting. No one, thank God!

Hooper used the government directory to look up the number, then dialed. "Senator Cherry, please. This is Special Agent Thomas Hooper."

"I'm sorry, sir," the woman said. "Senator Cherry is on the Senate floor. What is this about?"

"I'm not at liberty to say. When could I expect a return call?"

"Well, not today. Perhaps tomorrow morning?" The pitch of her voice rose slightly when she said "morning," making it a question and a pleasantry at the same time.

"I suggest you send an aide to find the senator. Tell the aide that if the senator does not telephone Special Agent Thomas Hooper at 893-9338 in the next fifteen minutes, I will send a squad of agents to find him and physically transport him to the FBI building. See that he gets that message or he is going to be grossly inconvenienced."

"Would you repeat that number?"

"893-9338."

The next call went to *The Washington Post* switchboard. "Jack Yocke, please."

After several rings, the reporter answered.

"Mr. Yocke, this is Special Agent Thomas Hooper of the FBI. I understand we have a mutual friend."

"I know a lot of people, Mr. Hooper. Which mutual friend are we discussing?"

"The one you just talked to, oh, ten or fifteen minutes ago."

"You say you're with the FBI?"

"Call the FBI building and ask for me." Hooper hung up.

In half a minute the phone rang.

"Hooper."

"Jack Yocke, Mr. Hooper. Trying to be careful."

"Our friend tells me that you discussed with him a conversation that one of your colleagues had over the lunch hour with Senator Cherry. Who is the colleague?"

"Ott Mergenthaler."

"And who else was a party to that conversation?"

Yocke gave him the names and the newspapers they worked for.

"Mr. Yocke, is my friend a good friend of yours?"

"Yes."

"Then I suggest you not mention that luncheon conversation, this conversation, or his name to another living soul. You understand?"

"I think it's clear."

"Good. Thanks."

"'Bye."

Hooper walked from his office to his secretary's desk. "Is Freddy back yet?"

"From Cuba? He got in about seven a.m. He's been over at Justice most of the morning."

"See if you can find him."

While Hooper was waiting he carefully and legibly wrote the three reporters' names and the newspapers they worked for on a blank sheet of paper. Freddy came in about five minutes later. "How'd it go in Cuba?"

"We got Zaba. And enough evidence to fry Chano Aldana."

"Great. But we have a more pressing problem. Senator Bob Cherry had lunch with these three reporters." He shoved his note across the desk. "Cherry hinted that the government knew everything it wanted to know about that car-bus crash the other night because it had an undercover agent in place."

"Aww, damn," Freddy said. "He was just briefed on that this morning and he's spilled it already!"

"Go to the director's office, tell the executive assistant what the problem is, and see if the director will telephone the publishers of those newspapers and kill the story. Report back to me as soon as possible."

"That may keep it out of the papers for a day or two, but that won't cork it. It's out of the bottle now, Tom."

"I'll talk to Cherry."

"Good luck. He's probably told a dozen people."

Hooper rubbed his forehead. "Go see the director."

He was still rubbing his forehead, trying to think, when the phone rang again, the direct line. "Hooper."

"Okay, it's me. I've calmed down a little. Sorry."

"Forget it, Harrison. Where are you?"

"Why?"

"I'm sending an agent in a car to get you. You're done."

"How'd the word get out?"

"We told the President and briefed key members of the congressional Oversight Committees. One of the senators then had lunch with a team of reporters and dropped some hints."

"Awww, fuck!"

"Where are you?"

"Now you calm down. Freeman patted me on the head after that incident. I'm in real tight now, man. He's got a meeting sometime tonight with Fat Tony Anselmo. Something heavy's going down. We're cunt-hair close, Tom. No shit."

"You are *done,* Harrison. I don't want to see you a corpse. Not only would death be bad for your health, it'd leave me with no case. We've got enough to take Freeman and his associates off the street for a few years, and I'm not greedy. You're *done."*

"Now look, Tom. I'm a big boy and I stopped wearing diapers last year. I'm not done until I say I'm done."

"Harrison, *I'm* in charge of this case. We can maybe keep Cherry's little luncheon chat out of the papers for a few days, but he's probably already run off at the mouth all over town. I don't know. He'll probably lie to me about it. This is your life you're betting."

"Two nights. Two more nights and then we bust 'em."

"You are a flaming idiot."

"That's what everybody says. Talk to you tomorrow."

The phone went dead.

Hooper hung the instrument up and sat staring at it.

When it rang again he let the secretary in the outer office take it. She buzzed him. "Senator Cherry, sir."

He pushed the button. "Senator, this is Special Agent Hooper. We need to have a talk. Immediately."

"I understand you made some threatening remarks a few minutes ago to one of my staff, Hooper. What the hell is going on over there anyway?"

"I really need to see you as soon as possible on a very urgent matter, Senator. I'm sorry if your secretary felt I was threatening."

The senator huffed and puffed a bit, but Hooper was willing to grovel, and soon the feathers were back in place. "Well," Cherry agreed finally, "I'm going out to dinner before I attend a reception at the French embassy. You could come by about sixish?"

"Senator, I know the unwritten rules, but I just can't come over. You'll have to stop by here."

The senator gave him a few seconds of frosty silence. "Okay," he said with no grace.

"The guard at the quadrangle entrance will be expecting you and will escort you to my office."

Special Agent Hooper was staring at the classified file on this operation when his assistant, Freddy Murray, returned from the director's office. Freddy pulled up a chair and reported:

"The director made the calls. The publishers agreed to kill the story unless it runs elsewhere, then they'll have to run it. That leak's plugged, at least for a little while."

"Thanks, Freddy."

"We got to wrap this operation up, Tom, and make some arrests. The pressure is excruciating and it's gonna get worse. While I was in the director's office he was on the phone to the attorney general. The AG has been talking to the President. Did you see this morning's paper?"

Hooper laid three documents on the table. "Why'd we start this operation, anyway?"

Hooper knew the answer to that question, of course, but he liked to think aloud. Freddy Murray thought this quirk of Hooper's a fortunate habit because his subordinates then knew where the boss's thoughts were going without having to ask. So he willingly played along. "To find out who in the bureau is on McNally's payroll."

"And what have we discovered?"

"Nothing."

"Correct."

"So." Hooper used the eraser on a pencil to scratch his head. "So."

"We've got enough to put McNally out of business," Freddy pointed out. "It's not like this operation hasn't borne fruit. Ford has filled our stocking with goodies. And the people in the front office are getting more desperate by the hour."

"Who are the three guys we thought might be dirty?"

"Wilson, Kovecki, and Moreto."

"Aren't these documents still on the computer?" Hooper pointed to them. Freddy looked at them. They were weekly progress reports to the assistant director. Harrison Ford's name was contained on each.

"I think so."

"Let's rewrite these reports. We'll construct four files, one for each of McNally's chief lieutenants, naming each of them in turn as our undercover operative. Then we let each man get an unauthorized peek at one of the files. What d'ya think?"

Freddy sat silently for a minute or so, turning it over and looking under it. "I think we're liable to get somebody killed."

"Listen, Harrison's dangling over the shark pit on a worn-out, fraying rope and blood is dripping into the water. The word is out—the feds have somebody inside. If McNally hears this rumor he'll be looking for the traitor—you can bet Harrison Ronald Ford's ass on that. Our first duty is to keep our guy alive, and our second is to find the rotten apples around here. We're about out of time, Freddy."

"I don't like it."

"You got a better suggestion?"

"Four files. Three suspects. Who's the fourth file for?"

"Bob Cherry."

Freddy scratched his crotch and picked his nose. "You're not playing by the rules," he objected, finally.

"There ain't no rules in a knife fight," Hooper growled. "Ask Freeman McNally."

"Why Cherry?"

"Why not? The shit started the rumor. Let's give him something to season it with. A name."

"What if our little conversation this evening goes well and he shuts up?"

"You had any dealings with this guy? He thinks he's one of the twelve disciples."

"Okay, so we let him get a sneaky peek at a bogus file. Then we talk to him? He'll come unglued—we call him in so we can bitch at him about his loose mouth and we leave secret files lying around unattended? He'll latch onto that like a pit bull with AIDS. He'll crucify us."

Hooper swiveled his chair and looked out the window. "Gimme something better."

"So we forget the file for the senator," Freddy said, musing aloud. "Let's play to him. We'll just stroke him and when everything's copacetic, introduce the name into the conversation. After all, he's entitled to be briefed. Let's brief the son of a bitch."

They got busy with the computer. The facts had to change on each report to fit the bona fides of the man they wanted to use. It took some serious brainstorming. They had two files constructed when Freddy said, "What if two or more names get back to McNally? Where are we then?"

They discussed it. After batting it back and forth, they decided that McNally would probably conclude that the FBI was engaged in funny business, which would discredit not only the names but the undercover agent rumor as well. They went back to work on the last file.

At noon Hooper sent his secretary home for the rest of the day. She was aghast. Hooper was insistent. "And don't mention this to anyone."

"But the personnel regulations!"

"See you Monday."

By three that afternoon Hooper and Freddy had drilled a hole through the plasterboard between the outer office and Hooper's office. They installed a one-way mirror on Hooper's side of the wall. The secretary's forgettable print was rehung on her side to cover the hole. Freddy trotted down the hall and borrowed a vacuum cleaner from a cleaning closet to clean up the dust and drywall fragments.

The suspects were called one at a time into Hooper's office to interview for the new positions in the division that Hooper had just yesterday recommended be created and filled in response to President Bush's recent announcements.

Wilson didn't look at the files on the desk in the fifteen minutes Hooper kept him waiting. When Hooper went into the office finally, Wilson flatly stated he wasn't interested in transferring from his present position. But he appreciated being considered.

They had better luck with the second man, Kovecki. He did glance at the target file. The name in his was Ruben McNally, the accountant. In fact, Kovecki looked at all three files on the desk. One of them was his personnel file, and he settled in to examine that closely. He was still looking at it when Hooper went in to interview him.

Moreto also looked. He selected the bogus file from the three on the desk and scanned it quickly. The name in his file was Billy Enright. Then Moreto went over to the window and stared out. He was at the window when Hooper entered the room.

In between interviews Hooper fielded a call from the director. "I want you to take your man to the grand jury on Monday. The prosecutors are doing the indictments this weekend. Monday night you start picking these guys up."

"Yessir."

"Hooper," the director said, "this comes straight from the White House. I expect you to make it happen."

At six-seventeen that evening the senator arrived. With the former Miss Georgia parked in the outer office visiting with a ga-ga young agent who was acting as the building escort, Tom Hooper and Freddy Murray gently cautioned the great man behind closed doors and gave him a fairly complete briefing on the operation, including the name of the undercover man, Ike Randolph. Most of the other things they told the senator were equally accurate but carefully tailored to fit the bare bones of the truth, which the senator already knew. They failed to mention the planned expedition to the grand jury Monday or the arrests they hoped to make within hours of obtaining indictments.

At seven thirty-two Hooper finally locked his office and he and Freddy headed for the Metro.

CHAPTER SEVENTEEN

* * * * * * * * * * * *

"THANOS Liarakos, please. This is Jack Yocke of *The Washington Post.*"

"I'm sorry, Mr. Yocke," the female on the other end of the telephone line told him briskly. "Mr. Liarakos isn't taking any calls from the press today."

"Well, we're running a story in tomorrow's paper about the extradition of General Julio Zaba from Cuba. The FBI brought him in from Havana this morning. The spokeswoman at the Justice Department said he'll be placed on trial here in Washington. They have a secret indictment handed down just yesterday from the grand jury. According to her and the press folks over at the White House, General Zaba was personally paid big bucks by Mr. Liarakos' client, Chano Aldana, to allow dope smugglers to use Cuban—"

"Really, Mr. Yocke. Mr. Liarakos is not—"

"Would he like to comment on this story?"

"If I say, 'No comment,' what will you say in the story you're writing?"

"I'll say that Mr. Liarakos refused to comment on the story."

The phone went dead. She had put him on hold.

Jack Yocke put his feet on his desk and cradled the phone between his cheek and shoulder. He cracked his knuckles. Aldana and Zaba. The A-to-Z connection. Too bad the *Post* wouldn't let him make a crack like that in print.

She came back on. "Mr. Yocke?"

"Still here."

"You may say this: In view of the gag orders issued in the Aldana case by Judge Snyder, Mr. Liarakos does not believe he is at liberty to comment on this matter."

"Okay. Got it. Thanks."

He was just finishing the story when the phone jingled. "Yocke."

"This is Tish. Sorry I couldn't get back to you earlier."

"Hey. I was wondering if you would like to go to dinner with me at the Graftons' tomorrow night? I meant to call you last week, but I got called out of town unexpectedly." The last sentence was a lie. He had intended never to call her again, but Mrs. Grafton had specifically asked him to bring Tish Samuels. He wondered what Mrs. Grafton's reaction would be if she heard Tish's little speech about her literary ambitions.

"I've been reading your Cuba stories. They're very good."

"Thank you. I was down there and all and real busy."

"You apologize too much, Jack. Yes, I'd like to go to the Graftons' with you. What time?"

You apologize too much. Only to women, Jack Yocke thought. Why is that?

Thirty minutes later he was in talking to Ott about General Zaba when he was summoned back to his desk by the telephone operator. "Your Cuban call is ready." He had a call in for Pablo Oteyza, formerly known as Hector Santana.

Yocke picked up the phone. "Jack Yocke speaking."

"Pablo Oteyza."

"*Señor,* I'm the *Post* report—"

"I remember you, Jack."

"Congratulations on being named to the interim government."

"Thanks."

"I sent you my articles on Cuba. Did you get any of them yet?"

"Not yet. The mail is still very confused. And I haven't yet heard a megaton detonation from the north, followed by a tidal wave of reporters, so I assume you honored your promises to me about what you would and would not publish."

"Yessir. I don't think you'll find anything embarrassing to you or the American government in the articles."

"Or my American friends."

"Right. *Señor,* I know you're busy. It's just been announced here that General Zaba was extradited and brought to Washington for trial. What can you tell me about him?"

"He was an associate of Chano Aldana. He used Cuban gunboats and naval facilities to smuggle cocaine. We gave the FBI agents all the evidence we have been able to assemble and let them interview Zaba's subordinates. Your people were very pleased."

"Will there be any other extraditions?"

"Perhaps. It will take time for the FBI and the American prosecutors to evaluate what they have. And to see if Zaba wants to talk. If the American government gets indictments for drug trafficking against other Cubans, my government will evaluate them and decide on a case-by-case basis. We made it plain to the FBI that people who were just following orders will not be extradited."

"Any truth to the rumor that Zaba's extradition was a quid pro quo for American economic aid?"

"Speaking for my government, I can say that the new government of Cuba and the government of the United States will cooperate on many matters. Economic aid is very high on our list of priorities."

"You sound like a politician."

"I *am* a politician, Jack. I look forward to reading your stories."

"Thanks for your time."

"Yes." Oteyza hung up.

Jack Yocke tapped keys on his computer to bring up the Zaba story, then began to make insertions.

To say that Harrison Ronald was apprehensive when he drove to work on Friday night would be an understatement. After his second telephone conversation with Special Agent Hooper, he had walked the streets for an hour, then reluctantly retraced his steps back to his apartment.

He had gotten out his slab-sided .45 Colt automatic and stuffed a full clip up the handle and jacked a round into the chamber. With the weapon cocked and locked and under the pillow, he tried to get some sleep.

He couldn't. He lay there staring at the ceiling and wondering who was saying what to whom.

Why in hell had he insisted on two more nights? Two more nights of waiting for someone to blow his silly brains out.

He had thought his nervous system had had all it could handle the other evening when he walked four miles from the Lincoln Memorial to McNally's northwest hidey-hole. He had told the tale of the evening's adventures to that little ferret Billy Enright, who left him sitting in a bedroom while he went to call Freeman.

He sat for an hour listening to every sound, every muffled footstep, waiting. Then Freeman had come in, inspected the bullet groove in his arm and cuts in his face and insisted that the wounds be cleaned and bandaged by a proper doctor. In the living room Billy had the television going, with the victims and blood and smashed car being shown again and again. When they had had their fill, Freeman and Billy drove him to some quack who had gotten himself banned for life from the practice of medicine by prescribing painkillers to rich matrons suffering from obesity and boredom.

All concern he was, Freeman that night. His face reflected solicitude, glee when he heard how Sammy Z had killed the guy in the backseat by crushing his larynx, laughter when he heard about the high-speed chase and the final, fatal crash. Keystone Kops stuff, slapstick. Ha ha ha.

"Ya did good, Z, real good."

"Sorry about your merchandise, Freeman, but I didn't think it was smart to go hiking down the street bleeding and all and carrying ten pounds of shit. And I had to ditch the car fast. It looked like Swiss cheese."

"You did right, Z, my man. Don't sweat it."

"Sorry about the car."

"Fuck the car. I'll get another." McNally snapped his fingers. "That

Tooley! I'd like to know who put that chickenshit cocksucker up to robbing me. No way that bubble-brain would dream that up by hisself."

"I'll ask around," Billy Enright promised. "Put the word out. Maybe offer some bread for info."

"Offer ten Gs," Freeman said, taking a thick roll of bills from his pocket. He divided it without counting and handed half to Harrison Ronald. "Here. I pay my debts. You were working for me, so I owe you. Here."

Harrison glanced at the stack and pocketed it. "Thanks," he said, with feeling.

"Make it five Gs," Freeman told Enright. "If we offer too much, people'll be dreaming up tales. Five's enough."

So Harrison Ronald was in tight with Freeman. Maybe. In any event, McNally had tossed him the keys to a four-year-old Ford Mustang, and that was what he was driving this evening. And that wad of bills, when he counted it back at the apartment, consisted of forty-three $100 bills.

In tight—maybe. Ford had no illusions about Freeman McNally. He would pay forty-three hundred dollars to see the look of surprise on his victim's face when he jammed a pistol up his ass and pulled the trigger.

If he had heard the rumor and decided Sammy Z was a cop, he would still be the same old Freeman McNally, right up until he grinned that grin and took care of business.

Take care of business. That was Freeman's motto. God, he took care of it all right!

Well, dealing coke and crack wasn't for the squeamish or indecisive. Nobody who knew McNally ever suspected he had either of those flaws.

As he threaded the Mustang through the heavy evening traffic—only seven shopping days left before Christmas—Harrison Ronald wrestled again with the why. Why had he demanded two more nights of this?

He had worried this question all afternoon and he still was not satisfied with the answer that fell out. He thought Freeman and the boys ought to be locked up for a serious stretch and he thought it was worth a big risk for somebody to accomplish that chore. But he had no personal ax to grind, other than the fact he loathed all these swine. Still, there were a lot of people in the world he would just as soon not spend time with. The discovery of another dozen or two wasn't earthshaking. No. The question was, Why did *he* want to risk his butt to put Freeman and friends and maybe one or two crooked cops where the sun don't shine?

Grappling with the why question made him uncomfortable. He wasn't a hero. The possibility that someone might see him as one was embarrassing.

Harrison thought that perhaps it was the challenge. Or some sense that he owed something. Payback. Something like that, probably. That wasn't too bad. But when he thought about it honestly—and he did do that: he was an honest man—he sensed a little bit of thrill at the excitement of it all. Living on the edge burned you out and scared the shit out of you and made you want to heave your guts at times, but it was certainly never dull. Every emotion came full blast, undiluted.

The thrill aspect made him slightly ashamed, coming as it did with a dollop or two of the hero juice.

Two more nights. Hang in there, Harrison Ronald, Evansville PD.

He parked the car in the alley and said hi to the guy standing in the shadows, hopping from foot to foot to keep warm. His name was Will Colby and he and Sammy Z had delivered crack on a half dozen occasions. Harrison rapped on the back door.

If they thought he was a cop, the reception inside was going to be very warm. As he waited for the door to open, he wiped the perspiration from his face with a glove and glanced again at Colby, who was looking up and down the alley. Colby seemed relaxed, bored perhaps.

Thirty degrees and a breeze, and he was sweating! Where's the thrill now, hero? He consciously willed his muscles to relax.

Ike Randolph opened the door and looked around.

"Hey, Ike."

Ike jerked his head and Harrison Ronald went inside.

As they went through the kitchen, Ike said, "Better get some coffee. You're out front tonight."

Harrison filled a styrofoam cup with steaming liquid. "When they coming?"

"Ten. Got a piece on you?"

"Nope."

"Get something from the bedroom and go on out front."

Harrison selected a .357 Smith & Wesson, checked the cylinder, then stuffed the weapon into the pocket of his pea coat. He had bought this coat because it was warm and had deep pockets and a large collar. There was sure a lot of standing around outside in this business. Just like police work.

With that irony in mind, he walked down the hall carrying the coffee, nodded at the guy with the Uzi, and went out the front door to the stoop.

Harrison had seen the guy out front before, but didn't know his name. "I got it. Anything happening?"

"Just cold as holy hell," the guy said, then went up the steps and inside.

So far so good. Another three minutes of life and a fair prospect of more. Amen.

He was still standing there at nine fifty-five when a dark gray Cadillac wearing New York plates pulled up to the curb in front and the man in the passenger seat climbed out. Fat Tony Anselmo. The man at the wheel killed the engine.

Anselmo glanced at Ford, taking in every feature with one quick sweep, then climbed the stairs and pushed the doorbell button. The door opened in seconds and he went in.

The man at the wheel sank into the seat until only the top half of his face was visible under his dark, brimmed hat. At twenty-five feet the features were hard to distinguish in the glare and shadows of the streetlights, but Harrison Ronald knew who he was: Vincent Pioche, hitter for the Costello family in Brooklyn and Queens. According to Freddy Murray, the FBI thought he had killed over twenty men. No one knew for sure, including Pioche, who had probably forgotten some of his victims. Brains weren't his long suit.

If you were going to make your living in criminal enterprises, Ford mused, you should either be a rocket scientist or mildly retarded. The people between those extremes were the ones in trouble. The thinking they did was both too much and not enough. Like Tooley.

That line of thought led him to consider himself. He had a high school diploma and two years of college. He could balance a checkbook and write a report. Tooley probably could have too, if he had had any reports to write.

Was he as smart as Freeman McNally, the Ph.D. of crack philosophy?

The very thought gave him goosebumps. The wind was cold and he had been out here over an hour. He began walking around.

Ike came out about ten-thirty and relieved him while he went inside for a break. He got another cup of coffee and hit the bathroom.

He was standing by the guard with the Uzi in the hallway sipping coffee when the door to the living room opened and Fat Tony came out. He already had his coat on. Freeman was behind him.

Freeman followed Tony to the door while Harrison trailed after.

Together they stood on the stoop and watched Tony Anselmo get into the car. As it drove off, McNally said, "There goes the two guys who killed Harrington and Lincoln a couple weeks ago."

Because he thought he ought to say something, Harrison Ronald asked, "How'd you hear that?"

"You can find out anything if you know who to ask and you've got enough money."

Freeman went back inside. Ike nodded and Harrison reluctantly descended to the sidewalk.

Yeah, with enough money to spread around you can find out anything, like who's the undercover cop in the McNally organization.

On Saturday morning at eight a.m. Harrison Ronald Ford met special agents Hooper and Murray in the motel in Fredericksburg. The first thing he did was give them the forty-three hundred dollars that Freeman had given him. The money, Hooper said, would go to a fund to finance antidrug operations.

As they sipped coffee, Harrison Ronald told them the news: "Freeman says Fat Tony Anselmo and Vinnie Pioche killed two guys named Harrington and Lincoln several weeks ago."

"How'd he find out?" Freddy asked.

"He says he asked the right person and used money."

"We'll follow it up. Right now I think those murders are being investigated by local police. To the best of my knowledge, they're wide open."

"Did he know why?" Hooper asked.

"Freeman didn't say specifically. Fat Tony spent an hour and a half with him last night. I think it's this money-washing business. It all fits." Harrison Ronald shrugged.

"Monday you're going to the grand jury. If they indict McNally and his gang, we start busting them Monday night."

Harrison Ronald nodded and inspected his hands. They were shaking.

"There's no reason for you to go back there tonight. Those clowns aren't going anyplace."

"Last night I got this tidbit on Anselmo and Pioche. That may wrap up two unsolved killings. Who knows what I might pick up tonight?"

"It isn't worth the risk," Freddy insisted, dragging his chair closer to the undercover man. "This undercover op rumor might land there today. Tonight they may decide to put a bullet into you for insurance."

"May, may, might, might. *Are you crazy?*" Ford's voice rose to a roar. *"They could have killed me anytime in the last ten months. I've been living on borrowed time, you asshole."*

Silence greeted that outburst. Eventually Freddy got up from his chair and went over to sit on the bed.

Hooper took the chair and dragged it even closer to Ford, less than two feet away.

Hooper spoke softly: "Why do you want to go back?"

"Because I'm scared. I've been getting more and more scared every day."

"You're burning out," Freddy said. "Happens to everyone. That's normal. You're not Superman."

"Freeman McNally ain't gonna die or get religion when you arrest him, Freddy. Even in jail, he's gonna continue to be the same old asshole. And sooner or later, his lawyer is going to tell him my real name. I have to learn to live with that or I'm done."

Hooper sighed. "Look. If killing you would let Freeman walk, he'd do it in the blink of an eye. But when he finally finds out he's been had, he's done regardless. And your real name will *never come out.* That I can promise."

The undercover man didn't seem very impressed. "Used to be, I got over the fear after a shift," he muttered. "Did a crossword puzzle or two, got some sleep, maybe had a drink, I'd get back to normal. Doesn't happen now. I'm scared all the time. Had to give up whiskey or I'd get stinking drunk and stay that way."

"There's no need to go back."

"I *need* to. Don't you see that? *I'm fucking scared shitless.* If I don't go back I'll be scared all my life. Don't you see? How am I ever going to sit in a patrol car by myself in downtown Evansville at night? How am I gonna stop a speeder and walk up on his car? They send me in to arrest some drunk with a gun, how am I gonna do that? I am fucking scared shitless and I got to get a handle on it or I ain't gonna be able to keep going, man. It's that simple."

Chapter Eighteen

* * * * * * * * * * * *

PRESIDENT Bush left for Camp David in the mountains northwest of Frederick, Maryland, around nine a.m. for a weekend retreat to hash out foreign policy issues with the secretary of state and the national security adviser. Before he boarded the helicopter, however, he had another session with Dorfman and Attorney General Gideon Cohen.

"What does this Zaba character know?"

"More than enough to convict Chano Aldana," Cohen told the President. "He had at least half a dozen personal meetings with Aldana that we know of—four in Cuba and two in Colombia. He gave orders to his subordinates to assist in shipping cocaine from Colombia to Cuba. He personally supervised at least four transshipments on to the United States."

"Is he talking?" Dorfman asked, a little annoyed that Cohen, as usual, was putting the cart before the horse.

"Not yet. Judge Snyder appointed him a lawyer yesterday. Guy named Szymanski from New York."

"The shyster that got those S&L thieves acquitted last week?"

"Yes. David Szymanski. He's got a national reputation and Judge Snyder called him and asked if he would serve. He agreed."

"Szymanski could dry up Niagara," Dorfman said acidly. "If Szymanski can't shut him up, this Zaba has a terminal case of motormouth."

"I talked to the secretary of state about this matter. He felt it was important that we get top-notch counsel for Zaba. We may well want Cuba to send us some more of these people to try, and we need to show the Cubans that anyone extradited will get quality counsel and a fair trial. That's critical. I personally asked Judge Snyder—"

"Okay, okay," George Bush said, breaking in. "Will Zaba talk or won't he?"

"I think he will," Cohen told him. "The Cubans put it to him this way: If he cooperated with us he could eventually return to Cuba a free man. When he gets back there he can always blame Castro."

"Who's conveniently dead," Dorfman remarked.

"No doubt Cuba will publicize his testimony as an example of the corruption of the old regime."

"No doubt," George Bush said. "You going to let him cop a plea?"

"If Szymanski asks, yes. Zaba will have to agree to testify against Chano Aldana. His sentencing hearing will be delayed until after the Aldana trial."

"Won't that give Aldana's lawyer something to squawk about?" Dorfman asked.

"Yes."

"How about this drug bust on Monday night? Is that on schedule?"

"Yessir."

"You and I and the director of the FBI will have a press conference Tuesday morning. Schedule that, please, Will."

"Yessir."

"And Will, go see that the reporters are moved back far enough so that I don't have to hear any questions on the way out to the chopper."

Dorfman departed. When they were alone, George Bush said, "Gid, I know that you and Dorfman strike sparks, but I need you both."

"The asshole thinks he was born in a manger," Cohen said hotly.

The President was taken aback. He had never heard Cohen blow off steam before—apparently lawyers at blue-chip New York firms didn't often indulge themselves. "That's true," the President replied with a wry grin, "but he's *my* asshole."

Cohen's eyebrows rose and fell.

"There's no way in the world I can please everyone. Dorfman attracts the criticism. He takes the blame. He takes the heat I can't afford to take. That's his job."

The attorney general nodded.

"This drug thing . . . We have to just keep plugging at it. We're trying and the voters will understand that. Only pundits and TV preachers expect miracles. And I don't want anybody railroaded. Our job is to make the damn system work."

Harrison Ronald got back to his apartment around noon. He locked and bolted the door and fell into bed with the .45 automatic in his hand. He was instantly asleep.

At five o'clock he awoke with a start. Someone upstairs had slammed a door. The pistol was still in his hand. He flexed his fingers around it, felt its heft, and lay awake listening to the sounds of the building.

When this was over he would go home. Home to Evansville and spend Christmas with his grandmother. He hadn't talked to her in five or six months. She didn't even know where he was. Tough on her, but better for him. She was getting on and liked to share confidences with her friends and minister.

Oh well. It would soon be over. One more night. When he walked out of this dump in three hours, he was never coming back. The landlord could have it—the worn-out TV, the clothes, the bargain-basement dinnerware and pots and pans, all of it. Harrison Ronald was going straight back to the real world.

He had leveled with Hooper about why he wanted to go back. He was going to have to learn how to live with fear—not just the fear of Freeman McNally—but fear itself. He had learned in the Marines that the only way to conquer this poison called fear was to face it.

Ah me. Ten months in a sewage pond. Ten months in hell. And this time tomorrow he would be out of it.

He lay in bed listening to the sounds and thinking about the life he was going back to.

Thanos Liarakos was in the den when he heard the kids shouting. "Mommy, Mommy, you're home!"

She was standing there in the front hallway with the kids around her, looking at him. Her hair and clothes were a mess. She just stood there looking at him as the girls squealed and pranced and tugged at her hands.

"Hug them, Elizabeth."

Now she looked at their upturned faces. She ran her hands through her hair, then bent and kissed them.

"Okay, girls," he said. "Run upstairs a while and let Mommy and Daddy visit. No, why don't you go out to the kitchen and help Mrs. Hamner fix dinner. Mommy will stay for dinner."

They gave her a last squeeze and ran for the kitchen.

"Hello, Thanos."

"Come in and sit down." He gestured toward the den.

She selected her easy chair, the antique one she had had recovered—when was it?—a year ago? He sat in his looking at her. She had aged ten years. Bags under her eyes, lines along her cheeks, sagging pouches under her jaw.

"Why'd you come back?"

Elizabeth gestured vaguely and looked at the wall.

"You didn't stay at the clinic. They called and said you walked away."

She took a deep breath and let her eyes rest on him.

"Still on the dope, I see."

"I thought you'd be glad to see me. The girls are."

"You can stay for dinner if you want. Then you leave."

"Why are you doing this to me?"

"Don't give me that shit! You're doing this to yourself. Look at yourself, for Christ's sake. You look like hell."

She looked down at her clothes, as if seeing them for the first time.

"Why don't you go upstairs, take a shower, wash your hair, and put on clean clothes. Dinner will be in about forty-five minutes."

She gathered herself and stood. She nodded several times without looking at him, then opened the door and walked out. Liarakos followed her to the foot of the stairs and stood there for three or four minutes, then he slowly climbed the staircase. He stood in the bedroom until he heard the shower running, then left.

He had said she would stay for dinner on impulse; now he regretted it. Could he manage his emotions for two hours? He loved her and he hated her, both at the same time. The irresistible tidal currents tore at him.

Hatred. In her foolish weakness and selfishness she abandoned everything for that white powder. Abandoned the children, *him*—yes, *him*—was it hatred or rage?

Love. Yes. If there were no love there would be no hatred. Just sorrow.

And then he was outside himself, staring at this man from an angle above, watching him walk, seeing the meaningless gestures and the twitching of the facial muscles, knowing the pain and knowing too that somehow none of it really mattered.

It didn't, you know. Didn't matter. The kids would grow into adults and make their own lives and forget, and he would keep getting up every day and shaving and going to the office. Age would creep over him, then decrepitude, then, finally, the nursing home and the grave. None of it mattered. In the long run none of it mattered a damn.

Yet there he was, standing there imprisoned on this tired old earth, being ripped apart.

"Lisa, tell your mother what you've been doing in school."

The child prattled about mice and gerbils and short stories. Elizabeth kept her eyes on her plate, on her food, concentrated on using the knife and fork at the proper time, on handling the utensils with the proper hands. She patted her lips with the napkin and carefully replaced it in her lap.

"Susanna, your turn."

The child was deep into a convoluted tale of fish and frogs when Elizabeth scooted her chair back a moment and murmured, "Excuse me." She bent down for her purse.

Liarakos snagged it. "I'll watch it."

His wife stared at him, her face registering no emotion. Then it came. A snarl which began with a twitching of her upper lip and spread across her face.

Liarakos flipped her the purse. She caught it and rose from her chair and went along the hall toward the downstairs half bath.

"You girls finish your dinner," he said.

"Is Mommy going to stay?"

"No."

They accepted that and ate in silence. They finished and he shooed them upstairs. Minutes later Elizabeth came back to the dining room, gliding carefully, her face composed.

He sat in silence watching her eat. She picked at the food, then finally placed the fork on the plate and didn't pick it up again.

"Don't you want to know where I've been?"

"No."

"Could you give me a ride or some money for taxi fare?"

"You can get wherever you're going the same way you got here. Good-bye."

"Thanos, I—"

"*Good-bye,* Elizabeth. Take your purse and go. Now! Don't come back."

"Thanks for—"

"If you don't go right now, I'll physically eject you."

She stared at him for several seconds, then rose. After half a minute he heard the front door open, then click shut.

Harrison Ronald looked at his watch for the forty-fifth time. Two hours and three minutes until he had to be there.

He examined his face in the broken mirror over the cigarette-scarred dresser—would they read it in his face? *He* could see it written all over his kisser, plain as a newspaper headline. Guilt. That was what was there. Old-fashioned grade-A guilt, the kind your momma always gave you, shot through with cholesterol and saturated fats and plenty of salt and sugar. *I did it! I'm the snitch! I'm the stoolie!* Whitey sent this chocolate Tom to tattle on all you shit-shoveling niggers and pack your black asses off up the river.

If Freeman asked him the question his face would shatter like frozen glass.

Two hours and two minutes.

Coffee? He had had three cups this evening. That was more than enough caffeine. No booze. No beer. No alcohol, period.

God, he was going to get stinking drunk tomorrow night. He was going to go on a world-class bender and stay yellow-puke drunk for three whole days.

If he was still alive tomorrow night, that is.

Two hours and one minute. A hundred-and-twenty-one minutes.

He picked up the automatic and ran his fingers over it. He would take it with him tonight. In ten months he had never carried a gun, but tonight . . . Maybe it would give him an edge, since they wouldn't expect it.

Two hours flat.

Captain Jake Grafton was feeling expansive. He had had a delightful day with his daughter, Amy, and had finished most of his Christmas shopping. Callie had gone by herself to buy Amy's presents and presumably one for Jake. He had glimpsed her sorting through his clothes this morning, probably checking sizes. This evening the captain smiled genially and let his eyes rest happily on Amy Carol, then on Callie at the other end of the dinner table. Two beautiful women. He was a very lucky man.

The captain's gaze moved down the table to Toad Tarkington, who was paying no attention to anyone except his wife, Rita Moravia, who sat beside him. Tomorrow Toad would probably have a crick in his neck. Rita was also the object of Amy's undivided attention. Amy adored the navy test pilot, but this evening as she regarded Rita a curious expression played about her features.

When Callie's gaze met Jake's, he nodded toward Amy and knitted his brows into a question. His wife shook her head almost imperceptibly and looked away.

One of those female things, Jake Grafton concluded, that men are not expected to understand or concern themselves about. He sighed.

Across the table from the Tarkingtons sat Jack Yocke and his date, Tish Samuels. Tish was a lovely person, with a pleasant smile and kind word for everyone. In several ways she reminded Jake of his wife, like the way she held her head, the way she listened, her thoughtful comments. . . . Tish also listened intently to Rita as she finished telling a flying story. When Rita concluded, Tish smiled and glanced at Yocke.

Whether the reporter knew it or not, the woman was obviously in love with him. Yocke seemed mellow, more relaxed than he had been the first time he was at the Graftons'. Or perhaps it was just Jake's mood that made him seem that way.

As usual when he was relaxed, Jake Grafton said little. He nibbled his food and took sparing sips of wine and let the conversation flow over him.

Callie turned to Yocke and said, "I've been reading your stories on Cuba. They are very, very good."

"Thank you," Jack Yocke said, genuinely pleased by the compliment.

Callie led him on, and in a few moments Yocke was talking about Cuba. Toad even tore his attention away from Rita to listen and occasionally toss in a question.

At first Yocke's comments were superficial, but it seemed as if the company drew him out. Even Jake began to pay attention.

". . . the thing that impressed me was the sense of destiny that the people had, the common people, the workers. They were gaining something. And then I realized that what they were talking about, what they wanted, was democracy, the right to vote for the leaders who made the laws. You know, we've had it here for so long that we've become blasé. It's fashionable these days to sneer at politicians, laugh at the swine prostituting themselves for campaign money and begging shamelessly for votes. And yet, when you're up to your eyes in dictatorship, being ordered around by some self-appointed Caesar with big ideas in a little head, democracy looks damned good."

His listeners seemed to agree, so Yocke developed the thought: "It's funny, but democracy rests on the simplest premise that has ever supported a form of human government: a majority of the people will be right more often than not. Think about it! Errors are part of the system. They are inevitable as the political currents ebb and flow. Yet in the long run, a shifting, changing majority will be right a majority of the time."

"Will these countries which are embracing democracy for the first time have the patience to wait for the successes and to tolerate the errors?" Jake Grafton asked, the first time during dinner that he had spoken.

Yocke looked down the table at the captain. "I don't know," he said. "It takes a lot of faith to believe in the good faith and wisdom of your fellow man. Democracy will stick in some places, sure. I think it needs to get its roots in deep though, or it'll get ripped up by the first big blow. There's always someone promising instant salvation if he could just get his hands on the helm and throttle."

"How about democracy in America? A fad or here to stay?"

"Jake Grafton!" Callie admonished. "What a question!"

"It's a good one," Yocke told her. "One of the common errors is to get rid of the system. We've got a lot of problems in America and two hundred and fifty million people advocating solutions. I should know—I make my living writing about the problems."

"You didn't answer the question," Toad Tarkington said, and grinned.

"I don't know the answer," Jack Yocke told him.

"I don't think anything could make us give up our republic," Callie declared.

"What do you think, Captain?" Tish Samuels asked.

Jake snorted. "The roots are in deep all right, but if the storm were bad enough. . . . Who wants coffee besides me?"

As Callie poured coffee, Jake saw Rita speaking softly to Amy. The youngster listened, her face clouding heavily, then she abruptly fled the room.

Jake folded his napkin and excused himself. He didn't get past Callie. She thrust the coffeepot at him, then followed Amy into the bedroom.

"How do you want it, Toad?" Jake leaned over the lieutenant's shoulder.

"In the cup, if possible, CAG."

"Rita, have you picked up any new lines to teach this clown? His act is getting real stale."

Rita grinned at Jake. "I know. I was hoping that since he works in your shop now you could give him some help."

"You work for Captain Grafton?" Jack Yocke asked Toad.

"Maybe I should go visit with Callie and Amy for a minute," Rita said, and rose from her chair. She came out of it supplely, effortlessly. Toad and Jake watched her until the bedroom door closed behind her.

"Yeah," Toad said to the reporter. "CAG can't get rid of me. Actually I have been of some small service to Captain Grafton in the past in his epic struggles to defend the free world from the forces of evil and all that. I suggested yesterday that he buy a Batmobile and I'd keep it over at my place until he needs it. He doesn't have a garage here."

"What do you two do over in the Pentagon?" Yocke asked.

"It's very hush-hush," Toad confided, lowering his voice appropriately. "We're drafting top-secret war plans to go into effect if Canada attacks us. We figure they'll probably take out the automobile plants in Detroit first. Surprise attack. Maybe a Sunday morning. Then—"

"Toad!" Jake growled.

Tarkington gestured helplessly at Tish Samuels, who was grinning. "My lips are sealed. Anyway, it's a real dilly of a tip-top secret, which as you know are the very best kind. If the Canadians ever find out . . ."

As they cleared the table, Jake said to Toad, "Rita seems to be fully recovered from that crash last year."

"She's got some scars," Toad said, "but she's amazed the therapists. Amazed me too."

They had the dishes in the washer and were in the living room drinking coffee when Amy and Rita came out of the bedroom holding hands. Both looked like they had been crying. Callie headed for the kitchen and Jake trailed after her.

"What was that all about?"

"Amy worships Rita and has a crush on Toad." Callie rolled her eyes heavenward. "Hormones!"

"Ouch."

Callie smiled and gave Jake a hug. "I love you."

"I love you too, woman. But we'd better get back to our guests."

"Aren't you glad we invited Jack Yocke?"

"He's a good kid."

Fear increases exponentially the closer you get to the feared object. Harrison Ronald made this discovery as he drove toward Freeman McNally's northwest Washington house.

He could feel it, a paralyzing, mind-numbing daze that made him want to puke and run at the same time.

He was paying less and less attention to the traffic around him, and he knew it but couldn't do better. That was another thing about fear—a little of it is necessary, keeps you sharp, makes you function at peak efficiency in potentially dangerous situations. But too much of it is paralyzing. Fear becomes terror, which numbs the mind and muscles.

And if the ratchet is loosened just a notch, the terror becomes panic and all the muscles receive one message from the shorted-out brain—flee.

He drove slower and slower. When the traffic lights turned green he had to will himself to depress the accelerator. A man in a car behind raced his engine and gunned by with his middle finger held rigidly aloft. Ford ignored him.

In spite of everything, he got there. He eased the car down the alley and into a parking place behind McNally's row house. The guard was standing in the shadow of a fence. Ford killed the engine. He was not going to retch, no sir. Under no circumstances was he going to let himself vomit.

"Now or never," he said aloud, comforted by the sound of his voice, which sounded more or less under control, and opened the door. The guard walked toward him with his hands in his coat pockets.

Oh, damn! *This is it!*

"You Z?"

"Yeah, man."

"Ain't nobody in there. You're supposed to go over to the Sanitary and pick up a load."

He stood there beside the car staring at the man. It didn't compute. Think, goddamn it! Think! The Sanitary Bakery . . .

"The guard'll meet you there."

Ford turned and reopened the car door. He seated himself, then tried to remember what he had done with the key. Not this pocket, nor this . . . here! He stabbed it at the ignition. Turn the key.

With the engine running a tidal wave of relief rolled over him. He pulled the shift lever back a notch and let the car drift backward, toward the alley.

Everything's cool. Everything's cool as a fucking ice cube.

Look behind you, idiot. Don't hit the pole.

As the guard returned to the shadows he backed out into the alley and fed gas.

The relief turned to disgust. He had sweated bullets all day, for what? *For nothing!*

Maybe he should just split. Why not? He had proved to himself he could make it through today. That was the main thing. Nothing's going to happen tonight, and why should he deliver another load of shit for Freeman McNally? The feds already had enough evidence for 241 counts on an indictment. Why add another?

What are you proving, Harrison? You've had no sleep, you've been scared shitless for ten months, you killed a guy, you got enough evidence to send McNally and friends up the river so long that crack will be legal when they get out, *but you have to be alive to testify.*

Why dick around with it another night? Don't lose sight of the main thing—*you've made it through today.*

But he knew the answer. He pointed the car toward Georgia Avenue and fed gas.

"How well do you know Captain Grafton?" Jack Yocke asked Toad Tarkington. It was about ten o'clock and they were standing on the balcony looking at the city. It was nippy but there was little wind.

"Oh, about as well as any junior officer can know a senior one. I think he personally likes me, but at the office I'm just another one of the guys."

"By reputation, he's one of the best officers in the Navy."

"He's the best I ever met. Period," Toad said. "You want paper shuffled, Captain Grafton can handle it. You want critical decisions wisely made or carefully defended, he's your man. You need a man to lead other men into combat, get Grafton. You want a plane flown to hell and back, nobody's better than he is. If you want an officer who will always do *right* regardless of the consequences, then you want Jake Grafton."

"How about you?"

"Me? I'm just a lieutenant. I fly when I'm told, sleep when I'm told, and shit when it's on the schedule."

"How does Captain Grafton always know what the right thing to do is?"

"What is this? Twenty questions? Don't you ever lay off?"

"Just curious. I'm not going to print this."

"You'd better not. I'll break your pencil."

"How does he know?"

"He's got common sense. That's a rare commodity inside the beltway. I haven't seen enough of it in this town to fill a condom, but common sense is Jake Grafton's long suit."

Yocke chuckled.

"Better watch that," Toad admonished. "Your press card may melt if you crack a smile. Your reputation as an uptight superprick is on the line here."

Jack Yocke grinned. "I deserved that. Sorry about those cracks the first time I met you. I was having a bad day."

"Had one of those myself one time," Tarkington muttered. He stamped his feet. "I'm getting cold. Let's go inside."

Harrison Ronald stood by the side of the Mustang and stared at the right front tire. Flat.

Traffic whizzed by on Rhode Island Avenue. When he felt the wheel pulling and heard the thumping, he had pulled into a convenience store parking lot.

Fate, he decided, as he opened the trunk and rooted in it for the jack and lug wrench. On the way to his rendezvous with destiny, Galahad's horse threw a shoe. How comes this stuff never happens in the movies?

He got the front end off the ground, but the lug nuts were rusted on. Damn that Freeman, he never had these tires rotated or balanced or aligned. Got so damned much money he never takes care of anything.

He needed a cheater bar or a hammer. Frustrated, he sat on the pavement and kicked at the end of the lug wrench. The wrench flew off, scarring the nut. He tried it again. And again. Finally the nut turned.

A police cruiser pulled into the lot and stopped in front of the store. Two white cops. They got out of the cruiser, stood for a moment or two silently watching Ford wrestle with the wrench, then went inside.

Jesus, didn't they see the outline of the automatic in the small of his back, under his coat? Those shitheads. A weapon was the first thing they should have been looking for.

As Ford kicked at the last nut, he glanced through the big plate-glass windows. The cops were sipping coffee and flirting with the girl behind the counter.

He skinned his knuckle and it started bleeding. Well, it wouldn't bleed long. The dirt and grease would get in the skinned place and stop the blood. His father's hands had always had chunks missing, cavities full of dirt and grease that slowly, ever so slowly, healed just in time to be ripped open again. As a kid he had looked at his father's thick, heavy hands and asked, "Don't they hurt?"

Dad, wherever you are, my hands are cold and hurt like hell and my ass is freezing from the pavement and my nose is dripping.

He wiped his nose on his sleeve.

So what did'ya expect? The cops'd help? Get real!

Jack Yocke found himself staring at Tish Samuels. He had been watching her for several minutes when he realized with a start what he was doing. He glanced around to see if anyone had noticed. Jake Grafton met his eyes. Yocke smiled and looked away.

Okay, so she's not *Playboy* beautiful, she'll never be on the cover of *Cosmo.* In her own way she's lovely.

Standing there watching her move, watching her gestures and body language, he remembered the Cuban madonna on the hood of the truck with the baby at her breast. How long had he looked at that girl? Thirty seconds? A minute? That woman had been life going down the road. In spite of war, revolution, poverty, starvation, she rode with courage from the past into the future.

He looked at Tish and tried to visualize her on the hood of that truck. She could ride there, he concluded. She's a survivor.

He poured himself another drink and settled on the couch to watch Tish Samuels.

Maybe he was just getting older. His ambitions somehow seemed less important than they used to be and he was rapidly losing faith in his own opinions. How many of his colleagues truly believed in the ultimate wisdom of the voters? Opinionated, egotistical iconoclasts—Jack Yocke marching bravely among them—they believed only in themselves.

Okay, Jack. If your meager brains and wisdom won't be enough, what will be? What *do* you believe in?

Musing thus, he found himself contemplating his shoes and in his mind's eye seeing the people walking on the road to Havana, walking as the dust rose and the sun beat down, walking into the unknown.

In front of the Sanitary Bakery Harrison Ronald turned the car around on a whim and backed it up beside the others. Six other cars. A crowd tonight.

He went to the door and knocked.

The man inside shut the door behind him and bolted it and jerked his head. "They want you upstairs, second floor, way down at the end."

The interior of the warehouse was dark, no lights. The only illumination came from streetlights outside through the dirty windows high up in the wall. He knew what was in here though and went along confidently as his eyes adjusted.

Second floor, down at the end. God, there was nothing down there but some empty offices with six inches of dust, dirt, and rat shit, and some broken-down furniture that was so trashed the last tenant had left it.

He checked the position of the automatic in his waistband at the small of his back and pushed against the thumb safety to ensure that it was still on. Wouldn't do to shoot yourself in the ass, Harrison Ronald.

He went up the stairs and turned left, toward the east end of the building. He could hear moaning. A male voice.

He stopped dead. Someone groaning, a deep, animal sound.

Harrison Ronald stood frozen, listening. There! Again!

He slipped his hand under his coat and touched the butt of the automatic again, then pulled his hand away.

No one in sight. Just the windows and the dim light and the black shapes of the pillars that hold up the roof. And that sound.

The terror seized him then. He started shaking as the low animal sound curled around him and echoed gently down the vast, empty, dark room. Someone past screaming, someone who had screamed his lungs out, who was now past words and pleas and prayers, someone who was past all caring. Someone who moaned now only because he still breathed.

There was something else. A *smell!* He sniffed carefully. Burned meat. Yes, burned meat, the smell of fried fat, acrid and pungent.

Oh, my God!

Harrison Ronald Ford walked forward. Toward the door cracked open and the light leaking out.

The moans were louder, and the voice.

"You betrayed your brothers, your brothers of the *blood*. Sold out to the honky fucks, sold out your flesh and blood, *sold out . . ."* Freeman McNally. Harrison Ronald recognized the voice. Freeman McNal— *"What did they pay you? Money? You'll never spend it. Women? You'll never screw 'em, not with what you got now. Ha!"*

McNally was insane. Crazy mad. His voice was an octave too high, on the verge of hysteria.

"Kill me."

Silence.

A scream. *"Kill me!"*

Harrison Ronald Ford pushed open the door. The stench was overpowering.

A naked man was tied to a chair in the middle of the room and above him an unshaded bulb burned. At least, he had once been a man. Strips of flesh hung from his frame. His crotch was a mass of raw meat. His face—Harrison walked closer to see his face—only one eye left—the other socket was black and burned and empty. On his chest were more burns. Amazingly, there was very little blood.

"Put the gun away, Sammy."

He looked around. Other men sat in chairs around the wall. On the floor was a laundry iron with bits of flesh still clinging to it, a wisp of smoke rising.

"Put the gun away, Sammy." It was Freeman. He was standing against the window. He had a pistol out and was pointing it.

Harrison looked down. The Colt was in his hand. He lowered it, then looked again at the man in the chair.

"Kill me."

"The shithead sold us out. He was whispering tales to the feds. He admitted it, finally."

He could kill them all. The thought ran through Harrison's mind and he moved his thumb to the safety. Five of them, seven rounds. Freeman first, then the others. As fast as he could pull the trigger.

Freeman walked over to Ford and stood looking at the man in the chair with his arms crossed over his chest.

"Isn't that some heavy shit? I've known him as long as I can remember. *And he sold me out."* Freeman snorted and shook his head. The sweat flew from his brow. "And all this time I thought it was you, Sammy. Shee-it!

McNally shook his head again and walked back to the window. There he turned and pointed his pistol at Harrison Ford. "You got a gun. Kill him." He said it conversationally, like he was ordering a pizza.

The tortured man was staring at Ford with his one eye. His hands were still tied behind the chair, or what was left of his hands. Traces of white showed through the seared flesh—bones.

"Shoot him," Freeman said, making it an order.

Harrison took a step closer. The eye followed him. Now the badly burned lips moved. He bent down to hear. "Kill me," the lips whispered.

Harrison thumbed off the safety. He raised the Colt and pointed it above the raw, oozing hole where the man's left ear had been. The ear itself lay on the floor by the iron.

"Sorry, Ike," Ford said, and pulled the trigger.

CHAPTER NINETEEN

* * * * * * * * * * *

IKE Randolph's body was in the trunk of the car when Harrison Ronald parked it on E Street in front of the FBI building. Freeman had told him to get rid of it, dump the body in the street somewhere. The mutilated corpse would certainly be a little point to ponder for anyone who someday might entertain the notion of crossing Freeman McNally.

Yeah, Freeman. Whatever you say, man. Four of them had tossed the body in the trunk and Harrison had driven away. He hadn't waved good-bye.

And he pondered the point.

The sun was up.

Sunday. Eight a.m. The streets and parking places were empty. In a few hours the suburban malls would open and the last-minute Christmas crowds would pack the parking lots and surge through the sprawling temples of retailing. The shoppers would swarm over the downtown malls too, but that was two hours away. Right now the only people on the streets were alcoholics and derelicts. Paper and trash from overflowing cans swept by the car, carried by the wind.

Harrison sat behind the wheel with the engine off and listened to the silence.

He had made it. He was still alive.

His hands shook.

The relief hit him like a hammer and he began to sob.

He was tired, desperately tired. The tears rolled down his cheeks and he lacked the energy to move.

Done.

Well, hell, I gotta get to Hooper. Give him the keys to Ike Randolph's hearse, then get some sleep.

He remembered to lock the car, then climbed the stairs to the FBI building and walked through the open foyer to the quadrangle. He went down the stairs to the quadrangle plaza and crossed to the kiosk where the Federal Security guard stood. The uniformed man watched him approach.

"Tom Hooper. Call him."

"And who are you?"

"Sam . . . Harrison Ronald Ford. Evansville, Indiana, police. He's expecting me."

"If you want to stand over there, sir, I'll call up and see if he's here."

He walked away so the rent-a-cop could watch his hands. He was too tired to stand. He sank down against the wall and crossed his arms on his knees and lowered his head to rest on them.

He was sitting like that, crying, when Thomas Hooper spoke to him six or seven minutes later.

"There's a corpse in the trunk of the car."

"Who?" Freddy and Hooper stared at Ford.

"Ike Randolph. They tortured him. He's a real mess."

The FBI agents looked at each other.

"We gotta ditch the body."

"Why?" Freddy asked, incredulous.

"We gotta, man," Harrison insisted.

"Now listen. We go to the grand jury on Monday. Monday evening or Tuesday they hand down murder indictments and we scoop up Freeman McNally and his lieutenants and lock them up. They won't get out on bail. There's no bail for murder. Then we give the grand jury all the rest of it and let them come up with a couple hundred counts."

Harrison was tired. "You listen. Freeman gave me tonight off. But if that body don't show up someplace, he'll smell a rat. The very first thing he'll do is check my apartment to see if I'm there. I won't be, man, I can guarantee you that. I ain't *ever* going back there. Then Freeman'll *know.* Maybe he'll skip. Maybe he'll be waiting with heavy ordnance when you go to bust him. Maybe he'll put out a contract on me. *I don't want to spend the rest of my life looking over my shoulder!"*

"We can't just go dump a corpse in the public street and—"

"Why not?" Tom Hooper asked.

"Well, hell, we're the cops, for Christ's sake."

"We dump the corpse and wait half an hour and call the police. Why not?"

Hooper was thinking of the grand jury and the lawyers. Just because the FBI wanted a quick indictment was no guarantee there would be one. It might take a week. And as he sat staring at Harrison Ford, he realized that he was going to play it Ford's way or the undercover man might go to pieces. Ford might not last a week.

"Where you parked?"

"Right in front of the building on E."

"Come on, Freddy. Let's go get this over with."

"At least let's pull the car into the basement and let the lab guys photograph the body."

"Are you fucking out of your mind?" Harrison roared. "The only reason, the *only reason,* I'm still alive after ten months of this shit is that nobody knew I was undercover. Now you're going to let the lab people see the car and the body and me? Do I look suicidal?"

"Forget it, Freddy," Hooper said. "We'll just be creative on our reports. Won't be the first time. Not for me, anyway."

In the car they talked about it. They drove down toward Fort McNair. On the east side of the army post was a huge, empty parking lot. Weeds growing up through cracks in the asphalt. Beer cans and trash strewn about.

The parking lot was bounded on the west and north by an eight-foot-high brick wall. Across the wall were huge old houses, quarters for senior army officers stationed in Washington. To the east, sixty yards or so away, were small private houses, but brush and trees obscured the view. A power relay station surrounded by a chain-link fence formed the southern boundary of the two-acre parking area.

They didn't waste time looking the place over. Ford backed up toward the brick wall and popped the button in the glove box to release the trunk lid. He left the engine running. All three men got out and went around back.

Freddy took one look and heaved.

"For the love of—"

"Look at his hands! They burned his fingers off!"

"Come on, you shitheads," Ford growled. "Grab hold."

They laid the corpse on the ground and got back in the car. Ford jerked the shift lever into drive and fed gas. Freddy retched some more.

"What I can't figure," Harrison mused, "is why Ike? Why'd he think Ike was the stoolie?"

"Remember Senator Cherry?"

"The mouth."

"Yeah. We told him Ike was our man inside."

Harrison Ronald braked the car to a stop and slowly turned to face Hooper, who was sitting beside him in the passenger seat. "You mean Ike was a cop?"

"Naw. He was just a hood. But we figured that since Cherry was talking out of school and there was little chance we could shut him up, we'd better do something to cover your ass. So we gave him a name—Ike Randolph."

Harrison faced forward. He flexed his fingers around the wheel.

"And Freeman killed him. That'll put him in prison for life. Too bad about Ike, but—"

"Freeman didn't kill Ike." Harrison Ronald said it so softly Freddy in the backseat leaned forward.

"What say?"

"Freeman didn't kill Ike. I did. Oh, Freeman tortured him, mutilated him, but he wanted to spread the fun around. He's that kind of guy. *I killed him.*"

"*You?*" Freddy said, stunned.

"It was Ike or me, man. If I hadn't pulled the trigger, I'd be a hundred and eighty pounds of burned dead meat this very minute. Just like Ike."

"Drive. Goddammit, *drive!*" Hooper commanded. "We can't sit here like three fucking tourists in the middle of the street. Everybody in town will get our license number."

Harrison put the car into motion.

"*You* killed him," Freddy said, still wrestling with it.

"What in hell did you think was gonna happen?" Harrison roared, sick of these two men and sick of himself. "Fuckhead! You *white* fuckhead! You *knew* if Cherry talked Ike Randolph was a corpse looking for a grave to fall into. And now he's dead! Well and truly dead, dead as I would be if anybody had whispered my name."

"Why didn't you dump the body before you came to us?" Freddy asked.

"I wanted you to see it. Ike was a pathological asshole, but he didn't deserve *that.* I wanted you coat-and-tie FBI paperpushers to see it and smell it and get it smeared all over your clean white hands. So sue me."

The ceiling was at least five thousand feet Henry Charon estimated as he drove up the interstate toward Frederick, Maryland. Hazy, five or six miles visibility. Not like out west where you can see for fifty miles on the bad days.

He knew where he was going, a little park along the Potomac. There should be no one there in December, a week before Christmas. The place had been deserted last week when he found it after consulting an aviation sectional map and a highway map. He had drawn some lines and done some calculating.

Just before he got to Frederick he exited the four-lane and turned south on a county road. The two-lane blacktop wound southward through fertile farming country of the Monocacy River valley. Neat homes and barns stood near the road and cattle grazed in the fields.

Henry Charon turned right onto a dirt road just past an abandoned gas station and proceeded west for 4.2 miles. The road he wanted was sheltered by a grove of trees. There!

No fresh tracks in the mud. And not too much mud. That was good.

He parked the car and pulled on his parka and gloves. Before he put his feet on the ground, he pulled a pair of galoshes over his hunting boots and buckled them.

It took him half an hour to check the area. No hunters or fishermen on the river, no one in the fields to the north.

The only house visible from the parking lot was a half mile or so away on the other side of the Potomac River, in Virginia. He checked the house with binoculars. No one about.

Occasionally a light plane flew over. Charon didn't look up. He was only sixteen nautical miles north of Dulles International and seven or eight miles north of Leesburg. Harper's Ferry was about fifteen miles to the west. So there were going to be planes.

He got the radios from the trunk of the car and went over to the pile of gravel near the bank, where he sat down. From this gravel pile he had an unobstructed view straight up and to the south and southeast from the zenith down to the treetops on the other side of the river, about ten degrees above the horizon. That was enough. More than enough.

He turned on each radio and checked the batteries. He had installed a fresh set in each unit this morning and he had others in the car, just in case. The needles rose into the green.

He selected the VHF frequency band on the first radio and dialed in the frequency for the northern sector of Dulles Approach, 126.1. With the antenna up and tweaked to the right just a little, reception was acceptable. On the other radio he selected UHF, and dialed in frequency 384.9. He was fairly confident they would be using VHF, but he wasn't taking any chances.

Both radios began spewing out the usual chatter between controllers and pilots. Charon arranged one radio on each side of the rock pile and adjusted the volume knob. They didn't need to be loud—he had excellent hearing in spite of the thousands of rifle shots he had listened to over the years without ear protection.

He got out the sandwich and coffee he had purchased at a fast-food emporium's drive-through lane this morning. He ate slowly, savoring each bite. The coffee cooled too quickly, but he drank it anyway. It was going to be a long afternoon.

Perhaps. Who knew?

All the preparation, all the planning was over. He was as ready as he would ever get. He thought about the past three weeks, about the plans he had made and contingencies he had provided for.

One chance in four. He had a twenty-five percent chance today, he concluded. As usual, the quarry had the advantage, which was just the way Henry Charon liked it.

Charon grinned. He finished the coffee and sandwich and carefully placed the paper and cup on the backseat of the car, where it couldn't blow out, yet where he could dispose of it the first chance he got.

Then he sat down again on the gravel and began listening intently to the radios.

He rose occasionally to scan with the binoculars, then resumed his seat.

This little park was on one of the two routes he thought it probable the helicopter carrying the President might take when flying from Camp David to the White House. He suspected that the helicopter would in all likelihood avoid the airport traffic area at Frederick and Gaithersburg. If so, it could pass those two airports to the east and enter Washington heading straight south for the White House, thereby overflying Silver Spring and Bethesda. On the other hand, if the chopper passed to the west of Frederick it would probably overfly this little park on the Potomac on its way straight down the river into Washington.

As he had studied the map Charon had come to favor the Potomac route. As the helicopter descended into the Washington area noise in populated areas would be minimized by flying down the river. That struck him as just the kind of consideration that a harried staffer would base a decision upon.

Still, he wasn't a pilot and he knew next to nothing about air traffic control. He hadn't had the time to monitor the route of other Camp David trips or to do the dry runs that would ensure success at the proper time. This whole thing was pretty shoestring. Yet the longer he spent in this area checking things out, the greater were the chances he would be seen and remembered.

So he would try this. If he got the opportunity, he would shoot. If not, he would look for another opportunity.

One chance in four. Maybe less. But enough.

He sighed and watched the birds and listened to the river when the radios fell momentarily silent. Occasionally he rose and used the binoculars to check the area. There were three picnic tables between the parking area and the riverbank. Near each table was a small stone barbecue grill. In the summer this would be a very pleasant spot for an outing, if you could get an empty table.

It was a few minutes after three p.m. when he heard the call he was waiting for. It came over the VHF radio.

"Dulles Approach, Marine One's with you climbing to three thousand out of Papa Forty en route to Papa Fifty-six, over." Charon knew those areas: Prohibited Area 40 was Camp David, Prohibited Area 56 was the White House–Capitol complex.

"Marine One, Dulles Approach, squawk Four One Four Two Ident."

A Cessna pilot made a call to Approach now, but his transmission went unanswered. Henry Charon turned off the radio, tuned to UHF, and put it back in the trunk of the car.

"Marine One, Dulles Approach, radar contact. You are cleared as filed to Papa Fifty-six, any altitude below five thousand. Report reaching three thousand and any change of altitude thereafter, over."

"Marine One cleared as filed. Report any change of altitude. We're level at three now."

"Readback correct. Cessna Five One Six One Yankee, go ahead with your request."

One last scan with the binoculars. He let them dangle around his neck. From the trunk he pulled out a roll of carpet. He put it on the ground and unrolled it. He took a second roll out and did the same.

Charon put one of the four-foot-long tubes carefully on the ground right by the gravel pile after he had inspected it for damage. The second he inspected and kept in his hands.

He arranged himself against the gravel so he had some support for his lower back, yet the exhaust from the missile would pass safely above the gravel. They would find this spot, of course, and the carbon from the missile exhaust would prove that it was fired here. He just didn't want the hot exhaust deflected onto his back. He put the missile launcher across his lap.

He sat there and waited, counting the minutes. If the chopper was cruising at a hundred and twenty knots, it was making two nautical miles a minute over the ground. He had figured the distance at twenty-four miles. Twelve minutes. With a tail wind or more speed, the time would be less. He would wait for eighteen minutes and if the chopper had not appeared it would have used a different route. And the wind was out of the northwest, so the chopper would have a tail wind today. Eighteen minutes, then he would leave and try something else.

The helicopter might not use this route. There was no way of knowing of course. He would soon see.

And the pilot of the helicopter didn't make the call to Dulles Approach from Camp David. He had lifted off a minute or two earlier and was climbing out on course when he called Approach. So less than twelve minutes.

The minutes passed as he scanned the sky. Six, seven, eight . . .

He heard the distinctive noise of a helicopter. He looked. The trees behind him would block his view until it was almost overhead.

He turned on the batteries in both launchers and grasped the binoculars.

There it was! High, to his left. Perhaps a mile east of his position.

He checked with the binoculars, thumbing the focus wheel expertly. Yes. A Marine VIP chopper, like the one he had seen on the White House lawn.

He lowered the binoculars and raised the missile launcher to his shoulder. Power on. Aim. Lock on. He squeezed the trigger.

The missile left with a roar.

Charon dropped the empty launcher and picked up the second one. Power on. Aim. Lock on. Shoot!

With the second missile on its way he tossed both launchers, the rugs, and the binoculars in the trunk of the car.

He looked up. The first missile had already detonated, leaving a puff of dirty smoke against the light gray overcast above. The chopper was falling off to the right, the nose swinging.

Whap! The warhead of the second missile exploded right against the chopper.

The helicopter's forward progress ceased and it began to rotate and fall, a corkscrewing motion.

Henry Charon picked up the remaining radio.

"*Mayday, Mayday! Marine One has had a total hydraulic failure and has lost an engine! We're going down!*"

"Marine One, Dulles, say again."

The pitch of the voice was higher, but the pilot was still thinking, still in control. The words poured out. "*Dulles, we've lost an engine and hydraulics. The copilot's dead. Two explosions, like missiles. We're going down and . . . uh . . . roll the ambulances and emergency vehicles. We're going down!*"

Charon snapped off the radio and carefully placed it in the trunk of the car on top of one of the rugs. He closed the trunk lid firmly.

He scanned the area. Nothing left lying about.

The assassin paused by the driver's door and looked again for the stricken helicopter. Much lower, falling several miles to the southeast with the nose very low . . . rotating quickly, like once a second. The crash was going to be real bad.

Henry Charon seated himself in the car, started it, and drove away.

CHAPTER TWENTY

* * * * * * * * * * *

HENRY Charon dialed the radio to a Washington news-talk station and pointed the car north, toward Frederick. A woman was debating with various callers the appropriateness of the federal response to the AIDS crisis. At Frederick he turned east on I-70. When he saw a rest stop, he pulled off.

He parked the car on the edge of the lot and removed the galoshes. These he put in the trunk. He carefully wrapped the spent missile launching tubes in the rugs and wound the rugs with gray duct tape. After closing the trunk and ensuring the car was locked, he walked fifty yards to the rest rooms and relieved himself.

Rolling again, he was listening to the radio when the announcer broke in with a bulletin:

"A United States Marine Corps helicopter carrying the President of the United States and several other high-ranking officials has crashed in northern Virginia north of Dulles Airport. Emergency crews from Dulles International are responding. We have no word yet on the condition of the President. No further information is available at this time. Stay tuned for further news as we receive it."

The radio station stopped taking calls. In short order the woman guest was off the air and two newsmen began discussing and speculating about the bulletin. They mentioned the fact that President Bush had spent the weekend at Camp David and was presumably on his way back to Washington when the accident occurred. They called it an accident. They read the list of the officials that had spent the weekend with the President and speculated about the reasons the helicopter might have crashed. The reasons they advanced all concerned mechanical failure or a midair collision. It was obvious to Charon that neither man knew much about helicopters.

He turned the radio off.

So it had started. The hunt was on and he was the quarry.

He turned off the interstate and followed the twists and turns of a county road for several miles until he reached a landfill. He pulled up to the booth.

The woman inside had the radio on.

"Five dollars," she said distractedly.

He took out his wallet and gave her the money. She pushed a small clipboard at him. On it was a form, a certification that he was not disposing of hazardous materials. False swearing, the form said, was perjury in the second degree.

"What's happened?" Charon asked as he scrawled something illegible by the printed X.

"President Bush's helicopter has crashed."

"You're kidding? Is he dead?"

"They don't know yet."

Charon handed the clipboard back and was waved on through.

More luck. His was the only vehicle there to dump trash. A snorting bulldozer was attacking a small mountain of the stuff while a huge flock of seagulls darted and swooped.

Henry Charon opened the trunk and got rid of the galoshes and the two missile launchers wrapped in carpet. He threw the cylinders down toward the base of a garbage pile that looked as if it would be next. Then he got the sandwich wrapper, bag, and coffee cup from the floor of the rear seat and added them to the garbage wasteland spread out at his feet.

He pulled the car out of the dozer's way, carefully avoiding the soft ground off the vehicle ruts. A pickup truck loaded with construction debris parked a little further down the cut and the driver began throwing off trash. He was still at it when the big dozer shoved a hill-sized pile of garbage and dirt over the rug-wrapped missile launchers.

Special Agent Thomas Hooper got the news at the FBI facility in Quantico. Hooper, Freddy Murray, and an assistant federal prosecutor were interrogating Harrison Ronald when the call came.

Prior to his assignment three years ago to the drug crimes division, Hooper had served for five years as special agent in charge of the FBI SWAT team. He was still on call. Use of the FBI for paramilitary operations was rare, but occasionally a situation arose. When the situation required more men than the SWAT team had available, the watch officer went down the standby list of qualified agents. He wanted Hooper to go to the crash site. He passed the news, the order, and the location in as few words as possible.

Hooper hung up the phone and found the other men were staring at him, no doubt in reaction to the look on his face. "The President's helicopter just crashed," he told them, "with him in it. I gotta go."

"Is he dead?"

"Don't know," Hooper muttered to his stunned audience on his way out of the room.

*   *   *

Jake, Callie, and Amy Grafton were returning to their apartment from a shopping mall when they heard the news on the radio. The family carried the packages upstairs and Amy ran for the television. Regular programming had been interrupted and the networks were using their weekend news teams.

Like tens of millions of viewers all over America, the Graftons got the news as the networks acquired it. Four people were dead in the wreckage and four were injured, three critically. Both the pilots were dead, as was the secretary of state and the national security adviser. One of those critically injured was the President, who had been flown to Bethesda Naval Hospital by another helicopter. Mrs. Bush, on vacation in Kennebunkport, was flying back to Washington.

Footage of the wreckage was shown, shot from about a hundred yards away.

Later in the evening witnesses to the crash were interviewed. One elderly woman working in her flowerbed had seen the craft fall. She searched for words as the camera rolled: "I knew they were going to die. It was falling so fast, twirling around, I closed my eyes and prayed."

What did you pray for?

"For God to take to Himself the souls of those about to die."

Amy decided she wanted to sit beside her father on the couch. He wrapped his arms around her.

In the newsroom of *The Washington Post* Jack Yocke was assigned to assist a team of reporters in writing a story assessing the presidency of George Bush, a story that would not run unless he died. Two weeks ago Yocke would have chafed at not being sent off willy-nilly to the crash site. Not this evening. As he called up the major stories of the Bush presidency on his computer screen and perused them, he found himself trying to get a sense of this man chosen by his fellow citizens to lead them.

World War II naval aviator, Texas oil entrepreneur, self-made millionaire, politician, public servant—why did George Bush want the toughest job in the world? What had he said? How did he approach the job? Why did he avoid the spotlight's glare? Did he have a sense of where America should go, and if so, what was it? These questions Yocke wrestled with, though he occasionally took a moment to read the wire service ticker and listen to the television.

He also took a moment to call Tish Samuels.

"Heard the news?"

"Isn't it terrible?"

"Yes."

"Oh, I feel for his wife," Tish said. "I admire her so. This must be extraordinarily tough on her, to be so frightened with the whole world watching."

* * *

The helicopter had crashed in a pasture just a hundred yards west of the Potomac, which flowed south at this point. In the glare of portable floodlights Special Agent Tom Hooper caught a glimpse of at least three dead cows. One of them was ripped almost in half. He asked the Virginia state trooper escorting him toward the helicopter.

"Shrapnel from the rotor blades," the trooper said. "The forward blades were still turning when it hit the ground."

The wreckage looked grotesque in the glare of the floodlights. The chopper had impacted nose low, so the cockpit was badly squashed. The crew hadn't had a chance. A team was cutting through the wreckage to get the last body out of the cockpit. Another team wearing army fatigue uniforms was examining the engines. The rest of the machine was almost as badly mangled as the cockpit, but not quite. Hooper marveled that four fragile human beings had survived the helicopter's encounter with the earth. Maybe.

The senior Secret Service agent was holding an impromptu meeting beside the machine. Hooper joined the group.

"The army experts are ninety-nine percent certain that this machine was struck by missiles. At least two. Probably heat seekers. We'll know for sure tomorrow when we analyze the warhead fragments."

"You're saying that this was an assassination attempt?" someone asked, the disbelief evident in his voice.

"Yes."

Hooper was stunned. He turned slightly to look at the wreckage, and now the evidence leaped at him—a hole and jagged tears in the right engine compartment, and another spray of small holes near the exhaust.

"When are you going to announce this?"

"That's up to the White House. None of *you* are going to say it to anybody. Now there's a ton of things that have to be done as soon as possible, so let's get at it."

The Secret Service assigned the FBI the job of locating the place from where the missiles had been fired. Hooper walked back toward his car and its radio with his mind racing. He would draw a circle with a ten-mile radius around this spot and seal it. Then he would search every foot of ground within the circle and interview every human being he could find. For that he would need people, as many as he could get. The local sheriffs and state police could help with roadblocks. But the searching, for that he would need a lot of people. Perhaps the Marines at Quantico could lend him some.

An assassin. He was out there somewhere. No doubt the Secret Service would redouble its efforts to guard the Vice-President and Mrs. Bush, but he would check to see if they needed more people.

So he got on the radio and began. He knew he would be at it all night and into tomorrow, and he was. Understandably, Hooper completely forgot about the grand jury and Freeman McNally. They would have to wait.

Henry Charon settled into the Hampshire Avenue apartment to watch television. He was munching a bag of chips and sipping a beer when someone knocked on the door.

He scanned the apartment. Nothing lying around that would incriminate him. Leaving the television on, he opened the door.

"Hello, Mr. Tackett," Grisella Clifton said. "Remember me? The building manager?" She was wearing a frumpy housedress and a bulky sweater.

"Oh, sure. Grisella, right?"

She nodded. "My television is on the fritz. May I watch with you?"

"Sure. Come in."

She settled in on the couch. He offered her some potato chips and beer. "I just couldn't. I'm not the least bit hungry. Isn't this whole thing so tragic?"

Henry Charon agreed that it was and plopped into the stuffed lounge chair.

"You're watching NBC? I've been watching CNN. They've been talking to some witnesses who saw the crash. What could have gone wrong with that helicopter?"

Charon shrugged. "We can change the channel if you like."

"If you don't mind. I think CNN is so . . . so newsy." Obligingly, he rose and turned the dial. "I just can't believe what happened to my set. The picture suddenly got all fuzzy. Just when there is something important on, it quits. Isn't that so typical?"

"Ummm."

"I do hope you don't mind this intrusion. But I just needed to be around someone. In the midst of life . . . It really bothers me, y'know?"

He nodded and glanced at her. She prattled on. He found he could hear anything important said on TV and still catch enough of her remarks to make appropriate responses.

She ceased talking when a doctor at Bethesda Naval Hospital came on the show. He explained the extent of the President's injuries in detail to the dozens of reporters and used a pointer and a mannequin to answer questions.

What if he survives? Charon asked himself. He had been paid to kill Bush, not put him in the hospital.

Not a word had yet been said on TV about an assassination attempt, but no doubt the Secret Service and FBI knew. The physical evidence of the helicopter would shriek murder to the first professional aircraft accident investigator who looked. Getting to Bush for a second attempt would be a real neat trick.

Listening to Grisella Clifton's nervous chatter—why was she nervous, anyway?—watching the images on the screen, he began to examine the problem. The armor might have a crack somewhere. He would have to think about it.

All over America, in hamlets and cities and on farms, people gathered around televisions or sat in automobiles with the radios on. The President of the United States lay in a hospital close to death, and two hundred and fifty million Americans held their breath.

It didn't matter if you had voted for George Bush or against him, whether you liked his politics, whether you even knew what his politics were. You sat and listened and were deeply moved as the condition of the President became known. He was seriously injured, with a concussion, broken ribs, a damaged spleen and a seriously fractured leg.

The surgeon at Bethesda reappeared on the television and ignored all the shouted questions. "We don't know. We don't know. We're running tests and we'll see." He paused, listened to the cacophony a moment, then said, "He's unconscious. His vital signs are erratic. We don't know."

He was not a king, not a dictator, but a fellow American who had been chosen to lead the nation for a period of four years. Four years—long enough for a skillful politician who understood the mood and spirit of the people to accomplish something worthwhile, yet not enough time for a fool or incompetent to do irreparable damage.

The nation had had all kinds of presidents in the 201 years since George Washington had taken the oath of office. Yet each of them had understood that they spoke for their fellow citizens, and by doing so they created in the American people a deep, abiding respect for the office of the presidency and the men who held it that seemed, in a curious way, to have little to do with the individual merit or personal failings of each temporary occupant. Americans expected the president to weigh the interests of everyone when he made a decision, to speak for all of them. From their congressmen and senators they expected partisanship; from their president they expected leadership. This working politician, this common citizen they raised to the high place, he became the embodiment of their unspoken hopes and dreams. In some vague, slightly mystical way, he became the personification of America. And of all it stood for.

So on this Sunday evening in December, all over America people collected themselves and took stock. Churches were opened so that those so inclined could pray and hear words of comfort. Parents told their children where they were and what they had been doing when they heard that John F. Kennedy had been assassinated. Switchboards jammed as millions decided to call home and touch base with their roots. In airports, shopping malls, and bars from coast to coast, as they gathered around television sets strangers spoke to each other.

There were incidents, of course. In Dallas a man in a bar cheered when an announcer said the President's life was in grave danger; he was severely beaten and, had he not been rescued by hastily summoned police, would probably have been beaten to death. An Iranian with a long-expired student visa lost his front teeth at a shopping mall in suburban Chicago after he loudly announced that George Bush deserved to die. In San Francisco a waiter dumped a tray of food in the lap of a self-styled animal rights activist who expressed a similar opinion. The activist repeated her remark to the manager who had rushed to apologize, and he summarily ejected her and apologized to his other patrons, who applauded loudly.

At nine-thirty that evening one of the network correspondents informed the White House press secretary's office that his network had a story that the dead pilot of the President's helicopter had mentioned explosions—"like missiles"—in his last transmission to Dulles Approach. The network was going with the story on the hour. Did the White House wish to comment.

Yes, it did. The press secretary said he would hold a news conference at ten-fifteen, and he asked the network to hold the story until after the conference. After a hurried consultation with New York, the correspondent agreed.

At ten twenty-two that night the White House press secretary appeared at the rostrum in the basement press room and squinted as his eyes adjusted to the glare of the floodlights. He held a paper in front of him and read from it. At his side were the directors of the Secret Service and the FBI.

"The Vice-President of the United States has authorized me to announce that the helicopter accident this afternoon which claimed the lives of five people was an assassination attempt. We assume—"

He got no further. People who knew better shouted questions at the top of their lungs.

The press secretary waited for the uproar to die. He swabbed his forehead with a handkerchief and continued to stare at the paper in his hand. Finally he resumed:

"We assume that the assassination attempt was directed at the President of the United States, although we have no direct evidence to support or refute that assumption. Apparently a party or parties unknown fired at least two heat-seeking missiles at the helicopter carrying the President, at least two of which appear to have inflicted major damage on the craft, rendering it unairworthy. The pilot immediately lost control. The crash occurred shortly thereafter. If you have questions, the directors of the Secret Service and the FBI are here to help me answer them."

"How do you know about the missiles?"

"The shrapnel from the warheads punctured the fuselage in many places," the director of the Secret Service said.

"Do you have any suspects?"

"Not yet."

"Do you have any clues?"

"None that we're going to discuss in public."

"Are arrests imminent?"

"No."

"Is it true that the pilot of the helicopter told Dulles Approach about explosions, like missiles, in one of his last transmissions?" This was from the network correspondent who had agreed to hold this story.

"Yes, that is true."

"Why wasn't this announced earlier?"

The press secretary was tired and had had a hell of a bad evening. He had little patience with questions like that. "We had to check it out. There are a couple of thousand rumors out there, including one that the pilot was drunk. We will release information when we have verified it and believe it is true. Not before."

"Was the pilot drunk?"

"Not to my knowledge. There will be autopsies on all the victims, of course."

Across the nation the mood of those still watching television, and they were many, turned gloomy. An assassin. A killer. Not an ordinary killer, but one who had directly attacked the United States of America.

All four of the networks seized the assassin angle with both hands. Film clips were aired of the Kennedy assassination. Pictures of Lincoln, Garfield, and McKinley were shown. Profiles of past presidential assassins and would-be killers were hastily assembled and aired. One network sent a crew to the New York residence of Jacqueline Onassis, Kennedy's widow, and camped outside with the camera running. The lady didn't come out.

At the *Post* Ott Mergenthaler stopped by Yocke's desk. The television in the corner was showing footage of Jack Ruby shooting Lee Harvey Oswald. "Wanta go get a sandwich?"

"Okay. I can take a break."

They walked to the elevator and took it down to the cafeteria. Normally at this time of night it was closed, but not this night.

"What do you think?" Yocke asked. "A nut like Oswald?"

"Not very likely. Crackpots don't shoot missiles."

"Remember a few weeks ago when they extradited Chano Aldana?

That 'communiqué' from the Extraditables in Colombia? 'We will bring the American government to its knees.'"

"I remember. If this is their work, they've made a good start."

"So what do you think?"

"I think nobody in Colombia has factored Quivering Dan Quayle into their calculations."

"As I recall, you called Quayle Bush's biggest mistake."

"That's just one of the nicer things I've said about him. I also said he was impeachment insurance for Bush."

They went through the serving line, helping themselves to cold sandwiches and hot coffee. When they were seated, Mergenthaler continued, "Quayle's a genuine nice guy, never been accused of being a deep thinker, no ideological cross to bear although he can mouth the conservative line and appears at times to believe some of it. He's just the kind of guy you'd like to include in a foursome on Sunday morning. Pleasant, affable, likes the kind of jokes dentists tell and can probably tell a few himself. Never worried about money a day in his life. If you hit your last ball into the creek, he'll toss you one with a grin and refuse to take a dollar for it."

Ott sipped coffee and munched some on his sandwich.

"Every observer who knows this guy says he grows into his job. People underestimate him—that's ridiculously easy to do—and he surprises them. He's got a modest amount of brains but never had to use them before he got into public office. So he learns how to be a congressman, how to be a senator, how to be a vice president. His staff feeds him lines to say and he says them. If Bush dies, Quayle will presumably learn how to be a president. Given enough time, enough good will by all concerned, he can probably learn how to do a mediocre job."

"He isn't going to have any time at all," Yocke said.

"That's my point. He's walking straight into a blast furnace. In addition to all the stuff Bush has been juggling, Quayle will have the drug crisis going full blast, hot enough to melt steel. People are going to want this kid who never made a tough decision in his life to *do* something. And you know what? I'll bet he will!"

Ott worked on his sandwich some more, then added, "If I was a doper in Colombia, I'd crawl into a hole and pull the hole in after me. The biggest temptation any man in the White House faces is to overreact. You got all those generals who'll want to go kick ass. If the Extraditables claim Bush as a trophy, the public is going to howl for blood. We may have a real rootin', tootin' *war* on our hands, mister. The hell with the S-and-L crisis, the hell with federal aid to education, the hell with balancing the budget. We're going to blow the whole wad on a trip to Colombia to burn out that hornet's nest. You watch. You see if I'm right."

"I don't think the Colombian dopers are behind this, Ott," Yocke said.

"Oh, I know, Aldana blew a lot of smoke. But that terrorist gig they've been running in Colombia won't work here. Not in America."

"I wish I had your optimism. If Quayle sends the Army and Air Force to Colombia to kick ass, *that* won't work. The people we're after will run and hide. We'd have to burn the damn place down and sift the ashes to get 'em. No, if the Colombians start murdering judges here and buying everyone who can be bought, America is going to change and change fast. *This will cease to be the America you and I grew up in.* I'm not sure what it will become. Frankly, I hope to God I never have to find out."

"Let's pray that George Bush doesn't die."

Ott snorted. "More to the point, we'd better pray that the Colombians don't claim they shot him down."

CHAPTER TWENTY-ONE

★ ★ ★ ★ ★ ★ ★ ★ ★ ★ ★ ★

Sitting in his room in the FBI dorm at the Quantico Marine barracks, Harrison Ronald Ford flipped through the Monday morning *Post* looking for the story about Ike Randolph's body. Most of the paper was devoted to the assassination attempt. That and a minute-by-minute account of Bush's life, including interviews with people who knew him when.

At first Ford thought it wasn't there, but he finally found the story on page B-7, three whole paragraphs: Body of a severely burned unidentified black male shot through the head found Sunday morning by a military policeman on a routine check of the perimeter of Fort McNair. Well, that was better than the anonymous phone call idea, though Ford was sure that someone had told the MP to go look.

He was disappointed. Likely as not Freeman and the boys would never see this little piddley story, considering what great readers they were. The whole damn crowd didn't invest a dollar a month in reading material. If it wasn't on the top half of the front page and staring at them through the glass of the newspaper dispenser, they would never see it.

Maybe one or two of the TV stations had picked up the story and run it when they were momentarily out of George Bush footage.

He tossed the paper on the desk.

Nothing was going right. The grand jury appearance had been postponed, Hooper was out chasing assassins all over Maryland and northern Virginia, Freddy was unreachable at the J. Edgar Hoover Building. And he was sitting here stewing. Wondering what was going through Freeman McNally's agile little mind.

It wouldn't be anything good, that was certain. When he didn't show up for work tonight, no doubt someone would check his apartment. At least he had had the good sense to leave the Mustang parked in front of the joint. That simpleton Freddy had wanted to take it back to the FBI lab. Harrison had told Hooper and Freddy in no uncertain terms what he thought of their intellectual ability.

His disappearance would not be something Freeman McNally would ignore. What was it he had said about Fat Tony Anselmo—you can find out anything if you know who to ask and have enough money?

Harrison stared out the window at the manicured lawn and trimmed trees.

The day was dismal. Overcast, threatening to rain.

And he was sitting here in plain view of anybody out there with a set of binoculars. He lowered the window blind and pulled the string to shut the louvers.

Then he threw himself full-length on the bed.

Ten months of this shit and he was still sweating it. Would it ever end?

"Did you watch any TV this morning?" Mergenthaler demanded of Jack Yocke on Monday morning. The older man stood at the opening of the cubicle with a wad of newspapers in his hand. He always read the New York *Times,* the Chicago *Herald Tribune,* and the Los Angeles *Times* every morning when he arrived for work.

"Fifteen minutes or so."

"Those idiots are canonizing Bush and he hasn't even had the decency to die. I got NBC's eulogy with my morning coffee. If he lives we'll have our very first saint in the White House. The Democrats won't even bother to have a convention in '92."

"Haven't you heard? The Democrats are talking about running Donald Trump and Leona Helmsley in '92."

"Stop laughing! I'm not kidding! I don't care how maudlin and saccharin those television twits get after he dies, if he dies. But if he doesn't, we're going to have to live with a politician the public gets all weepy just thinking about. Saint George. Yuck! Turns my stomach."

"Oh, I don't think it'll be that bad," Jack Yocke said slowly. "The public's memory is short. By '92 the Republicans will be spending millions trying to remind the voters that George almost gave his life for his country."

"Humph! By God, I hope you're right. This damn country won't work if we gotta start being nice to the politicians. And it won't work if we have only one viable political party." Mergenthaler stalked away toward his glassed-in office.

All across America this Monday morning the wheels of commerce turned slowly, if at all. Parents let children stay home from school and took a sick day themselves. The televisions stayed on. From coast to coast streets, stores, and factories were nearly deserted as everyone participated in the national drama by watching the talking heads on television.

Normal programming was preempted. Every fact, rumor, and tidbit about the shootdown and the President's condition was played and replayed, experts discussed the massive manhunt, politicians went from network to network for cameo appearances to assure the viewing audiences that the wheels of government were continuing to turn and to urge the public to remain calm.

Why these officials felt it necessary to urge the public to keep its wits was never explained. The only people who seemed outraged beyond endurance were a few elderly ladies who telephoned their local television stations to voice bitter complaint about the preemption of their favorite soap operas. Even so, there were fewer of these calls than television executives expected.

Amidst the speculation about the identity and motives of the assassins, a new element was slowly introduced. Tentatively, with circumspection at first, Dan Quayle began to get airtime.

He had appeared in the White House press room at seven-thirty a.m., in time to be carried live on all the morning shows, said a few carefully prepared words, then embarked in a heavily guarded motorcade for Bethesda Naval Hospital to see the President's doctors, since Bush was still comatose.

By midmorning the networks were heavily into Quayle. His wife, his kids, his parents, his school chums and former professors back in Indiana, all were paraded before cameras and all mouthed appropriate words. Those that didn't, didn't get on the air.

All the networks approached the subject in basically the same way. The popular perception that Quayle was a lightweight airhead was silently refuted by the carefully chosen words and pictures the network chose to air. Quayle was cast in a presidential light, spoken of with deference. Conspicuously absent this morning were the snide asides and giggles up the sleeves and lighthearted try-to-top-this reporting of his public misstatements and bloopers that had characterized media coverage of Dan Quayle since the day Bush chose him as his vice-presidential candidate.

In the *Post* newsroom Ott Mergenthaler noticed the collective corporate decision to polish Quayle's image and began making phone calls, trying to pin down producers and executives on why they made this decision.

Over in the Joint Staff spaces of the Pentagon, Toad Tarkington noticed it too. And when Toad noticed something, he quickly made everyone in earshot aware of it. Today, as usual in his new assignment, his listeners were all senior to him in years, rank, and experience, but that didn't seem to crimp the Toad-man's style in any significant way.

"Hoo boy, I'm telling you, they're grooming Danny the Dweeb for the big one. They ought to turn on the TV in George's room. If he saw this he'd leap out of bed and jog down to the White House."

"Mr. Tarkington," the Air Force colonel said in a tired, resigned voice, "please! Must you?"

"This is all a sick joke, right? Quivering Dan Quayle? The pride of the Indiana National Guard? Somebody call me when the commercial comes on. I'm gonna go buy some popcorn."

"Can it, Toad," Jake Grafton said. "Don't you have any work to do?"

"Yessir. As you know, I'm preparing a contingency plan to convert all the A-6s to Agent Orange spray aircraft so we can zap the South American cocaine fields. I figure if we mix the stuff with the gas, we can just fly over the fields with the fuel dumps on and—"

"Back to work."

"Aye aye, sir."

Judge Snyder was at least seventy, with thin hair and a thick waist and big, hamlike hands. He was tall, about three inches over six feet, but he appeared taller because he moved with that clumsy awkwardness that some big men have. Still, the word that came to most people's minds after they had met Judge Snyder was "crusty." Even his wife used that word when describing him to new acquaintances. The young lawyers with fashionably long, styled hair who practiced in front of him would have added another word—"profane"—although no one had ever heard him indulge in salty language in the presence of his wife. Clearly he was not of the generation of the buttoned-down, big-firm Mercedes drivers who constituted the majority of the lawyers who practiced in his courtroom.

When Thanos Liarakos entered the judge's office at ten o'clock on Monday morning, Snyder had a television going and was reading a newspaper. He held the paper up before him, spread wide, as he leaned back in his heavy swivel chair.

His office was full of books, with briefs and case files stacked everywhere. On the wall behind him was a framed piece of needlework. Inside delicate pink and yellow flower borders were the words SUE THE BASTARDS.

When the door closed Judge Snyder lowered one corner of the paper and frowned at his visitor. "Why aren't you at home, Liarakos, watching the damned TV with everybody else?"

"Seen enough of it, your honor," was the reply.

"Me too. Turn that damn thing over there off, will you?"

Liarakos did, then dropped into a chair. He took an envelope from his jacket pocket and extracted the contents, which he handed to the judge.

Snyder reluctantly folded the newspaper and laid it in front of him on his desk. He perused Liarakos' document.

"The prosecutor seen this?" the judge asked curtly.

"Yes, sir."

"What'd he say?"

"Well, he didn't want a say. Said he would abide by your decision."

"I *know* he'll abide by my decision. I want to know if he wants to argue before I make it."

"No. He doesn't."

"Well?" the judge said, holding the sheets between thumb and forefinger and waving them gently back and forth.

"It's a personal problem. I just don't think I can adequately represent Aldana and I want to be excused. There are dozens of competent, experienced criminal lawyers in this town and Aldana can afford any of them. Hell, he could hire 'em all."

"Why?"

"It's personal."

"Had some young puppy in here last week with a motion like this. It all came down to the fact he thought his client was guilty. This isn't any damned silly nonsense like that, is it?"

"No. It's personal."

"You sick?"

"No."

"In trouble with the law?"

"No, sir."

"Motion denied." Snyder tossed the paper back across the desk. It landed in front of Liarakos, who stared at it.

"It's my wife. She's a cocaine addict."

"Sorry to hear that. But what's that got to do with this motion?"

Liarakos raised his hands, then lowered them. He opened his mouth, then closed it and stared at his hands. "I want out. I can't in good conscience defend Aldana. He's entitled to a good defense and *I can't give it to him.*"

"Horseshit," Judge Snyder said. "How many lawyers are there these days who haven't had a friend become addicted to something? All these damn fools used pot in college. They go to parties and somebody has a sugar bowl full of powder for the guests who are 'with it.' I may be an old fart but I know what the hell goes on. Half the bar has your problem or some version of it."

Seeing the look on Liarakos' face, Judge Snyder's tone softened, "Now look. If I approve that motion, Aldana's new lawyer will think up fifty reasons why he needs a ton of extra time to study the government's case and file motions and I'll almost have to give it to him. Yet the government wants Aldana tried as soon as possible, for a lot of reasons that have to do with foreign policy and our relations with Colombia. Those reasons are good ones, in my opinion. I suggest you talk to your client. Tell him what you've told me. If he wants to get another lawyer, that's his business. It's *his* ass. But the new lawyer will get not one more day than you've got. Tell Aldana that too."

"I've already talked to him," Liarakos said. "He wants me."

"Did you tell him your wife was a cocaine addict?"

"Yes. I did."

The judge very much wanted to ask what Aldana's reaction to that revelation was, but he refrained. Attorney-client privilege. He contented himself with readjusting his fanny in his chair and easing the pressure on his scrotum. He also raised an eyebrow.

"He just grinned," Liarakos muttered. He stood up and walked around the room.

He was examining a law book when he said, "I probably shouldn't say this, but I will. My impression is that it really doesn't matter to Chano Aldana who his lawyer is. Apparently the man thinks he'll never go to trial."

"Had a dog like that once," Judge Snyder said, and lazily stretched his arms out as far as they would go. "Kept shitting on the carpet. His education was painful, but he finally got the message."

At two o'clock that afternoon Vice-President Quayle held a news conference. Television rating services later reported that more people watched this news conference than any previous one in the history of television.

When Quayle first walked into the glare of the television lights and looked at the sea of faces of the waiting media, he handled it well, his aides offstage thought as they watched him on a monitor. He looked calm, properly somber, in charge. He began by reading a short statement that expressed the nation's outrage at the person or persons who had attempted to take the President's life and the government's resolve to bring the perpetrators to justice. The aides nodded with every phrase. The Vice-President had rehearsed this little speech for a quarter hour, and it came off just right, they thought.

The first question was unexpected, however, and horrified the aides and William C. Dorfman, who stood among them staring at the monitor with his tummy hanging over his belt and a sheen of perspiration on his forehead. "Mr. Vice-President, a group calling themselves the Extraditables, who are known Colombian narcotics traffickers, has just claimed credit for shooting down President Bush. Does the government have any evidence to support or refute that claim?"

It was here that the worldwide audience got another look at that blank, frozen, wide-eyed stare that an inspired reporter had once dubbed "the deer in the headlights look."

"I . . . I hadn't heard that," Quayle said after a few seconds. "Did it just come in?"

"Yessir. From Medellín, Colombia."

"Well, I don't know," Quayle said lamely. "We are investigating— looking at evidence and all—I don't know. Ahh . . . of course, nut groups and criminals can say anything. We'll see."

The same reporter had a follow-up question. "What will be the United States government's response if the Extraditables' claim proves to be true?"

"Well, I don't know that it is true. As I said, criminals can say anything. If it's true, I don't know. We'll . . . ahh . . . I guess I don't want to . . . ahh . . . speculate about what we might do."

Offstage Dorfman nodded vigorously. He had impressed on the Vice-President the necessity of not committing himself or the government to any particular course of action on any matter. So far so good.

"Why," another reporter asked, "haven't the people who did this been apprehended?"

Quayle was ready for this one. "The various law-enforcement agencies are doing everything within their power to find the people who shot down the President. I am satisfied with the manpower and methods they are using. We will announce results when we have some that can be publicized without jeopardizing the ongoing investigation."

"Do you feel," a woman reporter asked, "that you are capable of properly fulfilling the heavy responsibilities that you have just assumed?"

"Well . . . I . . . I think I can do what needs to be done. I'm hoping right along with everybody else that George Bush recovers quickly and can reassume the responsibilities of his office." Here the Vice-President spoke sincerely, and quite effectively, Dorfman thought. This response had been carefully rehearsed. "No one wants George Bush to get well more than I do. I'm praying for him and I hope everyone else in America is too."

When it was over Dorfman led the entourage back toward the office spaces as he snarled at his executive assistant, "Get me a copy of that damned Extraditables press release. And get the CIA and State Department people over here on the double. I want to know what the fuck is going on and why the hell the press got it before we did. I want to know *now!*"

At the conference in the cabinet room that followed, Quayle sat at the center of the table where Bush normally sat and said little. Arranged around the table were the directors of the FBI, CIA, and DEA, the assistant secretary of state—the secretary had died in the helicopter crash that had injured the President—the attorney general, and the head of the Secret Service. Dorfman sat beside Quayle and did the talking. As usual, he was blunt.

"Are the Extraditables behind this?"

No one knew.

"By God, we'd better find out and damn fast."

"We're squeezing our sources now. We'll hear something soon."

"Squeeze harder. We've got to find out who is behind this attempted murder and get these people arrested. Right now the public is holding its breath. We can't get on with the business of government when ninety percent of the stuff in the newspapers and on the air is about assassins and victims. So the people who did this have got to be found. Find them."

Afterward Dorfman had a private conference with Dan Quayle, a man whom he would have despised if he had ever taken the time to think about him, which he hadn't. Dorfman occupied the center of the universe and everyone else merely orbited his star. Still, while he had never had any patience with people who lacked his intellectual gifts, lazy rich people who floated effortlessly along enjoying life's bounties had always brought forth the darkest side of his aggressive personality. Just now he had to steel himself to treat Quayle with what he thought was deference.

"This Extraditables claim," he muttered, "is political dynamite. No doubt this very minute someone is advocating an invasion of Colombia. The least misstep and we could have Colombians publicly assaulted in our streets. Remember the hostage mess in Iran ten or eleven years ago?"

Quayle remembered.

"And yet, if we don't take measured, positive steps to handle this mess, people will say that you're incompetent. Anything you do will be too much for some people, too little for others."

"I've been in politics for a while," Quayle said, a little annoyed at Dorfman. He disliked being patronized and that was all he ever got from Dorfman. He had spent the last two years assiduously avoiding the man.

Dorfman continued, trying to sound reasonable. "My role for the President has been to play the bad cop, the hard ass, the guy who says no. I suggest that until the President recovers enough to resume his duties, you continue to use me the same way. Let me play the heavy. When something positive comes along, you take the credit."

"That might have worked for George Bush, but it won't work for me," Dan Quayle said. "Not over the long haul. People think I'm incompetent, a featherweight." Dorfman tried to interrupt but Quayle kept going. "I'm not going to let you be de facto President while I sit on my thumb. That won't work."

"I know that, sir. I'm merely making a suggestion. You're the man in charge."

Quayle's innocent blue eyes zeroed in and didn't blink. "Governor, I'm going to lay it right on the line with you. Everyone knows that you wanted to be the vice-presidential candidate in '88 but Bush picked me instead. Everyone knows that you want the spot in '92. And everyone, including me, suspects that you've been lobbying the President to dump me from the ticket."

"I haven't," Dorfman said, his face reddening.

Dan Quayle continued as if he hadn't heard. "Right now I don't think it would be a good idea to replace Bush's team, at least until we get some idea of when the President might be capable of resuming his duties. But," Quayle added matter-of-factly, "this team had better get some results."

At four p.m. that afternoon Thanos Liarakos had a short visit with his client, Chano Aldana, in a cell. The guard was outside and the two were alone. Liarakos had long suspected these visitation cells were bugged but this afternoon he never gave possible listeners a thought.

"Your colleagues in Colombia are taking credit for the attempted assassination of George Bush."

Aldana merely grunted. Something like amusement played across his fleshy features.

"Well, did they do it? Or did you hire it done?"

"What's it to you, Mr. American lawyer?"

"I'm your defense counsel. I want to know if you're responsible for the attempt on the President's life."

Aldana snorted. Then his lips curled in a sneer. "You've got two daughters, right? What are their names—let me think—oh yes! Susanna and Lisa. Now listen very, very carefully, Mr. Thanos Liarakos, rich American lawyer with the clean white hands. You tell these people that if they don't send me back to Colombia, many more Americans will die. You silly people have been living in a dream world. I'm going to show you the hard, naked truth. And if you double-cross me, if you don't do exactly what I tell you, you won't have two pretty little daughters anymore." Aldana snapped his fingers. *"Do you understand me, Mr. Thanos Liarakos?"*

"Guard! Guard! I'm ready to leave." Liarakos pounded on the door. He wiped his palms on his trousers.

"You had better pay attention, Mr. Liarakos," Aldana hissed. "If you think I can't reach you or your daughters, that will be your last mistake. I got to George Bush. *I can get to anyone on this planet. Do you understand?"*

The door opened then and Liarakos went through, but not without looking back over his shoulder at the round, sneering face of Chano Aldana.

As he walked down the corridor he wiped his hands on his trousers again, then swabbed his face with his sleeve. He saw the sign on the door that said MEN and ducked in. Suddenly he had an overpowering urge to urinate.

The prosecutor, William Bader, and Thanos Liarakos twisted uncomfortably in their chairs across the desk from Attorney General Gideon Cohen. Liarakos had gone directly from the cell to the prosecutor's office, and the two of them had come here, to the Department of Justice. Liarakos had just finished his tale.

"What does he expect the American government to do?" Cohen asked, his eyebrows high in disbelief.

"Send him back to Colombia," Liarakos said curtly. "I told you that."

"No."

The attorney general leaned back in his chair and stared at Liarakos. Liarakos stared back.

"I want protection for my daughters," Liarakos said at last.

"Send them to their grandparents."

"Don't give me that crap! These people can reach anywhere! I *believe* the son of a bitch. I want *protection!"*

"Two FBI agents."

"Around the clock. In school and in the head. Every minute of every day."

"For a while, okay." Cohen nodded. "But we're going to hold Aldana incommunicado. You are the only human who talks to him."

Liarakos snorted. "You wish. The jailers will see him. We have to feed him. They'll tell him what's happening. He'll threaten and bribe them. How are you going to stop that?"

"Quantico," Bader suggested. "Let's let the Marines hold him in their brig down there. Move all the other prisoners out."

"Any objection, counselor?" Cohen asked.

"Do it." Liarakos stood.

"Not so fast," Cohen said, straightening in his chair. "I want you to talk to the FBI. He claims he's responsible for four murders and the attempted assassination of the President. He's threatened other people. You're going to repeat this word for word in a sworn deposition."

"No, I'm not. Attorney-client privilege."

"Waived," Cohen shot back.

"Like *hell!* I do a deposition like that and you'll have to find another lawyer to defend the cocksucker and Judge Snyder will have a pound of my ass. I've told you what my client wanted me to say. *That's it.* You tell the FBI and the White House and anybody else you care to. This hot potato is all yours. I'm done. And I'm leaving." Liarakos walked out.

Cohen was on the phone to the FBI before the door closed behind the defense lawyer.

At midnight Henry Charon locked the door to the Hampshire Avenue apartment and went down the stairs to the street. He walked the block to his car, unlocked it, maneuvered it carefully from his parking place, and drove away.

The evening was chilly and humid. Much colder and it might snow. He was dressed for the weather. Long underwear, hiking boots, a sweater and warm coat. Under his thin leather gloves he wore a set of latex surgical gloves, just in case.

Scrupulously obeying the traffic laws, Henry Charon drove to National Airport and parked in the long-term lot. He put the entry ticket in his shirt pocket and sat behind the wheel scanning the lot. It took him about three minutes to decide on the vehicle he wanted. Just as he was about to get out of his car, another car drove in. He waited until the driver had exited the lot, then got out and carefully locked his door and put the keys in his trouser pocket.

The car he had selected was a Toyota. Getting in took about half a minute. Charon slid a thin, flat metal shim down between the driver's window glass and the felt seal and fished carefully until he got the notch in the shim in the right place. Then he pulled. The door lock button rose with a click.

Inside the car he felt under the mat. No luck. Not that he really needed a key, of course. He could hot wire the car with about five minutes of work, but a key would be nice. He looked in the ashtray and the glove box and the little compartment for cassette tapes. A spare key was wedged in there under a Grateful Dead tape.

The car started on the first crank. Half a tank of gas.

Charon gave the attendant the ticket from his shirt pocket and a dollar on the way out. The attendant had a portable radio going, a news-talk station. As the attendant glanced at the ticket and rang it up, Charon heard a voice on the radio mention Dan Quayle. As the wooden arm in front of the car rose, Charon fed gas. The attendant hadn't even looked at him.

It took an hour to find the house he was looking for in Silver Spring, set back among tall, stately maples and some really large pines. No cars on the street. He drove down to the corner and out to the main avenue, memorizing the turns, then turned around and came back.

As he eased the car down the driveway he examined the house for lights. One was on behind drapes in a downstairs room—he could just make out the glow.

Charon left the engine running and slipped the transmission into park. He pulled off the leather gloves and laid them on the seat beside him.

The automatic was in one coat pocket and the silencer in another. It took about six twists to screw the silencer into place. He didn't check the magazine or chamber—he knew they were ready.

He opened the car door and stepped out, then pushed the door closed until the interior light went out.

A brick stoop, a little button for the doorbell. He could hear the tinkle somewhere in the house.

The breeze was chilly and the wind in the pines made a gentle moan. It was a sound he had always liked. Now he shut that sound out and listened for others, car doors or engines or voices.

Nothing.

The door opened. A man about sixty, thick at the waist, in his shirtsleeves. He looked just like his photo last week in *Newsweek* magazine.

Well, Charon thought, this was luck indeed.

"Yes?" the man said, cocking his head quizzically.

Henry Charon shot him dead center in the chest. The gun made a popping noise, not loud, a metallic thwock. As he fell Charon shot him again. With the man lying in the foyer on his side, his legs twisted, Charon stepped over and fired a slug into his skull.

Then he pulled the door closed and walked for the car.

He heard voices now. "Dad! Dad!" A woman calling.

Seated behind the wheel, Charon saw lights in the second story come on.

He pulled the shift lever one notch rearward, into reverse, then looked over his shoulder and backed down the driveway toward the circle of warmth from the streetlight. No cars coming.

Henry Charon backed into the street, put the car in drive, and drove at twenty-five miles per hour toward the avenue. He glanced at his watch. Two-nineteen a.m.

At three-oh-five he took a ticket from the automatic device guarding the parking lot entrance at National Airport and wheeled the car back into exactly the same stall he had taken it from. He replaced the key in the cassette tray, locked the car, then walked toward the terminal to get a cup of coffee.

He would let about an hour pass before he drove his own car past the attendant and handed him the ticket he had just acquired driving in. No use giving the man two short-time tickets in the same night. The second time he might look at the driver. Not that he would remember me, Charon thought, wryly amused. Nobody ever does.

During the night Harrison Ronald awoke with a start. He found himself fully alert, lying rigid in bed, listening to the silence.

And God, it was quiet. Nothing! He strained his ears to pick up the slightest noise.

Fully awake and taut as a violin string, he eased the automatic from under his pillow and slipped from the bed. He listened at the door. Nothing. He put his ear to the door and stood that way for several seconds, listening to the sounds of his breathing but nothing else.

The fear was palpable, tangible, right there beside him in the darkness. He could smell the monster's fetid breath.

Frustrated, listening to his heart thud, he glided noiselessly to the window.

He pulled the blinds back ever so slightly. The light on the pole between the trees cast weird shadows on the grass, which looked from this angle like the green felt on a pool table.

Too quiet. No wind. The tree limbs were absolutely still.

What had awakened him?

He held his wristwatch so that the dim glow coming through the gap in the blinds fell upon it. Three-fourteen a.m.

Not even a hum from the heating system. That was probably it. It was off.

In a moment the system kicked back on.

He felt the tension ebbing and walked back to the bed. He sat gingerly upon it and tossed the heavy pistol onto the blanket beside him. Rubbing his face, then lying full-length on the bed, Harrison Ronald tried to relax.

What was Freeman doing right now? Did he know?

Of course he knew. Or suspected. Freeman would be curious, with that alley dog asshole-sniffing curiosity that had to be satisfied, so he would take steps to learn the truth. He would talk to people and use money and sooner or later he would know. What then?

CHAPTER TWENTY-TWO

★ ★ ★ ★ ★ ★ ★ ★ ★ ★ ★ ★ ★

TUESDAY the world came unglued. Those were the words a senator used later to describe the day, and those words stuck in tens of millions of minds as the perfect description.

It started whenever you awoke and turned on your television to check on the President's condition at Bethesda and found yourself staring at a stark image of a suburban two-story Cape Cod house surrounded by tall pines and lit by floodlights. In the gray dawn half light, the surreal image looked ominous.

The troubling thing about the picture was not the ambulances, the flashing blue-and-white beacons, the uniformed policemen and the clean-cut FBI types in Sears suits, nor was it the sobbing grown daughter and her two children home to visit Dad for Christmas. No. The troubling thing about the image was that the house looked like something from the set of an old "Leave It to Beaver" show. As you stared at it you could see that it looked exactly like the one in the ads for house paint for great American homes "just like yours"—the perfect distillation of the American two-story dream house in Hometown, U.S.A. And the owner had been assassinated, murdered, when he opened his door to a stranger.

The owner, of course, was Somebody, Congressman Doyle Hopkins of Minnesota, majority leader of the House of Representatives. He had been shot three times at point-blank range.

A better crime to push the panic buttons of middle-class America could not have been devised. The sanctity of home, neighborhood, and family circle had been savagely violated.

The television newspeople, no fools they, played that theme for all it was worth. "Why did he open the door?" one of them asked rhetorically, as if every suburban householder had not done the same thing dozens of times, as if the evil intent of Hopkins' assailant had been written across his face so plainly it would have still been obvious in the stark shadows of the porch light.

But if you stayed glued to the tube long enough, eventually you were told that the President's condition was unchanged. The doctor in charge of the President's medical team held a morning press conference, but only a few minutes of that got on the air. The story of the hour was the killing of the House majority leader.

That was the story of the hour until nine a.m. Eastern time, anyway. At eight fifty-eight five heavily armed men walked into the rotunda of the Capitol building wearing heavy, knee-length coats. They shot the four security guards on duty with pistols before the security men could get off a shot, then extracted Uzis from under their coats and ran along the corridors shooting everyone they saw.

A reporter-camera team setting up to interview the Speaker of the House was the first to get this atrocity on the air, at nine-oh-one a.m., just in time to capture a gruesome vignette of one of the gunmen mowing down the woman reporter, then turning the weapon on the cameraman. As he was hammered into a wall with five slugs in his body the camera fell to the marble floor and was smashed.

A uniformed security guard near the Senate cloakroom was running toward the noise of gunfire with his pistol drawn when he rounded a corner and almost careened into one of the Uzi-toting gunmen. They exchanged shots at a range of five feet. In the roar of the Uzi on full automatic fire the report of the guard's weapon was lost. Both men went down fatally wounded.

There were four gunmen left alive. One of them charged into a subcommittee hearing room where people were gathering and emptied a magazine into the crowd. The noise of the chattering automatic weapon was deafening, overpowering, in this room which had been recently renovated to improve the acoustics. Only when the trip-hammer blasts ended could those still alive hear the screams and moans, and then they sounded muffled, as if they were coming from a great distance.

The killer stood calmly amidst the blood and gore and groaning victims and changed magazines. He emptied the second magazine into the prostrate crowd and was inserting the third one into his weapon when a guard appeared in the doorway and shot him with a .357 Magnum.

The first two rounds from the revolver hammered the gunman to the floor but the guard walked toward him still shooting. He fired the sixth and last round into the gunman's brain from a distance of three feet.

Sixteen people in the room were dead and seventeen wounded. Only three people escaped without bullet wounds.

Another of the gunmen was shot to death in the House dining room after he sprayed the diners with two magazines and used the third on the chandeliers. His weapon jammed. He was crouched amid a shower of shattered glass trying to clear the weapon when two guards standing at different doorways opened fire with their revolvers. The man went down with three bullets in him and was shot twice more as he lay on the floor.

One of the gunmen somehow ended up in the old Senate chamber which, mercifully, was empty. Didn't matter. He stood near the lectern and sprayed two magazines of slugs into the polished desks and speaker's bench. Then he threw the Uzi down, drew a pistol, and blew his brains out.

The only terrorist taken alive was shot from behind as he ran down a corridor on the second level. He had killed over a dozen people and wounded nine others before a woman guard leveled him with a slug through the liver.

Watching the pandemonium on television—every station in town had a crew at the Capitol within twenty minutes and two of them had helicopters circling overhead—White House chief of staff William C. Dorfman took the first report from the FBI watch officer over the telephone in his office.

"How many of them were there?"

"We don't know."

"Have you gotten them all?"

"We don't know."

"Casualties?"

"Don't know yet."

"Well, goddammit, call me back when you know something, you fucking idiot!" Dorfman roared and slammed down the phone so hard the plastic housing on the instrument cracked.

These temper tantrums were a character defect and were doing him no good politically. Dorfman knew it and was trying to control himself. Still . . .

One minute later the telephone rang again. It was Vice-President Quayle. "I'm going over to the Capitol. I want you to go with me."

"Mr. Vice-President, I don't think that's a good idea," Dorfman replied as he jabbed the button on the remote to kill the TV volume. "The FBI just told me that they don't know if the guards got all the terrorists. The nation can't afford to lose you to a—"

"I'm going, Dorfman. You're coming with me. I'll be at the Rose Garden entrance in five minutes. Have the cars brought around."

The line went dead.

"Yessir," Dorfman said to nobody in particular.

The administration was sitting on a bomb with a lit fuse, Dorfman realized, and the fuse was dangerously short.

Terrorists! Not in the Middle East, not in some Third World shithole that nobody had ever heard of, but *here!* Washington, D.C., the capital of the United States! The next thing you know wild-eyed lunatic ragheads will be blowing stuff up and slaughtering people in Moline and Columbus and Tulsa. My God!

At least Dan Quayle was smart enough to comprehend the gravity of the situation. That was undoubtedly why he wanted to personally view the carnage at the Capitol, console the survivors, and be seen by the American people doing it. That would help calm all those people from

Bangor to L.A. who were right now beginning to feel the first twinges of panic.

Dorfman regretted his first impulse to advise Quayle not to go. Quayle's political instincts were sound. He was right.

Dorfman called for the cars and had a thirty-second shouting match with the senior Secret Service agent on duty, who didn't give a tinker's damn about politics but did care greatly about the life of the Vice-President that was entrusted to his care.

He also took the time to call Gideon Cohen and tell him to meet the Vice-President's party at the Capitol and to bring the director of the FBI along with him.

Dorfman shared the limo with the Vice-President, who had brought along his own chief of staff, one Carney Robinson, an intense blow-dried type who in his previous life had made a name for himself in public relations.

Dorfman apologized to Quayle for advising him not to go to the Capitol. "This is wise," Dorfman said. Neither Quayle nor Robinson replied. They sat silently looking back at the people on the sidewalks looking at them.

After a bit Dan Quayle cleared his throat. "Will, use the phone there. Call General Land at the Pentagon and ask him to meet us at the Capitol."

Without a word Dorfman seized the instrument and placed the call.

Henry Charon woke up a few minutes after ten a.m. at the Hampshire Avenue apartment and made himself a pot of coffee. While he waited for it to drip through he took a quick shower, brushed his teeth, and shaved.

Then he dressed, even putting on his shoes and a sweater. Only then did he pour himself some coffee and turn on the television to see what the hunters were up to.

He stood in front of the screen staring at it, trying to understand. A group of terrorists? The Capitol?

He sat on the sofa and propped his feet on the chair while he sipped the steaming hot liquid in the cup.

Well, one thing was certain—the FBI and police were going to be thoroughly confused. That, Charon reflected, was more than he had hoped for.

It was also an opportunity.

He drained the cup and poured himself another while he thought about it. After a couple of sips he went to the window and stood looking down into the street. Not many people about this morning. A few empty parking places, though. Another gray day.

The FBI would be around before very long, either FBI or local police. They would be looking for terrorists and assassins, so they would be knocking on doors and asking questions. Nothing to fear there.

His mind went back to the Capitol. He remembered the office building just east of the Supreme Court. What was it, five or six hundred yards over to the Capitol?

Could he make a shot at that distance? Well, with the best of the rifles he had fired three shots into a one-inch group at a hundred yards, so theoretically at five hundred yards a perfect shot should hit within a circle five inches in diameter. Yet the impact point would be about fifty-six inches below the point of aim because the bullet would be dropping, affected by gravity. If he made a perfect shot. With no wind.

And the distance was precisely five hundred yards.

With the wind blowing and a fifty-yard error in his estimate of the distance, all bets were off.

Henry Charon didn't have to review the ballistics—he knew them cold. And he knew just how extraordinarily difficult it would be to hit a man-sized target at 500 yards, especially since the target man would not be cooperating by holding absolutely still. It would be a real challenge.

He stood watching the passersby below and the bare branches being stirred by the breeze and tried to remember what the field of view looked like from the top of the office building.

He went back to the little living room and stood with the cup in his hand watching the television. The Vice-President was on his way to the Capitol, the announcer said. He would be there shortly. Stay tuned.

His mind made up, Charon snapped off the television. He turned off the coffeepot and the lights, grabbed his coat, and locked the door behind him.

"How many dead?" Dan Quayle asked the special agent who had greeted them and escorted them through the police lines into the building as reporters shouted questions and the cameras rolled. Quayle had ignored them.

"Sixty-one, sir. A couple more are in real bad shape and will probably die. Forty-three wounded."

"Any idea who these people were?"

"Colombians, sir," the agent said. "On a suicide mission. One's still alive, barely, and he did some talking before he passed out from internal bleeding and shock. An agent who speaks Spanish took down what he could. Apparently these people were smuggled into the country this past weekend and told their target this morning."

"Paid to commit suicide?" Dorfman asked in disbelief.

"Yes, sir. Fifty thousand before they left, and fifty more to the widow afterward."

That stunned the politicians, who walked along in silence. The agent led them to a hearing room where seventeen men and women and the man who had killed them lay as they had fallen. The wounded had been removed, but photographers and lab men were busy. They didn't look up at the gawking politicos or the Secret Service agents who stood with pistols in their hands.

Quayle just stood rooted with his hands in his pockets, looking right and left. Spent brass casings lay scattered about, bullet holes here and there, blood all over, bodies contorted and twisted.

"Why?" Quayle asked.

"Sir?"

"Why in hell would anybody take money to commit murder and be killed doing it?"

"Well, this one guy—the one that's still alive—he said he has a wife and eight kids in Colombia. He used to have ten kids but two died because he couldn't feed them anything but corn and rice and he couldn't afford a doctor when they got sick. They live in a shack without running water. He had no job and no prospect of ever getting one. So when he got offered this money, he looked at the kids and figured it was the only way they were ever going to have a chance, so he took it. So he said, anyway."

"Sixty-one people murdered," Quayle muttered so softly Dorfman had to take a step closer to catch it. "No, that's too nice a word. Butchered. Slaughtered. Exterminated."

The agent led them from the room and down the hall toward the cafeteria. They passed several bodies in the corridors. Dorfman tried not to look at the faces, but Quayle did. He bent over each one for a second or two, then straightened and walked on. His hands stayed in his coat pockets and his shoulders sagged.

They were standing in the cafeteria when Gideon Cohen and General Land and several other military officers joined them. One of the officers was a navy captain, "Grafton" his name tag said, who took it all in, his face expressionless.

"This guy who's still alive—he said he thinks there were other groups smuggled in."

"How did they get here?"

"By airliner. They were met at the airport and taken somewhere and given food and weapons. This morning they were driven here in a van and dropped."

"Where are the others? What are their targets?" Dorfman growled.

"He doesn't know."

Attorney General Gideon Cohen spoke for the first time. "Aldana's lawyer says Aldana told him yesterday afternoon that he was responsible for the attempt on the President's life. That's confidential, of course."

"Bastard's lying," Dorfman said forcefully.

"I wouldn't bet on it," Cohen rumbled. "Our people in Colombia are hearing rumors, too many rumors."

Surrounded by Secret Service agents the group kept walking. "Let's find a place to talk," Quayle said. The Secret Service led them to an empty committee room—all the committee rooms were empty just now—checked it out, then stood guard outside the door.

Quayle dropped into a chair on the aisle. The others selected chairs nearby. As they were doing so the director of the FBI and another man came in.

"Did these people shoot down the President's helicopter?" Vice-President Quayle asked to get the ball rolling.

"You mean these very men killed here?" the FBI agent who had been escorting them asked. "The survivor denied it, for whatever that's worth."

The director of the FBI nodded at the agent who spoke. "You may go back to your duties."

The man rose, muttered, "Gentlemen," and left.

The director addressed Quayle. "Mr. Vice-President, I've brought with me today Special Agent Thomas Hooper. He's in charge of our antidrug task force and he's been working with the team that's looking for the people who shot down the President's helicopter. Before we came in we spent five minutes talking with the senior people who are working on this . . ." He gestured vaguely at the room around him. "Hooper, tell them what you told me."

Tom Hooper glanced around at the faces, some of which were looking his way, some averted. "What we've got here is a classic narco-terrorist strike. It was committed by people with a minimum of training, people you would classify as apolitical amateurs. It didn't really matter how many people were killed or wounded here—the publicity the event would get would be precisely the same. This atrocity was a *political* act.

"The attempted assassination of the President was very different in several significant ways. That was meticulously planned, carefully prepared, all to take advantage of an opportunity if one presented itself. In other words, a professional assassin."

"Just one?" someone asked.

"Probably," Hooper replied. "We've found the spot where the missiles were fired—a little picnic area beside the Potomac—and it appears that only one man spent the afternoon there. His tracks are all over. He wore some kind of rubber boots, but he appears to be of medium height, weight about one hundred sixty or so. Those are just tentative conclusions, of course."

"Who hired the assassin?" Dorfman asked.

"No idea, sir," Hooper said. "Guesses are three for a quarter, but I wouldn't bet against you if you thought the same people are behind all of this."

"Aldana," Dorfman said as if the very name were poisonous.

Dan Quayle spoke slowly, seemingly feeling his way: "The question is, what are we going to do to prevent any more of these slaughters?"

"We've got to find these other Colombians," Dorfman said.

"Heavy guards around all public buildings and likely places," somebody added.

"That won't stop these people." The words were spoken quietly but with force. Everyone looked at the speaker, Captain Jake Grafton. He continued, "All these people are after is an atrocity. They want publicity, fear, terror, to force the government to do their will. They'll find a target regardless. In Colombia they're blowing up department stores and banks and airliners. We've got all that plus shopping malls and these boutique emporiums, like the ones at the Old Post Office and Union Station. This close to Christmas . . ." His voice tailed off.

"I want to call out the National Guard," Quayle said. "We're going to have to guard the public buildings regardless, and as many of the shopping areas as we can find people for. And we can use the troops to search for these Colombians."

"Are you talking martial law?" General Land asked.

"I don't care what you call it."

"Troops will never find these terrorists, even if they're here," the chairman of the Joint Chiefs protested. "We can't have troops going door to door, searching every house. They aren't trained for that. That's what the FBI and police are for."

"FBI, what do you say?" Quayle directed his question at the director.

"These aren't ordinary times. We need quick results. To get quick results we need a lot of people. Yet when this is over the American people are going to hold the FBI and the military accountable if innocent people's rights are trampled on, injustice done. That's inevitable."

William Dorfman jumped in with both feet. "The American people will hold *us* accountable if these murdering swine aren't caught and caught damn soon. We've got to move heaven and earth to stop this slaughter or this country will come unglued. That's the *first* priority. Better to jail some innocent people and turn 'em loose later than let the guilty stay free."

"How about innocent people shot by nineteen-year-old kids with M-16s?" General Land asked Dorfman.

"Don't be a damn fool," Dorfman retorted. *"Your* job is to make sure that doesn't happen. If you can't do the job we'll—"

Dorfman had the sense to shut up just then, for the look on Hayden Land's face would have boiled water. Jake Grafton doubted if there was another man living who had ever had the temerity to tell the general to his face that he was a damn fool.

The silence that followed Dorfman's outburst lasted for a long moment.

"Why not use regular troops?" Gideon Cohen suggested with a glance at General Land. "Handpicked noncoms and officers? This *is* the federal district. I think that would be legal. Certainly justifiable. Even if it isn't legal, it'll be a while before a judge says so."

"No," Dan Quayle said. "National Guard." He stood. "When I get back to my office we'll announce it and prepare an order. In the meantime all nonessential government buildings should be evacuated, the employees sent home."

Quayle left the room first, surrounded by Secret Service agents.

Walking the corridors of the Capitol with General Land, Jake Grafton felt profoundly depressed. General Land apparently was in a similar mood. They paused by a body draped with a sheet that the forensic people had yet to get to and stood for a moment. Holes and blood in the wall, pieces of plaster and plaster powder on the floor. The toe of a woman's shoe was just visible under the edge of the white cloth.

She had been somebody, with a family and a job, ambitions and a future. Now she was a hunk of meat to be diced and sliced, mourned and buried.

We're all victims, Jake mused, the living as well as the dead. The America that had given birth to this woman and made her what she was would soon be changed in unforeseeable, incalculable ways by the white-hot fury of the forces that had been unleashed here this morning. The transformations caused by war—make no mistake, this *was* war— would be irrevocable. And Jake knew that the changes so wrought would not be welcomed by most Americans, himself included.

God *damn* these terrorists. He said it to himself as a prayer.

He was walking down the sidewalk carrying the toolbox in one hand and a four-foot length of ducting balanced on his shoulder when he realized that there were men on the rooftops. Henry Charon stopped at the corner and took a quick look upward at the tops of the buildings while he shifted the duct pipe to his other shoulder.

He had driven in from the east and had no trouble finding a place to park. A lot of people hadn't come to work today.

Keeping his gaze on the sidewalk, he proceeded to the entrance of the old office building and climbed the stairs. In the lobby he set the toolbox on the floor and punched the elevator button. The lobby was empty. Now if that office still was . . .

In the elevator he pushed the button for the top floor. The contraption wheezed and moaned, then with a hum rose slowly for several seconds. It lurched to a halt and the door opened.

The woman standing there gasped when she saw him and started.

"Oh, my God!"

Henry Charon smiled.

Horror contorted her features. "Oh, I'm *sorry!* Oh, my heavens, I am so sorry." The door started to close, but she popped in, beating it.

"What floor?" he asked.

"Five, please."

Charon pushed the button as she continued breathlessly, "I just didn't expect anyone to be in here. I'm so jumpy. All these terrorists and murders! My God! I should have stayed home. I am *so* sorry. What you must think."

"Forget it."

She gave him a big, embarrassed smile and got off at the fifth floor. He grinned at her again as the door closed.

The top floor was the seventh, and Charon got off there. The hallway was empty. He walked over to the door labeled STAIR and pushed at it. It opened. Satisfied, he went to the door at the rear of the hallway and laid down the duct pipe and toolbox.

The lock took half a minute. He sat the box and pipe inside, surveyed the empty room, then locked the door behind him.

Through the tree branches he could see the northern half of the Capitol's grand staircase that led up to the main entrance, which led into the Rotunda. The marble steps were covered with people. That was the door those suicide pilots from Colombia went in this morning. But Charon could see only half the stair. The other half was obscured by the Supreme Court building.

The window was dirty. He wiped the inside of the glass with his sleeve. Some of the dirt came off. Out of the corner of his eye he picked up a man on the roof of the Supreme Court building.

This would have to do.

Luckily it was winter and all the trees on the Capitol grounds had lost all their leaves. In summer the vegetation would obscure the scene from here.

The scoped rifle was carefully packed inside the duct pipe and padded with bubble wrap. He removed the weapon and the three long sticks that were also there. These had a piece of rope carefully wrapped around all three sticks, near one end, so when he spread the sticks apart the contraption became a tripod.

He loaded the rifle and laid it on the floor. Then he used a squirt bottle of window cleaner and a rag on the inside of the window glass. He did the entire window as he scanned the Capitol parking lot and every roof he could see.

Four men in sight on the roofs. Hundreds of people over there around the Capitol.

He had one of the radios in the toolbox. With the earpiece in his ear, he turned it on and played with it until he found the audio broadcast frequency of a television station. In fifteen seconds it was plain that the announcer was on the Capitol steps.

Listening carefully, Charon rigged the tripod and braced the rifle upon it. He turned the scope magnification to its highest setting, adjusted the parallax ring, then settled the rifle on the tripod.

He stood well back from the window, near the middle of the room. Swinging the rifle through the narrow field of view provided by the window sash, he was agreeably surprised at how much he could see. He was looking between tree branches though, and the breeze made them sway. The back-and-forth motion of the limbs made it more difficult to hold the reticle steady on target.

The announcer informed his audience that the Vice-President's party would soon be leaving the building. He didn't say how he knew.

If Charon made this, it would be one *hell* of a shot. Listening to the television audio, moving the crosshairs from person to person, he thought about some of the more memorable shots he had made. None of them had been this iffy, he decided. He wondered if he should really try this one. The images in the scope danced uncontrollably as the instrument's nine-power magnification exaggerated every twitch and tiny jiggle.

He settled the scope on a cop and took a deep breath, then exhaled smoothly and concentrated on holding the crosshairs of the reticle as steady as humanly possible on the center of the man's chest. Still, they moved around in a little circle. It was all he could do to keep the two filaments between the man's armpits. Just when he thought that was good enough, the man moved unexpectedly.

How long after he pulled the trigger would he have to clear the building? Sixty seconds? Less?

And the flight of the bullet would be affected slightly by the window glass. He couldn't open the window—an agent on a roof might see it and send someone to investigate. So he'd shoot through it. Impossible to say how much the glass would deflect the bullet. Maybe just enough to miss over this distance, a little more than a quarter mile. Maybe enough to throw the bullet ten or twelve feet off.

He thought about it as he turned the horizontal filament adjustment knob to compensate for bullet drop.

Okay. It's going to take a lot of luck to make this shot. A *lot* of luck.

What he really needed was a practice shot. Well, when you thought about it, he had had a lot of those. Thousands over the years. This one would have to do the trick.

Aha! The announcer: "Here is the Vice-President now."

Henry Charon straightened and worked the bolt, chambering a round. He snicked off the safety. He flexed his shoulders, set his feet, then settled the forearm of the rifle onto the tripod and grasped the junction with his left hand. He snuggled the butt into his shoulder and got the stock firmly in place under his cheekbone.

Now he swung the rifle toward the door of the Capitol. Someone had arranged a battery of microphones. The Vice-President ignored them and walked down the steps amid a phalanx of Secret Service agents carrying submachine guns in their hands. There was a corridor of sorts between the cameras and the people.

Behind Quayle—who was that? An army officer. And a naval officer, three or four civilians.

Charon tried to steady the rifle on the civilians, who were coming toward him down the steps. He couldn't shoot when they were moving: they were just too small at this distance. And until they stopped and stood still he couldn't even be sure who they were.

At the bottom of the stairs, right beside a limo, the Army officer stopped to talk to Dan Quayle. Okay, the civilians were joining the group. They were close together.

Who are they?

Dorfman! One of them is Dorfman. He's on the list. Who is the other? Aha! That's Cohen, the attorney general. Also on the list.

Quickly now. Breath deeply, exhale slowly, relax and squeeze, slowly and steadily. Steady . . . steady . . .

Damn tree limbs—swaying around . . . Squeeze slowly, gently, allow for the wind, keep the crosshairs cen . . .

The rifle fired.

The report in the closed room was deafening, like two sticks of dynamite. Part of the window glass blew out.

CHAPTER TWENTY-THREE

★ ★ ★ ★ ★ ★ ★ ★ ★ ★ ★ ★ ★

JAKE Grafton heard an audible thwock and turned, just in time to see Gideon Cohen spin half around and fall to the pavement.

The nearest Secret Service agent roared, "Everybody down," and the two agents closest to the Vice-President physically pushed him headfirst into the back seat of the limo. One of them dove in on top of him while the other slammed the door.

"Get down! Everybody down!"

Jake crouched, his eyes on Cohen. Was it just his imagination or did he really hear the report of a rifle several seconds after Cohen fell?

Cohen's groans were audible above the screams and shouts of the panicked onlookers, who were scattering or lying facedown on the steps and pavement. An agent was on top of the attorney general, bracing himself with his hands and knees so that none of his weight rested on the injured man.

"My God!" someone roared. "They tried to kill the Vice-President!"

"Get that fucking car outta here!"

The Secret Service agents pointed their Uzis at the crowd, searching. They were still standing like this five seconds later when the driver of the limo stomped on the gas and made the rear tires squeal as he accelerated away.

Three or four men were examining Cohen. Jake tried to see but couldn't.

Where? Jake rose to his knees and tried to look for the spot where the shot had come from. All he could see was the backs of Secret Service agents. He stood.

"Goddammit, get back down here, Grafton," General Land growled. "Never stand up in a firefight. Were you born yesterday?"

As he came out of the stairwell into the lobby Henry Charon bumped into a woman. He reached out and caught her and steadied her on her feet.

"Sorry," he said, and headed for the door to the sidewalk.

"Did you hear that explosion?" she called.

"Upstairs, it sounded like," he told her over his shoulder and kept going for the door.

That's odd, she thought, staring after him. He's wearing surgical gloves.

Out on the sidewalk Henry Charon walked north at a brisk pace, but not too brisk. Just a man who knows where he's going and wants to get there. He reached the corner and crossed, then paused and watched an unmarked car with a blue light on the dash and a siren wailing round the corner and screech to a stop in the middle of the block, just fifty feet past the building he had just come out of.

Charon wheeled and walked east. He passed a man jogging in the other direction, toward the Capitol. "Somebody tried to kill the Vice-President," the man shouted, pointing at a small transistor radio he carried.

Charon nodded and kept going. Behind him he could hear more sirens.

At two that afternoon Billy Enright, one of McNally's lieutenants, who had been watching television, went into the next room and woke Freeman McNally. Freeman got out of bed and padded in to watch and listen. Someone had taken a shot at the Vice-President, and the feds were calling out the National Guard.

Freeman called T. Jefferson Brody at his office. Normally he never used the phone here for business, since it was probably tapped, but now he was calling his lawyer. "It's me, Tee. You hear the news?"

"About the Capitol this morning? Holy damn! I heard all right."

"The National Guard. Quayle's calling out the Guard."

"Oh, that! Just to stand around at public buildings and stuff."

The problem with Brody, McNally told himself, was that he had no understanding of how things worked. "That's just the start," he told the lawyer patiently. "You talk to our friends, Tee. This Guard shit ain't good."

"How heavy do you want me to get?"

"Lay the wood to 'em, man. This Guard shit is really bad. Those soldiers ain't going to spend all their time shining their shoes and strutting around in front of the public library. Once they're here, they're going to try to shut down the business. I can feel it."

"You want me to go all the way if I have to?"

"All the way."

McNally hung up and went back to the television. In a little while he went to the kitchen and made himself a cup of coffee.

When Billy Enright came in five minutes later and helped himself to an ice cream bar from the freezer compartment of the refrigerator, Freeman was sipping coffee at the table.

Freeman waited until Billy had unwrapped his ice cream and dropped into a chair at the table. "Y'know," he said, "I think we got us a real window of opportunity here."

"What do you mean?"

"If the soldiers show up tomorrow or the next day, what are they gonna be doin'?"

"Looking for terrorists and assassins. Gonna be everywhere. We'll have to cool it for a while, maybe take vacations."

McNally waved that away. "Think about it. For a week or two all these guys are going to do is search for these Colombians and this dude who tried to off Bush and Quayle. Now is the time to solve some of our little problems so when the Guard *leaves* we can get back in business. That's what I mean. We've got a little time here to fix things up and believe me, anything the cops get just now will go right through the cracks. The Guards ain't cops. They're mechanics and shoe salesmen. The priority is going to be on catching these big Colombian terror dudes. Dig?"

"Yeah," said Billy Enright, lapping at a gob of ice cream that was threatening to run down the stick onto his fingers. "I dig where you're coming from."

Special Agent Freddy Murray was busy trying to coordinate the search for the assassin's trail when he got a call from one of his wiretap experts. "Just recorded a tape I want you to hear."

"Who?"

"Freeman McNally. Conversation with his lawyer."

"We can't use that."

"I know that. But you'd better listen to it. Pretty curious."

"Bring it up."

Murray got back to the task at hand. The FBI lab had identified the brand of tires on the vehicle the assassin had driven in and out of the picnic area on the Potomac that had been the site of the missile launching. Murray was assigning sectors in the Washington area, sending agents to interview every retail outlet for that brand of tire. If they had no success, he would expand the areas. And he expected no success.

This was classic police work, and given enough agents and enough time, would get results. The problem was that Murray had very little of either just now. Still, regardless of how loudly the politicians screamed and the deadlines they invented, the assassin would not be caught until he was caught. Sooner or later the elected ones would figure that out. Until they did, agents like Murray would have to just keep plugging.

He took three minutes to listen to the tape twice. Freeman McNally's voice, all right. Freddy would know that growl anywhere.

"What's that mean?" he asked the wiretap man. "'All the way'?"

"I dunno. The bit about the friends is plain enough. I want to put a tail on this T. Jefferson Brody to find out who he thinks 'our friends' are."

"We don't have anybody."

"One or two guys."

"No! We don't have *anybody* available. Log the tape and file it and let's get back to work."

"You're the boss."

The wiretap man was no sooner out of the room than the direct line rang. "Murray."

"Harrison Ronald. What's happening?"

"Turn on the TV," Murray snapped. He had no time for this.

"I don't mean that assassin shit! I mean the grand jury indictment, you twit."

"It's been put on hold."

"Remember me? The juicy little black worm that dangled on the end of your hook? For *ten fucking months?*"

"Maybe next week. I'll let you know."

"You'll call me. *Ha!* I'm supposed to just sit here with my thumb up my ass until you get around to locking these people up?"

"Harrison, I—"

"Just how far down your friggin' list am I, anyway?"

"Harrison, I know where you're coming from. But I don't set the priorities around here. I'll call—"

Freddy stopped when he realized Harrison Ford had hung up on him.

Congresswoman Samantha Strader was in her early fifties and wore her hair stylishly permed. Representing a congressional district carved from the core of her state's capital city, she held one of the safest Democratic seats in the nation and, in effect, was in Congress for life. After twenty years in the Washington vortex, Sam Strader embodied the trendy prejudices of upper-middle-class white women. She was pro-choice, anti-military, fashionably leftist, and ardently feminist. She viciously attacked the professional hypocrisy of her colleagues in Congress because she was absolutely convinced that she herself was pure of heart and free of taint. Political cartoonists found her enchanting.

This woman, who was extraordinarily sensitive to the slightest whiff of male chauvinism, also possessed the chutzpah to tell the press, "I have a uterus and a brain and I use both." On detecting a slight, fancied or otherwise, she didn't cast aspersions—she hurled them, lobbed them like grenades, usually when reporters were around to hear the detonations. Her victims, most of whom possessed a brain and a penis but had never seen fit to brag about either, wisely kept their mouths shut and bided their time.

Still, Sam Strader had no trouble envisioning herself, acid tongue, uterus, and all, ensconced in the Oval Office as the first woman President of the United States. She campaigned more or less continuously to try to convince others to see her the same way. Seasoned political observers with a less-biased perspective thought she had no chance of becoming President unless the Republican party, in a suicidal frenzy, nominated Jim Bakker for the job.

One of the reasons Strader's mouth often got her into trouble was that she had little tolerance for people she considered fools, a trait she had in common with William C. Dorfman, whom she also despised. High on her list of fools who goaded her beyond endurance was Vice-President Dan Quayle, whose own particular brand of foot-in-mouth disease was of a different strain from Strader's but, if anything, more debilitating.

This was the man who had said, "I stand by all the misstatements." There had been plenty of those, God knows. Once, when explaining why he would not be glad-handing around Latin America just then, he told reporters with a straight face, "I don't speak Latin." Quayle on the strategic significance of Hawaii: "It is in the Pacific. It is a part of the United States that is an island that is right here." He had spoken to the Samoans straight from the heart: "Happy campers you are. Happy campers you have been. And as far as I am concerned, happy campers you will always be."

Strader's very favorite Quaylism was this gem, from an address to the United Negro College Fund: "What a waste it is to lose one's mind—or not to have a mind. How true that is." On hearing this, Strader had sneered at the first reporter she met: "That's the voice of experience if I ever heard it."

On a visit to Chile ten months ago Quayle had purchased—in full view of a contingent of reporters—a souvenir doll with a flip-up dick. This light-hearted indulgence in the joys of crude male locker-room humor enraged feminists coast to coast, including Strader.

Dan Quayle was, in Strader's opinion, the living, breathing personification of all that was wrong with America. That the pampered, privileged son of a filthy-rich white man, one who had majored in "booze and broads" in college and emerged so dismally ignorant that he failed an examination for National Guard enlisted public affairs specialist, could go on to become a congressman, a U.S. senator, then Vice-President, and now, acting President, was enough to test the faith of even the most wildly optimistic.

Sitting here looking at Dan Quayle as William C. Dorfman explained why the presence of the National Guard was required in the District of Columbia, Sam Strader realized with a jolt what the future held. Quayle was stupid, practically retarded, and it was written all over his bland, expressionless face for anyone to see. And the whole world was looking! *She was going to be the next President of the United States.* The premonition gave her goose bumps.

Quayle sat in his chair beside the podium, Strader said later, like a neolithic about to receive an honorary degree from a bible college in Arkansas. Spread at his feet were two dozen senators and congressmen and reporters from every major television network, wire service, and most of the nation's major newspapers. And Quayle looked bored with the whole proceeding.

As Dorfman explained it, the Guard would augment the federal security police charged with guarding public buildings and maintaining order, thereby freeing FBI and police to search for and apprehend the assassins who had killed the secretary of state, the national security adviser, and the House majority leader, and injured the President and the attorney general. In addition they would apprehend any Colombian narco-terrorists who might still be lurking about.

The press was restless. Too many questions remained unanswered.

The instant Dorfman opened the floor the questions were shouted: Who was behind the violence? How had these Colombian killers gotten into the country? What assurance could the government give the American people and citizens of Washington that the violence was over?

"We are doing our best," Dorfman said, "to preserve the public order. Obviously various criminal elements are at work here and we are proceeding vigorously, within the limits of the law, to apprehend those responsible. And to protect—"

Quayle interrupted. He got to his feet and went to the podium. "Listen," he said. "If we knew who these people were and where they were we'd arrest them. Obviously we don't. We're doing everything we can. We will do everything we need to do. I promise."

"Will you declare martial law?"

Quayle exchanged glances with General Land, who was standing off to one side of the platform. "I will if I have to," he said slowly. "I'll do whatever has to be done to protect the public and preserve the Constitution."

"What about people's constitutional rights?" Samantha Strader asked in a strident tone that carried over the reporters' voices.

Quayle looked at her. His expression didn't change. "I'll arrest anybody who needs to be arrested and the courts can sort it all out afterward."

The politicians looked queasy. The print reporters scribbled furiously while the television people waved their hands and shouted, "Mr. Vice-President, Mr. Vice-President," but the press conference was over. Quayle was leaving. Dorfman, General Land, and their aides all followed. The reporters waited only until Quayle passed out of the room, then they charged for the main doors.

Watching it all from a far corner, Jack Yocke shook his head and made a few notes in his small spiral notebook. Nearby Sam Strader cornered Ott Mergenthaler. "Do you really think Dapper Danny made this decision, or was it good-buddy Jabba the Hut Dorfman?" she asked.

Ott mumbled something, and Jack Yocke grinned as he annotated his notebook. Ott hated it when people asked him questions—it nudged him off stride. But Strader's questions were pro forma: *she* was the elected one, following destiny's star.

"For five years," she continued, apparently oblivious to whatever pearl Ott let slip, "the Colombian druggies have used terrorism and murder against their government and their fellow citizens. They've blown up airliners, banks, slaughtered thousands. Everyone *knew* that someday narco-terrorism would come here." That statement lifted Yocke's eyebrows a millimeter. "Now the American people want to know, When it came, why were the macho muchachos in our government caught with their pants down?"

Yocke realized that someone wearing a uniform was standing beside him. He looked around into the face of Jake Grafton, who was apparently listening to Strader.

"Want to answer that one, Captain?" Yocke said, inclining his head an inch at the congresswoman.

"Off the record?"

"Way off."

Grafton's shoulders rose and fell. "They weren't unprepared. They just weren't ready, if you understand the difference. It's almost impossible for people who have known only peace to lift themselves to that level of mental readiness necessary to immediately and effectively counter a determined attack. The mind may say get ready, but the subconscious refuses to pump the adrenaline, refuses to let go of the comfortable present. We refuse to believe."

"Pearl Harbor," Yocke replied, nodding.

"Precisely." Grafton looked around toward a crew breaking down the electrical cable network for a battery of television cameras. "So what do you think?" Grafton added.

"I think Dorfman is finding out who's in charge."

Jake Grafton nodded. A smile flickered on his lips, then disappeared.

"You were on the Capitol steps this afternoon when Cohen was shot. Why didn't you get down and stay down?"

Jake Grafton shrugged. "I figured he'd only shoot once."

"That was a rather large assumption."

"As I said, the human mind works in strange ways. But what sane person would want to shoot me?"

"There's that," Yocke acknowledged. "But he shot at the Vice-President and missed. You could have collected another stray slug."

"Did he miss?" Grafton asked. "I got the gut feeling this guy hits what he aims at."

Captain Grafton turned and left, leaving the reporter scratching his head. He had the feeling that Grafton had wanted to say something else but changed his mind.

* * *

Senator Bob Cherry was in a hurry when he got back to his office that afternoon. After the press conference he and a dozen of his colleagues had spent an hour grilling William C. Dorfman, and Dorfman had been insufferable, as usual. How George Bush tolerated the man's presence, Cherry told himself, was an enigma that only a shrink could explain.

And then there was Dan Quayle, a man with the intellect and personality to be a mediocre deputy sheriff. In a rural county, of course. Cherry had been convinced for years that Quayle had been chosen for VP instead of Senator Bob Dole because Bush and Dole, who had fought hard for the presidential nomination, personally loathed each other. As if personalities mattered.

As Cherry charged through the outer office, he spotted T. Jefferson Brody sitting at the guest's chair at his aide's desk. Brody rose. "Evening, Senator."

"You want to see me?" Cherry asked as he made for the door to his office. Brody noticed the senator gave Miss Georgia a quick smile in passing and got one in return.

"Just a couple of minutes, Senator."

"Come on in. A couple of minutes is all I've got."

Brody did as he was bid and closed the door behind him. Cherry stripped off his shirt and tie as he stirred through the phone messages on his desk.

"What's on your mind?"

"The aide said you were over at the White House?"

"Getting briefed. At least that's what they called it. Jesus, what a day!"

"The networks say that Quayle is calling out the National Guard."

"Yep." Cherry found a clean shirt in the closet beside the washroom and put it on.

"My clients were hoping that you might oppose that move."

"Wouldn't do any good. Quayle's made up his mind. Not that I disagree with him. He's right about this, I think."

Cherry selected a tie from the rack and looked at his image in a mirror as he worked on knotting it. "Just out of curiosity, what's your people's beef?"

"My clients are the people who have contributed generously to your PAC and campaign fund, Senator."

Cherry made a face. He had assumed that. His estimate of Brody's political sophistication went down a notch. "What's their beef?" he repeated.

"Well, Senator, it's like this. They think it'll be bad for their business."

"Pretty damn shortsighted of them, isn't it? I mean, tourism and business travel to Washington will fall like a chunk of blue ice with all these killers running around loose. The sooner they're behind bars the safer everyone will be."

"That's just it, Senator. My clients don't feel that way. They think the FBI and Secret Service can find these people. Baldly, troops are bad for business."

"Sorry. They'll have to live with their disappointment."

Cherry selected a sports coat and pulled it on. He came back around to his desk and pushed a couple of the phone messages away from the others with a finger. "I am in a hurry tonight, Jefferson. I have a couple of calls to make before I leave."

"Senator, I don't think you understand."

"Understand?"

"I'm not asking you for a favor. I'm telling you." Brody grinned.

The senator straightened. His shoulders went back. "Are you leaving or should I call my aide to throw you out?"

Brody sagged back in the chair and threw one leg over the other. "It's funny, when you think about it. All those contributions, and you never once had anyone check to see who was actually giving you the money."

"What . . . ?"

"FM Development, that's a real Florida corporation, and the sole stockholder is Freeman McNally, a prominent local businessman. Maybe you've heard of him? ABC Investments, that's . . ."

Cherry collapsed heavily into his chair. He stared at Brody.

"I'm sure the FBI could give you a fairly extensive dossier on Freeman McNally, Senator. You have really screwed the pooch this time."

"What do you want?"

"I've told you. No National Guard. No troops."

"No." Cherry's face flushed scarlet.

Brody got out of his chair and sat on the edge of the desk. He leaned toward Bob Cherry. "You just haven't thought this through yet, Senator. When it gets out that you've been flying around the country wining and dining and sixty-nining Miss Georgia and paying your campaign bills with *drug* money supplied by Washington's biggest crack dealer, your career will immediately hit the wall. Splat! You'll be *finished.*"

"I'll give the money back. *I didn't know!* I'll—"

"Get real! You politicians sold out to the country-club types who ran out and bought savings and loans. You let them shoot craps with government-insured money—five hundred *billion* dollars down the sewer. You've maneuvered like drunken snakes to get yourselves big pay raises. You've voted yourselves the best pensions in the nation while you've looted the Social Security trust fund. *You've damn near bankrupted America.* The *voters* have to *pay* for all that! Their *children* will have to pay for it! Their *grandchildren* will have to pay! *They* aren't going to believe that Bob Cherry was so senile, so abysmally stupid that he didn't check to see who was stuffing the money into his pocket!"

Brody stood. He buttoned his jacket and adjusted his tie. "All you glad-handing backslappers do little favors for each other—a military base in this district, a sewer system there, a dam over here. Isn't that the way your exclusive little club works?"

Brody's voice dropped. "You get busy and call in some markers. Raise some hell. I'd better be reading in the newspaper about your courageous stand to keep democracy *in* the District and the soldiers *out,* or come Friday you'll be reading about some very interesting contributions made by big-name dope dealers to a certain senator."

Brody paused on the way to the door and turned around. "One more word of advice, Senator. People who cross Freeman McNally rarely live to brag about it."

T. Jefferson Brody's next stop was Senator Hiram Duquesne's office. He caught the senator on the way out the door.

"If you don't mind, I'll walk along down to the garage," Brody said.

He broached the subject of the National Guard troops.

"You know," Duquesne said, "if someone had suggested calling in the Guard this morning after the attack on the Capitol, I would have been against it. But after that shot at the Vice-President I'm for it.

"Gid Cohen's in bad shape. The doctor thinks he'll make it. Took that slug in the shoulder. Just missed his left lung by an inch." Duquesne shook his head. "The rifleman fired from a building five hundred and twenty-seven yards away. Left the rifle and a tripod and a toolbox. Just aimed, fired right through a closed window, dropped everything and walked away."

"Amazing," Brody agreed.

"I don't know what we're up against here, but this shit has got to stop. Quayle's doing the right thing. Didn't think that airhead had it in him."

"My clients want you to oppose this move. They don't want the Guard in the District."

"Sorry, Jefferson. This has gone too far for politics as usual. Quayle has the legal and moral responsibility and he is taking steps. The Senate will back him up every way it can."

Brody kept silent as they walked past the attendant at the entrance to the garage. He waited until they had reached Duquesne's car and the senator was fishing in his pocket for the key.

"My client is Freeman McNally. Perhaps you've heard of him?"

Senator Duquesne gaped.

"Freeman McNally. His reputation is a little unsavory, but he's a businessman. Pays his legal fees without a quibble. Contributes money to worthy causes. Gives freely to certain politicians. Like you, for instance. He's given you over twenty-five thousand dollars. Remember FM Development Corporation?"

"Why, you greasy, filthy son of a bitch!"

"Now, now, Senator, let's not get personal here. You were free to check to see where the money was coming from, and presumably you didn't bother. You were free to refuse the money. You never did."

"What do you want from me?"

"I told you. My client doesn't want the Guard in the District. He's contributed generously to keep you in the Senate and he thought you should pull out all the stops and help him out on this."

"And if I don't? Come on! Your kind of slime always has a stick handy if the carrot doesn't work."

"My client wants to see you right out front, Senator, waving the banner to keep the military out of the District. If the parade leaves without you . . . ." Brody shrugged. "You're going to have a difficult time explaining away twenty-five thousand dollars in contributions from Washington's biggest crack dealer, Senator. Really tough."

"Get out of my sight, you bastard." Duquesne balled his right fist and took a step forward.

"Think it over, Senator." Brody took a step backward. "If I were you I wouldn't throw away my reputation and a Senate seat over this. I'd bend a little and go on down the road."

Brody turned and walked quickly away.

"I'll see you roast in hell, Brody," the senator called after him.

Brody kept walking.

Captain Jake Grafton and his staff spent the evening at the Pentagon. They had much to do. The National Guard had already begun mobilizing at the armory adjacent to RFK Stadium, but the usual chain of command was about to be radically altered. Grafton and his colleagues drafted an order for the signature of Vice-President Quayle that placed the Washington Guard unit under the immediate operational command of the chairman of the Joint Chiefs, thereby removing ten or so layers of generals and their staffs from the chain of command. This change had been requested by the White House. The order would be signed first thing in the morning.

After the order had been sent to the chairman's office for review, and probably for redrafting, Grafton and FBI special agent Thomas Hooper got themselves a cup of coffee and spread a street map of metro Washington upon Grafton's desk.

Toad Tarkington, never one to be left out, pulled a chair around so he could see.

"I really don't have time for this," Hooper muttered. Jake knew that well enough. Hooper looked exhausted. His shirt was dirty and he had spots on his sports coat. He needed a shave. He probably hadn't been home in several days. But his superiors had sent him over here anyway.

Jake got a yellow marker from his desk drawer and begin putting yellow splotches on the map. He marked public buildings, the White House, the Executive Office Building, the Capitol, the Supreme Court, the FBI building, the Justice Department, the office buildings that were used by members of Congress.

Then he handed the marker to Hooper. "Your turn."

Hooper marked the courts, the jail, buildings used by various other government agencies. When he finished, he tossed the marker on the map.

"Twenty-six buildings," Tarkington said, ever helpful.

"Around the clock, at least three armed men at every entrance."

Jake pulled a scratch pad over and began figuring. "Anybody want to guess the average number of entrances for each building?"

"Six or eight," the Air Force colonel said from his seat on the adjacent desk.

They discussed it. They used seven.

"We don't have enough men. Nowhere near."

"Get more," Hooper said. "Men are the one asset you guys got lots of."

"Until we get more—and that will take some time—we'll have to put maybe one man at each entrance and keep mobile squads nearby to back them up."

Hooper shrugged.

"You realize," Grafton said, "that all we're doing here is setting up a shootout if the Colombians or anybody else wants to start something. These troops will be issued ammunition and they'll shoot. They'll have to. There aren't enough of them to do anything else, and they aren't trained to do anything else. Some of them will be killed. Bystanders will be shot. It's gonna be real messy."

"Better not be," Hooper said. "That's what you people are supposed to prevent."

"Let's trim the list. Protect only key buildings."

"No. I've got my orders. Protecting only key buildings merely sends the terrorists to unguarded buildings."

"Not if what they're after is a confrontation."

Hooper shook his head. "The object of terrorism is to show the impotence of the government. Give them an opening and they'll take it."

Toad Tarkington spoke up. "How about a trap? Apparently unprotected buildings with a couple squads of soldiers inside?"

"The buildings would have to be empty," Hooper pointed out. "But without a stream of civilians coming and going, any observer will immediately see that something is wrong."

"You're telling us that this is a no-win situation," Jake Grafton said.

Hooper raised his hands in acknowledgment.

"How did we get to this?" the colonel asked rhetorically. "Again?"

"You can't *win* fighting terrorists," Hooper said, trying to explain. "The politicians—this is just my personal opinion—will *never* allow you to move fast enough to get the jump on these people. Politicians are reactive, always looking for consensus."

"Bullshit," said Jake Grafton. "Politicians aren't stupid. *This is not a conventional war.* Every shot fired is a political statement. The politicos intuitively understand that and the guys in uniform had better learn it damn fast. Until we do, we're not even in the same ballgame."

Hooper looked skeptical. He rubbed his face and drained the last of his coffee.

Jake Grafton picked up the phone and called the chairman's office. Anybody who thought Hayden Land was going to let the terrorists pick and choose their targets, he told himself, didn't know Hayden Land.

The final fillip of the evening for loyal slaves of the big eye made the eleven o'clock news coast to coast. The networks had spectacular footage.

At approximately ten p.m. Eastern Standard Time four cars drew up to a three-story row house in northeast Washington—two cars on the street in front, two in the alley. The men in the passenger seats of the cars used Uzi submachine guns on the men guarding the house, then sat in the cars and fired a total of twenty-four 40-mm grenades through the windows, totally destroying the interior of the structure and setting the place afire. Then the cars drove away.

None of the witnesses could, they said, describe any of the cars or the men in them. No one could remember a single license number.

Police theorized on camera that the killers had used M-79 grenade launchers. They said the house belonged to a suspected crack dealer, one Willie Teal.

The fire in the background behind the policemen and reporters played on screens nationwide. It was quickly out of control and burned out half the houses on the row.

The following morning when the fire was completely out, officials found fourteen bodies in the house where the fire had started, the one that had been assaulted with grenades. This total did not include the four men shot to death outside. Police also found the twisted remains of over a dozen pistols, three submachine guns, and five pump shotguns. A briefcase containing almost five hundred thousand dollars was in the rubble with most of the bills still intact. Five pounds of cocaine somehow escaped the fire and was discovered in a hiding place in the basement by a fireman searching for smoldering timbers.

Harrison Ronald Ford watched the conflagration on television as he lay in his bed in his room at the FBI dormitory at Quantico. He sipped a soda pop and rubbed his Colt automatic occasionally and listened to the commentators try to sum up the violence and horror of the day.

One earnest female was expounding eloquently when he rose from the bed and snapped the idiot box off.

So Freeman McNally had decided to permanently settle Willie Teal's hash. Another little lesson for those who thought they could cross Freeman McNally and get away with it.

M-79 grenade launchers, 40-mm grenades through the window. Like this window.

He pulled back the edge of the venetian blind an inch or so and peeked out at the parking lot and the grass beyond.

What do you do when a grenade comes through the window into your bedroom at night? Do you huddle under the blanket? Pick it up and toss it back?

Hell no! You die, man! Bloody and perforated from hundreds of shards of steel, you die. Just like Willie Teal.

He was breathing hard. His heart was pounding and he was breathing too fast.

He turned off the light. In the darkness he got dressed, layering on sweaters and sweatshirts.

In the bathroom he tried to vomit and couldn't. His stomach felt like he had swallowed a stone. He closed the door, stuffed a towel under it so light wouldn't leak, and turned on the light.

The .45 automatic was loaded and had a round in the chamber. The hammer was back and the thumb safety on. Cocked and locked, the DI had called this condition, way back when.

He put the muzzle in his mouth and tasted it.

Go ahead. Save Freeman the trouble. You know that he didn't decide to annihilate Willie Teal and not lift a finger to solve his biggest problem—you.

He saw himself in the mirror. So pathetic.

He put the gun in his waistband and sat on the commode and sobbed.

CHAPTER TWENTY-FOUR

★ ★ ★ ★ ★ ★ ★ ★ ★ ★ ★ ★ ★ ★

ABOUT two in the morning Harrison Ronald heard the fire door on the first floor of the stairwell being opened. It made a metallic noise that was clearly audible here on the third-story landing of the Quantico FBI dorm, where he sat in the darkness with the slab-sided Colt in his hand. Nobody had ever oiled the push-bars on the heavy doors, thank the Lord.

Harrison Ronald eased his head between the rails and stared downward into the darkness, trying to see. There was nothing. Not a glimmer of light. There should have been light, of course, but Harrison Ronald had unscrewed all the bulbs over two hours ago.

Somebody was down there.

He closed his eyes and concentrated on what he could hear. He even held his breath. Yes, a scraping sound. A shoe sole on the nonskid of the concrete steps.

Harrison Ronald pulled his head back and sat absolutely still, the automatic held firmly in both hands.

This is really it, he told himself. Anybody with a legit reason to use this stairwell would not try to be quiet.

This is really it!

He sat frozen. Any movement he made the other man was bound to hear. His feet were out of position and his butt was cold, ice-cold, on the hard concrete step. He sat listening, breathing shallowly.

A light! The man below was using a small pencil flash, looking things over. Now it was gone.

Somewhere outside a car horn honked. It sounded far, far away.

The man was at the second-floor fire door. The intruder would have to push down the thumb latch on top of the grip, then pull the door open. The thumb latch would require some serious pressure since it mechanically moved the push-bar on the other side.

The latch clicked and the sound echoed in the stairwell.

The man below stood for the longest time, also listening.

Harrison Ronald didn't even breathe.

Then the door opened and the intruder went through. He let the door swing shut but stopped it before the latch clicked.

Was that right? That's what it sounded like to Harrison Ronald. He eased himself upright, massaged his cold, stiff bottom, and still trying to make no noise, crept across the landing and down the stair to the second-floor door.

He felt the steel door, slid his fingers across to the jam. Yes, it was ajar.

He eased his eye to the window in the door and looked down the hallway. The man was outside his door. A thick figure, medium height, carrying a long weapon.

Harrison Ronald moved away from the window and stood in the darkness, trying to think.

The man might not come back this way although he had left the door ajar. Even if he did, he might be expecting Ford to be waiting here. If the man goes into the room, Ford asked himself, should I go down the hallway toward the room? Back up to the third-floor landing? Or down to the first floor?

He took another look.

The man was bent over, working on the lock.

What if there is more than one man?

That thought froze Harrison Ronald. No, not a sound here in the stairwell. Maybe another man coming from the lobby, using the elevator or the stairway beside it. If so, where was he?

He took another peek through the window. The stout man was going through the door. No one else in the hall.

The man would come out of there in seconds.

What to do?

Amazingly enough, the simple expedient of avoiding the man never occurred to Harrison Ronald Ford. He had lived with fear too long. He sought now to surprise his enemy, confront him in a way that maximized the slim advantage that surprise bestowed on the aggressor. For Harrison Ronald intended to be the aggressor. Growing up black in the blue-collar neighborhoods of Evansville and as a young rifleman in the Marine Corps, he had learned the lesson well: attack—fiercely, ruthlessly, with iron-willed determination—always attack.

The door to Ford's room opened silently. A head peeped out and surveyed the dimly lit hallway. Now the stout figure emerged, moving lightly for a man so large, and came along the corridor toward the fire door standing ajar.

He opened the fire door and slipped through.

Crouching on the second step, Ford swung the edge of his hand with all his strength at the man's legs. The man pitched forward headlong. He made a sickening splat on the landing.

Ford was on him in seconds. His hands around the prone figure's throat, squeezing with all his strength. After a few seconds he stopped.

The man under him was absolutely limp. Sitting on his back, Harrison Ronald felt the carotid artery. Nothing.

He rolled the body over and felt gently in the darkness. The forehead was smashed in, pulpy. No blood, or at least no slick, smooth wet slimy substance.

Still breathing hard, still pumped with adrenaline, Ford grasped the dead man's arms and pulled the corpse up the steps. The weapon clattered away.

The body was heavy, at least two hundred pounds. Ford heaved and tugged with all his strength. He paused twice, but with one last mighty heave he managed to get the corpse to the second-floor landing.

He checked the hallway through the window in the door. Empty.

Wedging the door open, he tugged the body through and pulled it down the hallway, which, mercifully, was polished linoleum. He opened the door to his room and dragged the body inside, then raced back for the weapon on the stairs.

In his room, with the faint light from the parking lot coming through the window, he examined the man carefully. Even with his forehead smashed in, he was recognizable. Fat Tony Anselmo. There was a weapon in his coat pocket, a 9-mm automatic with a silencer as big as a sausage. The long weapon was a shotgun, a Remington pump with the barrel amputated just in front of the forearm. It was loaded.

Ford laid the shotgun on the bed and went through the man's pockets. A wallet containing cash, no credit cards. A lot of cash, mainly twenties. Ford put the wallet back in Anselmo's pocket. He quickly went through the other pockets. Cigarettes, lighter, a motel room key, some change, a small pocket knife, two wadded-up handkerchiefs. No car keys.

How had Anselmo gotten here?

Someone was outside waiting.

Ford checked the 9 mm. Loaded, with the safety on.

How long had Anselmo been in here? Five minutes? Four?

He stuffed the automatic in his belt. He was already wearing a jacket over a sweatshirt and sweater. The stairwell was unheated.

He opened the door slowly, checked the hallway, then slipped out. He headed for the stairs that led down to the lobby.

There was a man at the lobby desk, seated on a stool with his head down. Harrison Ford waited behind the fire door, watching him through the small window. The man was reading something on the desk in front of him. He turned a page. A newspaper.

A minute passed. Then another.

Come on! Don't just sit there all night, you knothead!

The desk man picked up his coffee cup and put it to his lips. He frowned, looked into the cup.

He rose from his stool and walked to his right, Ford's left.

The pot was in that little office across the hall. Quickly now!

Ford eased open the door, checked that the desk man was not in sight, then popped through and pushed the door shut behind him. He strode across the carpeted lobby and went through the outside door, closing it behind him.

He dropped behind the first bush he came to and looked around. Beyond this little driveway was the parking lot with the mercury-vapor lights shining down upon it.

Using the trees and shrubs for cover, he circled it as fast as he could trot, pausing and crouching several times behind large bushes for a careful scan.

He reached the vantage point he wanted, with all the cars between him and the entrance to the stairwell that Tony Anselmo had used. Crouching, staying low, he moved carefully parallel to the last row of cars with the 9-mm automatic in his hand.

Up there, on the second row. Wasn't that a head in that dark green car? Hard to tell. Perhaps a seat-back headrest. He moved slowly alongside a car, keeping it between him and the green sedan.

It took fifteen seconds to get to a place where he could look again.

Yes. A man. Apparently white.

He moved slowly now, going behind a line of cars, working closer.

He also checked the other cars. There might be someone else out here.

The door to the green sedan opened. Ford realized it when the interior courtesy light came on.

Then it went off. The man was standing beside the car.

On his hands and knees, Ford crept across the back of the last car in this row, the third one, and looked forward. The green sedan was in the second row, and the man was standing beside the driver's door, about forty feet from where Ford was hunkered. He was doing something. A weapon. He was stuffing shells into a shotgun.

Ford heard the distinctive metallic snick as the man worked the action, chambering a round. He turned his back to Ford and started toward the stairwell door.

Harrison Ronald Ford rose into a crouch, braced his hand against the side of the car, and steadied the automatic. The damn thing had no sights.

He quickly aligned the silencer and squeezed off a round.

The man staggered, tried to turn. Ford squeezed again. Another pop. And another.

The man went down. The shotgun clattered as he hit the asphalt.

Ford ran to his right, all hunched over, down about five cars, then charged across the driving lane into the second row. Alongside a car he threw himself on his face and looked under the parked vehicles. He could see a dark shape on the asphalt, obviously not a tire.

Harrison Ronald Ford leveled the automatic with both hands, trying in the gloom to sight along the rounded top of the silencer.

Shit! This is crazy! He could not see well enough to really aim, even if he had had sights.

He lay there breathing rapidly, staring across the top of the weapon at the dark shape five cars over. The seconds ticked by.

He was going to have to do something.

If he went back to the spot that he had fired from, the man would have a clean shot between the cars at him. If he went along the first row, the same thing would eventually occur.

If the guy were still alive and conscious, that is.

Harrison Ronald wiped the sweat from his face with a sleeve.

Fuck!

He was sure as hell going to have to do something.

He got to his feet and rounded the front of the car he had been lying beside. The green sedan was plainly visible. Moving carefully, silently— he was wearing rubber-soled running shoes—he went toward it with the pistol grasped tightly with both hands, the safety off.

Kneeling on the asphalt, Ford tried again to see the fallen man between the tires. He saw a piece of him the second time, apparently still in the same place and position.

He rounded the front of the green car with the pistol ready and fired the instant it covered the man sprawled there on his side beside the front tire.

He needn't have bothered. Vinnie Pioche was already dead.

When Jake Grafton left the Pentagon, Callie was waiting out front in the car. The buses and subways didn't run at these hours of the night. Jake climbed in and sighed. "I called home. Amy said you were here. How long have you been waiting?"

"Two hours."

"I'm sorry."

"Oh, Jake," Callie said as they hugged each other. "I was so worried about you today. Amy called me at school. She was distraught, almost hysterical. They've run film clips on TV, over and over, all evening. The attorney general getting shot, the Secret Service agents ready to blast the first person who twitched, and you're standing up and looking around like a damned fool."

"Story of my life," he muttered.

"Hug me again, Jacob Lee."

"With pleasure," he said and gave her another squeeze and a kiss. She drew away finally and looked at him with her arms around his neck. "Your mother called."

He nodded. There was nothing to say.

"Oh, Jake!"

Finally she released him and put the car in motion.

The radio was on. Something about a huge fire in northeast Washington.

"What's that all about?" he asked.

"Haven't you heard? Somebody attacked a row house. Set half the block on fire."

"When?"

"About ten tonight. Have you been working on this National Guard thing all evening?"

Jake nodded and turned up the radio volume.

"What's happening, Jake? Assassinations, battles . . . it's almost like a war."

"It *is* a war." After listening a minute, he snapped the radio off. "This is just the first battle. The have-nots versus the haves."

"Have you eaten?"

"No, but I'm going to drop you at the apartment building. I need the car for a while. There's somebody I need to go see."

"Oh, Jake! Not tonight! You need some sleep. Why, the sun will be up in a few hours."

Jake Grafton grunted and sat watching the empty streets.

"Let me come with you."

"You go home and stay with Amy. I'll be home in an hour or so."

"They had Mrs. Cohen on television tonight, coming out of the hospital after seeing her husband. And Mrs. Bush. And Mrs. Quayle. This whole mess, it's so *evil!*"

"Ummm," Jake said, still watching the occasional passing car, wondering vaguely who was driving and where they were going at this hour of the night. The problem, he knew, was that the Colombian narco-terrorists knew exactly what they were fighting for and they wanted it very badly. They wanted a place in the sun.

"What I can't figure out is why Dan Quayle called out the National Guard instead of bringing in Army troops."

"Who knows?" her husband replied. "Maybe he got tired of all the flak he caught in '88 about joining the Guard to avoid service in Vietnam. Maybe he's going to show everybody what a fine fighting outfit the Guard is."

"Doesn't that bother you, his avoiding Vietnam?"

Jake Grafton snorted. "I seem to recall that back then most of the guys my age were trying to avoid going to Vietnam. In some quarters the quest took on religious status."

"You went," she said.

"Hell, Callie, half the country is still discriminating against Vietnam veterans. The U.S. government says Agent Orange never hurt anybody."

"You went," she repeated.

Jake Grafton thought about that for a moment. Finally he said, "I was always a slow child."

His wife reached out and squeezed his hand. He squeezed hers in return.

* * *

Harrison Ronald Ford didn't hesitate. He wrestled the dead weight that had been Vinnie Pioche into the backseat of the green sedan. He tossed the shotgun into the front seat, then got behind the wheel. The keys were still in the ignition.

He started the car. Three quarters of a tank of gas.

How had two New York hoods gotten by the Marine sentries at the gate?

Leaving the car idling, he got out and walked around to look at the front bumper. Residing there was a nice blue Department of Defense officer's sticker. Clean and new.

Harrison got back behind the wheel. He closed the door and sat looking at the door that Fat Tony had gone through on his way upstairs to kill him as he waited for his heart to slow down and his breathing to get back to normal. His hands were still shaking from the adrenal aftershock.

These two worked for the Costello-Shapiro family in New York, the Big Bad Apple. Well, tonight they had been attending to a little chore for Freeman McNally.

Harrison had no proof of course, but he didn't need any. He *knew* Freeman McNally. Freeman had succeeded at an extremely risky enterprise by killing anyone in whom he had the slightest doubt. Why Anselmo and Pioche had agreed to do this little job for Freeman was an interesting question, but one that would probably never be answered. A favor for a new business associate? Good ol' Freeman. A friend indeed.

Ford got out of the car again and closed the door. He looked for the spent shell of the last round he had fired into friend Vinnie. It had been flipped fifteen feet to the right of where he stood. He pocketed it and went back through the lot to find the others. The search took three minutes, but he found them.

Back behind the wheel of the car, he picked up the automatic and popped the clip from the handle. Still held six rounds. He slipped the clip back in place and put the safety on.

Other men would come after him, of course. If Freeman could reach him here in the FBI barracks at Quantico he could reach him anywhere —in a police car in Evansville, a barracks on Okinawa, a hut on a beach in Tasmania—*anywhere.*

It took Harrison Ronald about ten seconds to decide. Not really. It took him ten seconds before he was ready to announce the decision to himself.

It's the only choice I've got, he told himself.

He had actually made the decision before he stuffed Vinnie in the backseat and picked up the shells, but now it was official.

Harrison Ronald put the car in gear and fed gas. He coasted through the parking lot, avoiding the little driveway that went up by the office, and headed for the main gate and the interstate to Washington.

It was funny, when you thought about it. He had been scared silly for ten months, day and night and in between, and now he wasn't. He should have been, but he wasn't. As he drove along he even whistled.

Jake Grafton parked the car three blocks from what was left of Willie Teal's place and walked. Fire trucks and hoses were everywhere. Cops accosted him.

He showed them his military ID. Since he was still in uniform, he was allowed to pass.

Standing across the street from Willie Teal's, Jake Grafton marveled. The entire row from here to the corner was a smoking ruin. Six firemen played water on the wreckage by the light of three big portable flood-lights. Behind a yellow police-line tape, several hundred black people stood watching, occasionally pointing.

Jake turned to the nearest policeman and said to him, "I'm looking for a reporter named Jack Yocke. Seen him around?"

"Young? Late twenties? Yeah. Saw him a while ago. Look over there, why don'cha?"

Yocke was interviewing a woman. He scribbled furiously in his notebook and occasionally tossed in a question. At one point he looked up and saw Grafton. He thanked the woman, spoke to her in a low, inaudible tone, then walked toward the naval officer.

"Somebody said the fireman had used enough water to float a battleship, but we certainly didn't expect to see the Navy show up to take advantage of that fact."

"Who did this?"

Yocke's eyebrows went up. "The police are right over there. They're working their side of the street and I'm working mine. My version will be in tomorrow's paper."

"Gimme a straight answer."

Yocke grinned. "Prevailing opinion is that Freeman McNally just put a competitor out of business. Off the record, with a guarantee of anonymi-ty, witnesses tell me four cars, eight men. They used grenade launchers. Just sat in the cars cool as ice cubes in January and fired grenades through the windows. The firemen and police are still carting bodies out of Teal's place. Ain't pretty."

"You about finished here?"

Yocke shrugged.

"I want to have a little talk. Off the record, of course."

"Is there any other way?"

Yocke led the way toward his car. Walking toward it he asked, "You hungry?"

"Yeah."

They went to an all-night restaurant, a Denny's, and got a seat well back from the door. The place was almost empty. After they had ordered, Jake said, "Tell me about this town. Tell me about Washington."

"You didn't come out here in the middle of the night to get a civics lecture."

"I want to know how Washington works."

"If you find out, you'll be the only one who knows."

"Okay, Jack Yocke, *The Washington Post*'s star cynic, let's hear it."

"You're serious, aren't you?"

"Yep."

Yocke took a deep breath and exhaled slowly, then settled himself comfortably behind his podium. "Metropolitan Washington is basically three cities. The first, and largest, is composed of federal government employees who live in the suburbs and commute. This is the richest, most stable community in the country. They are well paid, well educated, and never face layoffs or mergers or takeovers or competition or shrinking profit margins. It's a socialist utopia. These people and the suburbanites who provide goods and services to them are Democrats: big government pays their wages and they believe in it with all the fervor of Jesus clinging to the cross.

"The second group, the smallest, is made up of the movers and shakers, the elected and appointed officials who make policy. This is official Washington, the Georgetown cocktail-party power elite. These people are the actors on the national stage: their audience is out there beyond the beltway. They're in the city but never a part of it.

"The last group are the inner-city residents, who are seventy percent black. This group only works in federal office buildings at night, when they clean thcm. Thc city of Washington is thc biggest employer; forty-six thousand jobs for a population of about 586,000 people in the district."

Jake whistled. "Isn't that high?"

"One in every thirteen people works for the city. Highest average in the nation. But major industry dried up in Washington years ago, leaving only service jobs—waiters, maids, bus drivers, and so on. So the politicians create jobs, just like in Russia. The inner-city residents, like the suburbanites and the residents of every major inner city in the country, are also Democrats. They cling to big government like calves to the tit."

"So what the hell is wrong?" Jake Grafton asked.

"Depends on who you ask. The black militants and the political preachers—that's *all* the preachers, by the way—claim it's racism. The liberals—you have to be rich and white to have enough guilt to fit into this category—claim it's all the fault of a parsimonious government, a government that doesn't do enough. I've never met a liberal yet who thought we had enough government. This even though the district has one of the highest tax rates in the country and the federal government kicks in a thousand bucks a head for every man, woman, and child every year."

Jack Yocke shrugged grandly. "To continue my tale, the schools in the suburbs are as good as any in the country. The schools in the inner city are right down there with the worst—fifty percent dropout rate, crime, drugs, abysmal test scores, poisonous race relations—by every measure abominable. The average inner-city resident is ignorant as a post, poor as a church mouse, paranoid about racial matters, and lives in a decaying slum. He collects a government check and complains about potholes that are never filled and garbage that is never hauled away while the local politicians orate and posture and play racial politics for all they're worth and steal everything that isn't nailed down. He'll vote for Marion Barry for mayor even though he knows the man is probably a drug addict and a perjurer because Barry uses the white establishment as a scapegoat for all his troubles.

"Speaking frankly, the District of Columbia is a Third World shithole. The local leaders are quacks, demagogues, and outright thieves. Public schools and hospitals are appallingly bad, tens of millions of dollars of public funds have been stolen or squandered, charges of racism are endemic. The *Washington Monthly* magazine said the District has 'the worst government in America,' which is probably true. A U.S. senator called it the most corrupt *and* most incompetent urban government in America. With me so far?"

Their food came. The waitress asked if they needed anything else and they both shook their heads. When she was gone, Yocke continued:

"Except for tourism and government, the District has no other economic base, nothing to create middle-class jobs. Its people don't believe in self-help or education. They blame all their woes on the U.S. government. If this place were in Central America or Africa, Barry would have proclaimed himself 'maximum leader' or 'president for life.' Since they have the misfortune to be surrounded by the United States, however, they want this sixty-four-square-mile banana republic to become the fifty-first state."

"Why?"

"Why not?"

With his mouth full of a bite of BLT, Jake said, "Being a state won't help."

"Of course not. But Marion Barry can be governor and Jesse Jackson can be a senator. The Democrats will get a bigger majority in the House and Senate and three automatic electoral votes. What more do you want, for Christ's sake?"

"You really are a cynic, aren't you?"

"Oh, come off it, you overpaid nincompoop in a sailor suit. I've been a reporter in this town for three years. I go out every night and look at the bodies. I spend evenings at the emergency room of D.C. General with the abused kids, the wives beat half to death, the overdoses, the gunshot victims who won't tell who shot them, the rape victims. I stand in the courthouse halls and watch the attorneys plea-bargain, selling their clients' constitutional rights for a reduced sentence or probation. I go to the jails and look at the same old faces again and again and again. I talk to the victims of muggings, robbery, burglary, auto theft. Human carnage is the name of my game, mister. Who the hell do you think you are?"

"Three years," Jake Grafton sighed. "It's too long, yet it's not long enough."

The reporter suddenly looked tired. No doubt his day had been as long as Jake's. He said, "No doubt you'd feel better if I had said ten years. Let's change it. Ten years' experience it is."

"You're floating down a sewer in a glass-bottom boat, Yocke. Sooner or later you have to get in and swim."

"You think *I'm* to blame for some of this?"

"I read the paper. I haven't seen any of this with your byline."

"You ought to read the paper more carefully," Yocke said. He rubbed the stubble on his jaw. "There's a whole bunch of very talented people who think their mission in life is to write all of it—the good, the bad, and every subtle nuance in between. They put all of it in the paper. The hell of it is nobody pays any attention. It's like tossing pebbles into the Atlantic Ocean. Doesn't even disturb the fish."

Jake took a sip of coffee, then helped himself to another bite of BLT. After he'd chewed and swallowed, he said, "You've heard about the National Guard deal. How will that go, in this city you describe?"

Yocke took his time. He drank some coffee and slathered the remainder of his sandwich with more mustard. "I don't know. If the troops are just going to stand around public buildings looking spiffy and the shooters stay home, everything will go swimmingly. Absent a charge of child molestation, Quayle will be our next president."

"Why'd you say if?"

"You'd be home in bed, Captain, if that was all there was to it. Neither of us rode in yesterday on a hay wagon."

Grafton caught the waitress' eye and held his cup aloft. She brought the pot and gave him a refill.

After swallowing his last bite of sandwich, Yocke continued: "A lot of people in this town are fed up to here with these dopers and politicians. They've been demanding action and getting politics as usual. Something is going to give."

"What're you saying? There's going to be a revolution?"

"Packed emergency rooms, innocent people slaughtered, children starving and neglected and abused, jails packed full as sardine cans, cops fighting for their lives. Now I'll tell you, a *lot* of little people are sick and tired of going to funerals. They've *had* it. And you know what? I don't think the political cretins have a clue. They're dancing between the raindrops blaming the big bad Colombians and the white establishment and the National Rifle Association."

Jack Yocke threw up his hands. "Ah well, even Fidel Castro got the message finally, just before they shot him."

Jake nodded. "Yeah."

A few minutes later, Yocke asked, "Why'd you stand up today when they shot at Quayle?"

"Stupid, I guess."

"Captain, whatever you are, stupid isn't on the list."

"Wondered where the shot came from. Took a look."

Yocke's eyebrows went up and down once. "Well, thanks for the sandwich." He shoved the check across toward Grafton.

"Any time."

Approaching Freeman's house, for the first time in a long time Harrison Ronald did not feel the dread. He didn't drive by, of course. After the fracas earlier this evening over at Teal's Freeman would have a squad of men in front and another squad of men in back, some of whom would inevitably recognize Sammy Z.

Harrison parked two blocks away and walked.

The streets were silent and empty. Amazingly quiet. A gentle breeze made the tree limb shadows cast by streetlights stir and shake.

He was behind a car, crouching, when he got his first look at the end of the alley. A streetlight was on the pole. But there was no one in sight. No guard.

Odd.

Using the cars for cover he worked his way to the alley and looked down it. He couldn't see anyone.

He went down the alley with the automatic in his hand, flitting from shadow to shadow, pausing occasionally to look and listen. Nothing.

Even Freeman's backyard was empty.

Nobody home. Okay, where would he be? Three or four possibilities suggested themselves, and as he mulled them Harrison Ronald tried the back door. Locked. He pounded loudly on the door with the butt of the pistol and stood to one side.

Thirty seconds passed, then a minute. He put the muzzle of the silenced pistol against the lock and pulled the trigger.

Inside the lights were off. He proceeded slowly, warily. The house was empty.

In the weapons room he wiped the prints from the automatic, even popped the magazine out and wiped that off on a handy cleaning rag, and tossed it into the box with the others. He selected another automatic with a silencer already attached, loaded it, and helped himself to a couple more loaded magazines. He was about to leave when a silenced Uzi caught his eye. Why not? He took it and four magazines of 9-mm ammo.

Leaving the Uzi inside the back door, he pulled the door shut behind him. He trotted down the alley and the two blocks to the car, then drove it back.

He maneuvered it into the parking area and dragged Vinnie from the car. God, the body was heavy! The corpse hadn't been this heavy when he loaded it into the car. Or perhaps he had been too pumped to notice.

He put Vinnie in the easy chair in front of the television, then turned the set on. The rest of the lights he unplugged.

Another trip to the car for Vinnie's twelve-gauge, which he laid across the dead man's lap. The empty brass casings in his pocket he tossed around the room after wiping them.

When he started the car, he thought for a moment, trying to decide if there was anything else he wanted to do.

Yeah. Come to think of it . . .

Standing in the door to the living room, he sprayed a magazine of 9-mm slugs from the Uzi. Above the guttural buzzing of the silenced weapon the sound of the television shattering and the slugs slapping the plasterboard was plainly audible.

That magazine spent, he loaded another and went into the bedroom. Three bursts there, then into the kitchen where he finished out the magazine on the refrigerator and oven and dishes in the cabinets. He put another magazine in and emptied it in Freeman's bathroom into the toilet and the bathtub and the mirror and sink. The shattered porcelain and glass flew everywhere.

This was like pissing on Hitler's picture. Somehow it just wasn't enough.

He went back to the storeroom and got some more magazines for the Uzi. He looked around. Under the couch where the boxes of ammo were stored was a cardboard box half full of grenades. Harrison helped himself.

What would you have to do to make Freeman McNally pay enough? For what he did to the Ike Randolphs, for what he did to all the people he peddled his poison to, for all the unspeakable misery and pain this man gave the world so that he could line his pockets—*for what he did to Harrison Ronald Ford*—what would you have to do to McNally to even the balance in the ledger?

The filthy fuck would have to scream until his soul shattered.

Seven cars were parked outside the Sanitary Bakery warehouse, including Freeman's big Mercedes. No guards in sight outside. Maybe they were all inside having a snort and a drink, still celebrating the big party at Willie Teal's.

Sitting here in the green sedan looking it over—this was *really* weird—Harrison Ronald wasn't scared. Not the least. He felt good, real good, like he had had a snort. He had never told the FBI agents of course, and would never tell anyone else, but he had had to snort the stuff in front of Ike and Billy Enright, and a couple times in front of Freeman and his brothers, just to prove his bona fides. Feds and cops would never touch the shit, according to street wisdom.

It had been tough leaving the stuff alone after he had used it more or less regularly for several months. Excruciatingly difficult. But that wasn't the hardest part. He had been nervous, scared, all along, but after doing the coke he had his first real attacks of paranoia, and they hadn't ceased, no doubt because he had plenty to be paranoid about. All he had to fight it had been grit and determination. They weren't enough.

But now all those waves of panic and loose-boweled terror were gone. He had made up his mind. He was going to attack. Maybe die.

And he felt good, real good.

He parked the car on the north side of the warehouse by the chain-link fence where the garbage trucks were kept and locked it after he got out.

The neighborhood was quiet enough—only traffic sounds coming across the railroad tracks from New York Avenue. That and the low guttural snarls of the two Dobermans on the other side of the fence. He stood looking between the garbage trucks at the slab-sided black bulk of the building. There was a door over there somewhere. He had seen it before during the daylight.

He used the silenced pistol on the dogs. Two shots each. The Dobermans went down like they were sledge-hammered.

The gate through the ten-foot-high fence was held together by a big chain with a padlock on it. Two shots for the padlock, then sixty seconds to unwrap the chain, squeeze through, then wrap it again.

The door was nailed shut with a two-by-six across it. No doubt there was other timber on the other side. He tried to remember if he had noticed this door in his many walks through the interior. If he had, he would remember, but he didn't. Still, there was undoubtedly concrete and steel in there somewhere for the bullets to ricochet from. The sound of the full-metal-jacketed 9-mm slugs spanging through the old warehouse would certainly announce his arrival. And his intentions.

Well, here goes nothing.

He sawed the board in half with half a magazine from the Uzi, then kicked at the center of it with all his strength. It gave.

He kicked three or four times. The noise was loud here. It was probably echoing all over that huge mausoleum. Yet apparently something was holding the upper part of the door on the inside. He used the rest of the magazine on the point of resistance and kicked some more. It sagged.

Empty magazine out, new magazine in, Uzi ready, he gave one last mighty kick and the door flew open. Harrison Ronald dived through and rolled sideways, right into a wall.

He lay there for a second, his eyes adjusting to the gloom. He was under a stair that led up to the second-floor balcony. The main stairwell that led to the upper levels was off to his left. The room that the guard was in—that the front door opened into—was off to his right on the other side of the building.

He heard someone running.

Up, moving to his right along the wall, the Uzi ready. He could see the light coming from the doorway to the guard room. The door was open. The only other light in the place came from a naked bulb on the third-floor landing on the east end of the building. But it was so high and far away the light seemed to get lost in the cavernous space.

A flash and a loud report came from behind a box against the far wall. The bullet hit near Ford's head. He scuttled toward the darkness, away from the open door.

Another shot. And another.

He used the Uzi. A three-shot burst. Little flashes against the masonry where the jacketed bullets hit. He fired again, not trying to aim in the semidarkness, just walking the slugs in. The third burst drew a scream.

Ford was up and running for the stair at the east end of the huge room when two wild shots from the screaming man sailed by. He kept going, running hard, and was in time to see the vague outline of someone coming down the stairs.

Harrison Ronald triggered a long burst at the stairway as he ran. The figure slumped and went down. From fifteen feet away he triggered a short burst into the body, then took cover beside the stairway, breathing hard.

His heart was thudding like a trip-hammer, yet he felt good, oh, so good. He should have done this six months ago.

The first man he had shot was still screaming. And cursing, the high-pitched wail of a man in agony. Like Ike Randolph in his final moments.

Someone above him on the balcony fired at him and a shard of something struck his face. It stung. He wiped at it. Wet. Blood.

Whoever was up there was moving—he could hear him.

Harrison dug a grenade from his coat pocket, got the pin out, and holding the Uzi in his left hand, came out of the darkness running and lofted the grenade upward with a basketball sky-hook shot.

The damn thing might come bouncing down before it popped, but what the hell. End it here.

It didn't. The grenade went off with a flash and boom that was painful in this huge masonry echo chamber. A big piece of the wooden balcony rail came crashing down, the gunman in the midst of it. He landed with a splat a dozen feet from Ford and lay where he had fallen as the dust and dirt settled around and on him.

"Hey, down there!"

The shout came from upstairs.

"I don't know who the hell you are down there but you'd better stop this shit, man!"

It sounded, Harrison decided, like Billy Enright. Maybe at the head of the stairs.

The stairs were pretty conventional. They went upward to a landing against the outer wall, then turned 180 degrees and went on up to the second floor, the balcony level. And so on, a landing between each floor, up to the fourth floor. If Ford could gain the balcony everyone above him was trapped. This was the only exit from the higher floors.

He tiptoed up the stairs and stopped on the step prior to the landing. He took out another grenade and pulled the pin. Then he stood, listening and waiting.

"There's five of us up here, man, and we're all armed." It sounded like Billy was right around the corner at the head of the stairs, standing on the balcony. His voice was tense, wound tight. "I think," he continued, "that you're only one—"

Ford leaned around the corner and tossed the grenade.

"Fuck! You fuck—"

The concussion of the explosion was intensely painful in this confined space. Some of the shrapnel ricocheted against the wall and bounced off Ford, too spent to penetrate.

Harrison Ronald rounded the corner with the Uzi spraying and charged up the stairs two at a time.

Billy Enright sat with his back to the waist-high balcony rail, trying to hold his guts in with both hands. In the center of his ripped-apart face his eyes widened in recognition. He opened his mouth, but only blood came out. Then he slowly toppled sideways.

Ford heard a laugh. From someplace. Where? He moved back into the stairwell and scanned the balcony, trying to see.

"You get him, Billy?"

Freeman McNally.

"Naw, Freeman. Billy's lying here trying to hold his guts in. Maybe you got a cheerful word for him. He could use it right now."

Another laugh. "Well, well, well. If it ain't our good buddy the fucking stoolie, Sammy Z."

"I ain't a stoolie, Freeman. I'm a cop. The FBI put me in to get the goods on you. And I got 'em. Ten fucking months worth. They got it *all.* You're gonna be in jail until you're too old to get it up, Freeman, if you make it through tonight, which is very doubtful."

McNally laughed again. It sounded like he was somewhere above, maybe on the fourth floor, talking out of one of the interior windows.

"This ain't your night, Freeman. You get lucky and kill me, you're going straight to the butt-fuck house. I hear all those homos got AIDS, man. They'll be delighted to see your tight little cherry ass."

"Well, you got one thing right, Sammy. I am sure as hell gonna kill you."

"It's already been tried tonight, Freeman. I hope you didn't waste any money on Vinnie and Tony. They won't ever be able to pay you back."

Ford heard a noise above him, in the stairwell. Someone was coming down. "I'm gonna kill you slow, real slow," McNally said, "like I did ol' Ike. You're gonna fucking beg for a bullet, boy."

Ford ascended the stairs, both hands on the Uzi. He was four steps up when the top of a head peeped around the corner. Ford pulled the trigger and held it down.

The body plopped out from behind the wall onto the landing. Brains and blood were scattered all over the wall behind.

"Little hard to tell, Freeman," Ford called, "but I think you just lost a brother."

He paused and changed magazines, then stepped over the corpse and kept going. Ahead of him was the glare of the naked bulb on top of the landing. He shot it out. The pieces of glass fell with a tinkle, leaving the stairwell in total darkness. All he could hear was the moans of the guard on the warehouse floor.

Harrison Ronald waited for his eyes to adjust.

Finally, when he realized he could see all he was going to see, he eased his head around the corner and looked. It was like looking into a coal mine at midnight. Nothing. Same the other way.

He got out two grenades. Pin out of one, he tossed it down the hall to his left, then the other to the right. He had no more than got his hand back in when the first one went off. Then the second. Like two thunderclaps.

Silence.

Total silence. Like a tomb.

He wanted to talk, taunt Freeman about Ike, make the bastard suffer before he died. But he knew better. He stood silently, listening and trying to breathe slowly and noiselessly.

He was standing like that when he heard the explosion just behind him and felt the numbing shock of the bullet rip into him.

Harrison staggered. He dropped the Uzi and went to his hands and knees.

Something grabbed his throat and squeezed viciously. McNally had come down the staircase from above.

"I got him, Ruben, I got him!"

His neck—he couldn't breathe . . .

Ford reached back, groping desperately. His hand found its target and he grabbed all he could get and pulled with all his strength.

Screaming, Freeman McNally released his neck hold as Ford twisted and squeezed and tore, trying to rip his balls off. Screaming high and loud in unbearable pain as Harrison Ronald filled his lungs and physically lifted the man with his right hand as he levered himself up.

Harrison got his left hand on McNally's neck and pushed him back against the wall, then smashed his head again as he tried to literally rip the man's testicles from his body.

The scream was choked off in McNally's throat. Another smash into the wall and Ford lost his grip. He spun the man to a better angle and drew back his right hand to smash his larynx, just as someone arrived and fired a weapon.

Ford threw Freeman aside and lunged. The weapon flew and his fist connected with something soft. He struck savagely, again and again and again as hard as he could until the man he was pummeling went limp.

He was losing blood. He could feel the wetness. And he was weakening.

Neither of the other two men moved.

He fumbled in his pocket for the little penlight he had taken from Tony Anselmo. When was that?

Ruben McNally was apparently dead, his nose bone rammed up between his eyes.

Freeman's eyes stared at nothing, refused to focus.

Harrison Ronald felt Freeman's carotid artery. No heartbeat.

Furious, he rolled him over. A bullet dead center in the back, right between the shoulder blades. Shot by his own brother!

"You . . . you . . . you . . ."

Ford was also hit in the back and he knew it. Unless he got medical attention quickly he would probably bleed to death, hemorrhage into a lung or something.

"You . . . ," he told Freeman's frozen face, then couldn't think of anything to add. A wave of pain and nausea swept over him.

"Oh God, help me."

He got to his feet and started down the stairs, then tripped and almost fell. The flashlight hit the concrete and broke. It wasn't much of a light anyway. He kept going.

"God, forgive me for . . . for . . . please forgive me."

He tripped over a body and fell down the last flight of stairs. He lay there in the darkness with death creeping over him.

"No!"

Somehow he got to his feet and saw the light coming through the door to the guard's office a hundred feet away. He staggered in that direction.

The man behind the equipment box against the south wall was silent. Unconscious or dead. At least Ford didn't hear him as he shuffled by.

He got the phone off the hook and punched 911. "Sanitary Bakery warehouse," he told the operator as he threw the switch to electrically unlock the front door.

"The address and your name, please!" she said.

His legs were shaking and he was having trouble seeing. "Send the FBI and an ambulance. Better hurry. FBI . . ."

The phone slipped out of his grasp and he was falling.

"I'm dying," he said.

Then the blackness swept over him.

CHAPTER TWENTY-FIVE

* * * * * * * * * * * * *

THE subway and the buses didn't operate beyond the beltway on Wednesday morning, and tens of thousands of suburban commuters didn't hear the news on television or radio. Infuriated, many who normally rode to work on public transport tried to join the hordes who drove. This was a serious mistake. Troops and state policemen had blocked every beltway entrance to Washington and were making all vehicles attempting to enter or leave the district turn around. Only law-enforcement officers, people with military IDs, and emergency vehicles were being allowed to pass. Although many of those who normally worked in the city heard the news before they left their homes and consequently decided to stay home, the traffic jams that morning were monumental, even by Southern California standards.

All flights to and from National Airport were canceled. The trains and intercity buses were not running. Washington was isolated and troops patrolled the streets.

Not many troops at first. The National Guard was still mobilizing and had less than twenty-five percent of their men on duty. Regular army troops began arriving at three a.m. on C-141s and C-5s at Andrews Air Force Base. General Hayden Land had ordered in a division of infantry and two regiments of armored cavalry. It would take almost thirty-six hours to get all the men and their equipment to Washington.

During the night the Vice-President's original commitment to guard major public buildings had evolved into a show of overwhelming force. The plan recommended to General Land by the Joint Staff had been approved by the White House. No White House staffer wanted to be the first to say "enough," not when the primary criticism that continued violence would stimulate would be that the government had not done enough to prevent it. So the more-is-better recommendations of Jake Grafton and his group had been adopted all the way up the line.

By ten a.m. tanks and armored personnel carriers were parked near the major government buildings in the downtown area. By noon they were in front of every hospital in town. By two p.m. every traffic circle in the District had a tank parked in the flower beds beside the statue. The olive-drab monsters sat in pairs upon the Mall, the diesel engines idling in the chill December wind as the crews stood nearby drinking coffee from disposable cups and looking with wide eyes at the sprawling buildings bathed in the weak winter sun.

The men were dressed for the weather but they were still cold. Last night they had been in Georgia. They indulged themselves in a great deal of arm swinging and jogging in place.

At nine a.m. the Vice-President met with a delegation of two dozen congressmen and senators in the East Room of the White House. It was not a happy meeting. Legislators who lived outside the beltway were of course not present. Their colleagues demanded that representatives, senators, and members of their staffs have access through military lines.

Vice-President Quayle instantly agreed. "This," he explained, "was a glitch no one thought of last night."

"There's a hell of a lot of things you people never thought of last night," Senator Bob Cherry thundered. "Food—how are grocery trucks going to get into the city? How are sick people going to get in and out? Critical medical supplies? The radio says there are thousands of people stranded at National Airport and Union Station. Damn it, you can't just surgically remove this city from the rest of the United States and expect it to keep breathing. Won't happen."

"It'll only be until we can thoroughly search the city for terrorists," Quayle explained, looking from face to face. "Surely everyone can see the necessity for extraordinary measures."

"We gotta do *something*," someone muttered.

"Something won't hack it," Cherry boomed. "This military idea is half-baked. Won't work. Why does anybody think a bunch of kids wearing uniforms and carrying rifles can do what the FBI can't?"

"This may not work," Dan Quayle acknowledged. "But we're going to try it for lack of something better. We've got to stop the terrorism and violence. Stop it dead, once and for all. That's what I'm trying to do."

"But you can't just rip the Constitution into confetti," Cherry groused. "What about people's rights?"

"Senator," Quayle began patiently, "I'm well aware that Christmas is six days away and kids aren't out of school, and some people are being prevented from going to work and earning a living. I know this measure is a financial hardship on many and an outright disaster for others. My wife reminded me this morning that many employers cannot afford to pay their employees if they aren't working and a lot of those who can afford it won't bother. *I know* this measure is a real hardship on many. Still, it's necessary."

"In *your* judgment," Cherry said crossly.

"In *my* judgment," Quayle echoed, irritated with Cherry and all of them. He had been in Washington long enough to learn that there was nothing fair about politics: if ordering in the National Guard and the Army turned out to be ineffective or a disaster, he would be blamed; yet if the measure worked and the terrorists were apprehended, the advisors and staff would get all the credit for convincing Dan Quayle, the bumbling fool, to do the right thing.

"You should have asked the advice of the senior members of Congress *before* you called in the military," Cherry continued, not yet ready to let it lie. "I, for one, am more than a little peeved that we get summoned like ladies in waiting to come over here and listen to edicts from the throne."

Dan Quayle lost his temper. "Goddammit, Senator, everybody in this room knew about this yesterday. *I* have assumed the President's responsibilities during his disability and *I* am *not* going to run the presidency by committee."

"I'm not suggesting—" Cherry began, but Quayle ignored him and began talking into the microphone on the podium while referring to notes:

"I have appointed an independent nonpartisan presidential commission to oversee federal efforts to apprehend the people responsible for the atrocities of these past few days. This will be announced to the press as soon as we finish here. The commission will work closely with all the federal agencies involved to investigate all matters connected with these crimes. I want all the facts investigated and laid before the public. The commission will have the authority to pursue any line of inquiry it feels is germane. I will send a message to Congress today asking for a special appropriation so the commission can immediately hire staff and get to work. I certainly hope Congress will see fit to act quickly. I don't want anybody shouting cover-up when all the dust settles.

"Mr. Dorfman, please read the names."

Will Dorfman somehow didn't look his nasty, mean little self, Congresswoman Samantha Strader noted with a raised eyebrow. The troll actually looked human this morning—harried, a touch of exhaustion.

Dorfman read the list. The first name was that of the Chief Justice of the Supreme Court, Harlan Longstreet. That was fitting. Chief Justice Earl Warren had directed the inquiry into John F. Kennedy's assassination, but in spite of herculean efforts on the part of the investigators, nitpickers and conspiracy fanatics were still unsatisfied over twenty-five years later. Perhaps that was inevitable.

The eighth name Dorfman read was Sam Strader. When Dorfman had telephoned and asked her to serve she had been momentarily at a loss for words, a rare experience, not to be savored. "Why me?" she asked.

"Quayle wants this commission to be nonpartisan, and the only way we know to do that is to get people from all across the political spectrum to serve."

She mulled it for three seconds. Yes. Now, standing here watching

Danny the Dork prove that brains are not a prerequisite for public office, she was sure she had made the right decision.

She would have a delicious time tormenting those male chauvinist fascists at the FBI who, God knew, richly deserved far worse. More importantly, she would be able to make the blind world see that emperor Quayle wore no pants—this military witch hunt for someone to pin the blame on had all the earmarks of a debacle in the making. Last, but certainly not least, tens of millions of voters who had never heard of Samantha Strader soon would.

There was no reason that she shouldn't be the next president. After all, Quayle had the charisma of a fish. The real problem was getting the Democratic nomination, and if she could show what a woman could do to clean up this terrorist mess, she would have a leg up.

All in all, this was going to be an enjoyable, interesting project. As usual, Samantha Strader had not a scintilla of self-doubt: she believed in herself and her opinions with a white-hot zeal that would have looked good on a messiah. Despite the seriousness of the occasion Strader indulged herself in a luxurious grin.

Special Agent Thomas F. Hooper found his colleague Freddy Murray lounging beside the nurse's station outside the intensive care unit. "How is he?"

"Coming out of it. It'll be a few more hours. He surprised the surgeons. They thought he'd die on the table."

"Seven dead men in the warehouse and one in his room at Quantico. The maid found the body an hour ago when she went in to change the sheets. The lab guys are trying to put it all together and figure out who everybody is."

"I got ten bucks that says he killed them all."

"No bet."

Freddy Murray shook his head. "Funny, isn't it? Ten months— wiretaps, depositions, surveillance cameras, the whole enchilada—and all we got to show for it are seven corpses."

They stood silently, listening to the sounds of the hospital, the clicking, hissing, sucking, squeaking, groaning noises.

"The stiff in Harrison's room at Quantico is white. Not sure yet, but one of the agents thinks it's Tony Anselmo."

"From New York?"

"Yeah."

"We let this go on too long," Freddy Murray said after a bit. "We should've busted Freeman's bunch in September."

"Don't give me that! We didn't have enough in September."

"We let this go on too long," Freddy repeated stubbornly.

Tom Hooper let it lie. "Let's go sit down someplace. I only had three hours' sleep."

They collapsed on the sofa in the ICU waiting room, two doors down the hall.

Hooper sighed, then extracted a sheet of paper from his pocket and passed it to Freddy. "Ever seen this guy before?"

Freddy unfolded the paper. It was a copy of an artist's rendering of a face. A very plain face. At the bottom of the sheet this information appeared: "White male, approximately forty years of age, five feet nine or ten inches, clean shaven, short dark hair, dark eyes."

"Don't recognize him. Who is he?"

"The dude who shot Gideon Cohen yesterday. Maybe. A woman saw him in the lobby of the building as he was leaving. He was wearing surgical gloves."

Freddy looked at the picture again, trying to visualize that face on a real man. He started to hand the paper back, but Hooper waved it away.

"Keep it. We're getting thousands made. It'll be on television nationwide in an hour or so and in the papers this evening and tomorrow."

"It isn't that good a picture," Freddy pointed out.

Hooper shrugged. "You're a ray of sunshine."

"So what are you going to do about Harrison?"

"Do?" Hooper muttered, donning a slightly puzzled look.

"You gonna arrest him or what?"

"What would I arrest him for? What charge? Is there any proof that he's done anything illegal?"

"I dunno. That's why I'm asking."

"Get some cops up here—uniformed cops. I want a cop at the ICU door and one at the floor nurse's station twenty-four hours a day. And I want to hear immediately when Ford regains consciousness."

Hooper summoned all his energy and extracted himself from the soft couch.

"Where you going?" Freddy asked.

"Over to see what the hell those guys have turned up on the Willie Teal murders. You oughta see that place! Fourteen bodies! And we figured out which one is Willie. He was sitting on the crapper with his pants around his ankles when the grenades started coming in. Boy, is he ever dead!" Hooper scratched his head and glanced at his watch. "That search warrant for McNally's place ought to be signed by now. I'd sure like to find those grenade launchers."

Hooper looked at Freddy. "By the way, I haven't let them tell the press about these McNally killings. We'll hold onto that for a while and see what happens."

"What could happen? The McNally brothers wiped out the Teal outfit. Now they're dead. End of story."

Hooper grunted and walked out. Freddy watched him go, then headed for the pay phone. The police department was undoubtedly going to be delighted to furnish two officers around the clock.

There was a light. He could see the glare but his eyes wouldn't focus. Then the effort of holding his eyes open became too much and he closed them and drifted.

He had been dreaming and he tried to go back to the dream. It was July, that time of blue skies and hot, sticky days, and he was sitting on his grandmother's porch counting the squeaks as the swing went back and forth, back and forth.

He had the whole summer to loaf and play and yet the only thing he could think of to do was sit in the swing and listen to the chain squeak as it rubbed on the hooks in the ceiling.

His grandmother had been in the dream, sitting on the steps stringing beans, and it seemed important to see her again. Crazy as it seemed, with all the events of his whole life, the most important one, the memory that he treasured the most, was of a summer day when he was very young, swinging on the porch and watching his grandmother. So he tried to go back to the porch and the swing and the dry cracking sound as the beans snapped and . . .

But the light was back.

Someone was moving around.

"Harrison. Can you hear me?"

He tried to speak but his mouth was dry, like sandpaper. He licked his lips, then nodded a tiny bit. "Yeah," he whispered.

"It's me, Freddy. How you doing in there?"

"Where am I?"

"Hospital. You had a bullet in your back. You lost a lot of blood. They operated and got the slug and plugged up all the places you were leaking."

He nodded again, which was difficult. He was having trouble moving. He had no place to go anyway.

"Harrison, can you tell me what happened?"

He thought about it, trying to remember. It was difficult. The warehouse, driving around, all jumbled out of order. After a while he thought he had it straight. He said, "They came for me."

"Anselmo?"

"And the other one. White guy. Pi . . . Pioche."

That was right. He saw it clearly now. The stairwell, Fat Tony falling in the darkness, Freeman McNally screaming, the television shattering. . . . No. Something was mixed up some. . . .

That scream. It had been almost in his ear, painfully loud, the man in mortal agony. And Harrison Ronald had enjoyed it. He lay here now immobile, his eyes closed, remembering. Savoring that scream.

"What else can you tell me?"

Why was Freddy so insistent? "He screamed," Harrison said.

"Who?"

Who indeed! "Freeman."

"Why did you kill him?"

Why? Well, hell, you idiot, because . . . "Because."

"Hooper is gonna be over here in a few minutes to question you, Harrison. You killed eight guys. That's real heavy shit. Real heavy. I think you should think through what you're gonna say to Hooper very carefully. You dig me?"

Harrison sorted through it one more time. He felt like dog shit and he was getting sleepy again. "Nine guys."

"Nine?"

"Think so. It's pretty confusing."

He was drifting again, back toward the porch and the swing and the bright, hot days when he heard Freddy say, "You sleep now. We'll talk later."

"Yeah," he said, and tackled the problem of why his grandmother had white hair even back then. She was small and wiry and her hair was white as snow. It had been that way as long as he could remember.

"Senator Hiram Duquesne to see you, Mr. Hooper."

The secretary rolled her eyes heavenward and stepped clear so that Senator Duquesne could enter. He was fat—not plump, not overweight, but fat—in his middle sixties. His double chin swung as he walked. Embedded in the fleshy face were two of the hardest eyes that Tom Hooper had ever stared at. They swept him now.

The senator dropped into a chair and waited until the door was closed behind him. "I've just come from a conference with the director," he announced.

"Yessir. He called me."

"I want to report an incident. I want a report made and an investigation done. I want it all in writing and dated and signed and I want a copy."

Hooper grunted noncommittally. If FBI reports were going to be handed out the director would do the handing, not Hooper.

Just as Duquesne opened his mouth, the telephone rang. "Excuse me a second, Senator." He picked up the instrument. "Yes."

"Freddy is on the other line. Harrison is awake."

"Tell him I'll be there as soon as I can."

As he cradled the phone Duquesne said, "You could ask her to hold your calls."

"I don't have that luxury, Senator. Tell me about this incident."

Duquesne told him. From the first approach by T. Jefferson Brody several years ago to the incident last night in the parking garage of the Senate office building, he gave Hooper every incident and the details on every check. Hooper made notes and asked questions to clarify points. It took fifteen minutes.

Finally Duquesne announced, "There it is," and Hooper leaned back in his chair and reviewed his notes.

"I want this pimp Brody arrested," Senator Duquesne said. "I'll take the heat."

Hooper laid the legal pad back on the table. "What do I arrest him for?"

"Attempted bribery, extortion, I don't know."

"I don't know either. Assuming that all the contributions to the PACs he controlled were made according to law, and you have given me no information to suggest otherwise, there's nothing illegal about a notorious criminal making a political contribution. And people ask you to take positions on public issues twenty times a day."

"Brody didn't ask. He *threatened* me. I'm sure you can grasp the distinction between a request and a threat."

"Threatened you with what? *You* said *he* said he would call a matter of public record to the attention of the media if you didn't do what he wanted. I don't think that qualifies as a threat."

Duquesne's face was turning a deep brick hue. "Listen to me, you little badge toter. Don't give me one of those pissy nothing-can-be-done hog-crap sandwiches! I'm not going to listen to that!"

The expression on Hooper's face didn't change. "Senator, you have been had by a pro. Now listen carefully to what I'm going to say. By your own admission the man has done nothing illegal. He was the only other witness to this conversation, and believe me, he will deny everything that even throws a shadow on him."

Duquesne was taking it hard. His throat worked as he sat and stared at the desk between them.

"Now, here is what we *can* do. We can look into the accounting and see if he obeyed all the rules on his PACs and his contributions. That will take time but might turn up something. Brody sounds cute, but the law in this area is a minefield."

"That asshole wouldn't slip up like that," Duquesne said softly.

"The other thing we can do is put a wire on you and let you have another conversation with Brody. Maybe he'll say something this time that does compromise him."

"And me!"

"Perhaps. That's a risk you'll have to take."

"I don't like it."

"Who else has this man approached? How many other members of Congress has he tried to influence?"

"I don't know. But I seem to recall that somebody said he was giving money to Bob Cherry and three or four others."

"That'll be in their financial statements, right? We'll look and see if we can find these names."

"Where does that get us?"

"I'll be frank, Senator. It may take someone someplace they don't want to go. Freeman McNally is dead. He was killed last night."

Duquesne was speechless. "Who did it?"

"We're investigating. This information is confidential. We have not released the news of McNally's death and would like to hold on to it for a while."

Duquesne's color faded to a ghastly white. Out of the clear blue sky he had just supplied the FBI with a motive for the murder of a man who had just been killed.

Hooper watched the senator with an expressionless face. He well knew what Duquesne was thinking and it didn't bother Hooper a bit that he was thinking it.

"The good news," the agent said after he had let Duquesne twist a while in the wind, "is that Freeman has made his last political contribution. In the fullness of time, probably fairly soon, T. Jefferson Brody will hear of Mr. McNally's unfortunate demise. Of course he will still have a hold on you, but I doubt that he'll be foolish enough to try to use it. He impresses me as a very careful fellow."

"Cute. The bastard thinks he's cute."

"Ah, yes, don't they all?"

Freddy was standing beside the nurses' station listening to a man sitting in a wheelchair with his head swathed in bandages tell the cop all about his recent hair transplant. "You don't know how demoralizing it is to lose your hair. It's like you're visibly deteriorating, aging, you know?"

Hooper came through the door, took the scene in at a glance and led Freddy toward the waiting area, which was empty. Behind him the man was explaining, "It was male pattern baldness all the way. My God, I felt so—"

"How is he?" Hooper asked as he pulled the door to the lounge closed.

"Sleeping again. The nurse said he'll probably wake up in a little bit and we can talk to him then. She'll come get me."

"We found a body over at McNally's house. Vinnie Pioche, I think. And the place had been shot apart. Someone just stood inside the door of each room and sprayed lead everywhere. It's a real mess."

"Probably Harrison. He said Pioche came with Anselmo to get him. And he said he thinks he killed nine men, but it's real confusing."

Hooper fell into one of the chairs.

"Did he say why?"

"Because. He said he did it because."

"That's real helpful. Just what I need to feed to the sharks in the U.S. attorney's office."

"He's still under the anesthetic, Tom. He doesn't know what the hell he's saying."

Hooper grunted and stared at his toes. Then he took off his shoes and massaged his feet. "We should have wrapped this one up in September."

"We didn't have enough in September," Freddy said.

Hooper eyed him without humor, then put his shoes back on.

Fifteen minutes later the nurse opened the door and stuck her head in. "He's awake. Don't stay more than five minutes."

Harrison Ronald had his eyes closed when the FBI agents stepped up to his bed, but the nurse nodded and left them. Freddy said, "Harrison, it's me, Freddy. Tom Hooper is with me. How you feeling?"

Ford's eyes came open and slowly moved around until they found Freddy. After a moment they went to Hooper.

"Hey, Tom."

"Hey, Harrison. Sorry about this."

"It's over."

"Yeah."

Ford's eyes closed again. Hooper looked at Freddy, who shrugged.

"Harrison," Hooper said, "I need to ask you some questions, find out what happened. Why did you go to that warehouse anyway?"

The eyes focused on Hooper's face. They stayed there a while, went to Freddy, then back to Hooper. Harrison Ronald licked his lips, then said, "I want a lawyer."

"What?"

"A lawyer. I ain't saying anything without my lawyer's approval."

"Aww, wait a goddamn minute! I'm not charging you with anything. You're the sole witness to a serious—"

The word "crime" was right there on the tip of his tongue but he bit it off. He swallowed once. "All this has to be investigated. You know that. You're a cop, for Chrissake!"

"I want a lawyer. That's all I have to say."

Hooper opened his mouth and closed it again. He glanced at Freddy, who was standing with his hands in his pockets regarding the man in the bed.

"Okay. We'll get you a lawyer. I'll stop by tomorrow and see how you're doing."

"Fine. See you then."

"Come on, Freddy. We have work to do."

Harrison Ronald Ford went back to sleep.

CHAPTER TWENTY-SIX

★ ★ ★ ★ ★ ★ ★ ★ ★ ★ ★ ★

THE first man the soldiers killed was Larry Ticono. At the age of sixteen he had dropped out of the seventh grade after failing it three times. In spite of the nine years he spent in the public school system, he was illiterate. On those rare occasions when he was asked to sign his name he used an illegible scrawl.

Larry Ticono had been arrested three times in his short life—twice for possession of illegal drugs and once for burglary—but he had spent a grand total of only five days in jail. After each arrest he was released on his own recognizance. He returned to court only when the police picked him up again. One of his possession arrests had apparently fallen completely through the cracks and been forgotten. He had pleaded guilty to the other two charges and had received probation.

The wonder was that he had lived so long. He had a two-hundred-dollar-a-day crack habit and his welfare check was only $436 a month. The shortfall he made up by stealing anything that wasn't welded in place. Cameras, radios, televisions, and car stereos were his favorite targets. He sold his loot to fences for fifteen to twenty percent of their market value—not retail value when new, but market value used. He tried to avoid muggings, which were dangerous, but did them when nothing else readily presented itself.

Larry Ticono's life defined the term "hand to mouth." He slept under bridges in good weather and in abandoned buildings in bad. He rarely had more than twenty dollars in his pocket and was never more than three hours away from withdrawal.

This afternoon Larry Ticono's three-hour margin had melted to zero. He was on the edge with only $17.34 in his pocket. The corner where he usually purchased crack was empty. Although Ticono didn't know it, his suppliers were the retail end of the distribution network of Willie Teal, who had been forcibly and permanently retired from the crack business the previous night. So the street-corner salesmen had no product and were not there.

Frustrated and desperate, Ticono walked a half mile to another neighborhood that he knew about and tried to make a deal with a fifteen-year-old in a pair of hundred-dollar Nike running shoes. That worthy had not received his morning delivery from his supplier, an employee of Freeman McNally. The streetwise dealers sensed that something was wrong although they had no hard information. They had seen the troops coming and going and had heard the news on television, and they were worried. Many of them were drifting away, back to the welfare apartments and ramshackle row houses they called home.

When Larry Ticono approached the fifteen-year-old, that youngster had only four crack bags left and no prospect of readily obtaining more. So that young capitalist demanded forty dollars a hit.

The thought occurred to Larry Ticono that he should just mug the kid, but it vaporized after one look at the corner boss, a heavyset man standing by a garbage can watching. Larry knew beyond a shadow of a doubt that the guard had a weapon within easy reach and would cheerfully kill him if he so much as touched the youngster.

After trying futilely to bargain, he reluctantly turned away.

Two blocks later Larry Ticono threw a brick through a window of an electronics store and grabbed a ghetto blaster. He was promptly shot by a convenience-store salesclerk wearing a National Guard uniform. The blaster was just too large and heavy to run with at any speed.

The fifty-five-grain .223 bullet from the M-16 hit Larry high up in the center of the back, a perfect shot, which was pure luck because the clerk was wearing a pair of fogged-up glasses and had barely qualified with the M-16 in training. Before he threw the rifle to his shoulder and pulled the trigger the clerk had never killed any creature larger than a cockroach.

Still traveling at over three thousand feet per second when it pierced Larry Tocono's skin, the jacketed bullet expended a major portion of its eleven hundred foot-pounds of energy shattering his backbone and driving the fragments through his heart, exploding it. The slug then exited his chest and buried itself in a parked car sixty yards away.

Larry Ticono, age nineteen, was dead before his body hit the pavement.

The convenience-store clerk vomited beside the body.

Jack Yocke took in the scene at a glance a half hour later when he arrived. He busied himself taking names and trying to think of something to say to the clerk-private, who was sitting on the tailgate of an olive-drab pickup staring at his hands.

"I shouted for him to stop, but he didn't," the private said so softly Yocke had to strain to hear. "He didn't stop," he repeated wonderingly, amazed at the perverse ways of fate.

"No. He didn't."

"He should have stopped."

"Yes."

"He *really* should have stopped."

The reporter wandered over to a sergeant standing near the body smoking a cigarette. Some fifteen feet away a group of army or National Guard officers were conferring with a uniformed policeman. Yocke had yet to learn the nuances of the shoulder patches on the uniforms, which as far as he could see, were the only way to tell which service was which. The sergeant glanced at Yocke and continued to puff leisurely on his cigarette. He was thoughtfully surveying the faces of the watchers on the sidewalk across the street.

"I thought," Jack Yocke said, "that your people were supposed to fire their weapons only in self-defense."

The sergeant appraised him carefully. "That's right," he said, then went back to scanning the crowd.

"Yet as I understand it, the victim was running away when the private shot him?"

"Something like that, I suppose."

"So why'd he shoot?"

A look of disgust registered on the sergeant's face. "Who *are* you, anyway?"

"Jack Yocke, *Washington Post.* I didn't mean—"

"Shove off, pencil pilot. Before I lose my temper and ram that notebook up your ass."

"I'm sorry. No offense," Yocke said, then turned away. He shouldn't have asked that question. Why had he done it? Now he felt guilty. It was a new experience.

Disgusted with himself, he looked again at the private slumped on the tailgate and the body covered with a sheet, then walked to his car.

He had always been so confident, so sure of himself and his percep-tions. And now . . .

Six blocks away a group of people outside a closed liquor store—the military authorities had ordered them all closed—were throwing rocks at passing cars. One of them thudded into the side of the *Post*'s little sedan.

It's started, Jake Yocke decided. The supply of crack has dried up and the addicts are getting restless. He pointed the car toward the National Guard armory adjacent to RFK Stadium.

He didn't get very far into the building, of course. He showed his credentials and the soldier on duty let him into the press room, the first door on the right. There he found a half dozen government-issue steel desks, some folding chairs, and one telephone. And over a dozen of his colleagues, two of them from the *Post.* They were waiting for the press briefing scheduled for five p.m., fifteen minutes from now.

Yocke muttered at the people he knew—and he knew three or four of them—and found a corner to sit in. He sat there musing, thinking about the private who had killed a man when he shouldn't have, wondering if he, Jack Yocke, would have done any better. Maybe he wasn't really cut out to be a reporter. Stupid. He had made a stupid, insensitive remark, and now it rankled.

The reporters were waiting for Dan Quayle when he came out of Bethesda Naval Hospital. He could have avoided them but he didn't.

Ignoring the shouted questions, he stood still and waited until a battery of hand-held microphones were waving before him. "The President regained consciousness this afternoon for a short period of time. Mrs. Bush is with him. He is asleep now. The doctors believe his recovery will be rapid. He's in excellent health for a man his age and we have high hopes."

"Did you discuss the hunt for the assassin with him?" someone shouted.

"No," said Dan Quayle. Actually the President wasn't well enough to discuss anything, but he didn't say that. He thought about it and decided to let the monosyllable stand alone.

"Mr. Vice-President, what about the claim that the Colombian Extraditables are making, that they are responsible."

Quayle ignored that one. Then he heard a question he couldn't ignore.

"The Extraditables say that the terrorism will stop if you release Chano Aldana. Could you comment on that?"

"Said when?" Quayle asked, silencing all the other reporters.

"About an hour ago in Colombia, Mr. Vice-President. It just came over the wires."

Quayle thought about it. "We're not going to bargain with terrorists," he said. The crowd waited. The red lights on the fronts of the television cameras stayed on. "Chano Aldana is going to get a fair trial. As long as I am acting for the President, I promise you, I will use the full might and power of the United States government to accomplish that come what may."

"Are there any circumstances where you might release Aldana?" someone pressed.

"If the jury acquits him."

"Before trial, I mean."

"Not even if hell freezes over," Dan Quayle replied, and turned away.

"You know," Ott Mergenthaler said to Senator Bob Cherry, "the man has the personality of a store dummy, but I do believe there's some steel in his backbone."

Ott was in the senator's office and the two of them had just finished watching Quayle's performance. The senator reached for his remote control and killed the picture and sound after Quayle walked off camera and the network analysts came on.

Cherry sneered. "He's a medical miracle. He's got the brain of a penguin and the jawbone of an ass."

"Come off it, Senator. Say what you will, this crisis is not hurting Dan Quayle's reputation one whit. The public is getting a good look and I think they're liking what they see. I do, anyway."

"Ott! Don't kid around! You don't really believe this National Guard move was wise? For God's sake, man, I thought you had some sense."

"I do have, Senator, but I found out years ago that it does no good at all to proclaim the fact."

Had Cherry known Mergenthaler better, he would have stopped right there. When the columnist retreated to dry, edged retorts, he had been pushed as far as he was willing to go. Cherry pressed on: "Bush could control Dorfman, but Quayle can't. Dorfman is a shark and Quayle is a damn little fish. You don't seriously think that Dan Quayle is making the decisions over there, do you?"

"I hear he is," Ott said mildly, cocking his head slightly.

"Don't you believe it! Dorfman's pulling the strings. And I guarantee you the last thing Will Dorfman cares about is the U.S. Constitution. When is the Army going to leave? What about people's rights? Why hasn't the Congress been asked to authorize all this extracurricular military activity? The legalities—they've got the troops outside the federal district, out in Maryland for God's sake. The government will get sued for—"

"What's your real bitch?"

Cherry looked blank. "What do you mean?"

"You're blowing smoke. I've been writing a column in this town for fifteen years, Bob."

Senator Cherry took a deep breath and exhaled. "Okay, okay." He shrugged. "Quayle scares me. Real bad. If Bush dies we are in big big trouble."

"Next presidential election is in two years. Look at it as the Democrats' big chance."

Cherry writhed in his chair. "This country can't afford to drift for two years with a clown on the bridge. The only damn thing Quayle knows how to do is play golf."

"Bob, you're making a mountain out of a manure pile. True, Quayle's had a lot of bad press, some of it his fault, some of it because he's such an easy target to pick on and he's a darling of the conservatives. The man has an uncanny talent for saying the wrong thing. But this country is over two hundred years old! We can survive two years with *anybody* at the helm, be it Dan the Bogeyman or Hanoi Jane or my Aunt Matilda."

Cherry wanted to argue. After a couple more minutes Ott Mergenthaler excused himself. Out in the corridor he shook his head sadly. Assassins and terrorists and wholesale murder everywhere you looked, and Bob Cherry wanted to mutter darkly about Dan Quayle. Worse, he expected Ott to print it.

Cherry looks old, Mergenthaler told himself. His age is telling.

Querulous—that's the word. He's become a whining, querulous old man absorbed with trivialities.

The news conference at the D.C. National Guard Armory had barely gotten under way when it was abruptly adjourned. A junior officer announced that someone had attacked the crowd at the L'Enfant Plaza Metro Station. The brass hustled out. Among them was Captain Jake Grafton.

Jack Yocke fought through the press crowd to get to the door and charged for the street at a dead run. He ran along the sidewalk toward the entrance to the Guard's parking lot, just in time to see a government car coming out. He bent and scanned the passengers. Nope. The next one? Nope again.

Grafton was in the third car. Yocke jumped and waved his arms and shouted "Captain Grafton! Captain Grafton!" at the top of his lungs. The uniformed driver locked the brakes. Yocke jerked open the rear door and jumped in.

As the car accelerated away Jake Grafton and Toad Tarkington looked the reporter over.

"Riding your thumb today?" Grafton asked.

"I'm really glad you stopped, sir. Thanks a lot. If you don't mind, I'd like to tag along with you."

"The press regulations—"

"Yessir. Yessir. I know all about them. We have them stenciled on our underwear. Still, I'd like you to bend the rules a little and let me tag along with you for a few days. If you like, I'll even let you comment on the stories."

Jake Grafton's brow wrinkled and he looked ahead at the traffic the driver was threading through. Toad Tarkington gave Yocke a big grin.

Grafton held a walkie-talkie in his hand. The instrument was spitting out words too garbled and tinny for Yocke to understand. Grafton held the device to his ear for a moment, then lowered it back to his lap.

"You'll have to agree," Grafton said slowly, "not to do any stories at all until this is completely over."

Tarkington's grin faded.

"That's the *only* condition?" the reporter asked incredulously. "You don't want to comment on the story?"

"No. Just don't print anything until this is all over."

"No catch, eh?" Yocke said, still skeptical. Actually, all he wanted was a ride to L'Enfant Plaza. He sat now slightly stunned at Jake Grafton's willingness to go along with his spur-of-the-moment proposal. What was that old rule of thumb—if you ask ten women to go to bed with you, you'll only get your face slapped nine times?

"We can always let you out at the next corner," Toad told him sourly.

"Captain, you got a deal."

"Umm."

"What's happening now?"

"Some gunmen opened fire in the Metro Station at L'Enfant Plaza. Lot of people down, some of them soldiers. A real bloodbath."

"Colombians?"

"I don't know."

Yocke fished his notebook from an inside jacket pocket and flipped it open. As he scribbled and the car jolted, Toad said, "It's T-A-R-K-I-N-"

"I got it, Frog. What's your hometown?"

"Intercourse, Pennsylvania."

"Dry up, you two," Jake Grafton said, and held the walkie-talkie to his ear.

He was going to have to mention this little arrangement to General Land at the first opportunity. But he thought the general would approve. Just this afternoon the subject of the presidential commission had arisen, forced to the fore by a request from Congresswoman Strader for a military district headquarters pass, which was granted. The career officers who had been watching Ms. Strader's act for years suspected that she would be diligently searching for butts to kick at a postmortem later on, when both she and her colleagues would have the luxury of hindsight to enhance their wisdom. Alas, being second-guessed by Monday-morning quarterbacks went with the job.

When he saw Jack Yocke jumping up and down on the sidewalk, it occurred to Jake Grafton that it just might help to have an independent observer keep Ms. Strader et al. from playing fast and loose with the facts.

Jack Yocke was young and brash, but Jake Grafton had been reading the articles on Cuba and he was impressed. Yocke was a good reporter. He was observant and cared about people, and he could express himself well. He just needed seasoning. And a good reporter, Jake believed, would know a fact when he tripped over one. Yocke would do nicely.

These thoughts occupied Jake Grafton for about ten seconds, then he returned to the business at hand, a terrorist incident at a subway station. The general in charge was giving orders on the radio to the officer at the scene to storm the place as soon as possible. That struck Jake Grafton as logical. If these were suicide commandos like those who had shot up the Capitol building, the sooner they were killed the fewer the number of innocent people who would die.

The driver brought the car to a halt outside the main entrance to L'Enfant Plaza and the occupants jumped out and trotted toward a huddle of soldiers by the doors. The major general, Myles Greer, was conferring with a major. Jake could hear the sound of gunshots through the door, the ripping of automatic weapons fire. "How long?" General Greer asked.

"Another two minutes. I've got three men at the west entrance and I want ten there."

General Greer glanced at Grafton, who met his eyes. Greer had a tough decision to make and Jake Grafton knew it. And he was not about to use his position as General Land's liaison to influence that decision. The choice was simple and brutal: more soldiers meant more firepower, and the more firepower one accumulated, the fewer soldiers one was likely to lose. On the other hand, the shots they were hearing were being fired by the terrorists at unarmed civilians, and every second of delay meant that more of those civilians would die.

It took Greer about three seconds. "Let's go now," he said. The major gestured to the army lieutenant in battle dress and used the walkie-talkie.

Grafton spoke to the general, a question so soft that Jack Yocke almost missed it. "You got the subways stopped?"

Apparently satisfied with the answer, Grafton turned to two soldiers who were standing to one side. "You guys going to guard the doors?"

"Yessir."

"Gimme your rifle."

The young enlisted man looked toward his sergeant, who nodded. Toad Tarkington relieved another man of his weapon.

"I'm going with you," Yocke said.

Grafton didn't argue. The soldiers were moving out, the lieutenant in the lead. "Stay between me and Toad," Grafton said over his shoulder to Yocke as he trotted after them.

The men ran along a corridor of shops empty of people. The Army had already evacuated them. The corridor twisted and made several ninety-degree bends. The running men spread out, their weapons at the ready.

The sounds of gunfire were louder. As the corridor came to another bend the men came upon a soldier lying prone, his rifle covering the blind corner.

The lieutenant used hand signals. When his men were ready he leaped around the corner and two men followed him. Then the others, cautiously.

They were facing an open double door, and beyond it, escalators down. The popping of gunfire was louder, made painful by the echos from the concrete walls.

At the head of the escalator the sergeant opened fire on an unseen target below. He was firing single shots.

A spray of bullets from below showered sparks off the overhead and shattered one of the neon lights.

The sergeant fired a fully automatic burst, then charged down the escalator. Two men followed.

The lieutenant eased up, took a quick look, and with a gesture to the men behind him, followed.

Jake Grafton and Toad Tarkington, with Yocke between them, followed the soldiers.

The first dead gunman lay twenty feet beyond the end of the escalator.

An Uzi lay beside him. Around him were seven more bodies. Jack Yocke paused and watched as Jake Grafton went from body to body, checking for signs of life. Three men and four women. Several lay in little pools of blood. One of them had crawled for ten or twelve feet, leaving a bloody streak. As Grafton felt for the pulse of the last person he shook his head, then went off after the soldiers, keeping low. Yocke followed.

They were on a wide pedestrian walkway now, with the ceiling arching high overhead.

The walkway ended in a T-intersection, with walkways going right and left. The soldiers split up, running both ways. Jake Grafton looked over the edge, then ducked as bullets spanged pieces out of the chipped concrete.

Jack Yocke fell flat right where he was. The gunfire rose to a crescendo, then ceased. Yocke lay still in the sudden silence, waiting, his heart hammering.

Finally the reporter looked around. Toad was squatting nearby with his rifle at the ready. He was listening. Grafton was nowhere in sight.

Toad began to move.

Yocke followed him. They went to the rail and cautiously looked over. Grafton was below on one of the station platforms, listening to the Army lieutenant talk on the radio. Bodies lay scattered about. As they stood there looking at the carnage, Yocke heard the pounding of running feet behind him.

He dropped flat. Then he looked. Medics wearing white armbands displaying a red cross ran by carrying stretchers.

"Let's go down there," Yocke suggested. Toad shrugged.

Jake Grafton was sitting on the concrete with his back to a pillar, his rifle across his lap. If he noticed Yocke he gave no sign.

"Any of your guys hurt?" Yocke asked the lieutenant, who was assembling his men.

"One. Flesh wound. But two National Guardsmen charged in when the shooting first started and they got zapped."

"How many gunmen were there?"

"Five, I think."

"And the civilians?"

"Seven wounded, forty-two dead."

Yocke was poised to ask another question when the walkie-talkie squawked to life and the lieutenant walked away with the device to his ear.

The reporter looked around helplessly. Twisted and bloody bodies lay everywhere. Packages and attaché cases scattered about, here and there a shopping bag. He walked over to one woman and carefully picked up the wrapped Christmas presents that lay strewn randomly around her. There must be something, some gesture he could make to the arbiter of man's fate that would commend this woman's humanity. A prayer? But the grim god already knew. He placed the packages in a neat, pathetic pile beside the slack body.

She had been shot in the back, apparently as she tried to run from the obscene horror behind her.

Forty-two! My God!

Where will it end? Yocke wondered gloomily as a wave of revulsion and loathing swept over him. He averted his eyes and turned away.

Henry Charon stood in an empty third-floor office on L Street and scanned the traffic on the street below yet again. From where he stood he had an excellent view of the streetlight and the cars queuing there waiting for the light to turn green. And he could see the drivers.

The drivers sat behind the wheels of their vehicles waiting for the light to change with the look of distracted impatience that indelibly marked those who endured life in the big city. Some of them fiddled with their radios, but most just sat staring at the brake lights on the car ahead and occasionally glancing at the stoplight hanging above the intersection. When the light turned green they crept across the intersection and joined the block-long queue for the next light.

This was a good place. Excellent. A stand, like that one above the red-rock canyon where he had killed seven elk over the years. The elk would come up through the canyon from the aspen groves every evening about the same time.

He would be along soon. He was a creature of habit, like the elk. Regardless of traffic or weather, he always came this way. Or he had on the four evenings in the past that Henry Charon had watched. Yet even if he chose another route this evening—there was a chance that would happen, although slim—sooner or later he would again come this way. That was inevitable, like the evening habits of the deer and elk and bear.

Beside Charon was the rifle. This one was less than perfect; no doubt the stock was poorly bedded. But it would do. This would not be a long shot. No more than sixty yards.

A round was chambered in the rifle and the magazine contained three more. Henry Charon rarely needed more than one shot but he was ready, just in case. Although the habits of living things were predictable, random events happened to us all.

Henry Charon didn't move and he didn't fidget. He stood easily, almost immobile, watching. His ability to wait was one of his best qualities. Not waiting like the urban commuters, impatiently, distracted-ly, but waiting like the lion or the fox—silent, still, ever alert, always ready.

His eyes left the cars and went across the pedestrians and the people looking at headlines and making purchases at the sidewalk newsstand on the far corner beside the entrance to the Metro station. The vendor was warmly dressed and wore a Cossack hat with the muff down over his ears. His breath made great steaming clouds in the gloomy evening.

Charon's restless eyes scanned the cars yet again, then watched them creep across the intersection. One man blocked the crosswalk with his car when the light changed on him and he sat unperturbed staring straight ahead as pedestrians walked around the car, front and back, and glared at him.

Now he saw it—the car he was waiting for. Henry Charon lifted the binoculars to his eyes and adjusted the focus. Yes. It was *him.*

Charon looked at the cars ahead of his man with a practiced eye, estimating how many would get through the next green light. About six. That would bring this car down to third in line. Perfect.

Henry Charon laid the binoculars down and picked up the rifle. He checked the safety. Still on.

He looked again at the pedestrians, at the other cars, at the bag lady on the far side of the street rooting through a trash can.

The light changed and the traffic moved. One, two, three . . . six! Yes. The car he wanted was right there, third one back.

Henry Charon raised the rifle to his shoulder as he thumbed off the safety. The crosshairs came immediately into his line of vision without his even tilting his head. He put them on the driver, on his head, on his ear. Automatically Charon breathed deeply and exhaled. He was squeezing the trigger even before all the air had left his lungs.

The report and recoil came almost immediately. Charon brought the scope back into line and looked.

Good shot!

He laid the rifle down and walked briskly to the door, pulled it open and closed it behind him, making sure it locked. He passed the elevator and took the stairs downward two at a time.

Out onto the street—around the corner from where the victim sat dead in his car—and away at a diagonal. Charon stripped off the latex gloves from his hands and thrust them into the first trash can he came to. His car was in a garage five blocks away. He walked briskly, unhurriedly, scanning the faces of the people on the sidewalk with his practiced hunter's eye.

With all of the wounded and most of the dead removed from the underground Metro station, Jake Grafton, Yocke, and Tarkington went back the way they had come in. The chairman of the Joint Chiefs, General Hayden Land, was standing with the major general in the middle of a knot of people in uniform by the main entrance.

Grafton went over to the group and stood where General Land could see him and he could hear everything that was said.

Toad Tarkington stood near the door to the mall. He pointed the rifle he was carrying at the sky and examined the action. His face was intense, grim.

A question popped to mind as Yocke watched Toad. Would the naval officer have used it? No, he had made the mistake of asking the wrong question once already today, and as he looked at Toad, he thought he knew the answer. Yocke was still feeling the aftereffects of the adrenaline. Somehow, for a reason he couldn't quite fathom, Toad seemed the proper person to tell. "I was pretty pumped up back there."

"Uh-huh," Tarkington muttered and glanced at the reporter, then resumed his scrutiny of the weapon.

Yocke couldn't let it alone. "You know, you can watch a hundred movies and see the carnage every night in the hospital, but nothing prepares you for that feeling when the bullets are zinging by and you realize that every second could be your absolute last." He snapped his fingers. "Like that, life for you might stop right here. Like it did for all those folks down there on those subway platforms."

Toad finished his inspection of the rifle and held it, butt on his hip, pointed at the sky. He surveyed the knot of senior officers and the smooth-faced soldiers in battle dress and glanced up at the steel-gray sky. "I don't know how much life insurance you got," Toad said, "but if you're going to trail along behind Jake Grafton, you'd better get some more." Without waiting for a reply Toad wandered off to find the soldier who had lent him the rifle.

Yocke watched him go.

The brass was still in conference. And here comes Samantha Strader, as I live and breathe. She marched over to the group and joined it. His reporter's juices flowing, Jack Yocke managed to squeeze between the shoulders of two aides.

One of the men talking was not in uniform, although he had that look. Yocke whispered to the man beside him, who whispered back, "FBI. Guy named Hooper."

That would be Special Agent Thomas F. Hooper. Yocke made a note as Hooper spoke to General Land. ". . . they came in on a freighter last week. At least twenty of them, armed to the teeth, paid to commit suicide."

"So there's probably going to be more of this?" General Land said.

"Yes," Hooper told him.

"Do your sources have any feel for their targets?"

That was Jake Grafton speaking.

"Anywhere there are people," Hooper replied. "The more people, the better for them."

"Well, Captain?" General Land said.

"If we could just get everybody to stay home for a couple of days, sir, and use the time to search house-to-house—every building, every store, every apartment—a couple of days would do it. If we shut down all the public transportation and forbid everyone to use their cars, we could do it."

"FBI?"

Hooper pulled at his earlobe. "That's my recommendation too, General."

"General Greer."

Greer was the general in direct charge of the National Guard and army units, which had been integrated into one command. He considered for ten seconds. "That's probably the only way, I think. We've got to find these people and keep crowds from congregating while we do it. Those are the priorities."

"We're only four days away from Christmas," Congresswoman Strader noted aloud.

Land glanced at her, then back to Greer and Hooper. "Okay. You've got two days to find these people. Nothing moves inside the beltway unless it's a military or emergency vehicle. I want a concrete plan on how you're going to do this on my desk in three hours."

"General, I suggest we shut everything down at midnight," Jake Grafton added. "Be a nightmare trying to do it any other way."

"Midnight it is," said General Land. He didn't get to be a four-star general by being indecisive. "That'll give us eight hours to figure out how we're going to get this unscrewed."

Jack Yocke scribbled furiously, bitterly aware of the irony of his position. He was hearing the scoop of the decade only because Jake Grafton had made him promise not to print anything.

Then he became aware that somehow he was no longer in the circle of people. Apparently the group had moved, almost ten feet, no doubt because General Land had moved. Wherever the chairman was was going to be the center of the action. Yocke rejoined the conference.

". . . that negotiation is key to resolving situations like we had here today without bloodshed," Strader was saying, her voice firm and businesslike. Lecturing to the anthropoids, Yocke thought, and jotted the impression down.

General Land's reply was inaudible.

Strader's voice carried. "Why haven't you consulted with the FBI crisis-response team? They're expert at negotiating with terrorists and criminals in hostage situations."

This time Yocke caught the reply. "This was not a terrorist or a hostage situation, ma'am. These men were out to kill as many people as possible. This was an atrocity pure and simple and the men who did it knew they were going to die."

"*You* don't know that!"

"I know a *war* when I'm in one, *madam.*"

"And I'm telling you that you don't know *what* those men wanted because General Greer didn't take the time to *talk* to them. Those men might be prisoners if General Greer had *talked* instead of charging in willy-nilly shooting everybody in sight."

"Madam—" General Land began icily.

Strader chopped him off and bored in for the kill. "The aggressive behavior of *your* troops may be the reason those men shot all these civilians."

"General Greer did exactly the right thing. These people didn't *want* to talk." Land's voice had a razor-sharp edge. "They were too busy chasing down unarmed men and women and slaughtering them like rabbits. They might have laid down their arms, it's true, *after* they killed everyone in sight."

". . . lives at stake here."

"When are you goddamn dithering fools gonna figure out *you can't negotiate with people who don't want to negotiate?*" The general's voice was a roar, the anger palpable. "Now I've listened to all of the free advice I can stomach. I've got better things to do than stand here and shoot the shit with some civilian! Who the hell *are* you, anyway?"

"I'm Congresswoman Strader. I'm on the presidential commission to—"

"You can do your investigation later. Not now! Not here!"

"You wouldn't say that if I were a *man!* I've got a pass signed by—"

"Major," the general barked, "get her political ass out of my face, right fucking now."

"Yes, *sir!"*

Infuriated, her face the color of a scalded lobster, Sam Strader was firmly escorted away.

When Jack Yocke had the last of it in his notebook in his private shorthand, he looked up, straight into the bemused face of Toad Tarkington.

"What we got here," Tarkington said, "is a total entertainment package. Write that down too."

"Tarkington!" It was Grafton calling.

Yocke followed the young naval officer.

"Let's go," Jake Grafton said. He began trotting toward the military sedan. "Someone just shot the Chief Justice of the Supreme Court."

"Is he dead?"

"Apparently."

CHAPTER TWENTY-SEVEN

* * * * * * * * * * * * *

HENRY Charon parked the car a block from the New Hampshire Avenue apartment and walked. The streetlights were on and the sky was dark. Raindrops were beginning to splatter on the pavement and poing on the car roofs.

One of the cars near the apartment house was the green VW bug wearing its trendy bumper stickers. Ah yes, the sweater lady.

He paused in the entryway and used his key on the mailbox. As he suspected it contained the usual circulars and junk mail addressed to "Occupant." He put them in his pocket. He didn't want mail to accumulate in the box because very soon now someone would look through that little window. An FBI agent or police officer, or maybe a soldier, but *someone*. Someone hunting him.

He looked again up and down the street. The rain was getting heavier. Perhaps setting in for the night.

The cold felt good. When you live in the wild long enough you get used to the cold. You learn to endure it and never feel it. It's a part of everything and you fit in and adapt or you perish.

Henry Charon was good at that. He had learned to adapt. Becoming a part of his surroundings was his whole life.

So he stood for a few more seconds and let the cold and dampness seep over him as he listened to the tinny sound of the raindrops striking the cars.

Then he inserted his key in the doorlock and went inside.

The door to the first apartment was ajar and he could hear the television. This was where the apartment manager lived, the sweater lady, Grisella Clifton.

Wouldn't hurt to be seen for a moment. He paused at the door and raised his hand to knock.

She was seated in a stuffed chair in front of the television with a cat on her lap. Charon pushed the door open a few more inches. Now he could see the television. And hear the words:

". . . an artist's conception of the man who shot and wounded Attorney General Gideon Cohen yesterday at the Capitol in what may have been an attempt on the life of Vice-President Dan Quayle. This man is armed and very dangerous. If you see this man, do *not* attempt to apprehend or approach him, but notify the police immediately. At the bottom of the screen you will see a number to call if you think you might have seen this man. Please write this number down. And take a good, careful look."

On the screen was an artist's line drawing. Charon stared. Yes, the artist had got him. Probably from that woman he had met in the lobby as he was leaving the building. Who would have thought she had gotten that good a look? Damn!

The cat saw him and tensed. Grisella Clifton turned and caught sight of him.

"Oh! You startled me, Mr. Tackett."

"Sorry. I was about to knock."

She rose from her chair and turned toward him. The cat scurried away. "I'm so sorry. I guess I heard the outside door open, but I was just so engrossed in this . . . this . . ."

She turned back toward the television. The artist's effort was still on the screen. She looked from the television to Charon, then back to the television.

He saw it in her face.

She drew her breath in sharply and her hand came up to cover her mouth. Her eyes widened.

"Oh! My *God!*"

He stood there trying to decide what to do.

"You're *him!* You tried to *kill* Vice-President Quayle!"

"No, I didn't," Henry Charon said automatically, slightly irritated. He had been shooting at Gideon Cohen! And hit him too. That was one hell of a fine shot!

He saw her chest expand as she sucked in air. She was going to scream.

Without conscious thought he had balanced his weight on the balls of his feet, so now he pushed out toward her in one fluid motion with his hands outstretched.

Thanos Liarakos didn't know what made him turn his head to the right, but he did. She was sitting on a park bench there amid the naked black trees, the streetlight limning her.

He sat behind the wheel of the car staring, uncertain, yet at some level deep down very, very sure.

The man in the car behind laid on his horn.

Liarakos took his foot off the brake and let the car move. He went around the block looking for a parking place. Nothing. Not a single vacant spot. He jammed the gas pedal down and shot down the next street. Every spot full!

Around the corner, looking, the frustration welling rapidly.

He began to swear. The goddamn city, the goddamn traffic engineers and the goddamn planning board that let them remodel these goddamn row houses without driveways and garages—he cussed them all while he thought about Elizabeth.

There, a fireplug. He pulled in beside it and killed the engine. He hit the automatic door lock button on the door and was off and running even as the door slammed shut.

Elizabeth! Sitting out in the rain on a dismal cold night like this. Oh God—if there is a god up there—how could you do this to gentle Elizabeth? Why?

He jogged the last block and darted into the street to see around a tree that was in the way. In the process he was almost run over, but he dodged the delivery van and dashed across the traffic. Another Christian soul laid on his horn and squealed his brakes.

Liarakos paid no attention. On the edge of the park he halted and looked again.

She was still sitting there. Hadn't moved.

He walked forward.

As he passed a bench, still seventy-five feet from her, a derelict huddled there spoke: "Hey man, I hate to ask this, but have you got any loose change you could . . ."

She wasn't looking around. She was sitting there staring downward, apparently oblivious of the cold and the cutting wind and the steady rain that was already starting to soak Liarakos.

"Some loose change would help, man." The derelict was following him. He was aware of it but didn't bother to look behind him.

Her hands were in her coat pockets. The good coat she had worn to the clinic was gone, and in its place she wore a thin, faded cotton thing that looked as if it wouldn't warm a rabbit. Her hair was a sodden, dripping mess. She didn't look up.

"Elizabeth."

She continued to stare at the ground. He squatted and looked up into her face. It was her all right. The corners of her lips were tilted up in a wan little smile.

Her eyes moved to his face, but they looked without recognition.

"Man, it's a damn cold night and a cup of coffee would do for me, you know? I had some troubles in my life and some of them wasn't my fault. How about some Christian charity for a poor ol' nigger. A little change wouldn't be much to you, but to me . . ."

He found his wallet and extracted a bill without taking his eyes off Elizabeth. He passed the bill back.

"God, this is a *twenty!* Are you—"

"Take it. And leave."

"Thanks, mister."

Her face had a glow about it. Aww, *fuck!* She was as high as a flag on the Fourth of July.

"I tell you, man," the derelict said, "'cause you been real generous with me. She's in big trouble. She's strung out real bad, man."

"Please leave."

"Yeah."

The footsteps shuffled away.

He reached out and caressed her face, pressed her hand between his.

The rain continued to fall. She sat with her thin, frozen smile amid the pigeon shit on the park bench among the glistening black trees, staring at nothing at all.

"So what can you tell me?" Jake Grafton asked the FBI lab man.

"Not much," the investigator said, scratching his head. They were standing in the room from which the assassin had shot Chief Justice Longstreet. The rifle lay on the table. Everything in sight was covered by the fine dark grit of fingerprint dust.

"Apparently no fresh prints. We got a bunch, but I doubt that our guy left any. Be a fluke if he did."

"Where did the bullet hit the Chief Justice?"

"About one inch above the left ear. Killed instantly. Haven't got the bullet yet. It went through the victim, through the upholstery and the sheet metal and buried itself in the asphalt of the street. Rifle is a thirty-ought-six, same caliber and make as the one that fired the bullet into the attorney general. Same brand of scope, and I suspect, the same brand of gun oil and so forth."

The floor of the room in which they were standing had a fine layer of dust on it, and it showed tracks, a lot of tracks, so many in fact that the individual footprints ran together.

"Did you guys make all these?" Jake asked gloomily.

"No, as a matter of fact. Sort of curious, but the guy who did the shooting seemed to come into the room, go to the window, and stay there. He made some footprints, but not many, considering. He didn't have nervous feet."

"Nervous feet," Jake repeated.

The lab man seemed to be searching for words. "He wasn't real excited, if you know what I mean."

"A pro," Toad Tarkington prompted.

"Maybe," the FBI agent said. "Maybe not. But he's a cool customer."

The military curfew was announced at seven p.m., to take effect at midnight. Anyone on the streets between the hours of midnight and seven a.m. would be subject to arrest and prosecution by military tribunal for failure to obey emergency orders. Anyone on the streets *in a vehicle* between the hours of seven a.m. and midnight would also be subject to arrest. This curfew would be in effect for forty-eight hours, unless it was ended sooner or extended.

The order was news from coast to coast along with the murder of Supreme Court Chief Justice Harlan Longstreet and the subway massacre. The death toll continued to mount as two of the wounded succumbed to their injuries. One of them was a pregnant woman.

The mood of the nation, as reflected by man-on-the-street television interviews, was outrage. Politicians of stature were calling for an invasion of Colombia. Several wanted to declare war. Senator Bob Cherry was in the latter group. Ferried from newsroom to newsroom by limo, he abandoned his point-by-point criticism of Vice-President Quayle's efforts and lambasted the administration as unprepared and incompetent. He demanded the troops be pulled out of Washington and sent to Colombia.

On the other hand, Senator Hiram Duquesne and several of his colleagues journeyed to the Vice-President's office in the Executive Office Building that evening to offer their wholehearted support. They appeared before the cameras afterward and, in a rare show of unity, laid aside all partisan differences to praise the Vice-President's handling of the crisis.

Most of the people in the nation spent the evening in front of their televisions. One of those who watched was T. Jefferson Brody. He was sneering at Duquesne's image on the tube when the telephone rang.

The man calling he had never met, but he had heard his name several times and vaguely remembered that he did something or other for Freeman McNally.

"McNally's dead."

The news stunned Brody. There were a hundred questions he wanted to ask, but since he didn't know where the man was calling from—the line might be tapped—he refrained.

After cradling the instrument, he used the remote control to turn off the television.

Freeman dead! First Willie Teal, now Freeman.

T. Jefferson pursed his lips and silently whistled. Well, it's a dangerous business, no question about that. That's why they made so much money at it.

What was he doing for Freeman? Oh, yes, the senators. Well, that was spilt milk. But it was a hook he might use later on somebody else's behalf. If and when. He would see.

And because his mind worked that way, Brody's thoughts immediately turned to Sweet Cherry Lane, the big-titted, cock-stroking bitch who had conned and robbed him. Freeman had been unwilling to assist in that little project, but now Freeman and his reasons—whatever they were— were gone, leaving Brody in possession of the field. Bernie Shapiro hadn't been very enthusiastic either, but he would approach him again.

So T. Jefferson sat staring at the blank television screen and thinking graphic thoughts about what he would like to do to Sweet Cherry Lane.

His lips twisted into a smile. This Army curfew would be over in a few days, and then . . .

Ah, yes. And *then!*

At nine that night Toad Tarkington and Jack Yocke sat in a military pool vehicle with the engine and heater going, trying to stay warm. Yocke was behind the wheel. Since he knew the city so well Grafton had appointed him duty driver. Toad sat in the backseat.

The two naval officers had spent the evening at the Pentagon drafting the orders and plans for the chairman to sign and had picked up Yocke at the *Post* fifteen minutes ago.

Through the windshield they watched Jake Grafton and an army officer huddled over a map spread out on the hood of a jeep. The jeep was parked on the sidewalk under an apartment house entrance awning.

The rain continued to fall, drumming on the roof of the car in which Toad and Yocke sat.

"Grafton seems like an awful quiet guy for a successful military officer," Yocke said just to break the silence.

Toad snorted. "You're a reporter."

"What d'ya mean?"

"The guy can talk your leg off. You haven't heard him at the office! What you gotta have to get ahead in the military is credibility. People have to pay attention when you voice an opinion, they have to believe that you know what you're talking about. Grafton's got credibility with a capital C."

Yocke digested this information as he watched Grafton and the army officer. The army guy was wearing camouflage utilities, a thick coat, and a helmet. In contrast, Jake Grafton wore washed khakis, a green flight-deck coat, and a bridge cap with a khaki cover.

Yocke had had a good look at that green coat when Grafton got out of the car. It had grease stains on it in several places, no doubt souvenirs from one of the ships Grafton had been on. The trousers were no better. In spite of being washed so many times they looked faded, the grease stains were still visible. Sitting in the backseat, Tarkington was togged out about like Grafton, except that his heavy coat was khaki.

"Where do you navy officers get grease on your uniforms?"

"Flight deck," Toad muttered, and declined to say anything else.

Yocke looked at his watch. He would like to find a few minutes to call Tish Samuels. Maybe after the next stop.

Grafton came back to the car and climbed into the passenger seat. His coat and hat were dripping. He left the door ajar, so the overhead courtesy light stayed on. The captain extracted a map from his pocket and studied it. After a few moments he held it so the other two men could see it.

"Okay. They are searching door to door in these grids here and here and here." His finger rested on each in turn. "This third one they'll finish in about a half hour. There's just time for that battalion to do one more before knocking off for the night. Which one do you think they ought to do?"

Toad and Yocke stared at the map. "This is a little like roulette," Toad remarked.

"Yep," Jake Grafton said. "Go ahead. Pick a winner."

Yocke pointed. "Why not this one? It has some warehouses and some public housing projects. Those are likely. These projects—you could run four or five Colombians who don't speak a word of English into a room and they could stay for weeks with no one the wiser. And even if the neighbors are suspicious, they won't call the cops. They know better."

"Sold me." Grafton sighed. He got out of the car and went back to the jeep with the radio equipment.

In about a minute he returned. "Drive," he said.

With the car in motion, Jake turned to Toad. "Your wife home tonight?"

"Yessir."

"Think she'd like to ride around with us?"

"Sure. If we swing by that way, I'll run up and get her."

Toad gave Jack Yocke the address. When they pulled up in front, Jake said, "Tell her to put on a uniform, as old and grungy as she's got."

Toad nodded and walked quickly into the building.

"Nice of you to think of that," Jack Yocke said.

"She's only got ten more days of leave left, and I can't spare him."

"Off the record, way off, what do you do over at the Pentagon, anyway?"

Grafton chuckled. "Well, I'm the senior officer in a little group of seven or eight people that do the staff work on military cooperation with antidrug efforts."

"That doesn't tell me much."

"Hmm. For example, we more or less have one carrier in the Gulf of Mexico and eastern Carribbean on a full-time basis now. That was one of my projects. I lost."

"Lost? Isn't that a good idea?"

"That's just the trouble. Sounds like a terrific idea on the evening news or when some politician makes a speech in Philadelphia. Have a shipload of planes fly around over the ocean looking for boats and take pictures and call the Coast Guard when they see one. So a carrier home from six or seven months in the Mediterranean has to forgo maintenance and go sail around down there. The squadrons have money for a limited number of flight hours for each crew during the turnaround between cruises. With that money they have to train the new guys and keep the experienced crews sharp. Instead they spend the money to fly around in circles over the water. No one gets trained. The ships and planes don't get the proper maintenance. And when they're finished down south, we send them back to the Med."

"But it sounds good in Philadelphia," Yocke said. "Honestly, that *is* important."

"No doubt. But if we have to send untrained people into combat in Libya or the Middle East, they're going to *die.* They haven't had the necessary training. We'll lose airplanes we can't afford to lose. And even if we dance between the raindrops and don't have to fight, the ships will need more maintenance later, a lot more. Prophet that I am, I can tell you that when that day comes the money won't be available. Congress will say, Sorry about that. Haven't you heard about the savings-and-loan disaster and the deficit and the peace dividend?

"And our sailors and junior aviators don't want to spend their lives at sea. So they get out of the service and we have to spend megabucks to recruit and train new people. It's really a vicious cycle."

Grafton took a deep breath and exhaled slowly. "My group documents the cost of the choices. We explain the options to the decision makers. That's what I do."

Yocke wanted to keep Grafton talking. He changed the subject. "I've been looking at these soldiers today. They look pretty young to be carrying loaded rifles through the streets of a city."

"They *are* young. But they're good kids. They joined the Army to get a little piece of the American dream—a job, money for an education later, to learn a skill, to earn some respect. Young men have been joining the military for those reasons for thousands of years."

"Can they fight?"

"You bet your ass. They're as good as any soldiers who ever wore an American uniform."

"But they're not trained for the way you're using them."

"Nope."

The door to the apartment building opened and Rita Moravia and Toad Tarkington came out. Jack Yocke suppressed a grin. Moravia was a beautiful woman, but dressed in khaki trousers, a heavy coat, boater hat and flying boots, she didn't look the part.

"Hey, Rita," Jake Grafton said.

"Captain. Mr. Yocke."

"Jack. Please."

"Thanks for including me on your expedition. What's on the agenda?"

"Let's go watch the guys do a housing project." Jake consulted the map. "The Jefferson projects. You know where that is?" he asked Yocke.

"Yeah. I've been there before." Yocke pulled the transmission lever into drive and got the car under way.

* * *

The supermarket parking lot was unexpectedly crowded. Charon walked between the parked cars and by the people pushing shopping carts to the pay phone mounted on the wall, beside a row of newspaper vending stands. He glanced around to ensure no one was within earshot. The shoppers were too busy with their own affairs. Charon peeled back the leather glove on his left wrist to reveal his watch. Then he removed the telephone from its hook. He read the instructions. No coin needed for emergency calls. Saved a quarter, anyway.

He dialed 911.

The phone rang three times before a woman said, "Police emergency."

He spoke quickly, as fast as possible. "There's a woman being murdered in an apartment house on New Hampshire Avenue. I can hear the screams." He gave the address. "Better hurry." He hung up quickly and walked back to his car, which was parked in the darkest corner of the lot with a fringe of trees and shrubs behind, blocking the view. Still, anyone in the lot could see him clearly if they only took the time to look. Predictably they didn't.

He removed his gear from the trunk and carried it twenty feet away. Then he got out the plastique and the timing device and put them on the floor of the driver's seat. He inserted the fuse in the plastique and very carefully set the timer. He watched it tick on the LCD display for several seconds. Satisfied, he reached into the backseat and got the one-gallon milk jug. He put that on the floor beside the plastique and unscrewed the lid. Between the lid and the jug he had used a piece of plastic wrap to ensure a good seal. Now he peeled it off and tossed it on the seat with the red plastic screw cap.

The vapors from the gasoline in the jug would fill the interior of the car. When the bomb went off in an hour the gasoline vapors would enhance the explosion and ensure that a very hot fire resulted. If everything worked as he thought it would, there would be no fingerprints left for the police. The confusion and uncertainty caused by the bomb would also slow the manhunt.

He had rigged up a half pound of plastique. That was a lot. Maybe too much. Too bad he hadn't had time to play with this stuff and get a better feel for the proper quantity to use.

The car keys were still in the ignition. Better remove those. No use tempting some kid to break the window before this thing pops. He put the keys under the seat.

What else?

That's it. He pushed down the door lock and carefully shut the door. It clicked. He then pushed hard until it closed completely with another click.

The first police officers on the scene double-parked. The driver locked his car door and stood on the sidewalk listening while his partner walked around the car as he checked to see if the shotgun was loaded. It was. He ensured the safety was on.

"I don't hear any screams."

"Me either."

They had just started up the stairs when the building literally blew apart. Both officers died instantly. As the fireball expanded it seared the paint on cars a hundred feet away.

The backup officers two blocks away on New Hampshire saw the explosion and called it in. As the seconds ticked away the rubble heap that had been a building became a roaring inferno.

The first fire truck arrived four minutes after the explosion. Firemen flaked out their hoses and opened hydrants. More police cars rushed to the scene and additional fire trucks were directed in.

Sixteen minutes after the initial blast a green 1968 Volkswagen beetle parked a hundred feet away from the apartment building blew up. Investigators later estimated the car contained four pounds of Semtex, a Czechoslovakian plastic explosive. Pieces of the vehicle were found on the roofs of buildings as far away as a hundred and twenty yards.

Seven firemen working on a pumping truck parked beside the VW were killed in the blast. Flying debris decapitated a policeman fifty feet away. The glass in every window on the block that faced the street was blown in, cutting one woman so badly she bled to death. Over a dozen people were injured by flying glass and debris.

The police had sealed the block when Jake Grafton and his junior officers arrived. They stood for a few minutes at the police line and watched the fire in the center of the block rage unchecked. They could just see members of the police bomb squad going down the rows of parked cars, checking each one.

Jake Grafton sent Toad to make a phone call. The military had better have some EOD teams—explosive ordnance disposal—nearby if needed.

Bombs. Terrorists? Or our shooter that lacked the nervous feet?

Nervous feet. What a silly thing to say. The assassin didn't have nervous feet.

"Captain Grafton?" A uniformed patrolman asked the question.

"Yes."

"There's an FBI agent at police headquarters asking for you, sir. They want you to go down there, if you can."

"Sure. Tell them I'm on my way."

"Okay."

Jake looked around. Yocke was talking to Rita. He would know where police headquarters were. Jake had no idea.

It wasn't a real forest, of course. Here on the side of the ridge in Rock Creek Park where Henry Charon stood the traffic noise was loud. Too loud. It would drown out the noises he needed to hear if anyone came along. Not that that was very likely on a winter's night like this. Rain, cold, wind. Perfect.

He continued slowly up the ridge, making no noise at all as he moved across the wet ground without a flashlight. On his back was a pack that contained his supplies. A sleeping bag on a string hung from one shoulder.

His weapons were in a long gym bag he carried in his right hand. Three grenades, a disassembled rifle, and plenty of ammunition. Under his coat he carried a pistol. The silencer was in his pocket.

He found the little notch in the rocks without difficulty. His woods sense led him unerringly to it. He felt around carefully. Good! The cache in the crack above his head was undisturbed.

He lowered the bags to the ground and slipped away from the cave. He circled it in the darkness, taking his time, pausing often to listen and look. In ten minutes he returned to the cave and began unpacking.

He fixed a can of hot stew on a Sterno burner, taking care that the light of the small flame was not visible from the slope below. When he had finished eating and had cleaned up, he got the radio down from the crack where he had cached it and inserted the earpiece. Then he pulled out the antenna and settled down cross-legged in the dry, sheltered area at the rear of the cave to listen.

First the television audio. Since they were covering the crisis on a continuous basis, the networks had a habit of summarizing the news every half hour. He didn't have long to wait.

The chaos on New Hampshire Avenue exceeded his expectations. No fingerprints, no evidence for the police to sift from the apartment. Henry Charon smiled. He didn't smile often and never for someone else's benefit. His smiles were strictly for himself.

The military curfew was news to him and he listened carefully, thoughtfully, trying to calculate what it all meant.

Obviously the troops were looking primarily for terrorists, armed Colombians. If they discovered him it would be solely by accident.

When he had schemed and laid his plans he had never considered the possibility of troops. But he knew there would be unexpected complications so he was not unduly worried. As he sat there in the darkness thinking about it, it seemed to him that the thing to do was to stay holed up until the troops found the terrorists and life on the streets returned to normal. Then once again he could melt into the crowds.

The fact that his picture had been widely disseminated didn't concern him. He had spent too many years as an anonymous face. He had dealt at the same gas station in New Mexico for five years before the owner began to recognize and greet him. And in a city the size of Washington the inhabitants studiously ignore the faces they see, avoiding eye contact. This was no small town. Human nature would protect him.

He tuned the radio to another frequency band, the police band, and experimented until he heard the dispatcher. He would listen for an hour. That would give him a feel for what was happening in the city.

Of course, he could walk out of the District tonight and steal a car in the suburbs and be on his way back to New Mexico when the sun rose, but no. There were two names left on that list Tassone had given him—General Hayden Land and William C. Dorfman. Which should he try first?

Or should he forget about those two and make another try at Bush? About the only way to get Bush now would be to blow up the whole hospital. That would be a project! Impractical to hope one man could successfully accomplish such a project on short notice of course, but interesting to think about. This was getting to be fun.

And once again Henry Charon, the assassin, smiled to himself.

"All calls to nine-one-one are recorded," Special Agent Hooper explained. "I thought someone from the military might want to listen to this, just for the record, since you guys are sort of in charge right now."

"I like your delicate phrasing—'sort of in charge.'"

"Anyway, I called over to the Pentagon and they suggested you. The people at Guard headquarters said you would be wherever something was happening."

Jake let that one go by.

"Anyway, we'll have this tape analyzed by a computer for background noise, voice prints, all of it. We'll eventually get everything there is to get. But I thought you might like to give it a listen."

"Where?"

"Up here." Hooper led the way up a set of stairs. Toad, Rita, and Yocke trailed along behind Jake.

"There's a woman being murdered in an apartment house on New Hampshire Avenue. I can hear the screams. Nineteen-fourteen New Hampshire. Better hurry."

Hooper played the tape three times.

"He's talking too fast."

"He doesn't want to stay on the line very long."

"He's from the Midwest."

"He's white."

"He sure as hell isn't Colombian."

"Captain," said Tom Hooper, looking at Grafton. He had sat silently while Toad and Yocke hashed it over.

Jake Grafton shrugged. "He could have edited that down if he had wanted. Even talking fast, he stayed on the line longer than necessary."

"What do you mean?"

"He could have said as little as this: *'Nineteen-fourteen New Hampshire. I can hear the screams.'"*

"So?"

"So. You asked what I think. That's what I think."

"Maybe he's smart," Jack Yocke said. "Would the dispatcher have sent two officers over Code Red if all she had had was an address and reported screams?"

Hooper thought about it. "I don't know. I'll ask. Maybe not."

"So it's hurried and wordy and breathless. Unrehearsed, if you will. And it gets immediate action."

"It did," Hooper acknowledged. "Officers were there in three minutes. The bomb exploded thirty seconds later."

"Lot of fire," Rita Moravia commented. "I wouldn't have expected that."

"Probably gasoline," Hooper told her.

Jake Grafton checked his watch. He needed to get back to the National Guard Armory and talk to General Greer. And call General Land.

"You going to be in your office in the morning?" he asked Hooper.

"Yes."

"Could you give me a rundown on what you have on the assassin at that time?"

"Sure. But it isn't much."

"About ten."

"Ten it is," Jake Grafton said and turned his gaze to his entourage. "Well, children, the night is young. Let's get busy."

Henry Charon's sedan exploded right on schedule, just as Jake Grafton was leaving police headquarters. The glass in the huge windows of the nearby grocery store disintegrated and rained down on the unusually large crowd, people there to stock up on food for the next few days. Six people were injured, three critically. Miraculously, no one was near the sedan when it blew, but four parked cars were destroyed by the blast and the intense heat. The fire in the parking lot was burning so fiercely by the time the fire department arrived that the asphalt was also ablaze.

The assassin heard the calls on the police radio frequency. Satisfied, he turned the radio off and replaced it in the dry niche in the rock above his head, then slipped from the cave for another scout around. All he could hear were the sounds of vehicles passing below, and they were becoming infrequent.

The wind was cold, the rain still coming down.

As he undressed and crawled into his sleeping bag he reviewed the events of the last few days. Lying there in the darkness pleasantly tired, feeling the warmth of the bag, Henry Charon sighed contentedly and drifted off to sleep.

CHAPTER TWENTY-EIGHT

* * * * * * * * * * * * * *

WHEN Jake Grafton arrived at the National Guard Armory, over a dozen young men and three women were being led into the building in handcuffs. The troops escorting them pushed them roughly along with their rifle butts. One woman who refused to walk was being carried.

"Uh-oh," Jake muttered as Jack Yocke pulled into a parking place in the lot reserved for government vehicles. As he got out of the car he could hear them cursing, loudly and vehemently. One woman was screaming at the top of her lungs.

The screams followed him down the hall as he headed for General Greer's office.

The soldiers searching the Jefferson projects had run into problems, the general said. People refused to open doors, some had illegal drugs in plain sight, and some verbally and physically attacked the soldiers. The officer in charge, Captain Joe White-Feather, had arrested sixteen of the most vociferous and truculent. He also had, the general said, another eight men on a truck coming in. Some residents of the projects had sworn that these men were drug dealers, and indeed, several pounds of drugs and a quantity of weapons had been recovered by the soldiers.

"We can't *not* arrest them," the general said, and Jake Grafton glumly nodded his concurrence. In some complex, convoluted way, this whole mess was about illegal drugs and the people who sold and bought them. The soldiers were going to have to address the problem of the sellers and the users whether they or their superiors wanted to or not.

Captain Jake Grafton, naval officer, instinctively recoiled from the implications of the solution. Here was a law-enforcement function pure and simple, yet as the representatives of the government on the spot, the soldiers had to do *something*. But what? A problem needing a surgeon's scalpel was going to be addressed with the proverbial blunt instrument, the U.S. Army.

Jake Grafton reached for the phone.

Amazingly enough, no one on the Joint Staff had considered this possible complication. Career officers to a man, they had approached the problem from a purely military standpoint. The time crunch had demanded that logistics and the command, control, and communications functions—C^3—be addressed first. That was about as far as anyone had gotten. Yet the problem was reality *now*.

He got home that night at three a.m. Callie was waiting for him when he came through the door.

"Amy asleep?"

"For hours."

"Got any coffee?"

She nodded and led the way to the kitchen. When both of them had a cup in front of them and were seated at the kitchen table, she asked, "How is it going?"

He rubbed his face. "We're locking up everyone who resists military authority and everyone in possession of drugs. Holding them down at the armory. The jails are full."

"You're exhausted, Jake."

"Without a doubt, this is one of the worst days of my life. God, *what a mess!* We're all in over our heads—General Land, General Greer, me, every soldier on the street."

"Did you have any dinner?"

"Wasn't hungry."

She headed for the refrigerator.

"Please, Callie, I don't want anything. I'm too tired. I'm going to take a shower and fall into the rack."

"We saw you and Toad on television. Outside L'Enfant Plaza."

"An atrocity, like something the Nazis did to the Jews. I wouldn't have believed it if I hadn't seen it with my own eyes. *Evil.* You could feel it. Wanton murder on a grand scale."

She came over and put her arms around his shoulders. "What kind of people would do that to other people?" she murmured.

Jake Grafton just shook his head and drank the last of his coffee.

The next morning he stopped by the armory before he went to the FBI building. The rain had slackened and become a mist, under a low ceiling. The streets and wide boulevards looked obscenely empty. Jake passed an occasional military vehicle, some government cars, and the usual police, but nothing else.

All the stoplights were working. He stopped at one, but his was the only car in all four directions. He looked, then went on through.

He was stopped at a roadblock on Constitution Avenue. A soldier standing forward of the door on the passenger's side of the car held an M-16 on him while a sergeant checked his ID card.

The sergeant saluted. "You can go on now, sir."

"Let me give you a word of advice, Sergeant. The people we're after will start shooting at the drop of a hat. I suggest you get a couple more riflemen to cover each car as you approach it. And you might park a couple of your trucks sideways in the street here so they can't go barreling through without stopping."

"Yessir. I'll talk to my lieutenant."

Ninety-one people were now being detained at the armory. They were being held in unused offices and in the corridors and along the sides of the giant squad bay. The soldiers had been busy. They had obtained chain and padlocks from a hardware store somewhere and were securing belligerent people to radiators and exposed pipes and anything else they could find that looked solid.

Some of the new arrivals cursed and screamed and shouted dire threats, but the ones who had been there a while tried to sleep or sobbed silently. Some of them lay in their own vomit. "Withdrawal," one officer told Jake as he walked by trying not to breathe the fetid stench. The soldiers had a couple of military doctors and corpsmen attending these people. Pairs of soldiers took prisoners to the heads one at a time.

Forty or fifty of the prisoners appeared to be just people who had ignored the order to keep their vehicles off the street. These people were sober and well dressed and were busy complaining loudly to an officer who was interviewing them one by one, checking addresses and driver's licenses and writing all the information down, then turning them loose to walk home. The cars stayed in the armory lot.

Jake paused and listened to one of the interviews. The man was doing his best to browbeat the officer, a major. Jake signaled to the major, who left his interviewee in midtirade and stepped into the hall. "What are you doing with jerks like that?"

"Holding the worst ones," the major said, smiling. He jerked his thumb over his shoulder. "That one isn't too bad. He just can't get it through my head that the military order didn't apply to him."

After a hurried conference with General Greer and a look at the map of the city, Jake drove off to FBI headquarters. He picked up Toad Tarkington en route.

Toad sat silently beside Jake and stared at the empty streets and rare pedestrians.

The federal guard at the kiosk at the main entrance of the FBI building telephoned upstairs. Two minutes later a junior agent arrived to take them upstairs. "Not many people made it to work today," the agent told them and gestured toward the empty offices. "We have cars going around picking up people, but we'll only bring in about half of them."

Hooper was expecting them. He took them into his office and poured coffee from a coffee maker on his credenza. His clothes were rumpled and he needed a shave.

"What's your job, exactly?" he asked Jake.

"The general sort of added me to his staff temporarily. I'm really on the Joint Staff, along with Lieutenant Tarkington here and sixteen hundred other people."

Hooper had no reply. If the military bureaucracy were half as complicated as the FBI's, further questions would be futile. He glanced at his watch. "I've got about a half hour. Then I have to give a presentation to the presidential commission, or the Longstreet Commission, which is what I understand they're calling themselves now that Chief Justice Longstreet is one of the victims."

Without further ado he began: "As you may know, the President's helicopter was shot down with a couple of Stinger missiles. American manufacture. We're inventorying the Stinger missiles in every ammo depot nationwide and looking at every theft report we have, but we haven't got anything solid yet. We've talked to everybody in a ten-mile radius of the little park on the river that the missiles were fired from, but so far nothing.

"Our best leads are the rifles that were left after the attorney general and the Chief Justice were shot. The rifles are identical, Winchester Model 70s, bolt action in thirty-ought-six caliber. We've tried to trace them both and we've gotten lucky. Ten years ago the rifle that fired the shot that hit the AG was sold by a gun store to a dentist in Pittsburgh. He sold it six weeks ago via a newspaper ad. A man called him about the ad, then showed up an hour later, looked the rifle over, and paid cash. No haggling and no name.

"But we got lucky again. Sometimes it goes like that and sometimes you can't buy a break. The dentist described the man and he had a distinctive tattoo on his forearm. That came up a hit on the national crime computer. Guy name of Melvin Doyle, who as luck would have it was arrested three days ago in Sewickley, Pennsylvania, for beating hell out of his ol' lady. Doyle's done time for grand larceny, forgery, and a variety of misdemeanors."

Here he handed Jake a computer printout of Doyle's record. Jake glanced at it, then passed it to Toad, who read it through rapidly and laid it back on Hooper's desk.

"Our agents talked to Doyle last night. He was threatened with a federal charge of conspiracy to murder a public official charge, and he talked. He says he acquired three Model 70s for a guy he knew as Tony Pickle." He dropped another sheet in front of Jake. "This is Tony Pickle.

"Guy named Pasquale Piccoli, also known as Anthony Tassone. Grew up in the rackets, moved to Dallas in the midseventies. Was involved in S&Ls in Texas. Lately been living in Vegas."

He sat and stared at Jake.

"And," the captain prompted.

"And that's it," Hooper said. "That's all the evidence we have."

"The second rifle? Was it one of the three?"

"Don't know. Doyle didn't write down serial numbers."

"Doyle get anything else for Tassone?"

"He denies it. We're looking."

"Okay, now tell me what you think."

"Our Texas office is very interested in Tony Pickle. Seems he was sort of a Mr. Fix-it for some real shady S&L operators, most of whom are being investigated or are under indictment. It seems that two or three may have stepped beyond the usual bank fraud, kickbacks, cooked books, and insider loan shenanigans. It looks like they got into money laundering. Extremely profitable. Perfect for an S&L that was watching a ton of loans go sour and rotten."

"What does Tassone say about all this?"

"Don't know. We're looking. Haven't found him yet."

"Who," Toad asked, speaking for the first time, "were these S&Ls washing money for?"

Special Agent Thomas F. Hooper eyed the junior officer speculatively. "For the big coke importers. Maybe, roundabout, the Cali or Medellín cartels. That's the smell of it anyway. Lot of money involved." He pursed his lips for a second. "A *lot* of money," he said again, fixing his eyes on the picture of Anthony Tassone.

"Forgive our ignorance," Jake Grafton said. "But how much money does the FBI consider to be a lot?"

"Over a billion. At least that."

"That's a lot," Toad Tarkington agreed. "Even over at the Pentagon that's a lot."

After using every minute of Hooper's half hour, Jake and Toad left the FBI building at about the same time that Deputy Sheriff Willard Grimes pulled his mud-spattered cruiser up to the pump at the gas station—general store at Apache Crossroads, New Mexico. The deputy swabbed the windshield in the wind and bitter cold as the gas trickled into the cruiser's tank.

When he had the nozzle back on the hook, Willard Grimes went inside.

The wind gusted through the clapboard building as he forced the door shut. "Whew," he said, "think it'll ever get warm again?"

"'Lo, Willard," the proprietor said, looking up from the morning paper. "How many gallons?"

"Sixteen point six," Willard said, and poured himself a styrofoam cup full of hot, steaming coffee.

The man behind the counter made a note in a small green book, then pushed it over for Willard to sign. Willard scribbled his name with a flourish. He put twenty-six cents on the counter for the coffee.

"How's crime?" the man behind the counter asked.

"Oh, so so," Willard told him. "Gonna be trolling for speeders over on the interstate today. Sheriff told me to write at least five out-of-staters. Damn county commissioners are on him again to bring in some more fine money."

"You know," the proprietor said, "the thing I like most about living out here is that there isn't any real crime. Not like those big cities." He gestured toward the copy of the Sante Fe newspaper lying on the counter.

Deputy Grimes glanced at the paper. There was a drawing right below the headline. Someone's face. "That the guy who supposedly took a shot at the Vice-President?"

"Yeah. The President, the Vice-President, and half the cabinet. Cutting a swath through Washington, this one is. Making Lee Harvey Oswald look like a goldfish. And you know something funny? When I first saw that picture on TV last night, I said to the wife, I said, 'Darn if that don't look like Henry Charon, that lives up in the Twin Buttes area.' Crazy how a fellow's mind works when he sees a drawing like that, ain't it?"

"Yeah," said Willard Grimes, sipping the coffee and looking out the window at the lowering sky above the arrow-straight road pointing toward the horizon. He got out a cigarette and lit it as he sipped the coffee.

Oh yeah, now he remembered. Charon. Sort of a nondescript medium-sized guy. Skinny. Real quiet. Drives a Ford pickup.

Grimes ambled back to the counter and stared at the artist's drawing on the front page of the paper. He squinted. Naw.

"Couldn't be him, of course," the proprietor said. "Ain't nobody from around here going to go clear to Washington to gun down politicians. Don't make sense. Not that some of 'em couldn't use a little shootin'. The guy who's doing it is probably some kind of half-baked commie nut, like that idiot Oswald was. But Henry Charon? Buys gas and food here pretty regular."

"Couldn't be him," Deputy Willard Grimes agreed.

"Now if a fellow had it in for dirtball politicians," the proprietor said, warming to his theme, "there's a bunch that need shootin' a lot closer to home. Remember down in Albuquerque . . ."

Five minutes later, with another cup of coffee in his hand, Deputy Grimes was ready to leave for the interstate when a game warden drove up to the gas pump and parked his green truck. He came inside. Willard lingered to visit.

The game warden was eating a doughnut and kidding the proprietor when his eyes came to rest on the newspaper. "Don't that beat all," he exclaimed. "If that isn't Henry Charon I'll eat my hat."

"What?" said Willard Grimes.

"Henry Charon," the game warden said. "Got a little two-by-four ranch up toward Twin Buttes. I've chased that sonuvabitch all over northern New Mexico. He's a damned poacher but we could never catch him at it. That's him all right."

"How come you didn't say something yesterday?" Willard Grimes asked, his brow furrowing. "That picture must have been on TV a hundred times already."

"My TV broke a month ago. That's the first time I laid eyes on that picture. But I'll bet a week's pay that's Henry Charon. Sure as God made little green apples."

The envelope containing the lab reports from the Sanitary Bakery warehouse case had lain in the in-basket for four hours before Special Agent Freddy Murray had the time to open it. He read the documents through once, then settled in to study them carefully. Finally he pulled a legal pad around and began making notes.

The corpse of one Antonio Anselmo, white male about forty-five years of age with a partial dental plate, had been found in Harrison Ford's locked room at the FBI barracks on the Quantico Marine Corps base. The forward portion of his skull had been crushed. Death had been instantaneous. When the field lab people saw the body at eleven a.m. Wednesday, they calculated that Anselmo had died between midnight and four a.m.

Hair, bits of flesh, and minute quantities of blood were found on the landing of the stairwell nearest to Ford's room. Blood type was the same as Anselmo's. Threads of clothing and one shirt button had been recovered from the stairs. Marks on the lineoleum in the corridor that might have been made by a body.

Wallet—now this was interesting—both the wallet and a motel key bore partial prints of Harrison Ford.

A shotgun lay beside the body. It also had Ford's prints. And there was a minute oil stain on Anselmo's shirttail—a stain of gun oil. No other weapons in the room.

The second report went into great detail about the warehouse, with its six bodies and cocaine processing laboratory. Murray flipped through it uninterestedly.

He settled on the report concerning Freeman McNally's house. One body in the living room. Fifty-one-year-old white male named Vinnie Pioche. Shot three times, 9-mm slugs, two that entered the back and one that penetrated his right side, apparently while he was lying down. According to the coroner Pioche had been dead when the third shot struck him—no bleeding.

Then this ringer: the pistol that fired the slugs that killed Pioche was in the weapons room and contained no prints.

The report carefully detailed where each of eighty 9-mm rounds had struck in the lower floor of the house. Refrigerator, TV, bathroom—it was quite a list. There were diagrams and Murray referred to them several times as he read.

Cars outside the warehouse. One of them contained stains of human blood on the backseat. The blood matched Pioche's. The ignition key for this car had been recovered from Harrison Ford's pocket.

Now Freddy Murray went back to the report on the warehouse. He looked again at the coroner's detail of Freeman McNally's injuries. Scrotum partially ripped from the body, severe injury to the right testicle incurred just before death stopped the heart. Death caused by a bullet through the heart, a shot fired into his back from about four feet away.

Ruben McNally—half strangled and severely beaten, but the cause of death was internal bleeding in the brain caused when his nose bone was shoved into the cranial cavity.

Billy Enright . . .

Freddy sat back in his chair and whistled softly. Jesus. That was the only word that described it. Jesus!

He was still making notes an hour later when Tom Hooper came into the office and sagged into a seat.

"McNally?"

"Yeah."

"What do you think?" Hooper asked as he took off his shoes.

"Well," Freddy said slowly as he watched Hooper knead his right foot. "I'm struck by the many points of similarity between the McNally mess and the massacre over at Teal's."

Hooper didn't look up. "Bullshit," he said.

"No, I mean it, Tom."

Hooper dropped his right foot and worked some on his left. Then he put them both flat on the floor and looked at Freddy. "No."

"I admit there are a lot of *dis*similarities too, but it really looks to me like another gang wipeout. We are just damned lucky our undercover officer survived with only *one* bullet in the back."

Hooper pointed at the pile of reports. "Look at the one for Ford," he said. "Read me the analysis of the clothes the emergency room people took off him."

Freddy took his time. He found the passage, perused it, then said, "Okay, there's some blood, three different types, some brain tissue—"

"Now where in hell do you suppose he got that on him?"

"Tom, in places in that warehouse it was on the walls and in puddles on the floor. He rubbed against it somewhere."

Hooper put on his shoes and carefully tied the laces. That chore completed, he said, "You and I both know that Ford went into that warehouse and gunned those men. He beat one to death with his bare hands. He went there to do it. No other reason."

"Now you listen a minute, Tom. We got a ton of facts here but no story. A clever man could string all these facts together to tell any story he wanted to tell. I guarantee you that the lawyer Harrison Ford ends up with will be a damn clever man. If he gets indicted, even *I* am going to contribute to his legal defense fund."

Hooper said nothing.

Murray charged on. "You think it isn't going to come out that the bureau sent him in undercover? *Ha!* The defense is going to make us out to be a bunch of incompetent paper pushers who couldn't prosecute Freeman McNally and are now trying to hang our own undercover operative. My God, Tom! The next hundred people we try to recruit to go undercover are going to laugh in our faces!"

"Cops and FBI agents gotta obey the law too. Harrison went over the edge." The irritation was plain in Hooper's voice. "Why are we having this conversation?"

"Ford's mistake was not being in bed sound asleep when Tony Anselmo came calling with his sawed-off shotgun. Then he could have just died in his sleep and none of this mess would have happened."

"I know he killed Anselmo in self-defense," Hooper growled. "Nobody's suggesting charging him for that."

"You think that fight at the warehouse wasn't self-defense? My *God*, Tom. *He's got a bullet in the back.*"

Hooper got out of his chair and went over to the window. He ran his fingers through his hair. "So what are you suggesting?"

"I think Harrison Ford has done enough for his country. I'm suggesting we close the file on the McNally case and let Ford go back to Evansville."

"Just like that?"

"Just like that."

Hooper stood looking out the window.

"We should have busted McNally in September," Freddy said, more to himself than to his boss.

Tom Hooper had spent twenty-six years in the FBI. He thought about those years now and the various tough choices he had had to make along the way. Freddy irritated him with all this crap about September. They had handled this case right all the way, and circumstances beyond everyone's control had intervened. His thoughts turned to Ford—the man was not a good undercover agent. Oh, sure, he could think on his feet and he was brave as a bull, but he had too much imagination. He thought too damn much.

He stood at the window tallying Ford's sins. Goddamn that asshole, anyway. "Ford was planning to gun McNally and all the rest of them, then go back to his room at Quantico. He was going to call us and claim he and Anselmo had struggled and he had been knocked out. That's why he changed guns at McNally's house. We've got no proof that he killed Pioche. None! It's plausible that Anselmo killed him before he went to kill Ford. If Ford hadn't been wounded at the warehouse we might not have been able to place him there. All we would have had is a bunch of corpses."

"You think?" Freddy said behind him.

"I *know!* I can read that man's mind. He's no cop! He thinks like a goddamn jarhead. Attack! Always attack."

Hooper turned around. Freddy was perusing the lab reports.

"You listening to me?" he asked Freddy.

"I heard."

"Ford and McNally. They're just alike. Screw the law! The law is for those other guys, all those guys who can't get away with breaking it. They both think like that!"

Freddy folded the reports and stacked them neatly. He took his time with it and examined the pile to make sure it was perfectly aligned, with the files in proper numerical sequence. When he finished he spoke slowly, without looking at Hooper:

"McNally's out of business. Permanently. That, *I thought,* was our ultimate goal all along. And the government isn't going to have to spend a nickel trying him. No board and room in a heated cell for the rest of his life at the taxpayers' expense. No appeals. No claims of racial bigotry or oppression. It's all over."

He picked up the stack of files and held it out for Hooper. "Close the case," he said.

Just then the intercom buzzed. "Yes," Freddy said into the box.

"There's a call for Mr. Hooper from New Mexico. Another identification of that artist's drawing of the assassin."

"Tell her I'll take it in my office," Hooper told Freddy. He picked up the files and put them under his arm.

The first shots were fired at the soldiers in a poorer section of northeast Washington around two p.m. A detail had halted a beat-up '65 Cadillac containing two black youths and were marching them toward a truck when someone fired a shot. The soldiers dropped to the ground and began looking for the shooter. The two black youths ran. One of the soldiers in full combat gear ran after them. He had gone about fifty feet when there was another shot and he fell to the sidewalk.

His comrades sent a hail of lead into a second-floor window over a corner grocery, then kicked the door in and charged up the stairs. Inside the room they found a fifteen-year-old boy with a bullet-wound in his arm huddled on the floor. Beside him lay an old lever-action rifle.

"Why'd you shoot?" the sergeant demanded. "Why'd you shoot that soldier?"

The boy wouldn't answer. He was dragged down the stairs and, in full view of a rapidly gathering crowd, was thrown roughly into a truck for the ride to the hospital. Beside him on a stretcher lay the man he had shot.

"Honkey pigs," one woman shouted. "Arresting *kids!* Why you honkies here in our neighborhood anyway? Out to hassle the niggers?"

A brick sailed over the crowd and just missed a soldier. It took the soldiers twenty minutes to run the crowd off.

While this incident was playing itself out, a dope addict in a public housing project two miles away fired a shotgun through a closed door, striking the soldier who was knocking on it full in the face.

The second shot splattered harmlessly against the wall.

The soldiers kicked in the door while the addict wrestled with the lever to break open the double-barrel. His wife was sitting nearby in a chair. She watched silently as two soldiers with their M-16s on full automatic emptied their magazines into her husband from a distance of eight feet. The soldiers were hasty and inexperienced. Some of their bullets missed. However thirty-two of them—the coroner did the counting later— ripped through the addict before his corpse hit the floor.

CHAPTER TWENTY-NINE

* * * * * * * * * * * * * *

Wᴴᴱɴ darkness fell the number of incidents increased. The communications room at the armory became a beehive of activity as reports of shootings and angry crowds poured in over the radios.

At the Executive Office Building General Land conferred with the Vice-President. Lacking any other options, they agreed that more troops would be brought in and sent to each trouble spot. General Land ordered in a battalion that was on standby at Andrews Air Force Base.

Jake Grafton was at the armory poring over a map trying to learn which areas had been searched and which had not when he was called to the telephone.

"Captain, Special Agent Hooper."

"Yes."

"I thought you'd like to know. We've received over a dozen tentative identifications of the artist's conception of the assassin. Two in the Washington area and others from all over. We're checking all of them. But I thought you might want to swing by the local addresses. The agents are still there. You ready to copy?"

"Go ahead." Jake got out his pen.

When the captain had copied and read back both addresses, Hooper said, "I think the most likely ID is one out of New Mexico. Very definite. From a game warden and a gas station proprietor. They think the guy is a rancher out there and a suspected long-time poacher. Real good with firearms. Ran a guide service for out-of-state high rollers for the last seven or eight hunting seasons. A deputy sheriff went out to his ranch this afternoon and looked around. No one there. Doesn't appear to have been anyone there for a week or so."

"What's the name?"

"Charon. Henry Charon. The New Mexico Department of Motor Vehicles gives his date of birth as March 6, 1952. We've already got a fax of the driver's license photo. I've seen it. This could be our guy. We've got agents showing it to our witness now."

"Can I get some copies?"

"The agents checking out the local reports have copies. They'll give you one. We'll send some over to the armory as soon as we can."

"Like maybe a couple thousand of them."

"Well, we'll do what we can. Gonna take a little while."

"As soon as you can."

"Sure."

"How about the national crime computer? This guy have a record or some warrants?"

"We tried. Didn't get a hit. We're checking."

"Thanks for the call, Hooper."

"Yeah."

The nearest address was an apartment building on Georgetown Avenue. Jack Yocke drove. When they were stopped at a roadblock, he showed a pass signed by General Greer while Jake, Toad, and Rita displayed their green military ID cards. The sergeant examined the ID card photos and flashed a light in each of the officers' faces. Two men, both with M-16s leveled, stood where they could shoot past the sergeant.

"You may go on through, sir," the sergeant said as he saluted. Jake returned the salute as Yocke fed gas.

There was no parking place in front of the building, so Yocke double-parked. "A license to steal," he gloated.

"Toad, write him a citation," Jake said before he slammed the door.

The FBI agents were still talking to the apartment manager. Jake introduced himself. One of the agents took him out in the hall. He produced a sheet of fax paper with a picture in the middle. Much bigger than the little photo on a driver's license, the picture still had the same look: a man staring straight at the camera, his nose slightly distorted by the lens.

"The lady in here says this guy has been a tenant for about a month. We're waiting for a search warrant to arrive."

"But I thought this was the New Mexico driver's license photo?"

"It is. It's the same guy."

"Henry Charon."

"Interesting name. But not the one he used here. Called himself Sam Donally. She asked to see a driver's license when he signed the lease. She thinks it was Virginia, but isn't sure. She didn't write down the number. We're running Virginia DMV now. Without a date of birth it'll take a little time."

"Maybe he used the same date of birth. Easier to remember."

"Maybe."

"When did she last see him?"

"Four days or so ago. But she's only seen him about eight or ten times since he rented the apartment. He goes away for several days at a time. Says he does consulting work for the government. And—this is funny— of the ten other apartments in this building, six of the tenants are hcrc—and not one can positively identify either the photo or the drawing. Three thought it might be him, but only after I suggested that it might be."

"The manager expect him back at any definite time?"

"Whenever. He never says."

"So he could just come waltzing in any ol' time?"

"It's possible."

"Any chance he's upstairs now?"

"I went up on the fire escape fifteen minutes ago and peeked in. Place looks empty."

Jake stared at the picture. The face was regular, the features quite average but arranged in such a way that no one would ever call the owner handsome. He looked . . . it was hard to say. He looked, Jake decided, like everybody else. It was as if the owner of that face had no personality of his own. The eyes stared out, slightly bored, promising nothing. Not great intelligence, not wit, not . . . Nothing was hidden behind the smooth brow, the calm, unemotional features.

Wrong. *Everything was hidden.*

He took a copy of the artist's rendering from his pocket and held it beside the photo. Well, it was and it wasn't.

"Thanks," Jake Grafton told the agent.

In the car he showed the picture to the others. They immediately whipped out their copies of the line drawing to compare.

"Oh yes," Rita said. "It's him. It's the same man."

"No, it isn't," said her husband. "It could be, perhaps, but . . ."

"Let's go," Jake told Yocke. "The place on Q Street."

With traffic practically nonexistent, Yocke made excellent time. He ran every red light after merely slowing for a look. They drove past the Lafayette Circle address, Toad pointed out the error, and Yocke circled the block.

There was a parking place clearly visible fifty feet down the street, but Yocke double-parked in front of the main entrance. He gave Grafton a bland, slightly smug smile.

The captain sighed and got out of the car. "Toad, phone the armory and find out what's happening."

While the lieutenant used the telephone inside, Jake conferred with another agent in the hall. He was back in the car waiting when Toad came down the steps.

"Riots," Toad reported. "The lid is coming off."

"Any sign of the terrorists?"

"Nothing yet."

"Let's go back to the armory," Jake told Yocke and tapped the dashboard.

"Aye aye, sir. What did the manager say?"

"Wasn't the manager. He's gone for the holidays. It was one of the tenants. Identifies both pictures. Says the guy called himself Smithson. He couldn't remember the first name. Been here about a month."

"Only one tenant?" Rita asked. "What about all the others?"

"Just one. No one else is sure. The agents are going door to door."

"You'd think if one person saw him and was sure, they all would at least recognize the photo."

"You'd think," Jake Grafton agreed.

Assume these people are correct. Assume Henry Charon–Smithson–Sam Donally were all one and the same man. He had two apartments. No, make that at least two. What if he had three? Or four?

Grafton looked up at the buildings the car drove past. He could be up there right now, watching the street. But why had so few people seen him?

Let's assume the man is really Henry Charon from New Mexico. He comes to town, takes several apartments. Why? Because the hotels and motels were the very first places the police checked. Yet the minute his picture ran in the paper, he would have to abandon all the apartments. Wouldn't he? But that was a bad break. Unexpected. He worked like hell to ensure there would be no witnesses. But he *was* seen. That was always a possibility.

Apartments. He rented apartments about a month ago. The conclusion was inescapable—the attempt on the President's life was very carefully *planned*. Most attempts to kill the President were made by emotionally disturbed individuals, Jake knew, screwballs who acted on a sudden impulse when an opportunity presented itself. Charon or Smithson or Donally had carefully planned, bided his time. And he should have succeeded. This was the nightmare the Secret Service worked to foil— the professional killer who stalked his prey, the hunter of men.

It fitted. Charon was a poacher and a professional hunting guide. He knew firearms. He could shoot.

A hunter. A man at home outdoors.

Well, there were the alleys and the railroad yards. Maybe the places under bridges and overpasses where the bums hang out.

No. He would be seen and remembered in all those areas unless he went to great pains to look like a derelict. And to pass freely in the world of working people and tourists that was the rest of Washington, he would have to be groomed and dressed appropriately.

A master of disguise, perhaps? A quick change artist?

Jake thought not.

Was he still in Washington? Well, the assumption was that all these long-range shootings were done by one man, and if so, there appeared to be no obvious reason why he should have left. Unless he's finished what he came to do or decided to abandon the rest of his plan. Questions— there were too many unanswered questions.

The car entered one of Washington's traffic circles. As Yocke piloted the car around Jake Grafton caught sight of the statue amidst the trees and evergreens. These little parks, he thought, were about as close to the outdoors as the residents of Washington ever get.

Perhaps a camper, mounted on a pickup bed. Maybe one of those vacation cruisers with the little toilet and the propane stove. Surely Henry Charon from New Mexico would be at home in something like that.

What else? He was missing something. Henry Charon, a hunter and small rancher from New Mexico. He comes to the big city and only *three* people see him? See and *remember*.

The problem, Jake thought, was that he himself had lived too long in cities. He didn't see the city as Charon did, as alien territory.

No, he had that wrong. Charon saw the city precisely as he saw the forests and mountains. A hunting ground.

But where did that fact take him? Jake Grafton didn't know.

The conversation among his fellow passengers caught his attention now. "Why is it," Rita asked Jack Yocke, "that the newspapers and television give the impression that the whole city is in flames, with a million people rioting in the street? My mother called me last night in a panic."

"The television people are in show biz," Yocke told her lightly.

"Have there been any more 'communiqués' from Aldana's friends in Colombia?" Toad asked.

"Yeah," said Yocke. "They say they're going to blow up some airliners. They're going to bring this nation to its knees, they say. It's probably on TV right now. Be in tomorrow's paper."

Jake Grafton sat in glum silence. The aftermath of all this . . . God only knew. But, he suspected, the plight of the desperately hopeless, all those people without the education or pluck to make it in America—the natural prey of the Chano Aldanas—would be ignored in the hue and cry. Not that the poor were the sole consumers of illegal drugs or even the majority. Oh no. But they were the core of the problem, the loyal consumer base unaffected by changing fashion or public education. The poor were the least likely to get treatment, the least likely to have the social and financial and spiritual assets to escape the downward spiral of addiction, crime, and early death.

"We're going to have to legalize dope," Yocke said under his breath.

This comment produced an outburst from both Toad and Rita. Jake silenced them curtly. They were supposed to be fighting alligators: someone else was going to have to figure out a way to drain the swamp.

The situation room at the armory was packed with people, including General Land and his flag aides. Jake found time to quickly brief the chairman on the search for the assassin, then he got out of the way.

He stood there watching the brass do the math required to figure out how long it would take to search all the remainder of the city with the troops available. They knew as well as Jake that the people they were after might just walk a half block to a building that had already been searched.

General Land was acutely conscious of that possibility. He wanted street patrols to stop and examine the IDs of any suspicious characters. The D.C. police could help, but they had limited manpower.

The military presence was inexorably rising and would continue to rise until the terrorists were found. If they were here to be found. Score one for the narco-terrorists, Jake Grafton thought. If they had accomplished nothing else, the people inside the beltway were going to get a real taste of military dictatorship.

While these thoughts were going through Grafton's mind, Senator Bob Cherry and three other senators were voicing them on national television. Cherry dropped the bombshell toward the end of the program. Chano Aldana should be sent back to Colombia, he said, and then the terrorism would stop.

"The people of Washington, the people of this nation, should not have to submit to being wounded, maimed, and murdered just so the administration can have the satisfaction of prosecuting Mr. Aldana. The citizens huddle in their houses while the military makes war in the streets. We all admire persistence in the face of adversity, but at some point dogged insistence on observing all the arcane niceties of the law becomes foolhardy. Atrocities, bombings, assassinations—how much do we have to endure here in Northern Colombia? What price in blood and flesh does Dan Quayle think we should pay for Aldana's prosecution?"

Watching Cherry on a portable television in an armory office, Toad Tarkington muttered to Jack Yocke, "He's got a talent for rhetorical questions, doesn't he?"

"It's taken him far," Yocke replied.

Twenty minutes later Jake Grafton *saw* the map. It had been there for days and three enlisted men were diligently annotating it with pins and little symbols, but when someone stepped out of his way, suddenly it was hanging on the wall in his full view. And the thing he saw as he looked at it were all the areas that were not divided into blocks to be searched. For the first time he saw the open areas.

It was possible. Not very likely, but possible.

"General Greer, do you have a company I can borrow?"

The major general looked at him askance. "A company?" he growled. He didn't think much of naval officers—the damned boat drivers usually had only the vaguest grasp of *real* war, the land war. Just now he swallowed his prejudices. Grafton, he knew, was different. Liaison with the Joint Staff, Grafton had never tried to tell him how to do his job. Unlike fifty or so flag officers of all services who had been wasting huge chunks of his time with unsolicited advice.

"Yessir. A couple hundred troops. I want to walk them through Rock Creek Park."

The company commander lined his troops up in a parking lot of RFK Stadium across the street from the armory. As the sergeants counted noses and checked gear, Jake turned to Toad. "Go get rifles and a couple extra magazines for me, you, and Rita. And three walkie-talkies."

"What about Yocke?"

"He's a civilian." Right now the reporter was inside in the command post taking notes. If he didn't get out here on the double he was going to be left behind. His problem.

"Aye aye, sir," Tarkington said and trotted toward the armory.

The company commander, an army captain, asked Jake if he wanted to address the troops.

"No, you do it. Tell them we are going to be hunting a killer, the man who shot down the President's helicopter. They are to take their time, go slowly, use their flashlights. We'll do the Rock Creek Country Club first."

"You want this man alive, sir?"

"I'll take him any way I can get him. I don't want any of your men killed trying to capture him. Anybody who fails to stop when challenged, they can shoot."

"Your responsibility, sir?"

"My responsibility."

The army officer saluted and went to talk to his men.

Ten minutes later, with the enlisted soldiers aboard the trucks, the officers consulted the maps. Just as Jake and the two navy lieutenants climbed into their car, Jack Yocke came running.

"Welcome to the party," Toad told him.

The convoy moved slowly through the streets. Pedestrians were streaming in and out of the grocery stores, but the parking lots and streets lacked the usual glut of automobiles. The effect was jarring.

"I hear the stores are doing a land office business in liquor and contraceptives," Yocke remarked.

"Can't watch television all the time," Toad agreed.

"Oh, I don't know," Rita said. "The glare of the boob tube doesn't seem to affect your libido."

Jake Grafton sighed.

Senator Cherry and his aide drove back to the Senate office building in Cherry's car. Like many of the senators and congressmen trapped in Washington this close to the holidays—Cherry had told the majority leader a week ago that the chambers should adjourn early for Christmas and had been ignored—he had been issued a vehicle pass by the White House staff.

Two FBI agents were waiting in the hall outside Cherry's office suite.

Hooper he remembered. The other agent was named Murray. "Your door's locked," one of them noted.

"That's obvious," Cherry thundered derisively. "They gave me one lousy pass for one vehicle and *I* have to drive the damn thing. You think my receptionist is going to walk ten miles through the streets of this open sewer to unlock the door so you can have a nice place to wait?"

"No, sir."

The aide unlocked the door and the agents followed the senator into his office. After he had flipped on the lights and settled behind his desk, Cherry boomed, "Well?"

"Senator, we're trying to get a handle on the activities of a certain lawyer here in the District, fellow named T. Jefferson Brody."

Bob Cherry stared at them.

"It seems he made some campaign contributions that—"

"Did the White House send you over here?"

"No, sir. As I said, we're—"

"You just got a call from Will Dorfman, didn't you? Dorfman is trying to shut me up. *That asshole!* Well, it won't work! I am going to continue to say what has to be said. If Dorfman doesn't like it he can stick—"

"I haven't talked to *anybody* at the White House, Senator," Tom Hooper said with force. "I'm asking you, do you know T. Jefferson Brody?"

"I've met him, yes. I've met a lot of people in Washington, Mister . . . I've forgotten your name."

"Hooper."

"Hooper. I'm a U.S. senator. I meet people at parties, at dinners, they stream into this office by the hundreds. Just here in Washington I must have met ten thousand people in the last ten years. In Florida—"

"Brody. Jefferson Brody. He makes political contributions on behalf of people who want influence. Has he made any contributions to your campaign or any of your PACs?"

"I resent your implication, sir! You are implying that Jefferson Brody or someone owns a piece of me! You can haul your little tin badge right on out that—"

"I'm not implying anything, sir," Hooper said without a trace of irritation. He had dealt with these elected apostles on numerous occasions in the past. It was one of the least pleasant aspects of his job. "I'm trying to conduct an investigation into the activities of T. Jefferson Brody. If you don't want to answer questions or cooperate, your campaign finance statements are a matter of public record. We'll get them."

"I'm perfectly willing to cooperate with the FBI," Cherry said civilly. "But your timing couldn't be more . . . curious, shall we say? I appear on network television and take a strong stand against the administration about a matter of public concern. An hour later when I get back to the office the FBI is waiting for me. Nobody from the White House called you, you *say*. But what about your superiors? Did Will Dorfman call the director?

"I'll be blunt, gentlemen. I think Dorfman is playing hardball, trying to use the FBI to silence someone who is speaking out against the administration's handling of this terrorism debacle. I know how Dorfman plays the game. Next he'll start telling *lies* about me. He's done it before. He's good at it. The slander, the invidious lie—those are Dorfman's weapons against Bush and Quayle's enemies.

"Now you go back and tell your superiors that Bob Cherry can't be muzzled. You tell the director to call Dorfman and tell him Bob Cherry didn't scare. No doubt that perverted little troglodyte will think of a filthy lie and find an ear to pour it into. *But I'm going to keep telling the truth about Dithering Danny and that parasite Dorfman until the day I die.*

"Now get out. *Get out of my office.*"

Hooper and Murray went.

With the door closed, Bob Cherry sat for a minute or two lost in thought. Automatically he reached out and rearranged the mementos on his desk, handling them and brushing off any specks of dust that might have come to rest on them. This altimeter mounted on a walnut stand—a presentation from a Florida veterans association. The gold doubloon from a Spanish treasure galleon, the baseball signed by Hank Aaron, the fifty-caliber machine-gun round on an alabaster base—all these things had been presented to him by groups of Florida citizens who appreciated his loyal service in the Senate, his sacrifices on their behalf.

He rose from his chair and went around the room looking at the photos on the wall, dusting an occasional frame with a finger and here and there straightening one. He was in every photo. He had posed with presidents, with movie idols, with famous industrialists and writers and athletes. Many of the photos bore handwritten inscriptions safely preserved forever behind nonglare glass: "To Senator Bob Cherry, a real American." "To Bob Cherry, a friend." "To Senator Cherry, a true friend of the American working man." "To Florida's own Senator Bob Cherry, who believes in America."

After he had looked at every picture and made sure it was hanging correctly on its private nail, he lay down on the couch and closed his eyes. He would rest a while.

Going down in the elevator, Freddy Murray said, "You know, he might have gotten down off his high horse if you'd told him Freeman McNally was dead."

"I was going to," said Tom Hooper, "but the jerk never gave me a chance."

* * *

From a sound sleep Henry Charon came instantly awake. He lay in the darkness listening. He could hear the drip of water—the rain had begun again just as he drifted off to sleep—and the sound of branches rustling in a gentle breeze. Charon's eyes roamed freely in the dim half light that passed for darkness under that glowing overcast.

Something was not right. Something was out there in the night. Something that should not be there. It was very quiet. No traffic sounds at all from the road a hundred yards down the hill. No sound of aircraft overhead.

Yes. There it was again. Very faint.

He slipped out of the sleeping bag and pulled his boots on, then his sweater and waterproof parka. He reached down into the sleeping bag and retrieved the pistol.

In less than a minute he was completely dressed, the pistol in his pocket and the rifle in his hand. He swung the rucksack containing the hand grenades and ammo and the duffle bag that he would need to hide the rifle over his shoulder. Everything else he left.

Only now did Henry Charon check the luminous hands of his watch. Eleven thirty-four.

He carefully left the little cave and moved with sure, silent steps twenty feet around to his right, to a prominence where he could look and listen. He sank to the ground at the base of a tree so he would not present a clear silhouette, motionless, a part of the rock, a dark, indistinct shape in a dark, wet universe.

The glow of the city lights reflecting on the clouds was only thinly dissipated by the naked branches of the trees.

And he heard the noise again. A man, moving slowly and carefully, but moving.

Charon saw nothing. His ears told him what he wanted to know. One man, sixty or so yards away, around the slope and down a bit.

And coming this way.

Henry Charon didn't form hypotheses about who this intruder might be or why he was here. Like the wary wild animal he was, he waited. He waited with infinite patience.

Now he got a fleeting look at the man. A soldier, judging by the helmet and the bulky shape, indistinct among the brush and trees. The man was moving slowly, warily, listening and looking.

But wait! Above on the ridge—another man. Two of them.

He turned his head ever so slowly to acquire the second man. He could hear him but that was all.

The second man was closer than the one lower on the slope. That he had gotten this close without Charon hearing him was a tribute to his skill. The first man was much clumsier.

Charon had a decision to make. Should he wait and see if these men would pass him without detecting him or should he move away? If they were hunting him, which was likely, they would check out this overhang of rock and, if they were halfway competent, find the cave and his gear.

He mulled these questions as an animal would, without consciously thinking about them, merely waiting for his instinct to tell him it was time to move.

The first man he had heard came closer, now plainly visible as he moved between the trees and rock outcrops. He was carrying a rifle in his hands.

The second man was right up the slope even with Charon, judging by the sound. Charon did not turn his head. Only his eyes moved.

"Psst. Pssst!" The hissing came from the lower man. He gestured in Charon's direction, then said in a stage whisper, "There's some rocks to my left."

Charon remained frozen. The man who had whispered moved behind the tree that sheltered Charon, but he did not move to reacquire him. The man was less than a dozen feet away.

At this distance Charon could hear every step the man took. He could hear him breathing deeply, as one does when one is trying to get plenty of air and be quiet too. He could hear his clothing rustle. He could hear the gentle, rhythmic swish of the water in his canteen. He even got a faint whiff of the odor of stale cigarette smoke.

The man moved away from Charon's back, toward the cave. Still Charon remained motionless. Slowly, ever so slowly, he rotated his head to try to acquire the man above him on the ridge. Nothing. The man was behind the trees or just over the rocky crest. In any event Charon couldn't see him from where he had made himself a part of the earth.

A minute passed. The man behind brushed against the bushes, broke several branches.

"Billy! Billy! We got a cave here."

Seconds passed.

"Billy! There's a bunch of stuff in the cave."

"Say again."

Now the soldier behind Charon spoke normally. "There's a cave down here with a sleeping bag and some other stuff in it. Better report."

As the metallic sounds of a walkie-talkie became audible, Henry Charon moved. He moved straight ahead, back in the direction the men had come from. He kept low yet moved surely and silently and used the brush and trees and rocks to screen himself from the men behind him.

The voices of the two men around the cave carried. They were still audible though the words were indistinct when Charon halted beside the base of a large tree and scanned the terrain.

Other men would be coming up this slope to check out the cave. He had to get well away but he didn't want to move onto someone who was sitting motionless. So he paused to scan and listen.

He could hear someone down the slope. The person slipped and fell heavily, then regained his feet. He moved steadily without pause, working his way upwards toward Charon. No doubt he was trying to find the cave.

Charon slipped along, staying low.

He froze when he heard the sound of a walkie-talkie. Below, to the left. Another one!

He kept going parallel with the ridge line. After several hundred yards the ridge began to curve. Perfect. The road below would also curve since it ran along the creek. Charon turned ninety degrees left and began his descent.

Through the trees he saw the glint of light reflecting on the asphalt when he was still twenty-five yards away. His progress was slow now, glacial. He flitted from tree to tree, looking and listening. It took him three minutes to get across the creek, which was small but full.

Then he got down on his stomach and crawled toward the road.

The roadside was brushy with dead weeds and briars. Charon lay prone, listening.

Nothing.

Ever so slowly he raised his head. He was beside a crooked little tree that had all its branches tilted toward the road. The bare branches formed a partial canopy that left him in deeper darkness. He scanned right and left, searching the shadows.

Another minute passed as he tried to satisfy himself that no one was nearby.

He rose to a crouch and trotted across the two-lane asphalt toward the brush beyond.

"Halt!"

The shout came from his right, a surprised, half-choked cry.

Henry Charon sprinted toward the waiting darkness.

The impact of the bullet tumbled him. He rolled once and regained his feet, his left side completely numb. He gained the brush and charged into it and kept going as a bullet slapped into a tree just above his head and the boom of a second shot rang out. He hadn't even heard the first one.

There was no pain. Just a numbness that extended from his armpit to his hip. He could still use his left arm, but not very well. The rifle was still in his right hand. He hadn't lost it, thank God!

He attacked the hill in front of him, driving on both feet, fighting for air, not caring about how much noise he made.

They would be coming, that he knew. He had no illusions. No more than sixty seconds had passed before he heard the swelling noise of an engine coming down the road, then the squeal of its tires as the driver braked hard to a halt. Henry Charon went up the slope with all the strength that was in him.

* * *

The soldier was so nervous when Jake Grafton got out of the car that he couldn't stand still. He hopped from foot to foot, pointing up the slope.

"I shouted for him to halt but he didn't so I shot and he fell and got up and kept running and I shot again and dear God . . ."

"Show me."

The soldier led him to the spot where the man had fallen. Jake used his flashlight. He followed the soldier's pointing finger.

Specks of blood on the brush. "What's your name?"

"Specialist Garth, sir."

"You hit him."

Jake pointed his M-16 at the ground and fired three shots, spaced evenly apart. "You stay here," he told the soldier, "and tell your lieutenant to get people on the streets up there." He gestured toward the ridge he faced. "I think there're streets and houses up there."

"Yessir," Specialist Garth said, still swallowing rapidly and wetting his lips. "I hope—"

"You did right. You did your duty. Tell the lieutenant." Jake strode back to the car and tossed his hat in. "Toad, go down about fifty feet to the right. Rita, fifty feet left. We'll go up the hill. Keep your eyes peeled."

"What about me?" Jack Yocke wanted to know.

"Stay here with the car." The lieutenants were trotting to their assigned position. "Better yet, drive the car around and meet us up on top." And Jake turned and plunged into the brush.

Fifteen feet up the hill he regretted his impulse to have Yocke help. Having a car driven by an unarmed man waiting and ready for a desperate wounded man with a gun when he topped the hill wasn't the best idea Jake had had today.

Too late Jake Grafton turned around. Yocke was already driving away. "Damn."

Jake used his flashlight. He held it in his left hand and held the rifle by the pistol grip in his right, ready to fire. The trail in the wet earth was plain. Occasional splotches of blood.

If luck were a lady, this guy would be lying unconscious fifty feet up the hill bleeding to death. But Grafton had long ago lost all his illusions about that fickle bitch. The wounded man was probably tough as a man could be and would keep going until he died on his feet.

He's going to need a lot of killing, Jake Grafton told himself as he paused to scan the dark forest with his flash.

At the top of the hill was a chain-link fence topped by three strands of barbed wire. Behind it was a lawn and trees and a huge two-story house with lights in three or four of the windows. The fence was an impossible barrier for Henry Charon, who was bleeding and beginning to hurt.

He looked left and right, then went right on impulse. He moved quickly, still able to lope along although the shock of the bullet was wearing off.

The next house had a six-foot-high wooden fence, still too much for Charon. He kept going until he came to a small two-rail accent fence. He was across it and trotting across the lawn when he heard a car go by on the street.

Cars would mean police or soldiers. Charon went around the house and paused behind a huge evergreen to survey the area and catch his breath. He probed the wound with his hand. Bleeding. Behind him on the grass he could see the trail where he had come. Whoever followed would see it too.

The car that had gone by was not in sight, so Charon ran out onto the street and veered right. Pavement would show no tracks, although he was probably dripping blood.

He needed a place to hole up and dress the wound. Or to die if the wound was too bad. That was a possibility of course. He had seen it happen hundreds of times. A wounded animal would run for miles until it thought it had escaped its pursuer, then it would lie down and quietly bleed to death. Sometimes he had come up on them after they had lain down but while they were still alive. If they had lain too long they could not move. The shock and loss of blood weakened them, caused them to stiffen up so badly they couldn't rise. He wouldn't lie that long. He would be up and going before he got too weak or stiff.

But where?

He heard another vehicle, or perhaps the same one coming back, and darted down the first driveway he came to. The house was dark. Great.

He went around the garage and circled the house.

There might be a burglar alarm. Or a dog. He would have to take the chance.

He used the silenced pistol on the door lock. It took four shots, but finally it opened when he pushed against it with his shoulder and turned the doorknob.

He closed it behind him and stood listening. The darkness inside the house was almost total. He waited for his eyes to accommodate, then walked quietly and quickly from room to room.

Apparently empty. With the pistol in his hand he ascended the stairs.

The master bath was off the big bedroom. It lacked windows. He closed the door behind him and turned on the light.

His appearance in the mirror shocked him. The coat was sodden with blood. He stripped it carefully. God, the pain was getting bad! He had difficulty getting the sweater and shirt off, but he did.

The wound was down low, entry and exit holes about six inches apart, a couple inches above his hip point and around on his back. He could only see the entrance hole by looking in the mirror. No way of telling what was bleeding inside. If his kidney or something vital were nicked, he would eventually pass out from loss of blood and die. And that would be that.

As it was, all he could try to do was get the external bleeding stopped. And it was a bleeder.

How much blood had he lost? Easily a pint, maybe more. He felt lightheaded. There was no time to lose.

He snapped off the light and went out into the bedroom where he stripped the sheets from the bed. Back in the bathroom with the light on he used his knife to cut the sheet, then tore it into strips which he painfully and slowly wrapped around his abdomen.

This would work. If he could get the bleeding stopped he could move.

Jake Grafton followed the trail to the street. He stood there with Toad and Rita and surveyed the wet asphalt with his flashlight. The blood drops were quickly dissipating as the rain intensified.

Jake began to trot.

Jack Yocke pulled alongside. "Rita," Jake said, "go get the captain and the troops. Get them on trucks. Hurry."

Obediently she jumped into the car, which sped away.

A hundred yards later the blood spots were gone. Jake Grafton stopped and stood panting as he looked around.

"Where do you think he went?" Toad demanded.

"I dunno."

Jake used the flash again, shining it on the lawns and shrubs and tree trunks. "Probably in one of these houses, but he could have kept going. We're going to have to get the troops to surround this area and search it. If we can get them in position quickly enough, we can bag this guy."

"You think this man is the assassin?"

Jake didn't answer. It was a possibility. One thing was for sure— whoever it was didn't want to stop and chat.

From the bedroom window Henry Charon saw the flashlight on the street as he searched the closet for clothes. He pulled out some men's shirts and tried one on as he watched the two figures on the street. Much to his disgust, the man of the house was a fatty.

The second bedroom down the hall bore evidence of a male presence. A radio-controlled plane hung from the ceiling, some large posters of scantily clad pinup girls adorned the walls. Charon checked the closets. Yep. And the shirt fit. He rooted until he found a sweater and added that. The jeans were a little big, but he had a belt.

And there was a decent coat. Not a parka, but a warm one with a Gore-Tex surface.

When he had his boots back on, he went back to the master bedroom for the weapons and rucksack. Those two outside had walked fifty feet or so north and were obviously waiting.

Henry Charon had no doubt they were waiting for soldiers to arrive.

He went down the stairs and paused in the kitchen. The refrigerator. Pretty empty. Nothing but a loaf of bread and a half pack of baloney. The owners must be gone for the holidays. He stuffed the loaf in his pocket and wolfed down the baloney. The blood loss had made him ravenous. And food would help his body manufacture new blood cells.

He went into the front room and stood peeking through a crack in the drapes as he chewed and swallowed bread. He explored the bandage with his right hand. It wasn't sodden yet, but it would be after a while. He had extra sheet strips in the duffle bag.

Time to go.

Out in the backyard with the door pressed shut, he walked down the concrete walk to the swimming pool, which was covered for the winter. He was going to have to cross the grass.

He did so. The back fence was six feet high. He threw his bags over, then jumped and hooked a heel over the top. The pain in his side almost made him fall off. He struggled, then fell over the other side.

It was several seconds before he could move. It was so pleasant lying here on the soft ground, with the rain falling gently on his face. If he could just rest, sleep maybe, let this pain subside . . .

He struggled upright and got the bags positioned on his shoulders just as a dog in the nearby house began to yap.

He trotted past the left side of the house and got out on the street and kept going in a long, easy, ground-covering lope.

"What's that noise?"

"Dog barking somewhere," Toad said. He still had perfect hearing, much better than Grafton's.

"You stay here. Get the troops spread around, maybe out ten blocks if you have enough men."

Jake went down along the house they were in front of, trying to figure out where that dog was that was barking.

The backyard had a pool. He walked through the grass, looking for tracks with his flashlight. His boots sank into the soft earth. He went on toward the fence. That barking dog seemed to be across it and down a house.

He saw the tracks in the wet earth. Galvanized, Jake slung the rifle on his back and swung up. It occurred to him as he went over that he could have just made a fatal mistake.

The shot never came. He stood on the other side of the fence breathing hard, trying to listen. The dents in the grass went alongside the house.

Following, he stopped at the edge of the street and listened intently. He heard the faint sound of a man running, his boots hitting the pavement.

Jake Grafton ran in that direction. He was huffing badly, overheating from too many clothes. And he was sadly out of shape.

The street turned ninety degrees right in a wide sweeping turn. On both sides of the street were houses set well back from the pavement and partially obscured by yards full of huge bushes and evergreens.

As he rounded the curve Jake saw the man ahead. And the man ahead glanced back over his shoulder and saw him. Jake tried to run faster.

The man ahead broke like a sprinter. And he's got a bullet in him!

He was going to have to shoot. No question. He would never catch him. As he ran he flipped the safety off and thumbed the selector to full automatic. The distance between them was growing.

The man ahead was coming to a streetlight. Now!

Jake stopped and flopped down on his belly in the street. Too late he realized a gentle crown in the road obscured the lower half of the fleeing man's body.

Panting desperately, Jake aligned the sights as best he could. He squeezed the trigger and held it down as he fought to hold the weapon on target.

He let the entire clip go in one long, thunderous three-second burst.

Half blinded from the muzzle blasts, he rose into a crouch and stared, blinking his eyes desperately, trying to see.

The man he had been chasing was gone.

Disappointed beyond words, Jake sank into a sitting position in the middle of the street and tried to catch his breath. Oh God! Forty-five years old and tied to a desk. He still couldn't get enough air. His heart was thudding like he was going to die.

Three minutes later an army truck rounded the curve with a roar and squealed to a stop beside him. The sergeant on the running board leaped down and covered him with the M-16 while two men piled out of the rear of the truck and faced away with their weapons at the ready.

"Drop it."

Jake let the rifle fall. "I'm Captain Graft—"

"On your face, Jack, spread-eagle, or I'll cut you clean in half."

He obeyed. Wearing khaki trousers and a green coat, he sure didn't look like a soldier. Rough hands searched him and found his wallet, which they extracted.

"Sorry, sir. You may stand up now."

Jake rolled over and accepted an offered hand. When he was standing he asked, "You guys with Bravo Company, Second Battalion?"

"No, sir. Charlie, First Battalion. Sorry about—"

"Forget it. Let me use your radio."

Bravo Company was still assembling in Rock Creek Park. It would take another ten minutes or so, Rita estimated. She told him that the troops had removed all the equipment from the cave.

"Take it to the FBI. Special Agent Hooper."

Jake deployed the Charlie Company soldiers in the truck and searched the neighborhood where the fugitive had disappeared.

Nothing. The man was gone.

At one a.m. Yocke came by with Toad and Rita, and Jake climbed into the car. He was exhausted.

CHAPTER THIRTY

* * * * * * * * * * *

JAKE Grafton picked up Toad Tarkington at eight the next morning. They then drove over to the *Post* building to get Jack Yocke. He was wearing the same clothes he had had on last night.

"You sleeping up there?" Toad asked.

"You know how it is in the big city. Public transportation is the pits and if you drive you have to fight all the traffic."

"Want to borrow a toothbrush?"

"Thanks anyway. A guy in the newsroom had one and we all shared. You won't believe who is up there right now talking to Ott Mergenthaler." Without pausing, Yocke added, "Sam Strader."

That piece of news didn't seem to impress the two naval officers.

"And the powers that be have been on the phone more or less continuously with the White House. They want passes for our delivery trucks. Without them we can't publish."

Jake grunted. He was thinking about a cup of coffee, wishing he had one. None of the fast-food outlets or corner delis were open; their people couldn't get to work. Banning cars had shut this town down.

"The thing that has our guys going is that the authorities gave the TV people passes for their camera trucks."

"Each station got passes for two trucks," Jake said. "The *Post* and the *Times* have hundreds of trucks."

"Hey, I'm not arguing the case. I'm just filling you in on the news. That's my bag."

The silence that followed was broken when Yocke asked Jake, "How about a clarification of the ground rules between you and me. I agreed not to publish until 'this is over.' When will that be?"

"When all the troops leave and the civil government takes charge."

"My editor wanted to know. I left him with the impression I'm getting red-hot sizzling stuff."

"Are you?"

"Well, at least it's warm."

"Body temperature?"

"Not quite that warm. Tepid might be the word."

"What can we do," Jake asked Toad, "to give this intrepid lad some sizzle?"

"Let's think about that. I could tell you what Rita told me last night when I asked for some sizzle, but I doubt if it would help."

"Probably not."

Yocke was busy explaining what he meant by sizzle when the windshield popped audibly in front of the driver's seat and a neat hole surrounded by concentric lines appeared instantly, as if by magic.

Automatically Toad slammed on the brake.

"Floor it," Grafton said. "Let's get outta here."

Tarkington jammed the accelerator down. The next bullet missed the passenger compartment and penetrated the sheet metal somewhere with an audible thud. The report followed a second later.

Toad swerved and kept going. The first corner he came to he went around with tires squealing.

"Anyone hurt?"

"Not me," Grafton said and got busy brushing the tiny pieces of glass off the front seat. "You can slow down now."

"Someone's unhappy," Yocke said. "There's a lot of that these days."

"That asshole could have killed one of us," Toad groused.

"I think that was the idea," Yocke said dryly.

Toad Tarkington raised his lip in a snarl. Yocke was still insufferable.

At the armory Jake spent a half hour in the command center. Random shootings were occurring at at least a half dozen locations in the city. Troops were being directed to the affected areas to find the snipers.

"We got over a hundred druggies back there locked up and more coming in all the time," Major General Greer said. "If it's just withdrawal or possession, I'm shipping them down to Fort McNair. We're putting them in the gymnasium there until somebody figures out what to do with them. But the people with weapons, the people that are actively resisting our guys or carrying significant quantities of drugs, I'm keeping them here. We have to separate the wheat from the chaff some way."

"They're still carrying guns?" Jake asked.

"Oh yes. Apparently they're fighting each other *and* the soldiers. Just two hours ago we had a raging gun battle in the northeast section. Seven civilians dead and wounded by the time the soldiers got there. They were using automatic weapons."

"Any word on the terrorists?"

"Still looking. But even if we find them, my recommendation to General Land will be that we maintain martial law until this random shooting and gang warfare stops. We can't just walk out now and leave this mess to the cops."

Jake went back to the office General Greer had made available and got on the phone.

"I have something I want to tell you," Jack Yocke told Jake a half hour later when he and Tarkington finally got off the telephones.

Something about Yocke's tone caused Jake Grafton to raise his eyebrows.

Toad caught it too. "You want me to leave?" he asked the reporter.

"No. Maybe you both ought to hear this. You'll know what to do with it. Needless to say, it's not for public consumption."

"Off the record?" Toad asked, horrified.

Yocke's lips twisted and he nodded.

Toad tiptoed to the door, opened it and peeked out, then closed it and wedged a chairback under the knob. "Okay, fire away. But remember, even the walls have ears."

"How do you stand him?" Yocke asked Grafton.

The captain rested his chin in his hand and sighed audibly.

"Three or four weeks ago they had a revolution down in Cuba."

"We heard about that," Toad said.

"I figured I'd avoid the mob of reporters and travel down there in a slightly unconventional way, a way that would generate a story. So I went to Miami and walked in on a group of Cuban exiles that might be planning on going back. I promised them I wouldn't do any stories on how I got to Cuba. They weren't too thrilled about having me but they took me with them to Cuba. As I said, I promised not to publish anything about them. But I didn't promise not to tell the U.S. government."

"Okay." Jake nodded.

"At Andros Island in the Bahamas they loaded about three-dozen wire-guided antitank missiles aboard. That's where they said we were, anyway."

"Maybe you'd better tell us the whole story," Jake said, and pulled around a pad to take notes.

Yocke did. His recitation took fifteen minutes. When he was finished, both officers had questions to clear up minor points.

Finally, when everything seemed to have been covered, Jake asked, "Why are you telling us this?"

Yocke just looked at him. "Isn't that obvious?"

"You tell me."

"I think the U.S. government ought to look into where those antitank missiles came from. Maybe they were stolen from a government warehouse. Maybe—oh, I don't know. I'll bet they were stolen."

"Why didn't you go to the FBI?"

"Because I'm a reporter. If it gets around that I tell tales to the FBI, I'm finished. People won't talk to me."

"Why now?"

Yocke twisted. "I wasn't going to tell. But I know you fellows and now seemed like a good time."

"You could have been killed down in Miami," Toad pointed out.

"Well, I'm still alive."

"I'm trying to figure out why that is," Jake told him and leaned back in his chair and pulled out a lower desk drawer to rest his feet upon. "Why are you still among the living?"

"I told you what they told me."

"Hmmm. You think that was the real reason?"

"It sounded real good to me at the time."

"How does it sound now?"

Yocke cleared his throat and rubbed his lips as he considered the question. "It doesn't really hold water. Why should they trust me when a bullet would have solved their problem? They could have just dumped me out in the Gulf Stream. Nobody would have ever known and that would have been that. I don't know why they didn't, and I don't think the people in Cuba are going to give me any answer except the one they gave me then."

"Surely you've got a theory or two?"

"Well, yes. This business about General Zaba got me thinking. You know, it's easy to assume that our government is made up of a bunch of boobs who never know what's going on and screw up anything positive they try to do."

Jake's eyebrows rose a millimeter and fell.

"I've come to believe that most of the time you guys do your job right. It occurred to me that possibly one of the reasons General Zaba is in the U.S. to testify against Chano Aldana is because the U.S. government helped the rebels overthrow Castro."

"Interesting," Jake Grafton said.

"I think the reason I'm still alive is because the Cubans were CIA or knew that the CIA would not be pleased if American citizens got murdered."

Jake shrugged. "It's possible. But you haven't brought this up expecting me to find some answers, have you?" Jake asked.

"No. Just being a good citizen. I'm telling you on the off chance the U.S. government lost some antitank missiles and wants to find out where they went."

Jake Grafton laced his fingers behind his head. "Rest assured, we'll report this to the right people, but the investigation will be classified and we won't be able to tell you anything. Sure, if someone gets prosecuted for stealing antitank missiles you'll hear about it, but that's if and when."

Yocke raised a hand and nodded.

"Just passing the info along for what it's worth." He got out of his chair. "Now I have to go look in the command post room and call the office. If you guys go charging off, please come and find me."

"Sure."

After Yocke left, Toad went over to the door, waited about thirty seconds, then opened it and looked out. The hall was empty. He closed the door and stood with his back to it.

"I never thought he'd mention that to anybody."

"Guess his conscience got him," Jake Grafton said.

"Well, what do you think?"

"He's a pretty smart kid. I think he's ninety percent certain and is just making sure that Uncle Sam knows to cover the other ten. That's my feel." Jake shrugged. "But I don't know," he added, and put his feet on the floor and closed the desk drawer. "I guess we'll know what Yocke thinks if we see a story about it in the paper someday with his byline."

He tore three pages of notes from the legal pad and held them out for Toad. "Here. See these get to the CIA. Don't leave them lying around."

"Should I do a cover memo?"

"Yep. Top secret."

"The CIA guys are gonna think you raised this subject with him. They'll never believe he gave us this out of the blue."

"It was a good operation," Jake said after a moment. "Yocke doesn't really know anything. He just suspects. But Castro's out and we have Zaba, and Aldana is going to get what's coming to him. That's the bottom line."

"Yocke's a pretty good reporter," Toad said grudgingly.

Jake shooed Toad out with a wave of his fingers.

He called the telephone company and asked for Lieutenant Colonel Franz. The colonel was one of the officers from Jake's Joint Staff group. Jake had sent him to the telephone company yesterday morning.

"Colonel Franz speaking, sir."

"Jake Grafton. What's happening over there?"

"We're doing our best, sir, but we only have three people counting me. It's like trying to sample the Niagara River with a beer can."

"Uh-huh."

Franz sighed. Jake could hear him flipping paper, probably his notes. "All we do is listen to calls at random. No method. But we have heard three that seemed to be discussing sniping at troops. One concerned 'taking out' some rivals—I got that one. They must have had some kind of gear on the line that told them they were being monitored, because I only got ten or twelve words and one of them hung up while the other was talking."

"Exactly what was said?"

"'With Willie out the field is open so we got to take them out before—' Really, it was over before I even realized what I was listening to."

"Anything else?"

"One interesting thing. It seems there's going to be a rally this evening. The others have heard calls on that. Five calls altogether. You realize there could have been five hundred calls on that subject and we've intercepted five."

"A *rally?*"

"Yeah. That's the word they used. A rally."

"Where?"

"I don't know."

A rally? What in hell did that mean? Jake Grafton wrote the word on the pad in front of him.

"What d'ya think?"

"We could use some more people," Colonel Franz told him.

"Look around. Find out how tough it would be to turn off the whole phone system. There's got to be some switches around there someplace that would shut the whole thing down."

"Turn it off? Wow! Are you . . ."

"Just look around. I'll call you back."

Jake put in a call to General Land at the Pentagon. The chairman would be tied up for another quarter hour. His aide said he would leave him the message.

Jake doodled as he waited. Henry Charon. Apartments. Sleeping bags in caves. Poacher and small rancher.

Why is Henry Charon still in Washington? If he is. Jake wrote that question down and stared at it.

He called the FBI and asked for Special Agent Hooper.

"You had some excitement last night."

"He got away," Jake said. "Any developments?"

"The people in New Mexico got a warrant and searched Charon's ranch and took prints. Most of them were of one person and they match the prints on the stuff your people brought us last night from that cave in Rock Creek Park. It's definitely the same person."

"Any photos of this guy?"

"Nothing in the house in New Mexico. Not a one. We're looking."

"We need those driver's license photos as soon as you can get them over here."

"Be a couple more hours."

"How about this Tassone guy that the fellow in Pennsylvania sold the rifles to?"

"Nothing on him yet. Apparently no one in Vegas has seen him for a couple of weeks."

"How about here in Washington?"

"We're working on it."

"You going to put the Charon DMV photo on the air?"

"Be on the noon news."

"Tell me, if we shut down the telephone system, would you all be able to keep operating?"

Hooper paused before he answered. "Well, we have the government lines and dedicated lines for the computers and all. If those stay up, we'll be okay. And the local police have radios."

"Okay. Thanks. Call me if you get anything, will you? I'm at the armory."

"Found the terrorists yet?"

"You'll be the first to hear."

He had no more than hung up when the telephone rang again. General Land's aide was on the line. In a moment Jake was talking to the chairman.

"Sir, I'd like to recommend that we shut down the local telephone system. Apparently people are using it to plan attacks on the soldiers and on rival gangs. And somebody is trying to get up a rally for this evening."

"A rally?"

"Yessir."

"Bullshit. There'll be no rallys while we're trying to put a lid on things."

"Yessir. I'll pass that to General Greer."

"You talk to Greer about the telephone system. If he thinks shutting the system down is warranted, it's okay with me. Tell him I'll back him either way."

"Aye aye, sir."

Jake hung up the telephone and went off to find Major General Greer. He left the pad with his questions about Henry Charon lying on the desk.

His side hurt like fire. The pain woke him and Henry Charon lay in the darkness with his eyes open fighting it. He groped with his right hand until he found the flashlight and flipped it on.

The beam swung around the little cellar, taking in the supplies, the brick walls, the concrete slab ceiling.

He had gotten here at three a.m. after a four-mile trek through the alleys and backyards of Washington. He had successfully avoided the army patrols and a roving band of juveniles, but the effort had exhausted him. Never in his life had he been so tired.

With the pain of the wound and the cold and the wet and the exertion, he had wondered for a while if he would make it at all.

Now as he lay on the sleeping bag, still fully dressed in the damp clothes he had stolen last night, the pain knifed savagely through him, and he wondered if he could move. Only one way to find out. He pulled himself into a sitting position.

Oh *God!* A groan escaped him.

But he wouldn't give in. Oh no. Using his right hand, he pulled the battery-operated lantern over and turned it on. It flooded the little room with light.

He eased himself around so he could examine the sleeping bag where he lay. A little blood, but not much. That was good. Very good. The bleeding had stopped.

The best thing would be to lie still for a few days until that bullet hole began to heal, but of course that was impossible.

In spite of the pain he was hungry. He tried to order his thoughts and prioritize what he needed to do. He seemed to be mentally alert. That was also good and cheered him.

First he needed to administer a local anesthetic. He got out the first-aid kit and opened it. He could use his left hand if he didn't move his shoulder too much. The pain radiated that far.

It took three or four minutes, but he got a hypodermic filled and proceeded to inject himself in four places, above, below, and to the right and left of the wound. The contortions required caused him to break into a sweat and bite his lip, but the effect of the drug was immediate. The pain eased to a dull ache.

The roof of the old cellar was just high enough to let him stand, so he eased himself upright and stood swaying while his blood pressure and heart rate adjusted. He took a few experimental steps. He ground his teeth together.

He relieved himself into a bucket in the corner. He examined the urine flow carefully. Not even pink. No blood at all.

Food. And water. He needed both to replace the lost blood.

He rigged the Sterno can and lit it and opened a can of stew. While it was heating he munched on some beef jerky and drank deeply from the water can.

Still waiting for the stew to heat, he stripped off the clothes he was wearing. He pulled on dry trousers, but he left the shirt off. In a little while he was going to have to change this bandage. The wet clothes he hung on a convenient nail.

There! He felt better already.

After he had eaten the stew, he opened a can of fruit cocktail and consumed that. He finished it by drinking the last of the juice, then another pint of water.

Pleasantly full, Henry Charon lay back down on the sleeping bag. For the first time he looked at his watch. Almost twelve o'clock. Noon or midnight, he didn't know. But he couldn't have slept all day, clear through until midnight.

He pulled the radio over and turned it on. In a few minutes he had the television audio.

Noon. It was almost noon. He had slept for about eight hours.

He turned off the lantern to save the battery and lay in the darkness listening to the radio. He had the volume turned down so low it was just barely audible. He didn't want anyone passing in the subway tunnel outside to hear it—but that was unlikely. With the military in charge of the city all work on the tunnels had stopped.

So he lay there in the darkness half listening to television audio on the radio and thinking about last night. He had heard that officer on the road talking to the soldier who shot him as he climbed the ridge away from them. Really, that had been a stroke of terrible luck. Shot crossing a road! He had damn near ended up a road kill, like some rabbit or stray dog smashed flat on the asphalt.

He sighed and closed his eyes, trying to forget the dull pain in his back.

Any way you looked at it, this had been the best hunt of his life. Far and away the best. Even last night when the soldiers were chasing him and he was hurting so badly—that had been a rare experience, something to be savored. He had been out there on the edge of life, living it to the hilt, making it on his own strength and wits and determination. Sublime. That was the word. Sublime. Nothing he had ever done in his entire life up to this point could match it. Everything up to now had been merely preparation for last night; for slipping down through the forest between the soldiers, for going up that ridge wounded and bleeding and digging like hell, for throwing himself down in the street and rolling clear with the bullets flaying the air over his head, then running and scheming and doubling back occasionally to throw off possible pursuers.

Most men live a lifetime and never have even one good hunt. He had had so many. And to top it off with last night!

He was going back through it again, thinking through each impression, reliving the emotions, when he heard his name on the radio. He fumbled with it and got the volume up.

". . . has been tentatively identified as a New Mexico rancher and firearms expert. This man is armed and extremely dangerous. He is believed to have been wounded last night by troops in the District of Columbia as they tried to apprehend him. If you see this man, please, we urge you, do not attempt to approach him or apprehend him yourself. Just call the number on the screen and tell the authorities your name and address, and where and when you believe you saw him.

"Why Henry Charon apparently undertook to assassinate the President and Vice-President is not known at this time. We hope to have more for you from New Mexico on Charon's background later this afternoon. Stay tuned to this station."

Charon snapped off the radio. He lay in the darkness with his eyes open.

Not fingerprints. His prints were not on file anyplace. If they had his prints they had nothing. It must have been the drawing. Someone in New Mexico must have recognized it and called the police.

That conclusion reached, he dismissed the whole matter and began again to examine the events of last night in minute detail. After all, there was nothing he could do about what the police and FBI knew. If they knew, they knew.

Deep down Henry Charon had never really expected to make a clean escape. He knew the odds were too great. He had signed on for the hunt and it had been superb, exceeding his wildest expectations.

As the bullets had ripped over his head and the roar of the M-16 shattered the night, he had learned for the very first time the extraordinary thrill of coming face to face with death and escaping out the other side. The experience could not be explained—it defied words. So he lay here in the darkness savoring every morsel of it.

Eventually he would turn to the problem of what to do next, but not right now.

"These goddamn terrorists are in the District. You know it, I know it, everybody knows it. The question is what are they going to do next?"

Major General Greer stood with Jake Grafton looking at the map of the city that took up most of a wall. Greer was a stocky man, deeply tanned, with short iron-gray hair that stood straight up all over his head. He had made up his mind to be a soldier when he was nine years old and had seen no reason to change that decision from that day to this.

He glanced at Grafton. He expected a response when he asked questions aloud.

"They can wait for us to find them, sir," Jake Grafton said, "and shoot it out right there."

"That's option one," Greer said, nodding. This thinking aloud was a habit with him, one his staff was used to. Jake was catching on fast. Over in the corner, Grafton noticed, Jack Yocke was taking notes.

"Or they can select a target and hit it. Or two targets. Possibly three depending on how many and how well armed they are."

"Option two."

"They can hope we don't find them and give up the search."

"Three. Any more?"

"Not that I can think of."

"Me either. I like number two the best. That's the one I'd pick if I were them. I suspect a bunch of civilians paid to get killed won't do well just sitting and waiting."

Greer sighed. "As if we knew. Anyway, if they take option two, what will be their target?"

Jake let his eyes roam across the map. "The White House," he suggested tentatively.

"I have two companies of troops and ten tanks at Bethesda Naval Hospital. One company of troops around the White House and four tanks sitting there, one on each corner. Another company with tanks at the old Executive Office Building. Same thing at the Naval Observatory, where the Vice-President lives. Also at the Capitol on the off chance they'd hit that again, and at the Senate and House office buildings. What else?"

"I don't know."

"Join the crowd," said General Greer.

"What about the Marine base at Quantico?"

"Where they're holding Aldana? I think not. Chano Aldana doesn't strike me as the suicidal type. They'd never get him out alive. I've given orders to that effect. That's the last place they'd strike."

Only half the city had been searched so far. It was going very slowly. The troops were being sniped at from locations throughout the city. Five soldiers had been wounded and two were dead so far. And the soldiers were shooting back. Eleven civilians were dead so far.

Greer turned away from the map and ran his hand through the stubble on his head. He sank into the nearest chair. "Did you want something?" he asked Jake.

The captain told him about the eavesdroppers at the telephone exchange and what Lieutenant Colonel Franz had reported.

"A rally?" the general repeated.

"Tonight."

"Damnedest thing I ever heard. If it happens we'll break it up."

"I suggest we shut down the local telephone system. The people at the telephone company say it can be done. We know the people sniping at soldiers and other civilians are coordinating their activities by telephone. What this rally business means, I have no idea, but I don't like it. On the other hand, I'm told the television showed a photo of the guy the FBI believe is the assassin on the noon news, along with a telephone number to call if anyone sees him. They've been broadcasting similar appeals about the terrorists for two days. If we turn off the phones, we won't get any calls."

"Have you discussed this with General Land?"

"Yessir. He says it's your decision. He'll back you up either way."

"Haven't had any calls so far."

"No, sir."

"This rally business, that bothers me. The last thing we need is a bunch of innocent civilians wandering the streets en masse with all these criminals taking potshots at people. Hell, if something like that happens it could turn into a bloodbath."

Greer sat silently rubbing his head. "Turn the damn phones off," he said finally. "I'm going to screw this damn town down tighter and tighter until something pops."

CHAPTER THIRTY-ONE

* * * * * * * * * * * * * *

THE Longstreet Commission later listed many factors that contributed to the violence that occurred in Washington that day. However nobody disputed the assertion that the black population's long-cherished, deep-seated belief that they were victims of intentional racist oppression aggravated the situation and brought it to a boil.

Young males in street gangs—black males, by definition in the inner city—began breaking windows and looting stores, and when soldiers showed up, they threw rocks and bottles and everything else they could readily lay their hands on.

At first the soldiers fired their rifles into the air. When that didn't work, they waded in pushing and shoving and dragging the most belligerent to trucks for transportation to the armory.

Automobiles were set ablaze by the mobs, which became larger and more violent as television broadcast the madness. Inevitably some of the people on the streets were killed by soldiers, most of whom were no older than those who were screaming insults at them and hurling rocks. A television camera caught one of these incidents and instantly it became a rallying cry.

General Land ordered the television cameras off the streets, but by then it was too late. A dozen buildings in the poorer neighborhoods were ablaze and fire trucks and emergency crews were unable to get their equipment to the fires because of the rioting mobs. Some of the army officers decided to use tanks to try to cow the rioters, but the immediate response was to fill bottles with gasoline and stick blazing rags down the neck. These the rioters threw. After one tank was disabled and two men severely burned getting out of it, an accompanying tank opened fire with a machine gun. A dozen people were mowed down. The rioters fled in every direction, setting fire to cars and smashing windows as they ran. The whole scene played on television to a horrified nation.

The smell of smoke and burning rubber wafted throughout the city under the gray sky. Although one could smell the smoke almost everywhere in the city, the rioting was confined to the inner-city neighborhoods, the poor black ghettos, just as it had been during the major urban riots of the Vietnam War era. This did not occur by accident. Over half the twelve-thousand soldiers in the district were being used to protect the public buildings and monuments of official Washington. Still, the vast majority of rioters stayed close to home of their own accord, fighting and looting and burning in their own neighborhoods.

Generals Land and Greer rushed troops to every corner. The only option they had was to continue to increase the troop presence until the situation stabilized. The search for the terrorists was abandoned.

As the sun moved lower on the western horizon, the temperature of the air began to drop quickly from the daytime high of fifty-six degrees. In the armory General Greer and the staff watched the falling mercury as closely as they did the incoming situation reports. Perhaps cold could accomplish what the soldiers couldn't. Someone prayed aloud for rain.

With darkness approaching General Greer committed the last of his troops to the inner-city neighborhoods. Gunfire and flames still racked the city, but the number of people on the streets was definitely decreasing.

"Captain Grafton. We have a problem out front." The young army captain was apologetic. "General Greer said he's too busy and asked if you would handle it."

Jake laid down the pen he was using to draft a report for General Land. "Yes."

"It's out front, sir. If you would accompany me?"

In the hallway the junior officer told him, "We've got some people out here, sir, who want their relatives released into their custody."

"How many?"

"Only three. They had to walk to get here, and with the rioting and all . . ."

"Yeah. How many have you released so far?"

"We haven't released anybody, sir. We send the curfew violators and single-possession cases over to Fort McNair, but the rioters and looters and shooters we've kept here."

"These people the relatives want, what category are they in?"

"A looter, a shooter, and a possession case. The possession case is a woman. She was giving a guy a blow job in a car and since they weren't supposed to be in cars, our people searched them. The guy had some crack on him and she had some traces of powder and crack in her purse. So we brought them in."

The civilians were standing by the desk near the entrance to the equipment bay. Two were black women and one was a white man. Jake spoke to the oldest woman first.

"I'm Harriet Hannifan, General. I want my boy back." She was in her fifties, Jake guessed, stout, with gray hair. Her purse hung on her arm. Her shoes were worn.

"What's his name, ma'am?"

"Jimmy Hannifan."

Jake turned to the sergeant at the desk, who consulted his notes. "Looting, sir. He was throwing rocks through store windows. We caught him trying to run with a television. He dropped it and it broke all to hell and we caught him anyway."

"Your son ever been in trouble before, ma'am?"

"He's my grandson. Lord, yes, he's been in trouble at school and he runs with a bad crowd. He's only sixteen and wants to quit school but I won't let him."

"Bring him out here," Jake told the captain.

"How far did you walk to get here?" Jake asked Mrs. Hannifan.

"A couple miles or so."

"Pretty dangerous."

"He's all I got."

"And you, ma'am?" Jake said to the other woman, who was younger than Mrs. Hannifan but not dressed as well.

"It's my boy. He shot at some people. I saw the soldiers take him away."

Jake was tempted to refuse. But he hesitated. "How far did you come?"

"From Emerson and Georgia Avenue. I don't know how far it is."

"Five or six miles," the sergeant said. "Through all that rioting."

Jake nodded at the captain.

"And you, sir?"

"My name's Liarakos. I'd like to see my wife. The sergeant says she's been detained for drug possession."

"You mean you want her released?"

"No." Liarakos spoke forcefully. "I want to see her first. Then, maybe, but . . ." His voice trailed off.

Jake turned to the captain and said, "Bring those men to my office. And take this gentleman back to visit his wife." He asked the women to accompany him.

Back in his office with everyone seated, he sent Toad for coffee. Jack Yocke sat silently at the other desk.

The younger woman began to sob. Her name was Fulbright. "I know it's not your fault," she said, "but it's more than a body can stand, what with the drugs and the unemployment and the schools that don't teach them nothing. How can they grow up to be men living in this? I ask you."

"I don't know."

The silence grew uncomfortable as Mrs. Fulbright sobbed. Jake could think of nothing to say, and once he shot a glance at Yocke, hoping he would help. The reporter returned his look impassively and said nothing.

Toad brought the coffee just seconds before two soldiers escorted the men into the room in handcuffs. Men? They were just boys.

"You kids are leaving," Jake said, "because these women cared enough about you to risk their lives walking over here. You may not have much money, but you got something a lot of folks will never have—people that love you."

Both the youngsters looked uncomfortable, embarrassed. Ah, what's the use? Jake wondered. But maybe, just maybe . . . "Toad, when these ladies finish their coffee, drive these people home."

"My God, Thanos, why did you come?"

"I—"

She held up a hand so he couldn't see her face. He pulled her hand away. She was crying.

"You shouldn't have come," she whispered. "Oh, my God, Thanos, look what I've done to myself."

The room they had her in held five other women. It stank of vomit and urine. A half dozen bare mattresses lay scattered on the floor, but there was no other furniture. Elizabeth sat huddled on a mattress. Her clothes were filthy.

"I'm sorry, Thanos. I'm sorry."

"That's the first step on the road back, Elizabeth."

"I feel so dirty. So degraded! And I've crawled into this sewer all by myself. How can you even look at—"

"You want to go home? Without the dope?"

"I don't know if I can! But why would you—don't you know what I've done? Don't you know why I'm here?"

"I know."

She tore her hand from his grasp and held it in front of her face. "Please leave, for the love of—"

Liarakos rose and pounded on the door.

"Sir, I'd like to take my wife home."

Liarakos stood in front of Grafton's desk. Jake Grafton forced himself to look up into the man's face. "Fine," he said. "Where do you live?"

"Edgemoor."

"Isn't that over on the other side of Rock Creek Park?"

"Yes."

"Jack, go catch Toad. Tell him he'll have two more passengers. Go with him, Mr. Liarakos."

Liarakos turned to go, then looked back. "Thanks, I—"

Jake waved him out.

In ten minutes Yocke was back. "They all left with Toad," he said and sat down in the chair in front of Jake's desk. "Do you know who that man was?"

"Lee-something. I've forgotten."

"Thanos Liarakos. He's the lawyer representing Chano Aldana."

"Everybody has their troubles," Jake Grafton said, his eyes back on his report. The skin on his face was taut across the bones. His eyes looked like they were recessed even deeper into their sockets.

"You knew that when you first saw him, didn't you?"

"You're worse than Tarkington. Go find something to do someplace else, will you?"

Yocke rose uncertainly. He wandered aimlessly for several seconds, went out the door and down the hall, then out to the desk in the bay where the soldiers were checking in the prisoners. He waited until the sergeant finished logging in two more surly prisoners, then asked, "Mrs. Liarakos. Who was the man arrested with her?"

"Ah, I've got it here." The sergeant flipped through his book, a green, hardbound logbook. He found the entry. "Guy who refused to give his name. Stuff in his wallet says he is one T. Jefferson Brody, a lawyer if you can believe that. Three hours ago. He's in bay four if you want to talk to him." The sergeant gestured vaguely to his left.

Some of the prisoners were still drunk and belligerent. They shouted and raved obscenties. The smell of urine and body odor made the air heavy and lifeless. Yocke tried to breathe shallowly.

He looked into bay four, a waist-high enclosure with a stained concrete floor normally used for the repair of vehicles. The bay now held several dozen men who were shackled in place. Immediately across the corridor was another bay which contained women. The women sat with their backs to the men.

Yocke didn't recognize Brody. Dressed in a filthy blue suit, the lawyer was standing and straining against the chain around his wrist, screaming at the top of his lungs at the women's area. *You fucking cunt! I'll rip your fucking liver out with my bare hands. We won't be in here forever, you fucking bitch. Then you wait! I'll get you if it's the last thing I ever do!*

One of the soldiers walked over with a look of disgust on his face. "Hey *you!* Big mouth! I'm telling you for the very last time. Shut up!"

"That fucking cunt *robbed* me," Brody howled. "I'll—"

"Shut up, butt-face, or we'll gag you. You hear me!"

Brody fell silent. He stared fixedly across at the women's holding area. After a moment he sat down, but his gaze never wavered.

Jack Yocke turned away, slightly nauseated. Hell couldn't be any worse than this, he told himself, and shivered.

The first bomb exploded at six-thirty p.m. A truck packed with five tons of dynamite was driven through the fence at a huge electrical transmission substation on Greenleaf Point, near the mouth of the Anacostia River. The driver ran back through the hole in the wire as two soldiers chased him and fired their rifles. The driver disappeared into the low-income housing projects nearby. The soldiers were going back through the fence to examine the truck when its cargo detonated in a stupendous blast that was felt and heard for miles. The electrical substation was instantly obliterated. The lights went out in downtown and southeast Washington.

In the next fifteen minutes three more substations were attacked, effectively depriving the entire city of electricity.

"At least the damned TV stations are off the air," Toad Tarkington told Rita Moravia, who had just arrived at the armory on the back of an army truck.

While General Greer was responding to these attacks, a major natural-gas pumping station in Arlington was bombed. The explosion resembled a small nuclear blast. Then the place caught fire. In the darkness that fell on the city when the lights went out the glare of the raging inferno could be seen from rooftops all over the city.

At the same time the explosions were racking the city, an army platoon was ambushed and wiped out on the Capital Beltway by twenty men carrying automatic weapons. Three men in uniform waved the truck to a halt, then shot the driver and sergeant as they emerged from the cab. Some of the men were machine-gunned as they exited the back of the truck. A dozen survivors, trapped in the truck bed and unable to see out, threw out their weapons and surrendered. They were led down into the drainage ditch beside the freeway and shot. The weapons, ammunition, and radios were collected and loaded into the truck.

The attackers climbed into the back of the vehicle under the canvas covering and took their seats. In the cab two men examined the controls of the truck, which was still idling, managed to get the transmission into gear, and drove away.

The truck left the beltway at Kenilworth Avenue and proceeded south toward the city at about twenty-five miles per hour. Anticipating the enthusiasm of teenage soldiers, the Army had long ago installed a governor to prevent the engine from overrevving, yet the inexperienced driver couldn't get the transmission into a higher gear.

The two headlights behind metal grilles put out little light, but it was enough. The huge tires rolled easily over the potholes and broken pavement that commuters had accepted as their lot for years.

On the front of the truck was a huge steel horizontal beam, painted olive-drab like the rest of the vehicle. This beam was intended by the Army to enable the truck to push other, disabled, military vehicles.

At the Kenilworth–New York Avenue interchange a half dozen National Guardsmen were manning a roadblock. The driver of the hijacked truck didn't even slow down. The steel beam on the front delivered a glancing blow to the bus parked crossways in the road, shoving it aside as the truck careened on with the engine roaring. The men in back opened up with automatic weapons at the soldiers in the road as the truck swept past.

A third of a mile later the truck thundered by the sign that marked the boundary of the District of Columbia. It was a large white sign with blue letters artfully arranged above and below the logo of the Capitol dome. The sign read: WELCOME TO WASHINGTON, A CAPITAL CITY. MARION C. BARRY, MAYOR.

Henry Charon soaked the old bandage with water from the jug, then slowly unwrapped it from around his waist. It hurt too much for him to twist around to try to see the wound, so he didn't bother. He merely wrapped strips of the stolen sheet around his middle and tied them in neat knots.

Then he put on a flannel shirt and over that a sweatshirt.

The coat he had appropriated last night from the college boy was fashionable but certainly not utilitarian enough for Charon's taste. He hung it on a nail and donned a spare water-resistant parka. His well-worn leather hunting boots went on his feet over two pairs of wool socks.

He threaded a scabbard for a hunting knife onto his belt and positioned it so it hung into his rear hip pocket. When the belt was fastened and adjusted just so below the makeshift bandage about his middle, he inserted the thin-bladed razor-sharp skinning knife he favored into the scabbard and snapped the restraining strap around the handle.

Lastly he put on his cap, a wool-lined billed affair with ear flaps folded around the sides, just in case. The cap was a dark brown and bore the dirt and stains of many winters.

The silencer attached smoothly, effortlessly to the 9-mm pistol. He checked to ensure the magazine was loaded and pulled back the slide until he saw the gleam from a round in the chamber. Flicking the safety on, he slipped the weapon behind his belt in the small of his back. The grenades and two loaded magazines for the pistol went into the pockets of the parka.

He opened the duffle bag and checked the Model 70 Winchester. Still secure, properly padded, with a box of .30-06 ammo wrapped in bubble wrap. He zipped the bag closed and slung it on his shoulder.

What else? Oh yeah, the pencil flash. He tried it, then turned it off and stowed it in one of the pockets of the parka.

Not the radio. It would be nice but was too bulky. Food, water? A handful of jerky and a plastic baby bottle full of water—that would have to do. And the street map.

Anything else?

Gloves. He pulled them on slowly, good pigskin gloves that fit perfectly.

True, this would not be a stalk of Rocky Mountain Bighorn above timberline in subzero cold and blowing snow. Yet the quarry would be the wariest, most difficult game of all—man. Henry Charon grinned in delicious anticipation and turned off the battery-powered lantern.

*   *   *

The hijacked truck drove slowly through the gate into the armory parking lot and came to a stop beside three other trucks. The driver turned off the lights, killed the engine, and climbed down. On the other side the sergeant walked back and watched his men disembark from the bed.

The men didn't line up in formation. They immediately wandered away in twos and threes.

The parking lot was lit by emergency lights mounted on poles and powered by portable generators, which were noisy. The light was adequate, but barely.

The sergeant and a half dozen men walked toward the open door of the armory and passed inside. Two of the men halted inside the huge open bay and stared a moment at the prisoners shackled to the south wall. In the dim glare of the emergency lights that had automatically illuminated when the electricity failed the bay was quite a sight. Over two hundred sobbing, cursing, crying men and women were chained there. The noise was like something from a nightmare about an insane asylum.

After several seconds of silent observation, the intruders turned their attention to the soldiers guarding them, the men coming and going, the ladder that led up to a catwalk and more offices.

Another two of the men walked the length of the bay to the door on the other end while the sergeant and his remaining companions left the bay and walked into the hallway. Although the sergeant knew no English and couldn't read the posted signs, he immediately headed for the large double door standing open at the end of the hall that seemed to have a large number of people coming and going. He passed several Americans on the way, but they didn't give him a glance. With his dark, Latin complexion he fit right into this multiracial army.

The fake sergeant, with his two companions immediately behind him, paused in the large open doorway. Maps covered every wall and radios and telephones stood on the desks. In the center of the room behind a large desk sat a stocky man with two silver stars on each collar.

With a nod to his companions, the sergeant unobtrusively removed a grenade from the webbing across his chest and pulled the pin while the two men beside him did likewise. The three of them each tossed the grenades underhanded toward the center of the room and dove behind nearby desks for cover.

"Grenades!"

The shout galvanized the soldiers. Men were leaping and running and diving when the little hand bombs exploded. The shrapnel destroyed the emergency lighting.

The darkness and silence that followed the explosions was broken only by the high-pitched scream of some poor soul in mortal agony. Then the three intruders opened fire with their rifles.

Out in the squad bay the explosions were muffled but plainly audible. As the soldiers reacted the two terrorists near each door began, in a very businesslike fashion, shooting uniformed men as fast as they could aim and pull the trigger.

But there were too many soldiers. In less than twenty seconds the four intruders were dead.

In the parking lot the gunfire and staccato blasts of grenades continued unabated. One of the men from the hijacked truck reached an M-60 machine gun mounted on a swivel on the back of a jeep and began spraying the soldiers indiscriminately. He was soon shot, but another man took his place. Over eighty soldiers went down in the first thirty seconds of the firefight.

Inside the command post, most of the soldiers had been unarmed. Not that it mattered. The only light was the strobing muzzle blasts. Those soldiers who survived the grenades lay huddled on the floor as the bullets lashed and tore through the furniture and radios. By some miracle, all three of the terrorists fired their weapons aimed too high.

One officer had a pistol. When the automatic bursts stopped—he thought the intruders had expended all the shells in their magazines and were changing them—he opened fire with the pistol at the spots in the darkness where the muzzle blasts seemed to have been coming from. He hit two of the gunmen, but the third one successfully reloaded and killed him with a burst of six slugs.

This man emptied his rifle and reached for another grenade. Just as he got the pin out, a private ran up to the door behind him and gave him a point-blank burst from his M-16. The grenade fell, unseen by the private, who was killed in the explosion that followed a few seconds later. From the first grenade blast to the last, thirty seconds had passed.

Outside in the parking lot the battle lasted longer. Between the machine gun and bursts from M-16s on full automatic, the number of men who were down was staggering.

Still the soldiers who were unwounded or not wounded too severely fought back. In the confusion some of the Americans shot each other.

The shooting was still going on a minute later when someone began roaring, "Cease fire, cease fire." Then it stopped.

The sergeants were turning the bodies of the terrorists over and searching their pockets by the time that Jake Grafton got outside with his rifle. He had been in the head.

"They all look Latin, sir," someone said to Jake.

"Here's one still alive." The man the soldier was referring to was babbling in Spanish. He had a hole in the center of his stomach that was pumping blood. He was staring at the wound and repeating the rosary in Spanish.

"Colombia, *sí?*"

The wounded man continued his prayer. The soldier grabbed his shirt, half lifted him, and shook him violently. "Colombia, *sí?*"

"*Sí, sí, sí . . .*"

"I hope you die slow, motherfuck!" The soldier dropped the man to the pavement.

"How many did we lose?" Jake asked the major beside him as he stared about at the carnage.

"We're counting. Sweet Jesus, I think a lot of our guys shot each other. Everybody was shooting at everybody." The major's face wore an indescribable look of sadness. "God have mercy."

Jake Grafton felt a terrible lethargy. He wanted to just turn off his brain.

"General Greer's dead, sir."

Jake nodded slowly. Somehow he wasn't surprised. Toad, Rita, where were they?

He found them inside administering first aid to wounded men. Rita was working on a man with a sucking chest wound and Toad was trying to get the bleeding stopped on a man with a bullet through the thigh.

Jake left them and went to find a radio that still worked.

The radio was in the command post, its metal cover scarred by shrapnel. All over the room the medics and volunteers worked feverishly in the light of battery-powered lanterns and flashlights to save the living. The dead lay unattended in their own blood and gore. Jake Grafton fought the vomit back and held the flashlight as the technician tuned the radio to the proper frequency and made the call.

Minutes passed. The saliva in Jake's mouth kept flowing and he kept swallowing. His eyes remained firmly on the radio.

After an eternity the chairman's voice came over the speaker. Jake picked up his mike.

"Captain Grafton, sir. The terrorists found us. They just hit the armory about six or seven minutes ago. We think about eighteen or twenty of them. We haven't got a good count yet, but we think we've got about fifty U.S. dead and a hundred wounded."

Silence. What was there to say? When the words came it was a question: "Who's the senior army officer over there still on his feet?"

"Colonel Jonat, I think, sir. He's checking the wounded in the parking lot. General Greer and the two brigadiers that were here are dead."

"I'll be over there by helicopter as soon as I can. Right now the Vice-President wants to see me over at the White House. Tell the colonel to hold the fort."

"Yes, sir."

Jake went outside to find Colonel Jonat and get some air. The emergency generators continued to hum and the lights made grotesque shadows.

After a brief conversation with the colonel, who was organizing the transport of the wounded to the hospital, Jake bummed a cigarette. He was standing beside the door savoring the bitter taste of it when Rita came out. "I didn't know you smoked, sir."

Jake Grafton took another drag.

The distance was six hundred yards if it was an inch. Little quartering crosswind. Maybe ten knots. Let's see—the bullet would be in the air for about a second. How much would the wind cause it to drift? He tried to remember the wind tables. Ten knots was about seventeen feet per second. Forty-five degrees off—call it twelve feet in a second. The bullet would drift twelve feet every second it was in the air, *if* he was right about the velocity of the wind and the direction, and *if* the wind was steady throughout the flight of the bullet, which it wouldn't be.

And the trajectory drop—about nine or ten feet at six hundred yards. An impossible shot.

Only a damned fool would try a shot like that.

Henry Charon steadied the rifle on the concrete rail and stared through the scope at the armory. The average guy was six feet tall, so twice that distance would be twelve feet.

The people looked tiny in the scope, even with the nine-power magnification.

The assassin twisted the parallax adjustment ring on the scope to the infinity setting, then backed off a thirty-second of an inch. He settled the rifle again and braced it against his shoulder and studied the scene before the door of the armory.

He had come here because he knew that General Land would come to the armory eventually. Yet with all that shooting over there a while ago—the chairman of the Joint Chiefs should be coming shortly. All Charon had to do was wait. And make this shot.

Wait a sec—that guy standing there smoking near the door? Isn't that the officer from last night? Isn't *that* the man who was standing on the street outside the house under the streetlight?

It's him, all right. Same grungy coat and khaki trousers, same build, same shaped head.

That man hadn't fired the shot that had hit Charon, of course, but he had sprayed a clip full of .223 slugs within inches of his head. He had certainly tried. Wonder if he would try again, given the opportunity?

The thought amused Charon.

He backed away from the scope a moment, rubbed his eyes, then settled in with the rifle hard up against his shoulder. He thumbed off the safety and, just for grins, steadied the scope crosshairs about twelve feet to the right and twelve feet above Jake Grafton's chest. That was the spot.

He filled his lungs, exhaled, and concentrated on holding the rifle absolutely motionless while he took the slack out of the trigger.

Releasing the pressure on the trigger, Charon breathed several times as he thought about last night, about the feel of being chased.

But now—now was *after.* He was looking *back.*

What was he, Henry Charon, going to do with ten million dollars if by some miracle he got away? Sit on a beach somewhere and sip fruit drinks? Perhaps Europe. He tried to picture himself strolling the Left Bank or touring castles on the Rhine. Who was he kidding? He had never expected to get out of this alive. Thirty or forty years of boring anticlimax would be the same as prison.

He exhaled and steadied the crosshairs and ever so gently caressed the trigger with firm, steady pressure. Like all superb riflemen he concentrated on his sight picture without anticipating the moment of letoff. So he was agreeably surprised when the rifle fired.

Something stung Jake Grafton's upper left arm and he jerked. He looked. A hole. There was a hole in his coat! What . . .

He heard the report, a sharp crack.

"Take cover!" he screamed. *"Take cover!"* He pushed Rita down and fell on the pavement beside her. *"Fire coming in!"*

Where? He looked around. Against the skyline he could just see the hulking shape of RFK Stadium. Jake scrambled to his feet and began to run. A flash from the stadium high on the structure. Something buzzed by his ear.

Luckily he had hung onto his rifle. It held a full magazine.

As he ran through the gate and turned right for the stadium Jake shrugged off his coat and let it fall. Out of the circle of light and into the darkness, running hard, his heart coming up to speed too quickly and his breath not quickly enough, running . . .

A goddamn sniper! Some nut or dope addict? Or a diversion to pull the troops out of the armory?

Someone was following him, running along behind. He didn't look back.

The stadium was surrounded by a huge chain-link fence topped by barbed wire. Everything in this goddamn city had a fence around it! He made for an arch in the structure that he thought should be a gate. The fence would have a gate outside that. It did.

It was padlocked. He shot the lock. Then jerked it. No. This time he put the muzzle right up against one of the links in the chain and pulled the trigger. Sparks flew and slivers of metal sprayed him, but the chain fell away.

He tugged at the gate. Rita pounded up. She was carrying a rifle. She helped him pull the gate open.

"Get men to surround this stadium outside the fence. Tell them to shoot anybody coming out unless it's me."

"You think he's still in there?"

"I dunno. Keep moving. Don't be a stationary target." He went through the gate and ran for the arch.

Ramps led away to the right and left. Jake turned left and trotted upward.

On the second level he stopped to catch his breath and listen. The place was dark as a tomb.

Madness. This was madness.

Rita met a squad of soldiers running toward the stadium with their weapons at high port. "Surround it. Stay outside the fence. Captain Grafton's in there. Anybody else comes out, shoot them."

"No warning shots?"

"No. Shoot first. And take cover. This guy is a sniper. Try to get behind something in the darkness and lay very still." She pointed to the sergeant. "Go back to the armory and ask the colonel for a couple dozen more men. Spread them around."

"What are you going to do?"

"I'm going in there too." And with that she slipped through the gate in the fence and ran for the ramp.

Jake walked now, slowly and carefully with the rifle held in both hands and his finger on the safety. His eyes had adjusted all they were going to. He had had trouble the last few years with his night vision, but giving up smoking had helped a lot. His night vision was almost normal now. And he had just smoked a cigarette!

The place was so quiet. Black slabs of concrete, long corridors, huge doors that led out to the seats.

On the third level he turned and went out to the seats, where he could survey the interior of the stadium. There was a faint glow from the clouds, just enough to see the form of the place but not enough to see anyone on the other side of the playing field, if there were anyone there to see.

He hunkered down partially shielded behind a row of seats and scanned carefully, examining the geometric pattern of seats and aisles. After a minute he shifted position and began scanning in the other direction.

Nothing.

He was going to have to come up with a system. Something scientific. A plan.

Okay. He would go up to the top-level concourse and work his way completely around the stadium, occasionally taking the time to survey the seats. Then he would come down a level and repeat the procedure, and so on.

If the guy is in here . . .

But he probably isn't. Why would he stay?

Jake got up, staying low, and moved along the row. He would go out a different place than where he came in. No use being stupid about this.

He heard the bullet smack the seat near him and the booming echo of the report immediately thereafter. He fell flat and crawled, the rifle clunking against the seats.

Well, one thing's clear at least. He's still here.

Colonel Orrin Jonat sent a dozen more troopers to the stadium. With that dozen gone and the casualties and people to transport the wounded to the hospital and stack the dead, he was down to less than fifty men to guard almost four hundred *and* run the war.

First he took the time to arrange four teams of two men each around the armory. Not enough men, it was true, but all he could spare. It had also occurred to him that the sniper from the stadium might be a diversion. Still he had to balance that possibility against the other requirements. He was going to have to bring in a couple of companies from the streets. He didn't have enough men to get new radios in service and keep track of units on the streets.

Were these terrorists the last of them? he asked himself. If only he knew the answer to that!

The army lieutenant leading the squad across the vast, empty parking lots toward the stadium heard the shot from inside. When he got to the gate the sergeant there quickly briefed him.

"Maybe we should go in, sir?" the sergeant suggested.

"The navy people told us to stay out, right?"

"Yes, sir."

"So we got two good guys and at least one bad guy in there in the dark. If we send more people in, we'll end up shooting the wrong folks. It's inevitable. We just did *that* over at the armory. Not again. Deploy the men around the stadium. Anybody tries to sneak out, drill 'em dead."

Henry Charon was thoroughly enjoying himself. Standing at the mouth of one of the tunnels that led out from the concourse, he looked through the scope on the rifle. He could just make out the man on the other side of the stadium scuttling up the stairs toward the tunnel exit. This is a damn good scope, he told himself. It gathers the ambient light, allowing you to see better at night with the scope than you can with the naked eye.

Charon moved the crosshairs slightly to one side of the moving man and squeezed the trigger. The rifle set back against his shoulder with a nice firm kick as the roar filled the stadium.

He worked the bolt, then trotted back into the tunnel. He turned left at the concourse and jogged along.

He felt good. His side was hurting but not terribly so and he had adequate range of motion. He was fit. He could trot ten miles without breaking a sweat.

Henry Charon wondered if the other man was having as much fun as he was.

"Colonel, there's a bunch of people coming down the street."

Orrin Jonat looked at the soldier disbelievingly. "What?"

"A bunch of people. Not armed apparently. They're just walking this way."

"How many is a bunch?"

"Hundreds. We can't tell."

Colonel Jonat followed the soldier outside. He walked to the gate and looked down the street. Good lord, the street was filled with people.

He stepped back through the gate and got his people in. Then he had it closed. It was just a chain-link fence about six feet high. He asked the sergeant to install the padlock.

"I don't know where the lock is, sir."

"Go find it," Colonel Jonat said. "Or get one of those locks we've been using for the prisoners. Hurry."

He stood there waiting. The head of the column turned and a dozen people came toward the gate shoulder to shoulder.

"Open up."

The crowd was mostly black. Some white people, but predominantly black men and women. They ranged from young to fairly elderly. Some of the people were supporting others. There was even a man in a wheelchair. The man facing Colonel Jonat was about forty. He spoke. "Open up."

"This is a military installation. I'm the officer in charge, Colonel Jonat. I'm ordering you people to disperse. You may not come in."

"We're not armed, Colonel, as you can see. There are about a thousand people here and nobody is even carrying a pocketknife. Now open this gate."

"It's not locked, Tom," the man beside him said, pointing.

Where in *hell* is that sergeant?

"Open the gate or we'll open it. I'll not ask you again."

"What do you want here? Talk to me."

The spokesman stood aside. "Open the gate," he said to the people beside him. They laid willing hands on the gate and pushed.

Jonat jumped back out of the way. He backed up ten feet or so and soldiers with their rifles ready surrounded him. "Halt, goddammit, or we'll open fire!"

The crowd came through the gate and stopped two feet in front of the colonel. He could see more and more people gathering in the street. A thousand? He believed it.

"We want your prisoners."

"You aren't going to get them. Now get the hell off government property or—"

"Or what? You would shoot unarmed civilians who are just standing here? What are you, some kind of Nazi?"

Jonat tried to reason with the man. He raised his voice so that more people could hear. "Listen, folks. I don't know why you came, but I can't release these prisoners. They've shot at soldiers, killed some, looted, burned, sold drugs—you name it. I know Washington has been through hell the last few days, but these people will have to answer for what they've done. They will get a fair hearing and federal judges will treat them fairly. Please, go on home and let's get this city back to normal. Your sons and husbands will be treated fairly. I promise!"

"We want these people now."

"Out! Get out. Or I'll order these men to shoot you where you stand."

The crowd moved as one. They came forward, crowding, pressing. One woman walked up so close to the soldier beside Jonat that the muzzle of his M-16 was against her breast.

"Go ahead, Colonel," she said. "Tell him to shoot. He can't miss. I'll hold still."

She was a black woman, about thirty or so, with a strong, proud face. Orrin Jonat stared at her, but she was staring at the soldier who held the rifle. He was black too. He stared back, his jaw slack, his hand on the trigger of his weapon. "Could you do it?" she asked softly. "Could you murder me? Could you spend the rest of your life seeing my face and knowing that you killed me when I offer you no harm?"

The soldier picked the muzzle up, pointing the rifle safely at the sky, and took a step backward.

"Move back, Colonel. Move back." The spokesman also spoke softly, but with a hard edge to his voice.

Involuntarily the colonel retreated a step. As he did so the whole crowd moved silently forward. "Order your men to stand back, Colonel. You don't want to be the Reinhard Heydrich of Washington. Order them back."

"We *know* who these people are. We'll find them and arrest them again. They *will* answer for their acts. As *you* will."

"As God is my judge, I know you speak the truth, Colonel. Now stand back."

To his credit, Orrin Jonat knew when he was beaten. He spoke loudly: "Hold your fire, men. No shooting. Now back up."

The spokesman led the way through the door. He paused inside and looked at the bodies arranged in rows on the floor as people swarmed in behind him. Then he looked at the prisoners shackled to the wall. He motioned to his companions and they started forward.

Toad Tarkington was making a list of the dead from the information on their dogtags when the civilians came through the door, and now he positioned himself between the obvious leader and the prisoners. "Stop right there," he shouted. "Not another fucking step, buddy."

"Get out of the way." The man spoke calmly but with an air of authority.

The crowd surged past the man who faced Toad. Men, women, old people, they just kept coming.

Toad reached inside his coat and drew a pistol. He pointed it at the man in front of him and cocked the hammer.

"I can't shoot everybody, Jack, but I can sure as hell shoot you. Now stop these people or I blow your head clean off."

Out of the corner of his eye he saw something coming. He pulled the trigger just as the lights went out.

Jake Grafton stood in the third-level concourse listening. He was in total darkness, a spot so black he couldn't even see his hands. He closed his eyes and concentrated on what he could hear.

Some background noise from over toward the armory, but in here, nothing. Quiet as King Tut's tomb.

He opened his eyes and felt his way along the wall. Ahead he could see the glow where a ramp along the exterior wall came up. He paused. He would be an excellent target when he entered that faint glow. If there were anyone around.

He took a deep breath to steady himself, then moved forward.

Up a level. He would climb up a level.

Five minutes had passed since that second shot had spanged into the seat beside him as he scurried up the stairs for the safety of the tunnel. Too long. He should have moved more than the hundred yards he had come.

He should have set up an ambush. As long as this guy doesn't know where I am, Jake told himself, I've got the advantage.

But there was the ramp. Should he go for it or stay here?

His mouth was dry. He licked his lips and wiped the sweat from his forehead. Okay. To do it or not? The entrance to the ramp was only fifteen yards or so away.

He went for it as fast as he could. He rounded the corner and halted with his back against the wall, breathing hard. Then he heard it. A faint laugh.

Someone laughing!

"This is really too easy. You're not using your head, mister."

Jake ran up the ramp. As hard and fast as he could go. He came out on the top level and trotted along the concourse. After about a minute had passed he found a real dark spot and came to a halt. He stood there gripping the rifle tightly with both hands and listening.

Ambush. He needed to find a spot. Needed to sit and let this psycho come to him. Needed to wait if it took all night. But where?

He kept going. Fifty yards further along he came to another place where two ramps came up from below. There seemed to be more light than usual. Aha, the armory was down there and the emergency lights in the parking area were reflecting up here. Jake looked around. If he went along this corridor to the north, he could look back this way. If and when, bang.

His mind made up, he went down the corridor seventy-five feet or so and lay down against the exterior concourse wall, facing back toward the ramp area.

Of course his back was vulnerable, but if the sniper came that way, he would hear him coming. Maybe. The main thing was to stay put and stay quiet.

Who was this sniper, anyway? Could he be Charon? Naw, Charon was an assassin, out to shoot the big trophy cats. He wouldn't waste a bullet on a mouse.

Toad Tarkington was spinning. He was sitting in a cockpit of a violently spinning airplane and the Gs were pushing him forward out of the seat. The altimeter was unwinding at a sickening rate. He couldn't raise his arms or move. His eyes were redding out and he could feel the pain of the blood pooling in his head. Spinning viciously, violently, dying . . .

He opened his eyes. He was looking into the face of Jack Yocke.

Yocke pried open an eyelid and looked with interest. "You're going to be okay, I think. Your head's as hard as a brick. If I were you I wouldn't try to sit up yet though."

"What happened?"

"Well, a man hit you on the head with an ax handle. And you shot a man, fellow named Tom Shannon."

"He dead?"

"No. You got him in the shoulder. He's sitting right here beside you. If you turn your head you can visit with him."

Toad tried. The pain shot through his head so badly he felt himself going out again. He lay absolutely still and the feeling passed.

After a moment he opened his eyes and swiveled his head a millimeter, then another. Yocke was applying a bandage to a man who was naked from the waist up. They were on the floor of the armory bay.

Toad held his head and turned it. All the prisoners were gone! The three of them were the only ones in the whole room.

"How long I been out?"

"Fifteen, twenty minutes. Something like that."

"Damn you, Yocke."

"Hey, Toad." The reporter came over and stared down at him. "You could have killed Shannon."

"If he was the asshole in front, I was trying to. I'm damn sorry I didn't."

Yocke looked tired. "I didn't know you were carrying a pistol under that coat."

"I told you, being around Grafton, you gotta . . ."

"Lie still. You probably have a concussion."

"Jerk. Reporter jerk. *Spectator.*" Toad tried to sit. The effort nauseated him and made him so dizzy he had to steady himself with his hands on the floor.

When he opened his eyes he was looking straight at Shannon. "So you took 'em, huh? We'll get 'em back. Those fucking dirtballs won't get away with killing soldiers and all that shit just because a damn mob turns 'em loose."

Shannon just stared at him.

Yocke came over and used his fingers to part the hair on the back of Toad's head. He looked carefully. "You got a real bad goose egg, Toad."

"We'll find those assholes, Shannon, even if we have to flood this damn town and comb all the rats with a wire brush."

"Toad," Yocke said gently. "They didn't let those people go."

Toad Tarkington gaped. It didn't compute. He looked again at the maintenance bays where the prisoners had been held. It was empty. "What d'ya mean?"

"They didn't turn them loose, Toad. They're hanging them. All of them."

By some ironic quirk of fate, they brought Sweet Cherry Lane to the same light pole where they were hanging T. Jefferson Brody.

"Bitch, cunt, nigger slut! I hope we end up in the same furnace in hell so I can kick the shit out of you for a million years!"

The man in front of him put the noose around his neck while two women and two men held his arms. He struggled. *They couldn't do this to him! He was a member of the bar!*

"I got money. I'll pay you to let me go. Please! For God's sake."

He could feel the noose tightening as eight people in front of him pulled the rope. Holy shit! It was going to happen! They were *really* going to do it.

T. Jefferson Brody peed his pants.

Sweet Cherry Lane was standing there silently, watching him, as two men held her arms immobile and a third draped a noose around her neck.

"Why?" he croaked at her. "Why did Freeman McNally protect you?"

"I'm his half-sister," she said.

Before he could reply the people holding his arms let go and the rope around his neck lifted him clear of the ground. He grabbed the rope and held on with both hands as it elevated him higher and higher and the merciless pressure on his neck began to strangle him. He was kicking wildly, which caused him to spin slowly, first one way, then the other. His vision faded. Can't breathe, can't see, can't . . .

He heard a step. Lying there against the curved wall, he could hear a soft sound, followed by another. The sounds weren't like leather heels clicking on a wooden floor, but like something soft brushing against something that . . . The sound carried well against the wall. They were footsteps. That was all they could be.

Jake Grafton tightened his grip on the rifle and thumbed the safety off. He had it pointed at the ramp opening. As soon as this dude stepped into that square of faint light . . .

Another step. He was coming slowly, methodically, step by step. But how far away was he? How far would sounds carry around this curved concrete wall? Maybe a hundred yards, he speculated. Maybe twice that. Naw. Fifty was more like it.

The steps paused, then resumed.

He's coming.

Sweat dripped into Jake's eyes but he didn't move. He merely blinked and tried to ignore the stinging.

Suddenly he realized what a damn poor position he had chosen. He should have picked the doorway to a rest room to lie in, something that would have allowed him to look both ways. For the thought came in all its horror that the man he sought was probably behind him in the darkness.

Jake started to turn around.

"No, friend," the voice said softly. "Just hold it right there."

Jake froze.

"Well, we had ourselves a nice little hunt, didn't we? We stalked and stalked and now we are at the end."

"You'll never get away, Charon."

The man laughed. "I'll outlive you by quite a while."

He was behind Jake. But which side of the concourse? Probably near the exterior wall or his footsteps wouldn't have carried so well.

Jake tried to decide what to do. He knew to the depths of his soul that anything he tried would be futile. But he couldn't let this guy just shoot him like a dog! If he spun, he would have to rise to his knees and swing the rifle.

Jake thumbed the selector to full automatic fire. He turned his head, looking.

"You're thinking about turning and trying a shot, aren't you? Go ahead. I'll put the first one up your ass."

"Who hired you?"

Another soft laugh. "Would you believe I never asked? I don't know."

"How much did they pay you?"

"A lot of money. And you know something funny? I do believe I would have done it for nothing." Another chuckle.

The next time the guy spoke. While he was speaking Jake would spin and let this guy have a magazine-full of hot lead. "You really don't have to kill me, do you? You've had your fun."

"That's an interesting—"

A burst of gunfire strobed the corridor. Jake had just started to spin. He completed the maneuver and flopped down with the rifle aimed into the darkness in front of him.

In the silence that followed he heard something soft and heavy fall to the concrete. And he heard a sigh.

"Captain, don't shoot! It's me."

Rita!

He got up slowly, almost falling. Then a light came on. She had a small flashlight and she was shining it down on Henry Charon. He lay on his back, the rifle just out of reach of his right hand.

Jake walked up and stood looking down. He kept his rifle pointed at Charon and his finger on the trigger.

"How . . . ?" Charon said. He had been hit in the chest by at least three bullets. The red stain was spreading rapidly.

Rita seemed to understand. She flashed the light on her feet. They were bare. "I took my shoes off."

When she put the light back on Charon's face he was grinning. Then he died. The smile faded as the muscles went slack.

Jake bent down and felt for Charon's pulse. He straightened slowly.

"Come on," he said. "Let's go."

Rita extinguished the penlight. Together they walked along the concourse toward the light.

The bodies hung from every pole. Jake Grafton stared, trying to comprehend. Some poles had one, some had two. But they all hung lifelessly, stirring only as the cold night breeze moved them.

Inside the armory he found the soldiers gathered around Toad Tarkington, who was sitting on the concrete floor nursing his head. Jack Yocke was beside him talking to a civilian.

"You want anything in the paper about why you did it, Tom? You know they'll try you for a dozen felonies, perhaps even a dozen murders?"

The middle-aged, balding black man sitting on the floor was being worked on by a medic, who was strapping tape around a bandage arranged on his chest. Blood was smeared on his chest and trousers.

The man on the floor ignored the audience. He stared at Yocke. "Will you write it true? Write it the way I say it?"

"You know I will. You've read my stuff."

"The Jefferson projects. You remember?"

Yocke nodded. Oh yes, he remembered. The murder of Jane Wilkens by a crack dealer running from the cops. Another life lost to the crack business. "Jane," he said.

"Yeah. Jane." Shannon took a deep breath and grimaced at the pain. "It was my idea. We're all victims. We all lost somebody—a son, daughter, wife, maybe even our own souls. We *lost* because we expected someone to fight the evil for us and we waited and waited and they never did. Oh, they *talked,* but . . ."

He lifted his good hand and pleaded, "Don't you see, if we don't fight evil, we *become* evil. If you ain't part of the solution you're part of the problem—it's *that* simple. So we decided to take a stand, all of us victims.

"Then this terrorist stuff started. And the dopers started looting and shooting and trying to wipe out their competition so they could have a competitive advantage when it was all over.

"Now I tell you this, Jack Yocke, and you gotta write it just like this: I *hope* the talkers try me. I *hope* I get prosecuted. The people who don't want to be victims anymore will see how it *has* to be. We can't wait for George Bush or Dan Quayle or the hot-air artists. We can't wait for the police. *We* have to take *our* stand.

"I've taken mine. You kill my woman, you kill my kids, don't hide behind the law 'cause it ain't big enough. Justice *will* be done! *Right* will be done. There are just enough people like me. Just enough. You'll see."

The medic finished and spread a blanket on a stretcher. Four men lifted the wounded man onto it.

"I'm not good with words," the man told Yocke. "I never had much education. But I know right from wrong and I know which side I'm on. I've planted my feet. *Here* I am."

"What can one man do?" Jack Yocke asked.

"Lead an army, part the Red Sea, convert the world. Maybe not me. But here *I* stand until the world takes its place beside me."

The medics carried him away.

The chairman of the Joint Chiefs arrived by helicopter fifteen minutes later. Ten minutes after that the Vice-President arrived. Together they walked through the parking lot looking at the dangling corpses.

Jake Grafton went over to where Toad and Rita were sitting in chairs. "Come on. Let's go home. You got the car keys, Toad?"

"In my pocket."

"Rita, take the keys and bring the car up to the door."

"What about Yocke?" Toad asked as Jake helped him into the front seat.

"He's over with the heavies getting a story. Let's go home."

As the car exited the armory parking lot, Toad pointed toward the official party in the parking lot across the street. "Wonder what they're thinking?"

"They're politicians. Tom Shannon and the other citizens here tonight just delivered a message. They're reading it now."

CHAPTER THIRTY-TWO

* * * * * * * * * * * * *

Pᴇᴏᴘʟᴇ heard the news of the hanging on portable, battery-operated radios, then ran next door to tell their neighbors. The news seemed to drain whatever energy remained from the wounded city. The next morning it lay stunned, exhausted, its citizens cold and without power.

There was no rioting, no looting, no fires. The soldiers walked the streets without incident as crews worked feverishly to restore power to the residential neighborhoods. The bombed substations would require weeks to repair or rebuild, but emergency repairs began to restore power to a few areas by nightfall. In the areas without power, people were evacuated to schools and auditoriums where the Army installed portable generators. The people of Washington began to reach out to help each other.

Jake Grafton spent the day in a round of meetings as the federal authorities devised ways to thwart the terrorist threat from the Extraditables in the short term. Over the long term, the problem was the cocaine industry in South America.

The next day the ban against motor vehicles was lifted and people swarmed the city in a monumental traffic jam. That evening, after conferring with the directors of the FBI, DEA, and CIA and being advised that those organizations knew of no additional terrorists in the country, General Land started pulling out the troops.

He had Jake Grafton, Toad, and Rita come to his office and make a complete report. An hour later when the chairman signaled the interview was over, Jake asked for leave for himself and Toad. Rita was already on leave. The request was granted.

Out in front of the Pentagon Jake asked the two lieutenants, "You want to come over to the beach house and spend Christmas with Callie and Amy and me?"

They glanced at each other, then accepted.

All the troops were out of the city on the twenty-ninth of December. The following day George Bush was discharged from Bethesda Naval Hospital and returned to the White House.

He held a news conference that afternoon that was carried live nationwide. Attorney General Gideon Cohen sat beside him.

Bush said he felt good and was getting better every day. He wanted to take this opportunity to publicly thank Vice-President Quayle for his excellent stewardship during his incapacity, and he did so with the leaders of the House and Senate and all of the surviving Supreme Court justices in attendance. And he announced the formation of a presidential commission to study the nation's illegal drug problem and make recommendations on what needed to be done to solve it. Gideon Cohen was appointed chairman.

"I have asked the attorney general to chair this commission because he has been one of the harshest critics of our efforts to date. I know we can rely on him to give us a thorough, honest evaluation of our shortcomings. I promise you, we will ask the Congress to turn the commission's recommendations into legislation."

Then the President got down to brass tacks. "The drug problem is a complex social issue that is not going to go away by itself. Its causes include everything from poverty in Colombia and Peru to poverty and rotten schools in this country. The crux of the problem is that so many people have been left out of the world's evolving economy, people in the Third World, people right here in America. I don't know that there are solutions—certainly no easy ones—but I promise you this: we are going to face the problem."

Intended by the President to help calm the political atmosphere, which was rife with accusations and recriminations, the news conference had no such effect. It was too little too late.

Critics like Congresswoman Samantha Strader attacked the Army's handling of the crisis and damned Tom Shannon as a psychotic vigilante. He would have been stuffed into the same crack that held Bernard Goetz had he not been black. Unable to hurl the racist stink bomb, those who opposed tougher drug laws and tougher law enforcement and those with their own political agendas and ambitions united to demand that Shannon be tried, convicted, and hurried on his way to perdition.

Those who believed that the government hadn't done enough to combat illegal drugs rushed to Shannon's defense. It was wrong, they claimed, to martyr Shannon on the altar of the white man's guilt.

Jack Yocke's articles in the *Post* merely drew the lines for the combatants. Saint or sinner, Tom Shannon stood at the vortex of the developing firestorm. Curiously, he stood alone. After a quiet conference with his chief adviser, Will Dorfman, George Bush decided not to have the FBI or police attempt to discover the identities of the people who had accompanied Shannon to the armory. Those seeking to destroy Shannon were likewise not interested in having the stories of a thousand victims of the drug trade paraded before the public one at a time, night after night, ad infinitum. So Tom Shannon was the only man charged, for conspiracy with a person or persons unknown to lynch 382 people.

When Jack Yocke went to see him in the hospital, Shannon grinned. "Nobody wants to try us all, but they think if they try just me all the other victims will go away. Won't happen. Those people buried too many kids, buried too many husbands."

"What about legalization of dope?" Jack Yocke asked toward the end of the interview. "There's a lot of talk about that since Christmas. What do you think?"

"Personally I'm against it," Shannon said. "There's too many fools who'll get addicted. Off the record, though, I think that's what will have to be done. We've got to get the big money out of the business. If the money is gone the criminals will go. That'll stop the recruitment of kids just out of diapers to a life of using and abusing, a life of crime and ignorance and squalor. A whole generation of black kids is going down the toilet. It's an obscenity that's got to stop."

Remarkably, in spite of the hurricane-velocity winds building inside the beltway, life elsewhere in America returned quickly to normal. The soaps went back on television during the day and the sitcoms returned at night. Critics complained of the sexual innuendo that passed as humor this winter on the tube. A network executive said the critics didn't know what was funny.

The ball fell in Times Square on New Year's Eve and a great many people awoke the next morning with a hangover, but not as many as in past years, some pollster said in a headline story, because people these days were drinking less. Southern Cal won another Rose Bowl.

During the first week of January two former executives of a large Texas savings and loan pleaded guilty to twenty-eight counts of bank fraud and asked the court to put them on probation.

The wife of a well-known movie star sued her husband for divorce and claimed he was having an affair with his latest leading lady. The betrayed wife went from one syndicated morning talk show to the next telling her story and explaining to the sympathetic hosts the financial hardships that loomed as she tried to survive on half a million a month and keep the kids in school.

Iran had a little earthquake. Another ayatollah died while a blizzard stranded airline passengers in Denver, and Whitefish, Montana, reported record low temperatures.

The Democrats wanted to know when the administration was going to get serious about raising taxes and the Republicans wanted to know when the Democrats were going to get serious about cutting government spending.

Another congressman announced he was gay.

And the network that had rights to televise the Superbowl officially kicked off the hype with a show in which millionaire football players explained how their teams had overcome adversity this past year.

While all this was going on Senator Bob Cherry quietly resigned from the U.S. Senate. He told the Florida newspapers that he was tired and had done all he could for his country. Guessing who the governor would appoint to fill Cherry's seat became the diversion of the hour in Florida.

A fine wet rain, almost a mist, fell almost continuously in Washington that first week of the new year. Then the wind picked up and blew the clouds eastward out to sea.

Thanos Liarakos glanced again at the street sign and once again consulted his map. He drove slowly for several more blocks, then found the street he wanted. The trees in this suburban tract development were small and sticklike in the anemic sunlight. They would grow larger of course, but it would take twenty or thirty years for these neighborhoods to look settled, permanent.

He found the building he wanted and drove another half block looking for a parking place, then walked back. The sprawling one-story brick structure was surrounded on three sides by a chain-link fence. Inside the sturdy wire were sandboxes and swings and child-powered merry-go-rounds. And children. Lots of them, squealing, running, laughing.

Liarakos went in the front door and down the empty hallway. He paused outside the door marked OFFICE, squared his shoulders, then went in.

"Miss Judith Lewis, please. Is she around?"

The owlish-looking young woman with a heavy sweater and shiny pink lips sitting behind the desk noted his suit and tie, grinned perfunctorily, and said, "She has playground duty. Might be in back."

"And how . . . ?"

"Down the corridor to the first left and straight on out. You can't miss it."

"Thank you."

Judith Lewis was standing with her arms folded across her chest listening to a young boy tell a tale of woe, with much pointing and gesturing. She bent down and wiped his face and stroked his hair. As she did so the lower edge of her coat dragged in the dirt. That, Liarakos suspected, was not a detail that would bother Judith Lewis very much.

The child grinned finally and ran off to join his friends.

"Hello, Judith."

She turned and saw him, then rose to her feet. "Hello," she acknowledged without enthusiasm. She half turned away so she could watch the children. He approached and stood beside her, also watching the children.

"How was your holiday?" he asked.

"Fine." Her voice was hard and flat. She checked her watch.

"Beautiful youngsters."

"Recess is over in three minutes. Say what you came to say."

"Okay. That Cuban general, Zaba, knows enough to convict Chano Aldana. And he's talking, singing his heart out. I've been reading transcripts of his interrogations. If the prosecutors can get Zaba on the stand they can get a conviction."

"Why are you telling me all this?"

"Isn't it obvious?"

"I'm not going back to work for you, Mr. Liarakos. I thought I made that plain."

"What you made plain, Ms. Lewis, is that you thought Chano Aldana was the devil incarnate and ought to be locked up so he can't continue to murder and terrorize and sell poison to ruin the lives of children like these."

"You were equally definite in your opinion, Mr. Liarakos, as I recall." Her voice was acidic. "Like every wealthy, successful criminal, Aldana deserves the best legal defense money can buy, and that of course is *you*. And if you can hoodwink and bamboozle the jurors, it's your sworn duty to do so. Then you go home to your beautiful wife and children and eat a gourmet dinner and rest your weary soul, your duty well and truly done. Isn't that the spin you want on it? Oh, I haven't forgotten our last conversation, Mr. Liarakos. I doubt that I ever will. It brought into very stark relief all the doubts I've had through the years of law school and practice."

The bell rang. All the children charged for the door.

"If you'll ex—" she began, but he interrupted:

"I came to ask you to come back to work."

She stared at him as the schoolyard emptied and the last of the children disappeared inside.

"Listen, there's more to the legal profession than the Chano Aldanas of the world. Someone has to be in a position to help all these people who need someone to speak for them. Someone has to represent Jane Roe and Karen Ann Quinlan and John T. Scopes and all the rest of the folks who can't speak for themselves. That's why you went to law school, isn't it?"

"Yes, it is." She said it softly, almost inaudibly. She lifted the hem of her coat and brushed at the loose dirt that clung there.

"Where do you think you get the experience to help that one client in a hundred? You get it by going to court every day, wrestling with the prosecutors and the judges and the system. *Someone* has to know how to work the system."

She turned and faced the school.

"Someone has to care. Someone has to fight it every blessed day and do the best they can. If someone doesn't, the little people are going to go down the slop chute. Now I ask you, if *you* won't do it, who will?"

"You keep asking these goddamned rhetorical questions, Mr. Liarakos," she said bitterly. "And you're representing Chano Aldana."

"He paid the fee. The firm needs the money. I need the money. I'll do my level best for the bastard."

"Why?"

"Ms. Lewis, if you have to ask, you'd better stay here with the grade-school kids."

"Aldana is going to walk."

Liarakos snorted. "No, he isn't. Zaba knows enough to convict Aldana. I've been reading the transcripts of the interrogations. He's singing like a bird. They got everything chapter and verse. Names, locations, dates, amounts, quantities—everything. Zaba was the Cuban connection and he personally met with Aldana at least seven times. He even arranged for a couple of murders of DEA agents by Cuban intelligence. The prosecutors have got it."

"So. What are you going to do?"

"Me? I'm just going to give Aldana a hundred percent of my best efforts and the prosecutors are going to nail his guilty hide to the wall. Clarence Darrow couldn't get the sonofabitch off. There's no way. I've been doing this for a lot of years and I *know*. Aldana's guilty and the jury will see that and he'll go up the river for the rest of his natural life."

"And you?"

"I'll go home afterward, Ms. Lewis, and pour myself a stiff drink and give thanks that God created the jury system."

"But what if the jury *won't* convict Aldana?"

"Judith, you have got to believe in your fellow man or you'll have no hope at all. If the ordinary men and women on the jury won't convict him, why try to get him off the streets? If they won't convict him, they *deserve* him."

She kept brushing at the coat.

"You made a fine little speech in my office a few weeks ago, Judith. Something about the law existing to protect those who can't protect themselves. And here they are." He gestured toward the school building. "I thought you meant it."

She ran her hand through her hair.

She grimaced. "Are you sure?"

"I'll see you tomorrow at the office," he said. "Or the next morning. Whenever you can get there."

She kept brushing at her coat.

"Oh, and you and I have a new client. Guy name of Tom Shannon. A *pro bono* case."

"Shannon? Isn't he the man who led the lynch mob to the armory, the scapegoat they want to hang?"

"That's the man," Liarakos agreed. "You and he have a lot in common. He also says he knows the difference between good and evil."

He turned and walked toward the door to the school and went through it, leaving Judith Lewis in the middle of the empty playground staring after him, flipping at her coat hem automatically.

"God damn you," she whispered. "God damn you." And she began to cry.

She had thought she was out of it. And now this! The principal and the school officials—when they hired her she promised to stay. They were going to think her such a terrible liar.

She went over to the bench against the wall and tried to compose herself.

Well, tomorrow was impossible. She would call the school officials this afternoon, but she should give them at least one more day so that they could find someone else.

She used the hem of her skirt to wipe the tears from her eyes.

The doctor had a breezy manner. He radiated confidence and self-assurance. Apparently he had picked up the patois in Patient Relations 101.

"You're going to be fine. Every third day we'll change the dressing and inch the drain out. But I think you're well enough to go home."

Harrison Ronald Ford nodded and swung his feet back and forth as the doctor examined the surgical incisions in his back. He was perched on the side of the bed, which was too far above the floor for his feet to comfortably reach. Normally the nurse had a little stool placed just so.

"Hold still please."

Harrison obeyed. Since the doctor couldn't see his face, he grinned.

"Yes indeedy. Looking very fine. Gonna be a dilly of a scar, but maybe you can get a big tattoo back here and no one will notice. I have a rather extraordinary picture of a naked woman on a stallion I can let you look at if you want to consider classical artwork."

"Big tits?"

"Melons."

"Bring it in."

"Now if you have any trouble at all, you call me. Any time, day or night. And the people downstairs want you to continue in physical therapy every day. Make those appointments before you leave this afternoon."

"Sure."

The doctor came around to face him. "The nurse will be in in a moment to put a new bandage on you. I just wanted to check you one last time and shake your hand."

"Thanks, Doc."

They took him in a wheelchair to the administration office to finish the paperwork. The administrator asked for his address and telephone number and he gave them the apartment he had used as Sammy Z. "We'll see you tomorrow at ten in the morning."

"Sure." The doctor popped in and Harrison shook hands all around, one more time.

At his request they called him a taxi. It was waiting out front when he scribbled his name for the final time. With the nurse holding grimly to his elbow, he maneuvered himself out of the wheelchair and into the backseat. She supervised the cabbie as he placed the two bags in the trunk that Freddy Murray had brought up from Quantico. Harrison waved at her as the cabbie put the car into motion.

She gave him a distracted smile and charged back inside pushing the wheelchair.

"Where to, Mac?"

"National Airport."

"What airline?"

"Oh, I dunno. Don't have reservations yet."

"Well, you won't have no problem. Holiday rush is all over. Where you heading?"

"Evansville, Indiana."

"Go through Chicago or Cleveland?"

"One of those."

"Maybe US Air."

"Fine."

Harrison Ronald sat back and watched the cars gliding along under the winter sky. He had been in Washington, what? Almost eleven months. Seemed like forever.

The cab driver whistled for a redcap to handle the bags and Harrison gave him a two-dollar tip. The driver was right. He had no trouble getting a ticket on the next plane, which was scheduled to leave in an hour.

Harrison Ronald strolled to the boarding area and sat watching the businessmen and mothers with children. The men in suits were reading or writing reports, darting over to the pay phones and making credit card calls. The kids were hollering and scurrying about and demanding their mothers' attention. He sighed. It was so normal—so . . . almost like another world after all the stuff he had been through these last few months. He shook his head in wonder. Life does indeed go on.

Amazingly enough the airplane actually left on time. Most of the seats were empty. Harrison Ronald moved from his aisle seat to the window and took his last look at Washington as it fell away below.

It was over then. Really and truly over. No more terror, no more waiting for the ax to fall, no more sleepless nights wondering what Freeman McNally was hearing and thinking. Over.

What would he do now? He had been avoiding the issue but he examined it now as Washington slipped behind and the Alleghenies came into view like ribs.

The Corps—maybe. After he was healed up completely. He would go find a doctor to do all the therapy and bandage changing and drain pulling that the folks in Washington were worried about. Or perhaps he should go back to the cops. Maybe that. He would have to think about it some more. But now he felt so good, almost euphoric. It was hard to envision himself back on the street dealing with the would-be Freeman

McNallys, all the lazy losers who thought that everyone should hold still while they carved off a chunk without earning it.

He was tired so he reclined the seat and closed his eyes. The important thing was that he was going back to the front porch. Spring would come eventually, then the summer with its muggy heat. He would sit in the swing and watch his grandmother string beans and shuck corn for canning. Maybe go to the ballpark on hot summer evenings. Paint the house for her—that was what he would do. He thought about the paint, the smell of it with the heat on his back. It would be very good. And there would be plenty of time—all the time he would ever need. With these images in his mind he dozed off.

He awoke on the descent into Chicago. The plane to Evansville was a four-engine turboprop which entered the clouds as it left O'Hare and stayed in them until it was on final approach into the Evansville airport. Harrison was glued to the window looking at the Ohio River looping by the downtown and the streets and neighborhoods all neatly, perfectly square. He saw the high school he had graduated from and he saw the minor league ballpark where he had sold hot dogs all those summers growing up.

He took a cab from the airport.

The little house looked exactly the same. The swing was put away for the winter and the leaves were bare, but the grass had been mowed just before the cold stopped all growth. The house still needed painting. And the soffit under the eaves—he would fix those rotten places too.

The doctor had told him not to lift anything, so he had the cabbie put the bags on the porch. Then he tried the door. Unlocked.

He stepped in.

"Grandmom! It's me, Harrison."

"Who?"

Her voice came floating down the hallway from the kitchen.

He walked that way. He saw her before he got to the kitchen door. She was old and small and her hair was white. She didn't move too quickly anymore, but he thought he had never seen a more beautiful woman.

"Oh, Harrison! What a wonderful surprise! You're home!"

"Yeah, Grandmom. I'm home."

He took her gently in his arms.